Hearts Afire
and
Restless Hearts
Marta Perry

Doubleday Large Print Home Library Edition

Steeple
Hill ®

Published by Steeple Hill Books™

Contents

Hearts Afire

Hearts Afire
Marta Perry

DOUBLEDAY LARGE PRINT HOME LIBRARY EDITION

Steeple
Hill®

Published by Steeple Hill Books™

This Large Print Edition, prepared especially for Doubleday Large Print Home Library, contains the complete, unabridged text of the original Publisher's Edition.

STEEPLE HILL BOOKS

Steeple Hill®

ISBN-13: 978-0-7394-8848-5

HEARTS AFIRE

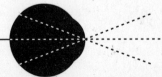

This Large Print Book carries the Seal of Approval of N.A.V.H.

Therefore we also, since we are surrounded by so great a cloud of witnesses, let us lay aside every weight, and the sin which so easily ensnares us, and let us run with endurance the race that is set before us.

—*Hebrews* 12:1

This story is dedicated to my granddaughter, Ameline Grace Stewart, with much love from Grammy. And, as always, to Brian.

Chapter One

Terry Flanagan flashed a penlight in the young boy's eyes and then smiled reassuringly at the teenage sister who was riding with them in the rig on the trip to the hospital.

"You can hit the siren," she called through the narrow doorway to her partner. Jeff Erhart was driving the unit this run. They had an unspoken agreement that she'd administer care when the patient was a small child. With three young kids of his own, Jeff found a hurt child tough to face.

The sister's dark gaze focused on Terry. "Why did you tell him to start the siren? Is Juan worse? Tell me!"

"He's going to be fine, Manuela." She'd agreed to take the sister in the unit because she was the only family member who spoke

English. "You have to stay calm, remember?" Naturally it was scary for Manuela to see her little brother immobilized on a backboard, an IV running into his arm.

The girl swallowed hard, nodding. With her dark hair pulled back in braids and her skin innocent of makeup, Manuela didn't look the sixteen years she claimed to be. Possibly she was sixteen only because that was the minimum age for migrant farmworkers to be in the fields. The fertile farmlands and orchards that surrounded the small city of Suffolk in southern Pennsylvania were a magnet for busloads of migrant farmworkers, most from Mexico, who visited the area for weeks at a time. They rarely intersected with the local community except in an emergency, like this one.

"Juan will need stitches, yes?" Manuela clasped her little brother's hand.

"Yes, he will." Terry lifted the gauze pad slightly. The bleeding had slowed, but the edges of the cut gaped.

The child looked up at her with such simple trust that her stomach clenched. *Lord, I haven't forgotten anything, have I? Be with this child, and guide my hands and my decisions.*

She ticked over the steps of care as the unit hit the busy streets of Suffolk and slowed. She'd been over them already, but somehow she couldn't help doing it again. And again.

She knew why. It had been two years, but she still heard that accusing voice at moments like this, telling her that she was incompetent, that she—

No. She wouldn't go there. She'd turn the self-doubt over to God, as she'd done so many times before, and she'd close the door on that cold voice. The wail of the siren, the well-equipped emergency unit, the trim khaki pants and navy shirt with the word Paramedic emblazoned on the back—all those things assured her of who she was.

She smiled at the girl again, seeing the strain in her young face. "How did your brother get hurt? Can you tell me that?"

"He shouldn't have been there." The words burst out. "He's too little to—"

The child's fingers closed over hers, as if he understood what she was saying. A look flashed between brother and sister, too quickly for Terry to be sure what it meant. A warning? Perhaps.

She could think of only one ending to

what Manuela had started to say. "Was Juan working in the field?" It was illegal for a child so young to work in the fields—everyone knew that, even those who managed to ignore the migrant workers in their midst every summer and fall.

Alarm filled the girl's eyes. "I didn't say that. You can't tell anyone I said that!"

The boy, catching his sister's emotion, clutched her hand tightly and murmured something in Spanish. His eyes were huge in his pinched, pale face.

Compunction flooded Terry. She couldn't let the child become upset. "It's okay," she said, patting him gently. "Manuela, tell your brother everything is okay. I misunderstood, that's all."

Manuela nodded, bending over her brother, saying something in a soft voice. Terry watched, frowning. Something was going on there—something the girl didn't want her to pursue.

She glanced out the window. They were making the turn into the hospital driveway. This wasn't over. Once they were inside, she'd find out how the child had been injured, one way or another.

Jeff cut the siren and pulled to a stop. By

the time she'd opened the back doors, he was there to help her slide the stretcher smoothly out.

They rolled boy and stretcher quickly through the automatic doors and into the hands of the waiting E.R. team.

Terry flashed a grin at Harriet Conway. With her brown hair pulled back and her oversized glasses, Harriet might look severe, but Terry knew and respected her. The hospital had been afloat with rumors about the new head of emergency medicine, but no one seemed to know yet who it was. All they knew was that the new appointment probably meant change, and nobody liked change.

She reported quickly, in the shorthand that developed between people who liked and trusted each other. Harriet nodded, clipping orders as they wheeled the boy toward a treatment room. This was usually the paramedic's cue to stay behind, unless the E.R. was shorthanded, but Terry was reluctant.

She bent over the child. "This is Dr. Conway, Juan. She's going to take good care cf you."

She looked around for Manuela, and found the girl near the door, her arms around her mother. Two men stood awkwardly to the side, clearly uncomfortable with the woman's tears. One, the father, turned a hat in work-worn hands, the knees of his work pants caked with mud from kneeling in the tomato field.

The other man was the crew chief, Mel Jordan. He'd driven Mr. and Mrs. Ortiz. He'd know if Juan had been working in the field when he was injured, but he wouldn't want to admit it.

Manuela came back to the stretcher in a rush, repeating Terry's words to her little brother. Taking in the situation, Harriet jerked her head toward the exam room.

"Looks like you'd both better come in."

Good. Terry pushed the stretcher through the swinging door. Because she didn't intend to leave until she knew what had happened to the child.

The next few minutes had to be as difficult for the sister as they were for the patient, but Manuela hung in there like a trouper, singing to Juan and teasing a smile out of him.

Finally the wound was cleaned, the stitches in, and Harriet straightened with a smile. "Okay, good job, young man. You're going to be fine, but you be more careful next time."

Manuela translated, and Juan managed another smile.

Harriet headed for the door. "I'll send the parents in now. Thanks, Terry."

This was probably her only chance to find out what had really happened at the camp. She leaned across the bed to clasp Manuela's hand.

"How was your brother hurt? What happened to him?"

Manuela's eyes widened. "I don't understand."

She bit back frustration. "I think you do. I want to know how your little brother cut his head. Was he working in the field?"

"What are you trying to pull?"

Terry swung around. The crew chief stood in the door, Dr. Conway and the anxious parents behind him.

"No kid works in the field. It's against the law. You think I don't know that?" Inimical eyes in a puffy, flushed face glared at her. Jordan had the look of a man who drank too much, ate unwisely and would clog his arteries by fifty if he had his way.

Dr. Conway pushed past him, letting the

parents sidle into the room with her. "What's up, Terry? Is there some question about how the boy was hurt?"

"I'd like to be sure." Ignoring the crew chief, she focused on Manuela, who was talking to her parents. "Manuela, what was your little brother doing when he was hurt?"

Manuela's father said something short and staccato in Spanish, his dark eyes opaque, giving away nothing. How much of this had he understood? Why hadn't she taken Spanish in high school, instead of the German for which she'd never found a use?

There was a flash of rebellion in Manuela's face. Then she looked down, eyes masked by long, dark lashes.

"He was playing. He fell and hit his head on a rock. That's all."

She was lying, Terry was sure of it. "When we were in the ambulance, you said—"

"The girl answered you." The crew chief shoved his bulky figure between Terry and the girl. "Let's get going." He added something in Spanish, and the father bent to pick up the boy.

"Wait a minute. You can't leave yet." They were going to walk out, and once that happened, she'd have no chance to get to the truth, no chance to fix things for that hurt child.

"We're going, and you can't keep the kid here."

The mother, frightened, burst into speech. Her husband and Manuela tried to soothe her. The boy began to cry.

Terry glanced to Dr. Conway in a silent plea for backup. But Harriet was looking past her, toward the open door of the exam room.

"What's the problem here?" An incisive voice cut through the babble of voices. "This is a hospital, people."

"The new E.R. chief," Harriet murmured to Terry, the faintest flicker of an eyelid conveying a warning.

Terry didn't need the warning. She knew who was there even before her mind had processed the information, probably because that voice had already seared her soul. Slowly she turned.

She hadn't imagined it. Dr. Jacob Landsdowne stood glaring at her. Six feet of frost with icicle eyes, some wit at Philadelphia General had once called him. It still fit.

He gave no sign that he recognized her, though he must. She hadn't changed in two years, except to gain about ten years of experience. Those icy blue eyes touched her and dismissed her as he focused on Harriet.

Harriet took her time consulting the chart in her hand before answering him. Terry knew her friend well enough to know that was deliberate—Harriet letting him know this was her turf.

Well, good. Harriet would need every ounce of confidence she possessed to hold her own against Jake Landsdowne.

Harriet gave him a quick précis of Juan's condition and treatment, giving Terry the chance to take a breath.

Steady. Don't panic. You haven't done anything wrong.

"The paramedic questions how the child was injured," Harriet concluded. "I was about to pursue that when you came in." She nodded toward Terry. "Terry Flanagan, Suffolk Fire Department."

She couldn't have extended her hand if her life depended on it. It didn't matter, since the great Dr. Landsdowne wouldn't shake hands with a mere paramedic. He gave a curt nod and turned to the group clustered around the child.

"The kiddo's folks don't speak English,

Doc." The crew chief was all smiles now, apparently smart enough to realize his bluster wouldn't work with Landsdowne. "Manuela here was saying that the little one fell and cut his head. Shame, but just an accident."

She wouldn't believe the man any farther than she could throw him, but Landsdowne's face registered only polite attention. He looked at Manuela. "Is that correct?"

Manuela's gaze slid away from his. "Yes, sir."

"Then I think we're done here. Dr. Conway, I'll leave you to sign the patient out." He turned and was gone before Terry found wits to speak.

Quickly, before she could lose the courage, she followed him to the hall. "Dr. Landsdowne—"

He stopped, frowning at her as if she were some lower species of life that had unaccountably found its way into his Emergency Room. "Well?"

She tried to blot out the memory of their last encounter. "While we were en route, I got the impression there might be more to this. If the child was injured while working in the field—"

"Did anyone say that?"

"Not in so many words."

"Then the hospital has no right to interfere. And neither do you."

He couldn't turn his back on her fast enough. He swept off with that long lope that seemed to cover miles of hospital corridor.

That settled that, apparently. She looked after the retreating figure.

Jake Landsdowne had changed more than she'd have expected in the past two years. He still had those steely blue eyes and the black hair brushed back from an angled, intelligent face, that faintly supercilious air that went along with a background of wealth and standing in the medical community.

But his broad shoulders appeared to carry a heavy burden, and those lines of strain around his eyes and mouth hadn't been there when she'd known him.

What was he doing here, anyway? She could only be surprised that she hadn't thought of that question sooner.

Jacob Landsdowne III had been a neurosurgery resident in Philadelphia two years ago, known to the E.R. staff and a lowly paramedic only because he'd been the neurosurgery consult called to the E.R. He'd been on the fast track, everyone said, the son of a noted neurosurgeon, being groomed to take over his father's practice, top ten percent of his med school class, dating a Main Line socialite who could only add to his prestige.

Now he was a temporary Chief of Emergency Services at a small hospital in a small city in rural Pennsylvania. She knew, only too well, what had happened to the socialite. But what had happened to Jake?

He'd changed. But one thing hadn't changed. He still stared at Terry Flanagan with contempt in his face.

"Glad you could join us, Dr. Landsdowne." Sam Getz, Providence Hospital's Chief of Staff, didn't look glad. *Let's see how you measure up,* that's what his expression always said when he looked at Jake.

"I appreciate the opportunity to meet with the board." He nodded to the three people seated around the polished mahogany table in the conference room high above the patient care areas of the hospital.

A summons to the boardroom was enough to make any physician examine his conduct, but Getz had merely said the board's committee for community outreach was considering a project he might be interested in. Given the fact that Jake's contract was for a six-month trial period, he was bound to be interested in anything the board wanted him to do.

Last chance, a voice whispered in his head. *Last chance to make it as a physician. They all know that.*

Did they? He might be overreacting. He helped himself to a mug of coffee, gaining a moment to get his game face on.

Getz knew his history, but the elderly doctor didn't seem the sort to gossip. In fact, Sam Getz looked like nothing so much as one of the Pennsylvania Dutch farmers Jake had seen at the local farmer's market, with his square, ruddy face and those bright blue eyes.

Dr. Getz tapped on the table, and Jake slid into the nearest chair like a tardy student arriving after the lecture had begun. "Time to get started, folks." He nodded toward the door, where two more people were entering. "You all know Pastor Flanagan, our fellow board member. And this is his cousin, Paramedic Terry Flanagan. They have something to say to the board."

Good thing his coffee was in a heavy mug. If he'd held a foam cup, it would have been all over the table. Terry Flanagan. Was she here to lodge a complaint against him?

Common sense won out. Terry would hardly bring up that painful incident, especially not to the community outreach committee. This had to be about something else.

The other people seated around the table were flipping open the folders that had been put at each place. He opened his gingerly, to find a proposal for Providence Hospital to establish a clinic to serve migrant farmworkers.

He pictured Terry, bending over the migrant child in the E.R., protectiveness in every line of her body. Was that what this was about?

He'd been so shocked to see her that he'd handled the situation on autopilot. He'd read equal measure of shock in her face at the sight of him. What were the chances that they'd bump up against one another again?

He yanked his thoughts from that, focusing on the minister. Pastor Flanagan spoke quickly, outlining the needs of the migrant workers and the efforts his church was making. So he was both Terry's cousin and a member of the board—that was an unpleasant shock.

This was what she'd done then, after the tragedy. She'd run home. At the time, he'd neither known nor cared what had become of her. He'd simply wanted her away from his hospital. Not that it had stayed his hospital for long.

The minister ended with a plea for the board to consider their proposal, and Terry stood to speak. Her square, capable hands trembled slightly on the folder until she pressed them against the tabletop.

Had she changed, in the past two years? He couldn't decide. Probably he'd never have noticed her, in that busy city E.R., if it hadn't been for her mop of red curls, those fierce green eyes, and the air of determination warring with the naiveté in her heart-shaped face.

That was what had changed, he realized.

The naiveté was gone. Grim experience had rubbed the innocence off the young paramedic.

The determination was still there. Even though her audience didn't give her much encouragement, her voice grew impassioned, and the force of her desire to help wrung a bit of unwilling admiration from him. She knew her stuff, too—knew how many migrant workers came through in a season, how many children, what government programs were in place to help.

William Morley, the hospital administrator, shifted uneasily in his chair as her presentation came to a close. His fingers twitched as if he added up costs.

"What you say may be true," he said. "But why can't those people simply come to the emergency room? Or call the paramedics?"

"They'll only call the paramedics in case of dire emergency." Terry leaned forward, her nervousness obviously forgotten in her passion. "Too many migrants are afraid of having contact—afraid their papers aren't in order or they're simply afraid of authority. As for the E.R., no one from the migrant camps comes in unless it's a case where the police or the paramedics become involved. They're afraid, and they're also dependent on the crew chief for transportation."

Jake heard what she didn't say. He hadn't thought too highly of the unctuous crew chief, either. But would he really refuse to transport someone who needed care? And did Terry, in spite of her enthusiasm, have the skills necessary to manage a job like this? He doubted it.

Morley was already shaking his head, the overhead light reflecting from it. If he'd grown that pencil-thin moustache to compensate for his baldness, it wasn't working. "Starting a clinic isn't the answer. Let the government handle the situation. We do our part by accepting the cases in the E.R. And, might I add, we are rarely paid anything."

"That's a point." A board member whose name escaped Jake leaned forward, tapping his pen on the table for emphasis. "We'd put ourselves at risk with a clinic. What about insurance coverage? When they come to the E.R., we have backups and safeguards. If Ms. Flanagan or one of her volunteers made a mistake, we'd be liable."

He thought Terry's cheeks paled a little at that comment, but she didn't back down.

"The hospital can establish any protocol it wishes for treatment. And I plan to recruit staff from among the medical professionals right in our community."

"How many people do you think have the time to do that?" Morley's head went back and forth in what seemed his characteristic response to any risk. "Really, Ms. Flanagan, I don't see how you can make this work in such a short time. Perhaps in another year—"

The mood of the board was going against her, Jake sensed. Well, he couldn't blame them. They didn't want to take a chance. He understood that.

"I have several volunteers signed up from my congregation," Pastor Flanagan said. "And I've spoken with the owner of Dixon Farms, the largest employer of migrant workers in the county."

"You're not going to tell me old Matthew Dixon agreed to help." Dr. Getz spoke for the first time, and Jake realized he'd been waiting—for what, Jake couldn't guess. "The man still has the first dollar he ever made."

If the minister agreed, he didn't show it. "He'll allow us to establish the clinic on his property. There's even a building we can use."

"If you can sell this idea to Matt Dixon, Pastor, you're wasted in the ministry. You should be in sales." Getz chuckled at his own joke, and Pastor Flanagan smiled weakly.

"That hardly solves the problem of liability," Morley said. "No, no, I'm afraid this just won't do. We can't—"

Getz interrupted with a gesture. "I have a solution that will satisfy everyone." The fact that Morley fell silent and sat back in his chair told Jake volumes about the balance of power in this particular hospital. "We need a volunteer from our own medical staff to head up the clinic. That's all." He turned toward Jake, still smiling. "I'm sure Dr. Landsdowne would be willing to volunteer."

Silence, dead silence. Jake stared at him, appalled. He could think of a hundred things that could go wrong in an operation like this, and any one of them could backfire on him, ending his last hope for a decent career. He had every reason in the world to say no, but one overriding reason to say yes. He had no choice. This wasn't voluntary, and he and Getz both knew it.

He straightened, trying to assume an expression of enthusiasm. "Of course, I'd be happy to take this on. Assuming Ms. Flanagan is willing to work with me, naturally."

Terry looked as appalled as he felt, but she had no more choice than he did. "Yes." She clipped off the word. "Fine."

"That's settled, then." Getz rubbed his palms. "Good. I like it when everything comes together this way. Well, ladies and gentlemen, I think we're adjourned."

Chairs scraped as people rose. Jake glanced at Terry, his gaze colliding with hers. She flushed, but she didn't look away. Her mouth set in a stubborn line that told him he was in for a fight.

He didn't mind a fight, but one thing he was sure of. Terry Flanagan and her clinic couldn't be allowed to throw him off course toward his goal. No matter what he had to do to stop her.

Chapter Two

"It's not the best thing that ever happened to me, that's for sure." Terry slumped into the chair across from Harriet in the E.R. lounge a few days later, responding to her friend's question about working with Jake Landsdowne. "It looks as if he's not any more eager to supervise the clinic than I am to have him. He hasn't been in touch with me at all."

Actually, she was relieved at that, although she could hardly say so. She'd tensed every time the phone had rung, sure it would be him.

"That's too bad. How are you going to make any progress if Dr. Landsdowne won't cooperate?"

Terry shrugged. "I've gone ahead without him."

"I'm not sure that's such a good idea." Harriet frowned down at her coffee mug. "He's very much a hands-on chief. He's been shaking up the E.R., let me tell you."

"I'm sorry." But not surprised. Jake Landsdowne had always been supremely confident that his way was the best way. The only way, in fact.

Harriet shrugged. "I expected it. Just be careful with him. I know how much this clinic means to you. You don't want to put the project in jeopardy by antagonizing the man."

Terry thought of Juan's frightened face, of the suppressed anger she'd sensed in Manuela. Of the other children she'd glimpsed on her trip to the migrant camp.

"I'll be careful." She had more reason than most to know she had to tread carefully. For a moment the need to confide in Harriet about her past experience with Jake almost overwhelmed her caution.

Almost, but not quite. She had to watch her step.

Please, Father, help me to guard my tongue. Telling Harriet would put her in an impossible position, and it wouldn't be fair to Jake, either. I just wish You'd show me a clear path through this situation.

"Did you know Dr. Landsdowne when you worked in Philadelphia? You must have been there at about the same time."

Harriet's question shook her. She hadn't realized that anyone would put the two things together, but naturally Harriet would be interested in her new boss's record.

"I knew him slightly," she said carefully. She wouldn't lie, but she didn't have to spell out all the details, either. "Mostly by reputation."

Anybody's life could be fodder for hospital gossip, and the handsome, talented neurosurgery resident had been a magnet for it. Still—

"Excuse me."

Terry spun, nerves tensing. How long had Jake been standing in the doorway? How much had he heard?

"Dr. Landsdowne." Harriet's tone was cool. Clearly Jake hadn't convinced her yet that he deserved to be her superior.

"I heard Ms. Flanagan was here." The ice in his voice probably meant that he knew she'd been talking about him. "I'm surprised you haven't been here before this. We need to talk about this clinic proposal."

Not a proposal, she wanted to say. It's been approved, remember?

Still, that hardly seemed the way to earn his cooperation. "Do you have time to discuss it now?"

He nodded. "Come back to my office." He turned and walked away, clearly expecting her to follow.

She'd rather talk on neutral ground in the lounge, but she wasn't given a choice. She shrugged in response to Harriet's sympathetic smile and followed him down the corridor. All she wanted was to get this interview over as quickly as possible.

The office consisted of four hospital-green walls and a beige desk. Nothing had been done to make it Jake's except for the nameplate on the desk. Maybe that was what he wanted.

He stalked to the desk, picked up a file folder, and thrust it at her. "Here are the regulations we've come up with for the clinic. You'll want to familiarize yourself with them."

She held the folder, not opening it. "We?"

His frown deepened. "Mr. Morley, the hos-

pital administrator, wanted to have some input."

She could imagine the sort of input Morley
would provide, with his fear of doing anything that might result in a lawsuit. Well, that
was his job, she supposed. She flipped
open the folder, wondering just how bad it
was going to be.

In a moment she knew. She snapped the
folder shut. "This makes it practically impossible for my volunteers to do anything
without an explicit order from a doctor."

"Both Mr. Morley and I feel that we can't
risk letting volunteers, trained or not, treat
patients without the approval of the physician in charge."

"You, in other words."

"That's correct." His eyebrows lifted. "You
agreed to the terms, as I recall."

"I didn't expect them to be so stringent.
My people are all medical professionals—I
don't have anyone with less than an EMT-3
certification. You're saying you don't trust
them to do anything without your express
direction."

Were they talking about her volunteers?
Or her?

"You can give all the sanitation and nutrition advice you want. I'm sure that will be appreciated. Anything else, and—"

His condescending tone finally broke through her determination to play it safe with him. "Are you taking it out on the program because you blame me for Meredith Stanley's death?"

She'd thought the name often enough since Jake's arrival. She just hadn't expected to say it aloud. Or to feel the icy silence that greeted it.

For a long moment he stared at her—long enough for her to regret her hasty words, long enough to form a frantic prayer for wisdom. "I'm sorry. I shouldn't have said that."

"No. You shouldn't." His face tightened with what might have been either grief or bitterness. He turned away, seeming to buy a moment's respite by walking to the window that looked out over the hospital parking lot. Then he swung back to face her. "What happened two years ago has nothing to do with the clinic." The words were clipped, cutting. "I think it best if we both try to forget the past."

Could he really do that? Forget the suicide of a woman who'd said she loved him? Forget blaming the paramedics who'd tried to save her? Forget the gossip that said he was the one at fault?

Maybe he could. But she never would.

He seemed to take her assent for granted. He nodded toward the folder in her hands. "Read through that, discuss it with your volunteers. Possibly we can arrange for the clinic to be in phone or radio contact with the E.R. when it's open. We'll discuss that later."

"Yes." Her fingers clenched the manila folder so tightly someone would probably have to pry it loose. All she wanted now was to get away from him—as far away as possible.

He picked up a ring of keys from the desk. "Suppose we go out and look at this clinic of yours."

"Not now." The words came out instinctively. "I mean...we can schedule that at your convenience."

His eyebrows lifted again. "Now is convenient. Would you like to ride with me?"

She didn't even want to be in the same state with him. "No. Thank you, but I'll need my car. Why don't you follow me out? The camp is a little tricky to find."

If she were fortunate, maybe he'd get lost

on the maze of narrow country roads that led to the migrant compound. But somehow, she didn't think that was likely to happen.

Jake kept Terry's elderly sedan in sight as they left the outskirts of Suffolk and started down a winding country road. He hadn't gotten used to the fact that the area went so quickly from suburbs to true country, with fields of corn and soybeans stretching along either side of the road.

He frowned at the back of her head, red curls visible as she leaned forward to adjust something—the radio, probably. He shouldn't have been so harsh with her. It wasn't Terry's fault that he couldn't see her now without picturing her racing the stretcher into the E.R., without seeing Meredith's blank, lifeless face, without being overwhelmed with guilt.

Just let me be a doctor again. That's all I ask. I'll save other lives. Isn't that worth something?

And did he really believe saving others would make up for failing Meredith? His jaw tightened. Nothing would make up for that.

Maybe that was why God stayed so silent when he tried to pray.

Meredith's death wasn't Terry's fault. But if someone more experienced had taken the call—if he had checked his messages earlier—if, if, if. No amount of what-ifs could change the past. Could change his culpability.

He pushed it from his mind. Concentrate on now. That means making sure Terry and her clinic don't derail your future.

It was farther than he'd expected to the Dixon Farms. The route wound past rounded ridges dense with forest and lower hills crowned by orchards, their trees heavy with fruit. Finally Terry turned onto a gravel road. An abundant supply of No Trespassing signs informed him that they were on Dixon Farms property. Apparently, Matthew Dixon had strong feelings about outsiders.

He gritted his teeth as the car bottomed out in a rut. Surely there was a better way to provide health care for the migrant workers. Wouldn't it make more sense to bring the workers to health care, instead of trying to bring health care to them? If Dr. Getz had given him any idea of what he'd been walking into that day at the board meeting, he'd have been prepared with alternatives.

Terry bounced to a stop next to several other vehicles in a rutted field. He drove up more slowly, trying to spare his car the worst of the ruts. Not waiting for him, she walked toward a cement block building that must be the site for the clinic. It was plopped down at the edge of a field. Beyond it, a strip of woods stretched up the shoulder of the ridge.

He parked and slid out. If he could find some good reason why this facility wasn't suitable, maybe they could still go back and revisit the whole idea. Find a way of dealing with the problem that wouldn't put the hospital at so much risk. To say nothing of the risk to what was left of his career.

Several people moved in and around the long, low, one-story building. Terry had obviously recruited volunteers already. The more people involved, the harder it would be to change.

Pastor Brendan Flanagan straightened at his approach, turning off the hose he was running. "Welcome. I'd offer to shake hands, but I'm way too dirty. I'm glad you're here, Dr. Landsdowne."

"Jake, please, Pastor."

"And I'm Brendan to all but the most old-fashioned of my parishioners." The minister, in cutoff jeans, sneakers and a Phillies T-shirt, didn't look much like he had at the board meeting.

"Brendan." Jake glanced around, spotting five or six people working. "What are you up to?"

"We recruited a few people to get the place in shape. Dixon hasn't used it for anything but storage in a couple of decades." He nodded toward what appeared to be a pile of broken farm implements. "It'll be ready soon. Don't worry about that."

That wasn't what he was worried about, but he wasn't going to confide in the minister. "I'll have a look inside."

He stooped a little, stepping through the door. The farmer certainly hadn't parted with anything of value when he'd donated this space.

"You must be Dr. Landsdowne." The woman who had been brushing the walls down with a broom stopped, extending her hand to him. "I'm Siobhan Flanagan."

"Another Flanagan?" He couldn't help but ask. The woman had dark hair, slightly touched with gray, and deep blue eyes that seemed to contain a smile.

"Another one, I'm afraid. I'm Terry's mother. Brendan recruited me to lend a hand today." She gestured around the large, rectangular room, its floors pockmarked and dirty, its few windows grimy. "I know it doesn't look like much yet, but just wait until we're done. You won't know the place."

He might be able to tell Terry the place was a hovel, but he could hardly say that to the woman who smiled with such enthusiasm. "You must look at the world through rose-colored glasses, Mrs. Flanagan."

"Isn't that better than seeing nothing but the thorns, Dr. Landsdowne?"

He held up his hands in surrender. "I'll take your word for it." She'd made him smile, and he realized how seldom that happened recently.

Somehow the place didn't seem quite as dismal as it had a moment ago. It reminded him of the clinic in Somalia. For an instant he heard the wails of malnourished children, felt the oppressive heat smothering him, sensed the comradeship that blossomed among people fighting impossible odds.

He shook off the memories. That was yet another place he'd failed.

Through the open doorway, he spotted the red blaze of Terry's hair. She was in the process of confronting an elderly man whose fierce glare should have wilted her. It didn't seem to be having that effect.

He went toward them quickly, in time to catch a few words.

"...now, Mr. Dixon, you can see perfectly well that we're not harming your shed in any way."

"Is there a problem?" Jake stopped beside her.

The glare turned on him. "I suppose you're that new doctor—the one that's in charge around here. Taking a man's property and making a mess of it."

This was Matthew Dixon, obviously. "I'm Dr. Landsdowne, yes. I understood from Pastor Flanagan that you agreed to the use of your building as a clinic. Isn't that right?" If the old man objected, that would be a perfect reason to close down the project.

"Oh, agree. Well, I suppose I did. When a man's minister calls on him and starts talking about what the Lord expects of him, he doesn't have much choice, does he?"

"If you've changed your mind—"

"Who says I've changed my mind? I just want to be sure things are done right and proper, that's all. I want to hear that from the man in charge, not from this chit of a girl."

He glimpsed the color come up in Terry's cheeks at that, and he had an absurd desire to defend her.

"Ms. Flanagan is a fully certified para-medic, but if you want to hear it from me, you certainly will. I assure you there won't be any problems here."

A car pulled up in a swirl of dust. The man who slid out seemed to take the situation in at a glance, and he sent Jake a look of apol-ogy. He was lean and rangy like the elder Dixon, with the same craggy features, but a good forty years younger.

"Dad, you're not supposed to be out here." He took Dixon's arm and tried to turn him toward the car. "Terry and the others have work to do." He winked at Terry, ap-parently an old friend. "Let's get you back to the house."

Dixon shook off his hand. "I'll get myself to the house when I'm good and ready. A man's got a right to see what's happening on his own property."

"Yes, but I promised you I'd take care of it, remember? You should be resting." The son eased the older man to the car and helped him get in, talking softly. Once Dixon was settled, he turned to them.

"Sorry about that. I'm afraid once Dad gets an idea in his head, it's tough to get it out. I'm Andrew Dixon, by the way. You'd be Dr. Landsdowne. And I know Terry, of course." He put his arm around her shoulders. "She used to be my best girl."

Terry wiggled free, but the look she turned on the man was open and friendly—a far cry from the way she looked at him. "Back in kindergarten, I think that was. Good to see you, Andy."

"Listen, if you have any problems, come to me, not the old man. No point in worrying him."

"There won't be any problems." He hoped.

Andrew smiled and walked quickly toward the driver's side of the car, as if afraid his father would hop back out if he didn't hurry.

The elder Dixon rolled down his window. "You make sure everything's done right," he bellowed. "Anything else, and I'll shut you down, that's what I'll do."

Shaking his head, Andrew put the car in

gear and pulled out, disappearing quickly down the lane, the dust settling behind the car.

Jake looked down at Terry. There were several things he'd like to say to her. He raised an eyebrow. "So, are you still his best girl?"

Her face crinkled with laughter. "Not since he took my yellow crayon."

He found himself smiling back, just as involuntarily as he had smiled at her mother. Her green eyes softened, the pink in her cheeks seeming to deepen. She had a dimple at the corner of her mouth that only appeared when her face relaxed in a smile.

These Flanagan women had a way of getting under his guard. Without thinking, he took a step closer to her.

And stopped.

I always told you your emotions would get the best of you. His father's voice seemed to echo in his ears. *Now it's cost you your career.*

Not entirely. He still had a chance. But that chance didn't include anything as foolish as feeling attraction for anyone, especially not Terry Flanagan.

*   *   *

Terry took an instinctive step back—away from Jake, away from that surge of attraction. Don't be stupid. Jake doesn't feel anything. It's just you, and a remnants of what you once thought you saw in him.

She turned away to hide her confusion, her gaze falling on the trailer Brendan had managed to borrow from one of his parishioners. Bren never hesitated to approach anyone he thought had something to offer for good works.

"Would you like to see the equipment we have so far?" She was relieved to find her voice sounded normal. "It's stored in the trailer until we can get the building ready." She started toward the trailer, and he followed without comment.

She was fine. Just because she'd had a juvenile crush on him two years ago, didn't mean they couldn't relate as professionals now. After all, half the female staff at the hospital had had a crush on Jake. He'd never noticed any of them, as far as she could tell.

"It's locked, I hope?"

The question brought her back to the present in a hurry. She pulled the key from her pocket, showing him, and then unlocked the door. "We'll be very conscious of security, since the building is so isolated."

He nodded, grasping the door and pulling it open. "About meds, especially. All medications are to be kept in a locked box and picked up at the E.R. when clinic hours start and then returned with a complete drug list at the end of the day."

Naturally it was a sensible precaution, but didn't he think she'd figure that out without his telling her? Apparently not.

"This is what I've been able to beg or borrow so far. There are a few larger pieces, like desks and a filing cabinet, that we'll pick up when we're ready for them." She pulled the crumpled list from her jeans pocket and handed it to him.

He looked it over, frowning. What was he thinking? His silence made her nervous. Was he about to shut them down because they didn't have a fully equipped E.R. out here?

"I'm sure it looks primitive in comparison to what you're used to, but anything is better than what the workers have now."

"It looks fine," he said, handing the sheet back to her. "I've worked in worse."

She blinked. "You have?"

He leaned against the back of the trailer, looking down at her with a faint smile. "You sound surprised."

"Well, I thought—" She blundered to a stop. She could hardly ask him outright what had happened to his promising neuro-surgery career.

"I didn't stay on in Philadelphia." Emotion clouded the deep blue of his eyes and then was gone. "I spent some time at a medical mission in Somalia."

She could only gape at him. Jacob Lands-downe III, the golden boy who'd seemed to have the world of medicine at his feet, work-ing at an African mission? None of that fit what she remembered.

"That sounds fascinating." She managed to keep the surprise out of her voice, but he probably sensed it. "You must have seen a whole different world there—medically, I mean."

"In every way." The lines in his face deep-ened. "The challenges were incredible— heat, disease, sanitation, unstable political situation. And yet people did amazing work there."

She understood. That was the challenge that made her a paramedic, the challenge of caring for the sick and injured at the moment of crisis.

The emergency is over when you walk on the scene. That was what one of her instructors had drummed into them. No matter how bad it is, you have to make them believe that.

"You did good work there," she said softly, knowing it had to be true.

"A drop in the bucket, I'm afraid. There's so much need." He glanced at her, his eyebrows lifting. "Hardly the sort of job where you'd expect to find me, is it?"

"I didn't say that."

"You were thinking it."

"Yes, well—" They were getting dangerously close to the subject he'd already said he wouldn't talk about. "Everyone said you were headed straight toward a partnership with your father in neurosurgery."

"Everyone was wrong." Tense lines bracketed his mouth. "I found the challenges in Africa far more interesting."

There was more to it than that. There had to be, but he wouldn't tell her. How much of his change in direction had been caused by Meredith's death?

It had changed Terry's life. She'd given up

her bid for independence and come running home to the safety of her family. Had he run, too?

Jake closed the doors and watched while she locked them, then reached out and double-checked.

She bit back a sigh. He couldn't even trust her to do something as simple as locking a door. How on earth were they going to run this clinic together?

Chapter Three

"Not a bad day, was it?" Terry glanced at her mother as they cleaned up after the clinic's opening day.

She probably should get over that need for Mom's approval. Most of her friends either called their mother by her first name and treated her like a girlfriend or else feigned complete contempt for anything a parent might think. She'd never been able to buy into either of those attitudes, maybe because Siobhan Flanagan never seemed to change.

Her mother turned from the cabinet where she was stacking clean linens. "No one would recognize this place from the way it looked a few short days ago. You can be proud of what you've accomplished."

Terry stared down at the meds she'd just

finished counting and locked the drug box. She should be proud. But... "Three clients wasn't much for our first day, was it?"

"It will grow." Her mother's voice warmed. "Don't worry. People just have to learn to trust what's happening here. And they will."

"I hope so." It was one thing to charge into battle to help people and quite another to fear they didn't want your help at all. "Maybe I've leaped before I looked again." Her brothers had teased her mercilessly about that when she was growing up, especially when she'd tried to rope them into one of her campaigns to help a stray—animal or human.

"Don't you think that at all, Theresa Anne Flanagan. You've got a warm heart, and if that sometimes leads you into trouble, it's far better than armoring yourself like a—like an armadillo."

Terry grinned. "Do you have any particular armadillo in mind?"

Siobhan gave a rueful chuckle. "That was a mite unchristian, I guess. I'm trying to make up for it, though. I've invited Dr. Lands-downe to your brother's for the picnic on Sunday."

"You've what?" She could only hope her

face didn't express the horror she felt. The
Flanagan clan gathered for dinner most
Sunday afternoons, and it wasn't unusual
for someone to invite a friend. But Jake
wasn't a friend—he was her boss, in a way,
and also an antagonist. She wouldn't go so
far as to think of him as an enemy, and she
certainly didn't want to think of those moments when she'd felt, or imagined she'd
felt, something completely inappropriate.

"What's wrong?" Her mother crossed to
Terry, her face concerned. "I know you think
he's a bit officious about the clinic, but if we
get to know him better—"

"I already know him. From Philadelphia."
Her throat tightened, and she had to force
the words out. "He's the one I told you
about. The one who blamed my team for
the death of the woman he'd been seeing."

The words brought that time surging back,
carrying a load of guilt, anxiety and the over-
whelming fear that perhaps he'd been right.
Perhaps she had been responsible.

"Oh, Terry, I didn't realize." Her mother
gave her a quick, fierce hug. "I'm sorry."

She shook her head. "It's all right. I didn't
tell anyone because—well, it didn't seem
fair to me or to him."

Mom sat next to her on the desk. "Has he talked to you about it, since he's been here?"

"Only to say he thinks we should leave the past alone."

"But the inquiry cleared you of any wrong-doing. He should apologize, at least."

Terry's lips quirked at the thought of Jake apologizing. "He probably doesn't see it that way. Anyway, if anyone's guilty—" She stopped, regretting the words already.

Her mother just looked at her. Better people than she had crumbled at the force of that look.

"We'd been called to the woman's apartment before. Two or three times. Always the same thing—she'd taken an overdose of sleeping pills or tranquilizers. We figured out finally that she was being careful. Never taking enough to harm herself. Just enough to make people around her feel guilty."

"And Dr. Landsdowne was the person she wanted to feel guilty?"

She nodded, remembering the gossip that had flown around the hospital. "They'd been dating, but I guess when he wanted to break it off, she didn't take it very well." A brief image of Meredith flashed through her mind—tall, blond, elegant, the epitome of the Main Line socialite. "I don't suppose anyone had ever turned her down before."

"Poor creature." Her mother's voice was warm with quick sympathy. "And him, too. What a terrible thing, to feel responsible for someone committing suicide. But what happened? You said she was careful."

"She took something she was allergic to." Terry's throat tightened with the memory. "We couldn't save her."

Her mother stroked Terry's hair the way she had when Terry had been a child, crying over a scraped knee. "That's probably why he blamed you. He couldn't face it."

Or because he did believe she was inept and incompetent. "I don't know, Mom." She pushed her hair back, suddenly tired. "I just know I've got to figure out how to deal with him now."

"Do you want me to cancel the invitation?" It was a testament to her mother's concern that she'd be willing to violate her sense of hospitality.

"No." She managed a smile. "I've got to get used to his presence. At least I'll be on my own turf there."

Her mother laughed. "And surrounded by Flanagans, all prepared to defend you."

"I don't need defending." The quick response was automatic. Her brothers had been trying to shelter her all her life. They'd never accept that she didn't need their protection.

"I know." Her mother gave her another hug and slid off the desk. "They mean well, sweetheart."

The sound of a horn turned Siobhan toward the door. "There's Mary Kate, coming for me. Are you heading for home now?"

"I just want to make one last check, okay?" And take a few minutes to clear her head. "I'll be right behind you."

"Walk out with me to say hi to your sister." Her mother linked her arm with Terry's.

Together they walked to where Mary Kate sat waiting. The back of her SUV was filled with grocery bags.

"Hi, Terry. Come on, Mom. I've got to get home before the frozen stuff melts."

"I'm ready." Siobhan slid into the car, while Terry leaned against the driver's side, scanning her big sister's face for signs of strain.

It had been ten months since Mary Kate

lost her husband to a fast-moving cancer—ten months during which she kept up a brave face to the world, even to her own family.

"How're you doing? How are the kids?"

"Fine." Mary Kate's smile was a little too bright. "They're looking forward to seeing you on Sunday."

"Me, too." She wanted to say something—something meaningful, something that would help. But, as always, words faltered against Mary Kate's brittle facade. She'd never relax it, certainly not in front of her baby sister.

Terry stepped back, waving as the car disappeared in a cloud of dust down the lane. Then she walked back into the clinic, mind circling the question she knew her mother had wanted to ask. Why hadn't she told them the whole story about what happened in Philadelphia?

Because I was trying to prove I could accomplish something independent of my family. Because I failed.

Pointless, going over it and over it. She pushed herself into action, cleaning up the last few items that were out of place, locking the drug box, putting Jake's list of rules in the desk drawer. The cases that had come in today were so minor she hadn't even been tempted to bend any of the rules. Not that she would.

The door banged open. Manuela raced in. Terry's heart clutched at the look on her face.

"Manuela, what is it?"

The girl leaned against the desk, breathing hard. "Juan. He's sick. He's so hot. Please, you have to come." She grabbed Terry's arm in a desperate grasp. "Now. You have to come!"

Jake's rule flashed through her mind. Staff will not go to the migrant housing facility alone.

"I have to," she said aloud. "I have to." She grabbed her emergency kit and ran.

Manuela fled across the rutted field toward the back of the string of cement block buildings that served as dormitories for the workers. Terry struggled to keep up, mind churning. Juan's cut could have become infected. That seemed the most likely cause for a fever, but there were endless possibilities. If she had to take him to the hospital, she'd also have to explain how she'd come to break Jake's rules in her first day of operation.

The sun had already slid behind the ridge that overshadowed the camp. It would be nearly dark by the time she finished. She should have thought to bring a flashlight. She should have thought of a number of things, but it was too late now.

Please, Lord. Guide me and show me what must be done.

A snatch of guitar music, a burst of laughter, the blare of a radio sounded from the far end of the camp. Words that she couldn't understand, cooking aromas that she couldn't identify—it was like being transported to a different country.

Manuela stopped to peer around the corner of the building, her finger to her lips to ensure Terry's silence. She didn't need to worry. Terry had no desire to draw attention to her presence.

But why was the girl so concerned with secrecy? If she'd fetched Terry without her parents' permission, that could be yet another complication to the rule she was already transgressing.

Manuela beckoned, and together they slipped around the corner and through the door. The room was a combination kitchen and living room, with a card table, a few straight chairs and a set of shelves against the wall holding plastic dishes and dented metal pots. An elderly woman, stirring something on a battered camp stove in the corner, stared at them incuriously and went back to her cooking.

Terry followed Manuela through a curtained door. At a guess, the whole family slept here on a motley collection of beds and cots jammed together. Juan lay on one of the cots, and to her relief, his mother sat next to him. Manuela grabbed an armful of clothes from the floor.

"Sorry." In the dim light, it seemed her cheeks were flushed. "Mama and I try to keep it neat, but it's hard."

"I understand." Six people were living in a room the size of the laundry room at the Flanagan house. No wonder it seemed cluttered. "Let's have a look at Juan."

Nodding to the mother, she bent over the cot. "Hi, there, Juan. Remember me?" She smiled reassuringly, trying to hide her dismay. His skin was hot and dry, his eyes sunken in his small face. She glanced at

Manuela. "Any chance we can get more light in here?"

Nodding, she switched on a battery-powered lantern.

No electricity, overcrowded conditions, inadequate cooking facilities—surely someone like Matthew Dixon could do better than this for his employees, even if they were here for only a short period of time.

She checked the boy's vital signs and cautiously removed the bandage on his head, relieved to find no sign of infection. "It doesn't look as if his injury is causing this, Manuela. Has anyone else been sick?"

Manuela translated quickly for her mother and then nodded. "Some of the other children have had fever and stomach upsets."

"Why didn't their parents bring them to the clinic?"

Manuela shrugged, face impassive. If she knew the answer, she wasn't going to tell.

"Tell your mother I'd like to have Juan checked out by the doctor." She glanced at her watch. "Since it's so late, maybe the best thing is to take him to the E.R."

The mother seemed to understand that phrase. Nodding, she scooped Juan up, wrapping him in a frayed cotton blanket.

Terry followed them out, hoping she was making the right choice. Harriet would come to the camp if she called her, but by the time she'd tracked her down, they could be at the E.R. Jake wasn't on duty tonight, so...

That train of thought sputtered out. Why exactly did she have his schedule down pat in her mind?

Mrs. Ortiz hurried outside. She stopped so suddenly that Terry nearly bumped into her. Mel Jordan, the crew chief, stood a few feet away, glaring at them.

"Where do you think you're going?" He planted beefy hands on his hips.

Terry stepped around the woman. "Juan is running a fever. We're taking him in to have the doctor look at him."

"You people aren't supposed to be here." He jerked his head toward the building. "Take the kid back inside. You don't want to go running around this time of night."

Mrs. Ortiz started to turn, but Terry caught her arm. Manuela moved to her mother's other side, so that the three of them faced the man.

"My car is at the clinic." She tried to keep her voice pleasant, suppressing the urge to rage at the man. "I'll run them to the hospital and bring them back. It's not necessary for you to come."

His face darkened. "I told you you're not supposed to be here, interfering in what doesn't concern you." He took a step toward her, the movement threatening. "Just get out and take your do-good notions with you. We don't need outsiders around here stirring up trouble."

Her heart thudded, but she wouldn't let him see fear. "You've got trouble already. The child is sick. You can't keep him from medical care. Or any of the other children."

It was obvious why none of the parents had brought their children to the clinic. Mrs. Ortiz trembled. Surely she didn't think the man would dare become violent....

And if he does, what will you do, Terry? Once again you've leaped into a situation without thinking.

Well, she didn't need to think about it to know these people needed help. What kind of a paramedic would she be if she walked away? One way or another, she was getting this child to a physician.

A pair of headlights slashed through the dusk as a car bucketed down the lane. Distracted, the crew chief spun to stare as the car pulled to a stop a few feet away, the beams outlining their figures.

She was caught in the act. She wouldn't have to take Juan to a doctor. Jake had come to him.

Jake took his time turning off the ignition and getting out of the car. He needed the extra minutes to get his anger under control. One day into the program, and Terry had broken his rules already.

She'd also, from the tension in their stances when his headlights had picked them out, put herself in a bad situation. There had been something menacing about the way the crew chief confronted her, moderating Jake's anger with fear for her.

The man—Jordan, he remembered— swung toward him. "What is this? A convention? Don't you people have enough to do without bothering us?"

Jake let his gaze rest on the man until Jordan shifted his weight nervously. Then he turned toward Terry.

Her shoulders tensed, as if expecting an assault. But no matter how tempted he might be, he owed Terry a certain amount of professional courtesy.

"What do we have, Ms. Flanagan?"

Her breath caught a little. "Juan Ortiz, age six. You'll recall he was treated in the E.R. Temp 103, upset stomach, dehydrated. I was about to bring him to the E.R. when Mr. Jordan intervened."

He knew enough about Terry to know she couldn't turn away from a sick child. His gaze sliced to Jordan. "Why were you trying to keep them from taking the child to the hospital?"

Jordan's face twisted into a conciliatory smile. "Look, it was just a misunderstanding. I'd never do a thing like that."

He felt Terry's rejection of the words as if they were touching. Well, they'd deal with Jordan later. The important thing now was the child.

"Let's go inside and examine Juan. Then we can see what else is necessary."

The girl, Manuela, explained to her mother in a flood of Spanish, and they all trooped into the cement block building that appeared to be home.

A few minutes later he tousled Juan's hair. "You're going to be fine, young man." He glanced at Terry, naming the medications he wanted. "You have all that at the clinic?"

She nodded. "I'll run over and get them."

"Wait. I'll drive you." And we'll talk. He turned back to Manuela. "I'm writing down all the instructions for you. It's very important to give him liquids, but just a little at a time. A couple of sips every ten or fifteen minutes. You'll make sure your mother understands?"

"Yes, doctor." She straightened, as if with pride. "I will take care of Juan myself. Everything will be done exactly as you say."

"Good girl. You sound as if you'd make a good doctor or nurse one day."

He saw something in her face then—an instant of longing, dashed quickly by hopelessness. He'd seen that look before. It shouldn't be found on children's faces.

"I would like, yes. But it's not possible. This is my life." Her gesture seemed to take in the fields, the building, the people.

"But, Manuela—" Terry began.

He shook his head at her and she fell silent. Now was not the time. But her expression made him fear Terry was taking off on another crusade.

"Well, you can practice your skills with

your little brother." He handed her the instructions. "Do you understand all that?"

She read through it quickly and nodded.

"Good girl. He'll be a lot more comfortable
once we get his fever down. We'll be back
in a few minutes with the medication, okay?"

"Okay." Her smile blossomed, seeming to
light the drab room.

He glanced at Terry. "Shall we go?"

She picked up her kit. "I'm ready."

They walked to the car in silence. He'd intended to read the riot act to Terry once
they were alone, but by the time they were
bouncing down the lane, his anger had dis-
sipated.

She was the one to break the silence.
"Why did you come?"

He shrugged. "I wanted to check on how
the first day went. Instead I found your car
there, you gone. This seemed the likely
place."

"You mean you expected me to break the
rules." She sounded ready for battle.

"Let's say I wasn't entirely surprised."

"The child was sick. What did you expect
me to do?"

"You should have called me. Look, Terry, I
understand why you went, but that's not ac-

ceptable. If it happens again, I'll pull the plug on the clinic."

Her hands clenched into fists on her knees. "You're pretty good at that, aren't you? Cutting your losses."

The jab went right under his defenses, leaving him breathless for an instant. He yanked the wheel, pulling to a stop in front of the clinic. Before she could get out, he grabbed the door handle, preventing her from moving. They were very close in the dark confines of the car.

"I thought we were going to leave the past behind." He grated the words through the pain.

"I'm sorry." It was a bare whisper, and the grief arced between them. "I shouldn't have said anything."

"No. You shouldn't have."

This was no good. They were both trapped by what had happened, and he didn't see that ever changing.

Chapter Four

Terry walked back into the clinic, aware of Jake pacing behind her. Why didn't he just leave and let her take care of getting the meds to Manuela? The last thing she needed was to have him trailing along behind her as if she couldn't be trusted to do a simple thing like this.

And does he know that he can trust you, Theresa? The voice of her conscience sounded remarkably like her mother. You certainly haven't shown him that you'll follow his rules so far.

Even worse, she'd brought up the past that both of them knew they'd have to ignore if they were to have any sort of working relationship. She had to do better—had to find a way to curb her tongue, along with that Flanagan temper that flared too easily.

She took a small cooler from the shelf and began filling it with ice.

"The antibiotic doesn't have to be refrigerated."

He was second-guessing her already. She would not reply in kind, but her lip was going to get sore from biting it if she had to be around Jake too much.

"I know. I thought Manuela could give Juan some ice chips to suck on."

He gave a short nod and took the cooler from her, holding it while she scooped the rest of the ice in. "Where is the drug box?" His voice sharpened. "Surely you didn't leave it here with the clinic unattended."

She held back a sarcastic reply with more control than she'd thought she possessed. She met his gaze. "It's locked in the trunk of my car."

"Good." He snapped the word, but then he shook his head. "Sorry. That wasn't an accusation."

She supposed that was an olive branch. A good working relationship, she reminded herself. You don't have to like the man, just get along with him professionally.

"I know. Believe me, being responsible for that drug box is at the top of my list." She hesitated. How much more should she say about what had happened tonight? "My family always accuses me of leaping before I look. I guess I proved them right tonight, didn't I? I reacted on instinct."

That was an apology, if he'd take it that way.

"Fast reactions are important for first responders like paramedics—"

She had a feeling there was a *but* coming at the end of that sentence. "Don't forget I'm a firefighter, too. Sometimes it's tough to keep the jobs sorted out."

He blinked. "I didn't realize that. In the city, being a paramedic is a full-time job."

"It's what I'm doing most of the time, but our department isn't all that big. When an alarm comes, I do whatever I have to." She smiled. "Can't let the rest of the family down."

Now she'd confused him. "The rest of the family?"

"All of the Flanagans are associated with the fire department in one way or another. My father and one of his brothers started the tradition, and our generation just carried it on. Even my cousin, Brendan, the one you met at the board meeting—"

He nodded, frowning a little, as if that board meeting wasn't the happiest of memories.

"Brendan's the pastor of Grace Church, but he's also the fire department chaplain. He manages to put himself in harm's way a little too often to suit his wife. The others— well, you'll meet them all at the picnic on Sunday."

This was the point at which he could make some excuse to get out of Mom's impulsive invitation. He probably wanted to.

"I'll look forward to that." He paused, his arm brushing hers as he reached for the lid of the cooler. "Unless that's going to be uncomfortable for you. If you'd prefer I not come, I'll respect that."

He was too close, and she was too aware of him. Instead of looking up at his face, she focused on his capable fingers, snapping the cooler lid in place as efficiently as he'd stitch a cut.

An armistice between them—that was what she needed. Maybe letting him see the Flanagans in full force would help that along. Besides, as Mom had said, they'd all be on her side, whether she wanted their help or not.

The silence had stretched too long between them. He'd think she was making too much of this.

"Of course I want you to come." She met his gaze, managing a smile. "You're new in town. We all want to make you feel welcome." Even though she'd rather he'd found any hospital in the country other than Suffolk's Providence Hospital to work in.

"I'll look forward to it, then."

"Fine. I'll write up the directions to my brother's farm for you." A truce, she reminded herself.

She began sorting the intake forms that had been left on the desk. "I'll just put these away and then run the meds over to the camp on my way out. If you'd like to leave, please don't feel you have to stay around."

"I'll take the meds over." He shook his head before she could get a protest out. "It's not a reflection on you, Terry. I just think it's safer if you don't go over there tonight. In fact, no one should be at the clinic alone."

"Shall I add that to the rules?" She couldn't keep the sarcasm out of her voice, and his mouth tightened.

"The rules are designed to keep everyone

safe. Including you. But you have to follow them."

"I know." Stop making him angry, you idiot. "Next time anything comes up, I'll call the hospital first."

"No, call me. You have my cell number, don't you?"

She nodded. "But you weren't on duty tonight. Wouldn't you rather we call the E.R.?" And now she'd let him know that she was keeping tabs on his schedule.

"That doesn't matter. I'd prefer to be called, so I know firsthand what's happening here. The welfare of the patients and the staff are my responsibility."

That almost sounded as if he cared about the clinic, instead of finding it an unwelcome burden foisted on him by the hospital administration.

"I'm glad you feel that way. It's good to know we can count on you."

She glanced at him, but he wasn't looking at her. Instead he was frowning at the cement block wall, as if he saw something unpleasant written there.

"My responsibility," he repeated. Then he focused on her, the frown deepening. "Look, it's just as well you understand this. Anything that goes wrong at the clinic is going to reflect on me in the long run. And I don't intend to have my position jeopardized by other people's mistakes. Is that clear?"

Crystal clear. She nodded.

It really was a shame. Just when she began to think Jake was actually human, he had to turn around and prove he wasn't.

"Dr. Landsdowne, may I have a word, please?"

The voice of the hospital administrator stopped Jake in his tracks. It felt as if William Morley had been dogging his steps ever since the migrant clinic program got off the ground. He turned, pinning a pleasant look on his face, and stepped out of the way of a linen cart being pushed down the hospital hallway.

"I'm on my way down to the E.R., Mr. Morley. Can it wait until later?"

Morley's smile thinned. "I won't take much of your time, Doctor. Have you read the memorandum I sent you regarding cutting costs in emergency services?"

Every department in any hospital got periodic memos regarding cutting costs from the administrator—it was part of the administrator's job. Morley did seem to be keeping an eagle eye on the E.R., though.

"Yes, I've been giving it all due attention." How did the man expect him to assess cutting costs when he'd only been in the department for a couple of weeks?

Morley frowned. "In that case, I'd expected an answer from you by this time, detailing the ways in which you expect to save the hospital money in your department."

Jake held on to his temper with an effort. He couldn't afford to antagonize the man. "It's important to take the time to do the job right, don't you agree? I'm still assessing the needs and the current staffing."

"Perhaps if that were your first priority, you'd be able to get to it more quickly."

He stiffened. "The first priority of the chief of emergency services is to provide proper care for the patients who come through our doors."

"Well, of course, I understand that." Morley said the words mechanically and leaned a bit closer, as if what he had to say was a secret between the two of them. "However, the hospital has to make cuts if it's going to remain solvent. We can't afford to have money bleeding out of the E.R. every month.

We need an E.R. chief who can make it run efficiently. I hope that's you."

Money wasn't the only thing bleeding in the E.R., but it seemed unlikely Morley was ever going to understand that. The threat was clear enough, though.

"I'll work on it. Now, if you'll excuse me—"

Morley caught his arm. "Another thing— I'm sure you're spending more time than you'd like dealing with this migrant clinic."

Jake nodded. The need to approve every step taken by trained nurses and para- medics was tedious, but he couldn't see any other way of dealing with the situation.

"It occurs to me that something might come up—perhaps has already come up— that the board would find a logical reason to postpone this effort until another time."

The man was obviously fishing for any ex- cuse to shut down the clinic. Jake's mind flashed to the incident two nights earlier when Terry had gone to the migrant hous- ing, clearly breaking his rules. If he told Mor- ley about it, the daily hassle of supervising the clinic might be over.

But he couldn't do it, no matter how much the clinic worried him. He'd promised Terry another chance. His mind presented him with an image of Terry's face, stricken and pale when he'd lit into her team, accusing them of negligence in failing to save Meredith.

No. He owed her something for that.

The wail of a siren was a welcome interruption. He gave Morley a perfunctory smile. "There haven't been any problems there yet. Now, if you'll excuse me, I'm on duty."

This time he escaped, pushing through the swinging door into the E.R.

The paramedics wheeled the patient in just as he arrived. Terry and her partner. He'd just been thinking of her, and here she was.

Terry gave him a cool nod as her partner reeled off the vital statistics—an elderly woman complaining of chest pain and difficulty breathing. He focused on the patient, who looked remarkably composed for someone brought in by paramedics.

He nodded to the nurse. "We'll take it from here."

Terry patted the elderly woman. "You listen to the doc now, Mrs. Jefferson. Everything will be fine."

"Thank you, dear. I don't know what I'd do

if I couldn't count on you." The woman beamed at the paramedics.

He flashed a glance at Terry, who was fanning her flushed face. Her red curls were damp with perspiration and her neat navy shirt was wrinkled. "Stick around for a few minutes. I'd like to speak to you."

She nodded, and he helped push the stretcher back to an exam room.

It didn't take more than a few minutes to determine what he'd already suspected—there was nothing wrong with the woman that merited a trip to the emergency room. The fact that the nurse also knew Mrs. Jefferson well enough to know she'd like grape juice just confirmed it. He left the woman happily drinking her grape juice and went in search of the paramedics team.

He caught up with Terry in the hallway. "Where's your partner?"

She swung toward him, resting a frosty water bottle against her temple. "Jeff's restocking the unit. Do you want me to get him?"

"Not necessary. I can say what I need to say to you." And he shouldn't be noticing how those damp red curls clung to her skin. Terry didn't mean anything to him except an obstacle to be overcome. "That woman shouldn't have been brought to the E.R. There's nothing wrong with her."

"That decision isn't really up to the paramedics, is it? We don't practice medicine."

He glanced around, but no one was in earshot. "Are you throwing my words back at me?"

Terry's face crinkled into a sudden smile. "Sorry. It's just that we all know Mrs. Jefferson is a frequent flyer."

"Frequent flyer?" He understood, all right, although he hadn't heard them called that— those people who called the paramedics when they got lonely or needed attention.

"Look, she lives alone in a third-floor walkup and her air conditioner just broke. I suppose she got a little scared. Anybody might in this heat. It happens."

"I know it happens, but it shouldn't." This was exactly the sort of thing Morley had been talking about. "It wastes the hospital's resources."

Terry looked unimpressed. "I don't work for the hospital, I work for the city."

He planted his hands on his hips. It was probably a good thing, for Terry's sake, that she didn't work for the hospital.

"That's not the point. We have to cut costs in the E.R., and every patient that's brought in here for no reason eats into our budget."

"She probably doesn't need a thing except to rest in a cool place for a while. That's not going to take any of your budget."

"She can find a cool place in a movie theater." He stopped short, realizing he was letting himself get into an argument with a paramedic. "Take her home. Now."

Terry looked at him as if she could hardly believe her ears. "You can't expect us to haul her back to that hot apartment now. Give me a few hours. I'll call Brendan and see if he can't get someone to donate a new air conditioner."

Brendan Flanagan, her minister cousin. The board member. Being caught between a board member and the hospital administrator was not a good place to be. For a moment longer he glared at Terry, annoyed at her ability to put him on the spot.

But this was a no-win situation. "All right. But she's not staying for supper. You and your partner get back here for her before five, or I'll call her a cab."

"Right. We'll do that." She spun, obviously

not eager to spend any more time in his company.

He stood for a moment, watching the trim, uniformed figure making for the door. At the last moment she stopped, turned and pulled something from her pocket.

She came back to him and held out a folded slip of paper. "I nearly forgot to give you this." She stuffed it in his hand and hurried out the door.

Jake unfolded the paper. It was a carefully drawn map, designed to take him to the Flanagan picnic on Sunday.

He didn't suppose he could get out of that picnic without offending several people, including one who was on the hospital board. But he suspected that, if Terry had anything to say about it, he wasn't going to enjoy himself.

The hot day had given way to a sticky, humid evening, with clouds thickening. A shower would be nice, Terry thought hopefully as she slid out of the car. But if they did get one this time of year, it would be a thunderstorm. She walked toward the back door of the comfortable house that had sheltered three generations of Flanagans.

Mom was in the kitchen, wiping cookie dough off the table. The aroma of chocolate chip cookies filled the air, and red geraniums rioted on the windowsills. She looked up, smiling as always. Mom always made you feel as if you were the best thing she'd seen all day.

Terry put one arm around her mother's waist while snagging a handful of still-warm cookies with the other hand.

Mom kissed her cheek and gave a laughing swipe at her hand. "Someday you're not going to be able to eat like that, Terry."

"Then I'd better take advantage of it while I can. Umm." She slid onto the stool next to the pine table. "Which of your grandchildren do I have to thank for the cookie baking today?"

"Mary Kate dropped the children off while she did some shopping. She's insisting she has to look for a job, and she needs some interview clothes that make her look like a physical therapist instead of a mom."

Terry sank down on the kitchen stool. "That wasn't the life she and Kenny had planned. They always felt it so important that she stay home with the children."

"Life changes when we least expect it."

Her mother took a package of chicken from the refrigerator and opened it. "Losing Kenny hit Mary Kate hard. She hasn't discovered all her strength yet."

Terry blinked. "What do you mean? She always seems to keep her feelings under control."

"I'm not sure what I mean." The admission was unusual for Mom, who'd always seemed the source of all answers to Terry. "At first I thought she was coping well with Kenny's death. Now, I'm not so sure. She's hiding something behind that cheerful face she puts on."

"Have you tried to talk to her?" That was a silly question. Of course Mom would have tried.

Mom's hand slowed on the piece of chicken she was breading, as if she'd forgotten what she was doing. "She's not willing to let me in. Maybe you ought to talk to her."

"Me?" Terry nearly choked on her cookie. "Mary Kate treats me like I'm about eleven. She'd never confide in me. And I doubt that I could give her any good advice, especially since..."

"Since what?"

She shrugged, evading those wise eyes. "You know. Having Jake Landsdowne around hasn't exactly done great things for my self-confidence."

"Terry, you know perfectly well that you're very good at what you do. You shouldn't let that man's opinion matter so much to you."

"I know, I know. But he's in charge—at least of the migrant clinic." She stood, shrugging. "Well, no point in talking about it. I'll set the table. Is it just the three of us tonight?"

"Just us."

Time was, they'd been hard put to fit the whole family around the dining room table. With her three brothers and cousin Brendan married now, supper was a much quieter affair most of the time, although people still seemed to show up at suppertime with the flimsiest of excuses.

She carried service for three through the swinging door into the dining room and began laying the table automatically.

Her mother didn't understand. Terry had been confident of her abilities before, when she'd gone off to Philadelphia to try her wings on her own, without the support of her big, loving, interfering family. That confidence had been shattered into a million pieces by what happened when Meredith Stanley died, and since then she'd struggled to put it back together, one patient at a time.

Now Jake was here, and she had to see him nearly every time she went to the E.R., had to cope with his criticisms of the way she was running the clinic, too. Small wonder she kept second-guessing herself.

Her mother pushed through the swinging door, a bowl of tossed salad in her hands. She set it down and gave Terry a searching look. "What is it? I can see something else has happened."

"I never could keep secrets from you, could I?" She managed a smile.

Her mother clasped her hand warmly. "You have a warm, open, loving spirit. That's not a bad thing, although maybe it opens you up to hurt sometimes. Now tell me."

"It's not a big deal, I guess. We had a call from Mrs. Jefferson today." She didn't need to identify the woman further. Her mother had heard about all their regulars. "Her air conditioner had broken, and she was sweltering in that walk-up apartment."

"Poor thing. What did you do about it?" Of

course Mom understood she'd had to do something.

"We took her in to the E.R. And I called Brendan. He managed to get an air conditioner from somebody, and he was over there installing it by the time we took her home."

"What was the problem, then?"

"Jake. Dr. Landsdowne. He knew there wasn't anything wrong with her, and he wanted us to take her straight back home. Said the E.R. couldn't afford to have people there who didn't need the care."

Her mother gave her a shrewd look. "I take it you had words about it."

"We did." She shook her head. "I keep trying to get along with him—honestly I do. I've prayed and prayed about it." Although if truth be told, mostly she was praying not to run into him. "Anyway, he finally agreed to let her stay for the afternoon. You'd have thought I was asking him to give her free plastic surgery for the rest of her life."

"Now, Terry, I'm sure he wasn't that bad. I heard about his service in Somalia. Surely that means his heart is in the right place."

"I guess so. But he's doing a good job of hiding it from me."

"Then maybe that's what we'd better take to the Lord." She took both Terry's hands in hers. "All right?"

Terry nodded. Mom had always taught them that they could pray anytime, any-place, and the more often, the better.

"Lord, we want to bring this situation with Dr. Landsdowne to you." Mom sounded so warm when she prayed, as if she were hav-ing an intimate conversation with a dear friend who already knew all her troubles. "We know he and Terry can find a way to get along, if only he'll show us the spirit that took him to do Your work in such a difficult place. Please open his heart, and open ours to see who he really is. In Jesus's precious name. Amen."

Mom's warmth and faith surrounded her, and some of the tightness she'd been hold-ing on to slipped away. Mom's prayer hadn't quite been what she'd have prayed, though. She wasn't so sure she wanted to know Jake any better than she already did.

Chapter Five

"Hey, Aunt Terry, play football with us!" Terry's niece Shawna punctuated the request by flinging the foam football straight at her. Terry grabbed it instinctively, nearly falling out of the lawn chair she'd positioned under the oak tree that shaded the yard at Gabe and Nolie's farm.

"C'mom, Shawna, it's too hot for football." In fact, lounging in a lawn chair watching the rest of the Flanagan clan scurry around getting the weekly picnic together sounded just right, if a little lazy.

Shawna, Mary Kate's eight-year-old, was the ringleader of the Flanagan grandchildren. She gathered the others around her, blue eyes sparkling, dimples flashing, and Terry knew her moments in the lawn chair were going to be short-lived.

A moment later, the chair collapsed under the rush of small bodies, leaving Terry laughing helplessly, tickling or kissing any niece or nephew she could reach.

"Is that your idea of helping?" Seth, her second-oldest brother, reached into the tangle of bodies and pulled out Davy, his son, giving him a kiss before setting him on his feet. "Getting the kids so riled up they won't want to eat?"

"Hey, I'm going to help them work up an appetite." She scrambled up, tossing the football in the air. "You want to help?"

Seth gave her the quick grin that had always made him everyone's buddy. "Thanks anyway. I promised to help Gabe get the ice-cream maker ready."

Even his promotion to captain in the fire department hadn't changed Seth's easygoing, steady outlook. In fact, since he'd married Julie, providing himself and Davy with the person they needed to make their family complete, she'd seldom seen him without a smile on his face.

She faked a punch at his midsection. "Looks like married life agrees with you. Next thing you know, you'll be growing a paunch."

"No chance." He patted his flat stomach. "Davy keeps me hopping, and when the new baby comes, I'll probably be walking the floor at night."

He glanced toward the picnic table, where Julie was helping Mom spread the table-cloth. The soft yellow top Julie wore accentuated her rounded belly.

The blaze of fierce love in his face startled Terry. Maybe Seth wasn't so calm and collected as all that, at least where his love was concerned.

He ruffled her curls, something her brothers had been doing to emphasize their height for years. "When are you going to take the plunge? Hasn't Mom rounded up any likely prospects for you yet?"

"Mom knows better."

"What about this new doc who's coming to dinner today? Julie and I thought maybe—"

"No chance." She couldn't say the words fast enough. Mom wouldn't have told anyone but Dad about her history with Jake, so maybe it was natural that they'd jump to that conclusion. "He's just one of Mom's good deeds. I think she's hoping it will make him a little easier to get along with at the migrant clinic. He's been driving us crazy with all his rules."

Seth put his arm around her shoulders. "Want us to throw a scare into him? The Flanagan boys can still look pretty fierce if we want to."

"Like you used to scare off all my boy-friends? No, thanks." She ducked away from him, hoping he was deceived by her light tone. "If you want to know why I'm still single, just blame it on yourself. Go get the ice cream ready. And shout when you need someone to turn the handle. All the kids want a chance."

Laughing, Seth walked toward the farm-house. Terry tossed the football to Mandy, Ryan's little stepdaughter. She couldn't look at Mandy now, laughing and chattering a mile a minute, without remembering the first time she'd seen her, when Ryan had carried her out of a burning building. Mandy was one of God's small miracles, now a part of their lives to stay.

She'd been kidding when she'd told Seth he'd scared off all her boyfriends, but there was an element of truth in that. Much as she loved her brothers, they could be a bit over-whelming. Any boy would have been wary of running afoul of Gabe, or Seth, or Ryan, or even Brendan, the cousin who'd been raised as one of them.

Not that she thought they'd try to scare Jake. Or that he'd scare if they did. But they'd always been so protective of Terry, their baby sister. She'd always known she had them to fall back on.

That should be a good thing, shouldn't it? But on the one occasion when she'd left Suffolk to try life on her own in the big city, she'd failed.

Terry calmed an argument between Shawna and Michael, her little brother, and sent Michael running toward the paddock for a long pass. The donkey lifted his head, watching the small figure running toward him. Toby was used to their shenanigans by this time.

She didn't want to think about that time in Philadelphia, because every time she did, it brought her right back to Jake. She glanced at her watch. He was late. Was it too much to hope that he wasn't coming?

Michael hurtled back to her, his face red.

"Listen, guys, I think we'd better stop and have a nice cold drink, okay? It's getting too hot to run around."

A chorus of groans greeted her, but she shepherded them toward the table, where a thermos of lemonade and another of iced tea sat waiting, and supervised the process of pouring lemonade into paper cups.

"Let's play another game, Aunt Terry, please?" Shawna leaned against her, wheedling. "It doesn't have to be a running game."

Terry dropped a kiss on Shawna's red curls. "I have a better idea. See Grandpa sitting there relaxing? Go ask him to tell you a story."

"Yeah, a story." Michael ran toward Dad, lemonade sloshing in his cup, and the others followed.

Dad gave them a mock fierce frown as they interrupted his discussion with Brendan of his favorite football team's chances, but she wasn't fooled. There was nothing Dad liked better than a fresh audience of little kids for his stories. Only Gabe and Nolie's one-year-old, asleep on a blanket in the shade, was still too young to understand Grandpa's tales.

Nolie, Gabe's wife, set a bowl of potato salad on the table. "We were going to start bringing the food out, but I guess your friend from the hospital isn't here yet. Should we wait awhile?"

"No, let's go ahead. Maybe he'll be here by the time it's ready." And maybe he wouldn't be.

She ought to be ashamed of herself. During worship that morning, she'd achieved a sense of peace, asking God to use her in this situation for His good ends. Now, it seemed, she was already frittering away those good intentions by hoping Jake wouldn't show up at all. She closed her eyes for a quick prayer.

I'm sorry, Father. I mean well, You know that. I just keep getting in the way of my own prayers. Please help me to deal with Jake the way You want me to, and guide my words and my thoughts when I'm with him.

Gravel churned under car wheels. She opened her eyes. Jake's car came up the farm lane and pulled to a stop along a row of lilac bushes. Her stomach gave a little jolt. God was giving her an immediate opportunity to test her resolve.

Jake cut the engine and sat motionless for a moment. He'd thought seriously about calling Mrs. Flanagan with an excuse, but decided that would be the coward's way out. Any excuse he'd made would simply look as if he didn't want to encounter Terry again after the clashes they'd had recently.

He couldn't do that. He might wish Terry were a bit more amenable to direction, but she was a good paramedic, and she was certainly devoted to her patients. That was the bottom line—patient care. That was something Morley, the hospital administrator, didn't seem to understand.

More to the point, he couldn't afford to antagonize a board member like Brendan Flanagan. His position was precarious enough already without doing that. So he'd go through with this, and he'd make a good impression on the Flanagan family if it killed him.

He got out and started toward the farmhouse. This didn't look like any working farm that he'd ever seen, not that he knew much about it. From the lane, green lawn stretched toward a white frame farmhouse with a wide, welcoming porch. Beyond was a garage whose double doors stood open, exposing what looked like some kind of obstacle course.

There was a cottage, like a smaller replica

of the main house, its front door flanked with rosebushes, and a red barn whose white-fenced paddock held a few animals he couldn't identify from this distance.

But it was the lawn that drew his attention. The scene was like a Flemish painting— people dotted across the grass, adults and children both, rustic wooden tables spread with white cloths for a picnic. Surely all those people weren't Flanagans. He'd expected a quiet family meal with maybe eight or ten people at the most. There were at least twice that many, it seemed, and they were all staring at him.

He hadn't felt this awkward since he'd started a new school in the eighth grade. Well, that was stupid. His confidence wasn't so badly damaged—he could still meet a bunch of strangers and make a good impression.

Terry detached herself from the group and came toward him. In jeans and a bright yellow T-shirt, she looked younger than she did in uniform. She moved reluctantly, he suspected. He could hardly blame her. Things between them had been difficult, to say the least. She'd probably have rescinded her mother's impulsive invitation if she could.

"Welcome to Nolie's Ark." If her smile was forced, it didn't show. "Did you have any trouble finding the place?"

"Not at all. The map brought me directly here." He'd noticed the unusual sign, with its fanciful ark loaded with all sorts of animals. "Why Nolie's Ark?"

Terry's dimples flashed. "Wait until we've shown you around. Then you'll understand. And Nolie's because the farm belonged to my sister-in-law before she and Gabe married. He wouldn't let her change the name."

"Gabe is your brother?" He had a feeling keeping everyone straight would be a job.

"The oldest. Come and meet everyone."

He fell into step with her. "I thought this was just going to be family today. I didn't expect such a crowd."

Terry's grin widened. "It is family. Sorry, I guess someone should have warned you about the size of the Flanagan clan. I'm afraid we can be a little overwhelming at first."

"Just at first?"

She chuckled. "You might have a point."

They'd reached the table. Apparently aware that they'd been staring at him, people began talking to each other again. He was just as happy not to be the center of attention.

Terry led him to the man at the grill loaded with sizzling hot dogs and hamburgers. "This is my brother, Gabe."

"Your big brother," Gabe corrected, extending his hand. "Welcome to our home."

Tall, with dark hair and blue eyes, Gabe didn't look much like Terry, but Jake saw a strong resemblance to Mrs. Flanagan. A handsome yellow Labrador retriever sat at Gabe's side.

"Thanks for inviting me. I appreciate the chance to get to know a few people." And possibly mend a few fences with a board member while I'm at it. He'd already spotted Brendan at the end of the table, bouncing a toddler on his lap.

"That's my wife, Nolie." Gabe nodded toward a slender blonde in a denim skirt and blue shirt, who was lifting the lid from a large casserole dish. "They've just put the food on, so why don't you find a seat. Terry can introduce you around while we're eating." He grinned, and now Jake saw the resemblance to Terry. "That might be easier than trying to remember a whole string of names."

Nolie clinked a glass, and the chatter slowly

died out. He slid onto the end of a bench
next to Terry as Pastor Brendan folded his
hands. Heads bowed around the table.

"Father, You've given us another beautiful
day to share Your bounty together, and we
ask Your blessing and care for those who
aren't as fortunate as we are. We thank You
for this food and the hands that prepared it.
We ask Your blessings on this family and on
the new friend You've brought into our midst
today. In Jesus's name. Amen."

A chorus of amens sounded around the
table. One of a pair of small redheads tugged
at Brendan's sleeve. "You didn't say God
bless the animals, Uncle Brendan."

"You're right, Michael, I didn't." He bowed
his head again. "And bless the animals, too.
Amen." He grinned. "Let's eat."

Serving dishes began to fly around the
table at what seemed the speed of light.
Mrs. Flanagan, across from him, snatched a
bowl of potato salad from her oldest son
and offered it to Jake.

"Please, have some." She gave him the
sweet smile that had lured him into this
family meal. "You have to fend for yourself
around here or you won't get a thing."

"Now, Mom, we're a little more polite than

that." Terry passed a crock of baked lima beans. "The speed just comes of having eight people around the table when we were growing up, four of them growing boys."

"Eight?" he echoed faintly as an airborne biscuit was snatched midair by Pastor Brendan, of all people.

Terry nodded, passing a bowl of coleslaw. "My sister Mary Kate is the oldest." She nodded to a slightly older version of herself, leaning across to fork chicken onto the plate of one of the children. "The two little redheads are hers—Shawna and Michael."

"Which one is her husband?"

Terry's face went somber. "Kenny died nine months ago. Liver cancer. Things went so fast I'm not sure she's accepted it, even now."

"That's rough." He caught the wave of sorrow she felt for her sister, a little startled that he responded to her emotions so quickly.

"Yes. It is." Her gaze was fixed on the roll she was buttering. "Gabe comes next— that's his and Nolie's toddler, Siobhan, sitting on Brendan's lap. They run this place."

"As a farm?" he ventured.

She smiled. "Not quite. Nolie trains service animals and then works with disabled individuals to bring them together with the right animals. That's how Gabe and Nolie met."

He glanced toward the dog, lying quietly behind Gabe, brown eyes watchful. "You mean the dog—"

"Max is a seizure alert dog. Gabe's a firefighter, injured in the line of duty. Now he helps Nolie with the animals and teaches at the fire academy."

"Dr. Landsdowne, glad to meet you." The bluff, hearty man who sat next to Siobhan Flanagan must be Terry's father. Clearly, that was where she'd gotten the red hair and freckles, although her father's hair was turning white. "I'm Joe Flanagan. Theresa's falling down on the introductions."

Jake reached across to shake hands. "A pleasure to meet you, sir."

"I'm just trying to introduce Jake slowly—" Terry stopped, flushing. "I mean, Dr. Landsdowne."

"I think it better be Jake when we're not on the job, don't you?" he said easily.

"Jake." Joe's handshake was firm. "Terry, the man's a doctor. I'm sure he can keep a few names straight." He nodded toward the other side of the long table. "That's Seth, our next son, with his wife, Julie. Little Davy belongs to them. And you know Brendan."

"I met him through the hospital board. Isn't he Terry's cousin?"

"My brother's boy. We raised him after his parents died. His wife, Claire, is an old friend of Nolie's. Then comes Theresa, and Ryan is the youngest, though he and Terry are so close in age they've always been like twins. That's him, with his wife, Laura, and their daughter, Mandy."

The names swam around in his mind. Maybe Terry's method would have been better. He turned toward her, but Gabe's little girl had toddled over to her, and she scooped the baby up in her arms.

"This is little Siobhan." She nuzzled the soft blond curls on the baby's neck. "She's our latest addition. Isn't she beautiful?"

She smiled at him, face glowing with love for her tiny niece. It was like leaning near a warm fire on a cold night, and the urge to draw closer surprised and cautioned him with its strength.

"Beautiful," he agreed. Joe had turned away to talk to someone else. "You really are all following your father's footsteps. I suppose he expected that."

"Oh, I guess he'd have been proud of us, no matter what we wanted to do. It just runs in the family."

The way being a doctor ran in his family, but it wasn't as if he and his sister had had a choice. The Flanagan kids apparently felt they did, but chose it anyway.

Otherwise, the Flanagan crew was as different from his family as it was possible to be. He couldn't imagine this babble of cheerful noise at any Landsdowne family gathering, and his sister's children would be tidied away long before the adults sat down at a linen-covered table for a meal prepared by the cook and a little civil conversation.

"Do you do this sort of thing often? Get together with the whole family, I mean." He gestured at the crowded table.

"Every Sunday," Terry said. Her eyes narrowed. "I suppose that sounds odd to you."

"Well, it—" It did sound odd, at least in his experience, for grown children to be so close to their parents, but he could hardly say so. "You seem to depend on each other a great deal."

"What's wrong with that?" The snap in

Terry's voice told him she'd taken offense. "We're a family. Naturally we stick together. Or don't you think that's natural?"

Why on earth did she have to take offense at everything he said? He'd come here to mend fences, not start a war. "I didn't mean—" he began calmly, but Mrs. Flanagan stood up and caught Terry's hand.

"Terry, come along and help me with the dessert. You can finish your conversation later." She practically dragged Terry away from the table.

Wise woman. She'd seen trouble coming and headed it off, but he'd still somehow have to convince Terry that he hadn't been criticizing. She seemed constantly ready to think the worst of him. Of course, she'd say she had good reason for that.

"Keep your hand flat, Mandy." Terry put a carrot on her small niece's palm. "You don't want Toby to think your fingers are carrots, do you?"

Mandy giggled, stretching her arm through the paddock rails toward the gray donkey. Toby, used to children, waited patiently until her hand uncurled, and then delicately took the carrot.

"It tickles," Mandy declared. "I love Toby, Aunt Terry."

"I love Toby, too." She gave Mandy a quick squeeze.

"Who is Toby?" The voice came from behind her. "Your boyfriend?"

Mandy and Michael both started to giggle, giving her time to tamp down her irritation and plant a smile on her face before she turned toward Jake. Really, couldn't the man see that she didn't especially want to spend her day off with him?

"Toby's the donkey," Michael explained, recovering first. "Aunt Terry doesn't have a boyfriend. She's a paramedic."

"I don't think the two are mutually exclusive, are they?"

"Michael thinks so." She ruffled Michael's curls, as red as her own. "He's almost seven, so he knows all about it."

Jake leaned over the fence to pat the donkey, listening to the children prattle on about how smart and how sweet he was, and giving her time to catch her breath. Had she overreacted to Jake's comment about the family? Possibly, but she was rather sensitive to the topic of being dependent on her family. He'd hit a sore point without even knowing it.

And probably he'd meant the comment to be just as condescending as she'd taken it. She didn't know what a family like the Landsdownes did together—sat around and talked about complicated surgical procedures, maybe. They probably didn't feed carrots to donkeys, as Jake was doing right now under Mandy's careful tutelage.

"Keep your hand flat," Mandy cautioned, parroting Terry's words to her as she straightened out his long, gifted fingers with her small hand. "You don't want Toby to think your finger is a carrot."

"Certainly not," he agreed. He tilted his head, smiling at Terry as the donkey nibbled the carrot.

She could only hope her face didn't express what she was feeling. She was so accustomed to a frown when Jake looked at her that the easy, relaxed smile knocked her back on her heels. The man had charm when he bothered to use it, which wasn't very often, at least with her.

"Hey, Michael and Mandy!" Gabe shouted from the porch. "Come quick if you want a turn with the ice cream."

The two bolted for the porch, not bothering to say a word.

Jake dusted off his hands. "Guess we know where we stand in the scheme of things. Somewhere below ice cream."

"They love to turn the crank." And they'd left her where she didn't want to be, alone with Jake. "Shall we go and join them?"

She took a step, but he stopped her with a hand on her arm.

"Your mother said you'd show me around," he said. "Why don't we start with the barn?"

That made it impossible for her to refuse, and he knew it. "It's just a barn," she tried feebly.

"I'm a city boy. Humor me."

She managed a smile that was probably more of a grimace and started toward the barn. Well, if he wanted a tour, she'd give him one.

"Nolie says the barn was built in the early eighteen hundreds, and not much has been done to it since then except for basic repair. The style is typical of Pennsylvania German barns. You'll see them all over the county. People know about the Amish in this area, but plenty of the other early settlers were German, too."

"I take it they built to last." He actually sounded interested.

"Seems that way. You really ought to talk to Nolie about it. She's the expert. Her family came over from Germany on William Penn's heels, from the sound of it."

She pushed the heavy door open. Gabe had probably closed it to keep the little ones out. She stepped inside, eyes adjusting gradually to the dim light. The lofty interior was cool after the bright sunshine outside.

"Just a barn," she said, swinging her hand in a gesture meant to take in the stalls, the loft, the stacked hay bales, even the ginger barn cat that leaped softly from a manger, as if to ask what they were doing there.

Jake brushed past her, approaching the chestnut quarter horse that stood in the closest stall. "Why isn't this handsome fellow out in the paddock today?"

She moved reluctantly to join him, and Eagle came over to have his face scratched. "Tact on Nolie's part, I imagine. If Eagle were out where the kids could see him, they'd want to ride him, and most of them are too small. She's just started giving lessons to Shawna, and she probably doesn't want to start a fight over who's big enough."

"Tactful," he agreed, patting Eagle's shining neck. "Now suppose *you* stop being tactful and tell me why you're upset with me."

That startled her into looking up at him. His face was grave and attentive, as if he really cared how she felt.

That was certainly unlikely. He'd never shown much consideration for her feelings before.

"If you must know, I didn't like being made to feel as if my family were somehow odd because we like to spend time together. I'm sure it's more fashionable to dismiss your parents as irrelevant, but we happen to appreciate ours."

His hand stilled on the horse's neck. "You're right."

"You mean you *were* being condescending."

His lips tightened. "Stop putting words in my mouth, Terry. No, I mean you're right to appreciate your parents. If I had parents like yours, I hope I'd feel the same way."

"Oh." He'd taken the wind out of her sails. "Well, I didn't expect—"

"You didn't expect anything but the worst from me." He swung to face her, close against the rough wood of the stall. "I know we've had our differences, but I thought we'd agreed to put that behind us. Still, you constantly put the worst interpretation on everything I say. Like the situation with your frequent flyer the other day."

Well, she was on solid ground there, whether he agreed or not. "We had to bring her to the E.R. It's not like she did any harm by being there, whether she needed medical care or not."

"Maybe so, but I'd just endured a lecture from the hospital administrator on cutting costs. If he has his way, the E.R. budget will be cut, and someone who really needs care could be turned away."

"Morley." The man's penny-pinching was notorious. "I'm sorry, but what else could I have done? I couldn't walk away and leave her in that stifling apartment." Surely he could see that.

"No. I guess you couldn't." He was looking at her so intently that she felt as if she were under a microscope. "You have a warm heart, and after meeting your family, I understand it." He put his hand over hers on the stall bar, and she seemed to feel his touch shimmering across her skin.

"There's—" Her breath got tangled up, and she had to start again. "There's nothing wrong with having a warm heart, is there?"

"Not a thing. Not a single thing."

He was so close that his breath touched her cheek, so close that she could see the tiny dust motes flickering in the shaft of sunlight that surrounded them. Eagle moved slightly in his stall, his hoofbeat muffled against the straw.

Jake leaned closer, and for an insane moment she thought he was going to kiss her. Then a shout from Gabe startled them and they pulled apart.

"Terry, Jake, the ice cream is ready. You better come before it's all gone."

"Be right there," she called back. She swung toward the door. "We'd better go. They'll eat it in no time flat."

She would not look back at Jake. She wouldn't wonder if he was annoyed at her brother's bad timing.

Maybe it wasn't bad timing at all. Maybe Gabe's interruption had been right on target to keep her from making a fool of herself.

Chapter Six

Jake took the bowl Gabe handed him automatically and stared at creamy vanilla ice cream studded with chunks of peaches. What had just happened to him, aside from the fact that these people expected him to eat a bowlful of cholesterol and calories?

He'd let his guard down far too much with Terry, practically coming right out and saying that he envied her for the family life she'd been blessed with. The opposite, obviously, was that he hadn't.

He put a spoonful in his mouth, and the rich flavor exploded on his tongue. Not good for him, of course, but very good to the taste. Like Terry.

The children were jumping up and down next to him, demanding seconds from the metal ice-cream bucket, nestled in its tub of ice. He took a few steps away from the melee, moving deeper into the shade of the huge oak tree.

Terry wouldn't understand his attitude toward his family. How could she? She only knew what everyone at Philadelphia General had known—just what people had always thought about Jacob Landsdowne III.

Born with a silver spoon in his mouth. The golden boy who had everything going for him, ready to step right into his father's prestigious practice. The guy who really had it made, not like the poor jerks who had to fight every step up the medical ladder and still ended up with a crushing load of debt they'd probably never be able to pay off.

The thing was, those people had never known what the payback was for everything he'd been given—the equally crushing load of obligation, the necessity of being perfect. He didn't want them to know. After all, he had a little pride left.

Across the lawn, Joe Flanagan was laughing, clapping Seth on the back over something. One of the children ran to him, and he caught her up and tossed her into the air, catching her in a bear hug.

No, with a father like hers, Terry wouldn't

understand. She probably wouldn't believe that a father could turn his back on his only son for the sin of being imperfect.

Well, enough self-pity. He'd wallowed in that long enough during those weeks in the hospital when he'd come back from Africa. He was finished with that.

This job was his last chance to reestablish himself as a doctor, and he couldn't let anything stand in his way. He had to succeed. And success meant not only proving himself as a doctor but also performing that delicate balancing act between good medicine and hospital profits, between Morley and his balanced books and Pastor Brendan and his good works.

So this picnic wasn't about the excellent food and certainly not about moments alone with Terry. He backed quickly away from the memory of standing so close to her in the barn, sunlight tangling in her red curls, her face tilted up to his.

Last chance. The words echoed in his mind. He had to focus on his goal, eliminating every distraction, especially ones with red hair and a stubborn streak a mile wide.

Pastor Brendan sat at the table, alone for the moment. Carrying the ice cream, he walked over and sat down across from him. "Not indulging in ice cream today, Pastor?"

"Brendan, remember?" Brendan patted his stomach. "I already had a serving of my wife's chocolate soufflé, and I'm stuffed. Claire is teaching herself to cook by working her way through a French cookbook."

"Lucky man."

"I am that." Brendan smiled, his gaze moving to the slim, dark-haired woman who was helping to clear the table. His gaze lingered there for a moment and then came back to Jake. "So, tell me how the clinic is working out. Are you managing to juggle that with your other responsibilities?"

"I've decided to give up sleeping." At the other man's look of concern, he shook his head, forcing an amused expression to his face. "No, just kidding. Terry has her volunteers so well organized that things are running very smoothly."

Except for such problems as Terry's unauthorized visit to the migrant housing, but he didn't think he'd mention that. If she hadn't told her family, he wasn't going to.

"I'm not surprised." Brendan glanced at Terry, who was pushing a small nephew on the swing tied to one of the oak's branches while she carried on a conversation with Seth's wife. "Terry's always been superb at running her various crusades."

"You mean she does this all the time?" It sounded as if Brendan could give him some valuable insight into what made Terry tick.

"From the time she was a kid, Terry's always been a crusader." He smiled, shaking his head a little. "Oh, maybe some of them were tilting at windmills, but her heart was always in the right place. It still is."

"Yes," he said softly, watching her without intending to. Terry's laugh looked as light-hearted as that of her nephew. "I can see that."

"She used to drag us into her battles, willing or not. Save the whales, save the park, provide Thanksgiving dinner for the hungry...whatever it was, Terry gave it her all."

"I guess the fact that she became a paramedic was a foregone conclusion, then. She wants to save people."

Brendan nodded. "Don't get me wrong, she was a good firefighter, still is. But she's never been content with just putting a fire out. She wants to fix things for people."

"Sort of like her cousin Brendan, then," he said.

Brendan chuckled. "Maybe you have a point there. My church was moving in the direction of helping the migrants already, but Terry just pushed us a little faster. And once I saw what those people are dealing with—" He nodded toward Mary Kate's little redheads, chasing each other around the table with apparently boundless energy. "I'm thankful our little ones don't have to live like that, so that obligates me to help."

"I take it you know Matthew Dixon pretty well, since he attends your church."

"Attends? Not very often. But the Dixons have belonged to Grace Church since it was founded."

Jake chose his words carefully. "I'm concerned that we not start any problems with him through the clinic. He seemed rather short-tempered on the subject the one time I saw him."

"I don't think you have to worry much about that. At least not about Matthew coming around looking for problems. He hasn't been well for the past year or so, and Andrew's really the one who's handling everything."

"Poor old fellow." Siobhan slid onto the bench next to him, abruptly joining the conversation. "He knows he's slipping. It must be terrible to feel you have to depend on your children that much."

"Don't worry, Mom." Terry came up behind her and slung her arm around her mother's shoulders in a quick hug. "When you start losing it, I'll still be there to help."

"Not if I get there first," Brendan said, smiling at his aunt.

Siobhan waved her hand as if waving them off. "The one I keep thinking about is that young girl, Manuela. She seems so bright and hardworking. It's a shame she can't even consider a career in medicine."

So Terry had told her family about Manuela's dreams. He watched her as she slid onto the bench next to him. Did that mean she'd also told them about her unauthorized visit?

Brendan nodded, glancing at the children who were gathering on a blanket in the shade, apparently to listen to a story Nolie was telling. "I'd hate to think any of our crew wouldn't feel they could be anything they wanted to be, if they worked hard enough."

"Wait for it," Terry murmured as Gabe and Seth came over to join the conversation.

"You're about to see the Flanagan jugger-naut in action."

He turned toward her, grateful to see a friendly smile. Whatever had almost hap-pened in the barn, Terry either hadn't no-ticed or was willing to ignore. As he should. "Juggernaut?"

"They tease me about my crusades, but they're just as bad. Listen to them."

Terry was right. The conversation had be-come general, with people throwing in ideas about how they could help the Ortiz family, and Manuela in particular.

"Are they always like that?" he said softly, just for the pleasure of seeing Terry smile, seeing her gaze go soft with affection for her family.

"Always. Trust me, they're born meddlers, all of them."

A shaft of sunlight, filtered through the leaves of the oak tree, touched Terry's skin, highlighting her freckles and making her green eyes almost golden. He ought to look away—

"So, can we count on you, Jake?" Bren-dan's question brought him back to earth with a bump.

What had he missed while he was thinking

about the color of Terry's eyes? Obviously the question implied that they wanted something from him. "Well, um, what exactly would you want me to do?"

"Just take the opportunity to talk with the girl, that's all. See how serious she is about medicine, what the possibilities are for her. Once we know that, we'll know better if we can do anything to help her."

The last thing he needed was further involvement with the Flanagans and their causes. "Why doesn't Terry talk to her?"

"You're the doctor," Terry said quickly. "Haven't you seen the awe in her face when she looks at you?"

Siobhan was nodding eagerly. "I've tried, but she won't open up to me. I'm sure you're the right person for the job, Jake."

He didn't want to. He didn't have time to. But clearly, he had to agree.

"I'll give it a try, but I'm not promising anything."

Brendan clapped him on the shoulder as if he were a hero, and the others chimed in, talking eagerly about what they might do.

"Juggernaut," Terry murmured. "I told you."

He looked at her, an unwilling smile tugging at his lips. For just a moment understanding flowed between them, strong as the August sun.

He looked away quickly. What had happened to his resolve to stay focused on the job?

Terry grasped the gurney, helping Jeff push through the E.R. doors as the patient continued to protest.

"I'm perfectly all right." The woman clasped her handbag to her chest and glared at Terry. "Just felt a little dizzy, that's all. There's no need for all this fuss."

"Just let the doctor check you out," Terry soothed. "It won't take long." Unless it was the heart attack she suspected, despite the patient's protestations.

Harriet and a nurse joined them the moment they rolled through the doors. She'd already spoken to Harriet on the radio, so the team was ready for their arrival.

"Female, fifty-seven." Terry kept her voice calm for the patient's sake, but instinct told her this was the real thing. She gave the stats quickly. "Experienced shortness of breath, cold sweat and dizziness on her way to work."

"I've just been tired lately, that's all. I haven't been sleeping well. It's nothing."

"Maybe so, but we'd like to be sure of that," Harriet said.

Her gaze met Terry's, and she knew Harriet was thinking the same thing she was—possible heart attack. Too many women didn't realize that their symptoms weren't necessarily the same as a man's. The patient was in good hands with Harriet.

She watched as they headed into the treatment room. Harriet mouthed "good call" over her shoulder as they pushed through the door.

Jeff grinned at her. "Nice job convincing her, Ter. For a while there I thought she was going to hit you with her bag."

"I saw you stayed out of the line of fire," she retorted, hoping Jeff didn't notice the fact that she was glancing around uneasily, hoping not to spot Jake. "You restock while I do the paperwork."

"In a hurry?" He lifted an eyebrow. So he had noticed. They'd been partners since she joined the department, her self-confidence battered by what had happened in Philadelphia. Jeff, with that deceptively laid-back manner and the calm, sure way he had of assuming she knew exactly what to do, had played a big part in helping her bounce back. She'd have adopted him as an older brother, if she didn't already have too many of those.

"Never mind." She grabbed the run report. "Just get us out of here in five minutes, and I'll treat you to coffee."

"Done." Grinning, he headed for the supply room.

Terry leaned on the counter and started filling out the paperwork automatically. She must have been too obvious, if Jeff noticed it. She'd better be more careful.

In the three days since the picnic, she'd managed, through a bit of evasive action, to avoid encountering Jake at all. She just wasn't all that confident of her ability to see him without thinking back to those moments in the barn—moments when she'd been convinced he was going to kiss her.

Well, he hadn't. And she'd behaved perfectly normally for the rest of the picnic, so he couldn't possibly know how embarrassed she'd been.

She smiled and moved a step away as a white-haired hospital auxiliary member set a vase of yellow mums on the counter. Like it or not, she couldn't keep on avoiding Jake forever. She had to get control of her feelings.

Had she been unwittingly sending him signals that day? A flush crept into her cheeks at the thought. Surely not. And yet, why else had it happened? Unless she was completely kidding herself—imagining something that Jake hadn't felt at all.

Somehow she couldn't quite buy that. She'd heard his breath quicken, seen his eyes darken. That had been real.

No matter what Jake had or hadn't felt, one thing was perfectly clear. She couldn't keep telling herself that her feelings were just the remnants of a long-ago crush. She was attracted to the man, despite all the things she disliked about him. Stupid, but whoever said attraction was a rational thing?

She scrawled her signature at the bottom of the run report and handed a copy to the receptionist. Maybe that wasn't what she'd expected to happen at the picnic, but some good had come out of it, too. The family had gotten to know Jake a little, and he'd agreed to help with Manuela. Two positives, to balance one big negative.

Maybe she should stop trying to avoid the man. If she did, perhaps she'd stop blowing his image up in her mind. She could start seeing him as a human being.

She shoved away from the counter. What was taking Jeff so long? There hadn't been that much restocking to do. She crossed the receiving area toward the supply room. She was ready for her morning coffee, even if he wasn't.

She'd nearly reached the door when she saw the stocky figure of her partner heading toward her, empty-handed.

"What's up? Aren't you finished yet?"

He shook his head. "We're finished, all right. We aren't permitted to restock the unit from the hospital supplies any longer."

"What? We've always done that. Who says we can't?"

"I do." Jake came through the door quickly, his lab coat flapping at his movement. His lean face was set, as if he were ready to do battle. "It's a new hospital policy."

"Since when?" She couldn't keep the edge from her voice. "We've always—"

He made a slicing motion with his hand, cutting her off. "It doesn't matter what you've always done, Ms. Flanagan. The E.R. has been directed to cut costs, and that's what we're doing. I'm afraid you'll have to sacrifice along with the rest of us."

That formal use of her name was probably a warning, reminding her of the difference in their status. Count to five, she warned herself. Better yet, count to ten.

"It hardly seems fair to penalize the paramedics." It took a determined effort to keep her voice calm. "After all, some of our materials stay here, one way or another, every time we deliver a patient."

Something, some small flicker in his eyes, told her she'd scored with that point. Then his mouth tightened.

"Sorry. You can do a direct replacement of any sheets that are left here. That's all."

Generous of him, since otherwise the hospital would end up with all their sheets. "What about other supplies? We always—"

He took a step toward her, his tall form screening her from the interested gazes of the E.R. receptionist, one custodian and two candy stripers who'd paused to watch. "Don't say another word." His voice was low, and those blue eyes were arctic. "Don't push me into a situation where I have to file a complaint about you, Terry. I don't want to do that."

Didn't he? She clamped her lips shut tightly. Could have fooled her on that one. She glared back at him, but in the end, it was her gaze that dropped.

Because like it or not, he was right. She couldn't have an open battle with him in front of staff members, no matter what she felt. She swallowed hard and managed to nod.

All right. When there was no choice, you'd better accept the inevitable as gracefully as possible. Maybe a complaint from the fire chief about the new policy would make Jake reconsider.

She walked quickly toward the door, her partner closing in behind her as if he couldn't wait to get out of there, either. Whether or not the chief could get this policy reversed, one thing was now clear. Her naive thought that maybe she and Jake could be friends had been blasted to pieces.

By the time she reached the clinic late that afternoon, Terry felt like the ragged end of a rope. They'd done two nursing home transports, gone clear across town on a false alarm, dealt with one combative drunk who'd taken a swing at Jeff, and hauled a reluctant elderly man with a possible broken leg down three flights of stairs. Just another day, but her back ached and the success she'd had with the heart attack patient had receded to the back of a long list.

"You can't get the big save every day," Jeff had commented when he'd headed for his car at the end of the shift. "At least we didn't lose anybody today."

He was right, of course. And she knew herself well enough to know that her irritability wasn't caused by the job. It had its roots in her encounter with Jake.

She pulled into a rutted parking space at the side of the clinic. At least neither of the other two cars already parked there belonged to him. Maybe she could go back to evading the man, since nothing else seemed to work.

She planted a smile on her face and headed for the door. It was nearly five, and experience had shown them that the next couple of hours would be the busy ones, as workers came in from the fields. This was also the first day they were running a bus, borrowed from the church, to the smaller migrant camps in the area, and they had no way of knowing how many people would show up on that.

She paused for a moment as she pulled open the screen door, just to enjoy the sight. What had once been a junk-filled shed now looked like a real clinic. The whitewashed walls and bright lights were the biggest factor, but the small touches her mother had engineered certainly made a difference—bright posters on the wall, a basket of fruit on the desk, a homey braided rug in the waiting area.

Jim Dawson and Carole Peterson, an EMT and a nurse practitioner who had been among her first volunteers, were at the battered desk going over paperwork.

"Hi, Terry." Jim grinned. "I know that aching back stance. How many people did you haul downstairs today?"

She stopped rubbing the small of her back. "Just one, but he weighed enough for three."

Carole waved a form. "If we get anyone from the other camps, should we indicate which one on the intake form?"

"I hadn't thought of that, but it sounds like

a good idea. Will you make a note of it on the volunteer hot sheet?"

Carole nodded. The hot sheet had become their lifeline, letting each volunteer know what new issues or solutions had come up during the previous shift. Working with volunteers required a totally different approach from working in the E.R. Had Jake figured that out yet? She doubted it.

The door from the back room swung open, and Manuela hurried through, arms loaded with clean towels. The stack began to tremble, and Terry hurried to help her.

"*Hola,* Manuela. It's good to see you. Are you giving us a hand today?" Maybe this would be a good opportunity to talk to the girl about her hopes, rather than depending on Jake to get around to doing it.

"You didn't know?" Manuela's grin nearly split her face.

Terry blinked. That had to be the first time she'd seen a genuine smile from Manuela, who normally carried more than her fair share of trouble. "Know what?"

"I have a job helping at the clinic. I work every day now. Dr. Jake hired me."

"No. I didn't know." When had all this happened? And why hadn't Jake said anything to her? Surely, as the clinic organizer, she should have been consulted.

Sour grapes, the voice of her conscience commented. You're just jealous because you didn't think of it.

Manuela began stacking towels with as much reverence as if the future of medicine depended on how straight they were. "Dr. Jake came last night to the camp. He talked to me, and he talked to my parents." Her face clouded slightly. "Papa was not sure this was a good thing, but Dr. Jake is paying me more than I could make in the fields, so he agreed."

"That's wonderful." She forced warmth into her voice. Of course she was happy for the girl, and she had to admit, it was an inspired idea. If Manuela did have the makings of a medical professional, they'd find out. "We certainly can use you."

"You will show me how to do things, won't you, Terry? I want to do everything perfectly."

For wonderful Dr. Jake's sake, no doubt. "Of course I will." She gave the girl a quick hug. "We'll make a paramedic out of you yet. Or do you have your sights set on something else?"

"That would be great, to help people the way you do. But I don't think it will be possible. Papa says I must remember that we will be leaving in a few weeks." She smoothed her hand over the surface of a towel. "This won't last."

Terry's throat tightened. Manuela deserved her chance, and she was a jerk for feeling irritated just because it came from someone else.

"No matter how long you're here, you'll learn a lot. Once you've learned something, nobody can take that away. It will go with you wherever you are."

Manuela nodded happily. "And I have Dr. Jake to thank for it."

She kept the smile pinned to her face with an effort. Maybe she'd better go and inventory supplies before she blurted out something she shouldn't about Manuela's new hero.

The storeroom was clean, quiet, and well-organized. Taking the clipboard that hung inside the door, she began checking supplies, jotting down notes as to anything they might need.

Unfortunately, that just reminded her of the episode with the supplies at the hospital. Really, how did Jake expect them to do their work, when—

Okay, enough. She was letting the man take over her thoughts far too much.

Forgive me, Father. I'm obsessing about something I can't control. And I'm actually envious that Jake thought of a way to help Manuela and I didn't. Please, forgive me.

There, she'd said it. Unfortunately she knew perfectly well that there was another step she had to take. She had to thank him for thinking of this gift for Manuela, to say nothing of the fact that he was undoubtedly paying her out of his own pocket. Even if they disagreed on other things, in this he deserved credit.

And she'd have a chance to make good on her decision, because she could hear his voice in the other room. Squaring her shoulders, she marched through the door.

Jake stood at the desk, talking with Carole and Jim. In jeans and a rugby shirt, he looked considerably more casual than he had at the E.R. that morning, but no less intimidating. He didn't turn, but she thought his shoulders stiffened when she approached.

The words didn't seem to be coming, but

fortunately for her, the bus pulled up just then. Word of the clinic's work must be spreading through the camps, because at least twenty people began filing through the door.

Thank You, Lord, she murmured silently, and hurried forward to begin triage, as Manuela rushed to translate. *Thank You for giving us this opportunity to help.*

An hour later, things had calmed down considerably. She found herself assisting Jake as he stitched a cut on the forehead of an elderly field worker. She watched his precise, even stitches and tried to find the words she had to say. She may as well blurt it right out.

"I wanted to say—"

He glanced at her, and she was momentarily thrown off her stride by the frosty edge in his gaze.

She cleared her throat. "You're doing a great thing for Manuela. I know she appreciates it. And I do, too." She shouldn't sound so reluctant. "I wish I'd thought of it."

"The important thing is that it happens, not who thought of it." His voice was cool.

"I know that." At least, she knew it rationally, if not emotionally. "She's so excited, and she really is an asset. I just—I know you must be paying her out of your own pocket. Maybe I can get some donations—"

"Forget it. I can handle it."

"Right. Okay." She took a breath. Of course he could handle it. He probably had a sizable trust fund backing up whatever he decided to do. It must be nice to be able to give without feeling a pinch.

Or was it? She handed him the dressing. Did it mean more when what you gave pinched you a bit? She hadn't given that any thought before, but it was something to ponder. Jesus had certainly thought more of the poor woman who'd given her last two pennies than the rich who gave out of their abundance.

Jake finished the job, nodded in satisfaction, and turned to her as the patient moved away. "You don't think much of me, do you, Terry?"

She fumbled the tray, nearly knocking over the antiseptic. "I don't know what you mean. I just told you how much I appreciate what you're doing for Manuela."

"Did you?" His smile was wry. "Somehow I had the feeling you were thinking something else."

She took a deep breath. She needed to do this right. "I know we've had our share of disagreements." That was putting it mildly. "But you've gone the extra mile for Manuela, and I'm grateful."

He looked at her for a long moment, as if measuring the depth of her sincerity. Then he nodded, and his face seemed to relax a little. "Look, I think we need to clear the air about what happened earlier."

For an instant she thought he meant those moments in the barn, and panic swept through her. Then she realized that he must be talking about the incident at the E.R.

"If we're clearing the air, I have to go on record that I think your new policy is wrong."

"I think it's wrong, as well."

She could only gape at him. "Then why are you doing it?"

Again that wry smile. "Do you really think I have free rein with what happens in the E.R.?"

"Why not? You're the boss, aren't you?"

"It's not that simple." He frowned, and she had the sense that he was choosing his words carefully. "I'd like this position to become permanent, but in order for that to happen, I have to please a lot of people.

And one of them happens to be very concerned with cutting costs in the E.R."

"Morley. I know. But why—"

"But surely it doesn't have to be your program that feels the pinch?" His eyebrows
lifted.

"I didn't mean that, exactly." Hadn't she?

"I'm going to have to do some things I
don't want to do, I'm afraid. I'm willing to
take the heat for that." His gaze held hers.
"But I'd like to know you'd give me the ben-
efit of the doubt, at least some of the time.
What do you say?"

What could she say, especially when he
was looking at her as if what she thought
really mattered to him?

"All right." She couldn't seem to look
away from his face, and she didn't want to
think about what that betrayed about her
feelings. "I promise."

Chapter Seven

"There you go, sweetheart." Terry smiled at the tot who'd just received her immunization, getting a shy grin in return. The child might not understand what she'd said, but she did understand the red lollipop Terry passed out as a reward for getting immunizations up to date.

The little girl skipped away. The next child in line looked at her lollipop, screwed up his face and edged toward the chair. Terry guided him into place gently.

"This would be a lot easier if we had Manuela here to translate," she said, passing the premeasured immunization to Jake.

He nodded, frowning a little, and then replacing the frown with a grin as he approached the child. *"Hola, amigo."* He darted a glance at Terry. "That's the extent of my

Spanish, I'm afraid. Is this the first time
Manuela has missed a shift?"

"She's always here waiting when we open
the doors. I don't understand it." She glanced
toward the door, but no Manuela appeared,
eager and smiling. "I hope nothing's wrong."

"We can check on her later if she doesn't
show up." He knelt next to the child, and
she watched as he deftly gave the injection.

"You know, we can take care of the immunizations if you have something else to do."

She'd called in plenty of volunteers for the
immunization day, not knowing how many
children would show up. More than she'd
have imagined, by the looks of it. Brendan
had organized the bus service, and they'd
advertised at all the camps.

"Don't I give the injections well enough to
suit an experienced paramedic like you?"
His eyebrows lifted, but she could see he
wasn't really offended. Their truce had held
for almost a week, which had to be a
record.

"You're doing fine," she assured him. "I
just meant it seems like a waste to have a
neurosurgeon give childhood immunizations."

"I'm not that any longer." He said the

words without any particular inflection, giving no clue to his feelings. "Besides, it's always good to keep your skills sharp." He ruffled the child's hair and sent him to Terry for his lollipop.

"Like Seth over there, trying to remember his high-school Spanish." She nodded toward the sign-in desk, where volunteers tried to take histories and determine what immunizations each child needed.

"He's giving it a valiant effort, I must say. But we could use Manuela there, speaking of skills."

They'd set up three immunization stations, but the slowdown at the sign-in desk meant they had a short break between clients. "Yes, we could. I had some volunteers from the advanced Spanish class at the high school, but I didn't think we'd need them today. By the time I realized we needed them, I couldn't get them out here in time." She welcomed the next mother and child pair. "I wish I knew what happened to Manuela."

Jake knelt next to the little boy, who'd tensed up enough to guarantee the shot would hurt. "Hey, come on, buddy. Relax." He put his stethoscope in the boy's ears. "Want to listen to your heart?" While the boy's attention was distracted, he deftly gave the injection.

"Now that's skill," Terry said, smiling at the child. "No tears at all."

"Glad you appreciate it." Jake straightened.

"Hey, I always appreciated your skill, even back when you were the high-and-mighty neurosurgery consult and I was just another nameless EMT." Too late, she realized she shouldn't have mentioned that again.

But he didn't seem bothered, glancing up from the chart with a slight smile. "Trust me, you were never nameless. An EMT with that mop of red curls could only be called Flanagan. You lit up that place like a torch every time you walked in."

She was absurdly pleased at the comment. "Frankly, I never considered the red hair an asset."

"Combined with that air of naive innocence, it was unmistakable."

Now that wasn't a compliment, although it was true. She'd been decades younger in experience and outlook when she'd arrived in Philadelphia. Eager to prove herself, thinking she had everything under control. She hadn't.

"Terry?" Jake was looking at her, eyes frowning. "What's wrong?"

"Nothing." She forced a smile. "I'd just resent that if I didn't know it was probably true. I gave a new meaning to *green* then."

She couldn't go any deeper than that, because it led into places that would hurt both of them and destroy this fragile balance. If he didn't realize how bruised she'd been when she'd run back to Suffolk, so much the better.

He was looking at her as if he might pursue the subject, but fortunately she spotted Manuela, hovering outside the screen door. "There's Manuela. Why is she standing out there?"

"Let's find out." Jake started toward the clinic door, and she hurried after him.

The moment she got close enough to see Manuela's face, she knew something was very wrong. No tears—just a set, despairing expression that was somehow worse than tears.

"Manuela, what is it?" She caught the girl's arm, but she stood stiffly, not yielding. "What's wrong?"

Jake guided them away from the clinic door, under the shade of the sycamore tree that stood at the building's corner. "We were worried about you when you didn't come in today," he said quietly. "What happened?"

"I cannot come." Manuela seemed to force the words out. "I just came to tell you that I must not work for the clinic any longer."

"If this is because of your father—"

The girl swallowed hard, shaking her head. "No. Not my father's doing."

Further questions hovered ready to burst from her, but Jake shook his head warningly. "Just tell us in your own way," he said. "Whatever it is, we'll help you."

"You can't help. I should have known—" She stopped, gulping back a sob.

Terry's heart twisted. Known what? That this small thing was too good to be true?

Manuela took a deep breath, straightening her shoulders as if to say she could bear whatever she had to. "The crew chief came to see us."

A ripple of anger rushed through Terry. She should have realized they weren't finished with that man yet. "What is he trying now?"

"Not him." The girl shook her head. "He just brought the message. He said to my father that Mr. Dixon was angry with us. That it was illegal for me to work at the clinic."

She exchanged glances with Jake over the girl's head. Why would Dixon get involved in this? Manuela's family wasn't here illegally, and surely they weren't breaking any laws by paying Manuela for doing chores around the clinic. It wasn't as if she were working long hours or handling dangerous materials.

"Why illegal?" Jake asked. "Did he say why Mr. Dixon thought that?"

"Mr. Dixon said that our contract that allowed us to be here to work was with them. That we must not work for anyone else. He was very angry, so my father says I must not come anymore." She tried for a brave smile, but it trembled. "I thank you for helping me to learn. I'm sorry."

She started to turn away, but Terry grasped her arm, mind racing a mile a minute. "Wait a minute, Manuela. I'm not at all sure he's right about that. We can do something. Jake, tell her."

"I'd like to help, but I don't know what we can do." His gaze evaded hers.

It didn't matter. She knew what he was thinking. That if this came to the hospital board's attention, it would reflect on him. It had been his idea.

"We can't sacrifice Manuela's future for the sake of expediency."

Jake met her eyes now, his look level. "It's not a question of expediency."

Jake had a job at stake, so he said. Maybe she couldn't believe his position really hinged on something so trivial, but she had to respect that. Still, her hands weren't tied.

"Look, I can understand why you might not want to be involved." She kept her voice even. This didn't have to lead to a fight. They could talk about it like colleagues, not enemies. "You can stay out of it. I'll go to see Matthew Dixon myself."

"No." His fingers closed over her arm. Before she could jerk away, he spoke again. "*You're* not going to see Matthew Dixon. *We* are."

In the few minutes it took to drive over the back roads to the Dixon farmhouse, Jake managed to second-guess himself at least thirty times. Did he really want to do this? What if Dixon turned around and complained to the chief of staff about him? Or worse, complained to Morley?

The lane curved around a clump of sumac bushes, their plumes red as flames, and the house came into view. A brick center section, its color worn to a soft rose over probably a couple of centuries, had wings of white frame going out on either side. A generous porch spanned the front.

The house should look welcoming, but instead it seemed faintly forlorn. The lane was rutted, and the porch sagged a bit at one end. No flowers filled the beds to either side of the front walk, and a crumbling brick wall enclosed what had probably been a side garden.

"They could use a load of gravel," Terry commented as they bumped to a stop.

"It looks as if Mr. Dixon hasn't been keeping the place up very well." He sat with his hands on the wheel, staring at the house. "Is he badly off?"

Terry shrugged. "I'm not sure any farmers are doing really well now, but Dixon has always been thought to have plenty of family money. I remember that Andy and his sisters went away to a private academy when the rest of us headed to Suffolk Middle School."

He glanced at her. Terry's temper had

nearly gotten the better of her at Manuela's tale, but she seemed to have it under control now. She was frowning a little, her forehead crinkling and her green eyes clouded.

"So, did you miss him when he went away?"

Her wide-eyed gaze met his. "Andy? Get serious."

"He said you were his girlfriend." Even in this situation, he couldn't resist the urge to tease her a little. Was that what all those siblings of hers did?

"I don't know why he was goofing off like that. He barely noticed me when we were in elementary school. Girls weren't big on his agenda then."

"What was?"

"Sports, I guess. And having the best of everything. Whatever the new fad was, Andy had to have it first."

"Seems funny he settled down here again after school. You'd have expected him to head for the bright lights." The way Terry had. Did she regret coming back to Suffolk?

Her mouth firmed a little, almost as if she guessed what he thought. "I suppose Andy felt his father needed him. This is a big operation." She glanced toward the barn. It needed a coat of paint, too. "Or at least, it was. If Matthew Dixon is having financial troubles, that could account for the condition of the workers' housing. Well, are we going in?" She grasped the door handle.

"Wait a second." His hand brushed her shoulder. "When we get in there, let me handle talking to Mr. Dixon."

He could feel her tense through that lightest of contacts, her shoulder tightening against his fingers.

"Why?" She sounded ready for battle. "My family has known him for years."

And you're the stranger here. She didn't add that, but she was probably thinking it.

"That didn't seem to help you the last time you confronted him, did it?"

Her frown deepened. "That was odd, now that I think about it. I'd have expected him to recognize me as a Flanagan, even if he didn't remember my name. I guess I'm not as memorable as I thought."

He let his finger touch a strand of coppery hair. "Maybe it's not that. Have there been any rumors about Dixon's health?"

"Not that I know of." Her gaze met his. "Are you thinking some form of dementia?"

"It's possible. That might explain the son's protective attitude."

She nodded slowly. "I guess so. Brendan might know something, as their pastor, but he wouldn't say. Maybe we ought to talk to Andy, instead."

"Manuela said the orders came from the old man. Let's start with him, in any event." He opened the door. "I don't suppose you'd consider waiting in the car?"

"No, I wouldn't."

She slid out, and he rounded the car to join her. They mounted the three steps to the porch, their footsteps thudding in the silence. The glass-paneled door stood open behind the barrier of a flimsy screen door.

He knocked, the door rattling in its frame. Nothing. He tried again, harder. A voice, sounding far away, called something he couldn't distinguish. He glanced at Terry.

"Do you suppose that meant come in?"

"Let's take it that way."

She yanked the screen door open and stepped inside. He followed her into a center hallway, papered in a floral pattern that looked as if it would have been right at home in the 1930s. A staircase mounted to the second floor, and archways on either side of them led into a living room and dining room furnished with dark, heavy pieces.

"Mr. Dixon?" Terry called. "Are you here?"

This time they got a livelier response. A door at the back of the hallway swung open, and Andy Dixon strode through. He checked his steps momentarily at the sight of them and then came forward, smiling, his hand extended.

"Terry. Dr. Landsdowne. This is an unexpected pleasure. What can I do for you?"

Impatient, Jake cut across Terry's polite response. "We'd like to speak to your father, please."

Andy's open face clouded, and he glanced toward the second floor. "I'm afraid you can't. He always rests in the afternoon. Can't I help you with whatever it is?"

"We'd prefer to talk with him." He glanced at his watch. Nearly five. "Won't he be getting up soon?"

"I'm afraid not." Andy's voice lowered, and he took a step closer to them. "The truth is, he's not up to handling much of anything these days. So if you need something, I'm afraid you'll have to make do with me."

"We're worried about Manuela. Manuela

Ortiz." Terry burst into speech. "Mel Jordan told her parents that your father objected to her working at the clinic."

He should have known Terry wouldn't be able to stay out of it. "We've been paying Manuela a small amount to help out," he explained. "It's useful to have her to translate to the patients, and we couldn't understand why your father would object to that."

"This must be some sort of misunderstanding. Look, let's go out on the porch and talk. I don't want to risk Dad hearing. He gets upset over nothing these days."

He ushered them out onto the porch. Giving them a very polite version of the bum's rush? Jake couldn't help but wonder how the Dixon family's chain of command fit together. Was Andy really in charge, as he seemed to imply?

"That's better." Andy closed the door behind them, his pleasant face creased with worry. "Really, I'm sorry about this. Of course there's no problem with the girl—Manuela, is it?—working at the clinic."

"Apparently Jordan thought there was." He didn't care to be caught in the middle over who was in charge here.

"Jordan has no business speaking to my

father at all." Andy's voice sharpened. "I've told him that. Please don't worry about it. I'll take care of everything."

"Thank you, Andy." Terry's voice was warm, and she seemed to accept everything the man said at face value. There was no reason why that should annoy him, but it did.

"I'd just like to be certain that your father isn't going to complain about us to the hospital."

"Believe me, I'll make sure that doesn't happen." Andy glanced at his watch. "I don't want to rush you, but I do have some things to do—"

"Of course." Terry shot him a look that demanded politeness. "We're very grateful, Andy. And Manuela will be so relieved."

"Yes. Thank you."

"My pleasure." Lifting his hand in farewell, Andy went back into the silent farmhouse, closing the door firmly behind him.

Terry frowned at him. "What's wrong? We got what we wanted. You should be happy."

"I am. It's fine." He started toward the car. It was fine, wasn't it? So why did he have this nagging worry that the situation with the Dixons could explode in his face?

* * *

Jake stood for the final blessing as the worship service ended. Brendan, formal in his black robe, spread his arms wide, as if to embrace the entire congregation of Grace Church. Jake felt himself giving in to the warmth and tried to resist. Then the organ music swelled, and Brendan was walking quickly to the back toward the sanctuary.

Jake slid the hymnal back into its rack. He still wasn't sure why he'd come to worship this morning. Maybe it should be credited, or debited, to Brendan's persistence. He could hardly tell Brendan that he preferred to do his wrestling with God in private these days. Maybe he could leave—

But Siobhan Flanagan slipped through the pews, slim and agile as a girl, to cut him off. "Jake, how nice to see you this morning. How did you like the service?"

It was impossible to resist the warmth of her smile. "Very much. Brendan is an excellent speaker." He'd rather talk about Brendan's speaking ability than the topic of the sermon.

"...we are called to do the good work God

has already prepared for us to do," Siobhan quoted. "That's one of my favorite verses."

"It seems a rather frightening one to me." The words came out before he had a chance to remind himself that he didn't intend to open up about his private spiritual health.

"Why?" Her air of interested attention robbed the word of any intent to pry.

"I suppose because it puts a heavy burden on the individual. If you don't do the work God planned for you, who will?"

"True. But I always see it that since God planned it, He also prepares us to do it." Her smile flashed. "Well, enough serious theology for the moment. Let's go to Fellowship Hall before all the coffee is gone."

She linked her arm in his, clearly not taking no for an answer. He let her draw him into the flow of people heading out the door to the left of the pulpit.

He wouldn't argue with Siobhan, but he wasn't sure she was right. He'd thought he'd known what God wanted of him, but either he'd been wrong or God had changed His mind.

Fellowship Hall was an expanse of beige carpet and beige cinder block walls, bright-

ened by colorful banners between the windows. The buzz of conversation was nearly
deafening. It sounded as if these people
hadn't seen each other in weeks.

Siobhan tugged him directly to a serving
table laden with cookies, coffee cake, fruit,
cheese, even vegetables and dip. A person
could make a meal of what was spread out
for the coffee hour, and it looked as if some
people were.

Well, he'd have his coffee and speak to a
few people, so no one could accuse him of
being unfriendly.... Now why did a certain
redhead's face pop into his mind at that
thought?

Siobhan had been caught by an elderly
woman who seemed intent on volunteering
her for a rummage sale, so he took a few
steps away, scanning the crowd. Some-
what to his surprise, he saw a few people
from the migrant camp. Perhaps Brendan
had sent the bus for them. They'd been
corralled by a smiling couple and ushered
to the food table as if they were the guests
of honor.

When he spotted Terry's red curls, he realized he'd been looking for her. A niece and

a nephew hung from each hand, and she was laughing down at them.

Something warm seemed to unfurl in his heart at her expression. Terry, of all people, ought to be married with children of her own by now. They'd look like her, with those red curls and green eyes.

Terry's gaze met his, and now the smile was for him. He couldn't leave without speaking to her. He'd just say hello, and then he'd be free to leave. He made his way through the crowd to her side.

"Looks as if you have an anchor on each arm," he said.

"I have a pest on each arm," she said with mock ferocity. "Go on, you two. Go get another cookie. Your mom will really appreciate the sugar high."

They ran off. She watched them for a moment before turning to him. "Is everything all right?"

"Of course. Why wouldn't it be?" She couldn't know he found it difficult to be here.

"I thought you might have run into Matthew Dixon. He hardly ever comes to church, but he's here today."

He glanced around the room. "Maybe I should speak to him. Where is he?"

"Over there." She drew in a breath. "He's talking to Dr. Getz. I'm not sure that's a good idea."

"I'm sure it's not," he said grimly. "I suppose I should see just what they're talking about."

"If he's complaining, it's probably about me. I'll come, too."

He almost told her he'd handle it, but they weren't in the hospital now. This was her turf, not his. Besides, for some ridiculous reason it felt good to have someone next to him as he approached the two men.

"It's been terrible, that's what it's been." Dixon, lean as a rail in a navy suit that looked as if it didn't get much use, glared at Sam Getz.

Jake felt as if he'd been punched. Dixon was complaining about them to the chief of staff. How was he going to explain this away?

"It was that late frost," Getz said. He glanced at them with a smile. "Not that Dr. Landsdowne would know what a late frost does to the apple harvest. He's a city boy."

Dixon gave Jake a short nod, his eyes a little uncertain, as if not sure he knew him.

"Dr. Landsdowne is in charge of the clinic," Terry said. "And I'm Terry Flanagan. Remember me?"

"Joe Flanagan's girl. 'Course I remember you. Didn't I see you someplace lately?"

The old man was failing, obviously. More surprising was the fact that his son had let him out alone. But even as he thought that, he spotted Andy working his way through the crowd, balancing two coffee cups.

He could only be relieved. Dixon didn't apparently remember anything about the situation with Manuela. Or at least, didn't know that he and Terry had interceded. Presumably Andy was handling the situation.

Getz clapped him on the shoulder, startling him. "I'll tell you why I wanted this young man to head up our emergency services, Matt. He gave up an important position to work in an African medical mission. Anybody who'd do that has his priorities in the right place."

He froze. He couldn't look at Terry. She knew why he'd really gone. If Getz found out, he'd lose that respect for Jake's priorities in a hurry.

"I guess somebody has to do it." Dixon's voice was grudging. "I wouldn't want to go rushing off to Africa."

Jake gave him a meaningless smile. All he could think was that he wanted to get out of here.

But Getz's hand still clasped his shoulder. "You know, hard as it is to believe, I was actually in medical school with Jake's father. He went on to fame and fortune, and I'm right back here where I grew up. Funny world, isn't it?"

Funny wasn't the word for it. His stomach was churning, the coffee turning to acid. Getz. And his father. There couldn't be a worse combination.

It's a coincidence. Stop overreacting. No one here knows about your relationship with your father. No one ever will.

But Terry was looking at him with concern in her face, and he was afraid she was beginning to read him entirely too well.

Chapter Eight

Terry glanced out one of the small windows at the clinic. The sky was dark with low clouds, the air so heavy it was almost hard to breathe. The narrow lane that led toward the migrant housing lay dusty and empty.

Manuela sat in one of the metal chairs in the waiting area, bent over the heavy book in her lap. Her long hair, loose today, hung down over her shoulders like a curtain, and she twisted a lock around her finger.

"Looks like we're not getting any customers today." She slid onto the chair next to the girl, the metal clammy to the touch. "We may as well close up early."

Manuela seemed to come back from a long way away. "¿Que? Oh, yes, I see." She closed the book slowly. "I'm sorry if I am wasting time. Do you want me to do some-thing?"

"Reading isn't wasting time. Are you studying something for school?"

Her dark lashes swept down, hiding her eyes. "Not exactly. I'm not in school."

"Well, not now, I guess. But school will start next week." Hard to believe the sum-mer was over already. The days had been flying by since she'd been busy with the clinic.

"I won't be going." Longing showed in her face for a brief moment. "My father says we won't bother to start school here, since we will be leaving in a few weeks."

"I see." Tread carefully, she warned her-self. You don't really know what life is like for Manuela. "You're studying on your own, then."

Manuela drew her hands away to show her the cover of the book she held. It was a tenth grade biology text. "Your mother got this book for me. So I could try to keep up with my studies. She says if I want to go into a medical field, I must do well in science."

Trust Mom to come up with some practical way to help Manuela. Guilt pricked at her. She'd been so preoccupied with the clinic that she hadn't followed through on her intention to do more to help Manuela realize her dreams.

"I'm glad she did that. Isn't it hard to study something like science in English?"

"Something that's hard is worth doing. Besides, I love it." She flipped open the book to a chart showing a diagram of the human body. "Look. This shows how the blood travels in the body, and there's another that shows how the heart works."

"I wish I'd been that enthusiastic about learning things when I was your age." Manuela should have her chance to achieve. If only she could stay long enough to get some uninterrupted schooling.... "Isn't it possible for your family to stay a bit longer, so you can start school here?"

She shrugged. "Some workers will stay through the fall, to work the fruit harvest, but so far my father has not been chosen."

"Who decides that?" She was beginning to have a bad feeling about this.

Manuela didn't look at her. "The farmer says how many workers he needs. The crew chief gets to pick."

And Jordan wouldn't pick her father, that was what she didn't say. Because Terry had

made too many waves. It had never occurred to her that Jordan had the power to
retaliate against the Ortiz family.

"I see." She suppressed the words that
sprang to her lips. She couldn't hold out
false hope to the girl. "If Mr. Dixon wanted
your father to stay, would he?"

Manuela nodded. "But it's up to Mr. Jordan."

"Maybe so. But maybe Mr. Dixon would
intercede with him."

"If you asked him?" Manuela's eyes
shone. "Would you, Terry?"

"I'm not sure he'd listen to me, but maybe
if my cousin Brendan talked to him." She
put her hand over the girl's. She didn't want
to encourage Manuela too much, but surely
a little hope was good for her. "Would you
like to go to school here?"

"More than anything. I'm always so far behind when I am able to attend school."
Manuela's fingers clung to hers. "If I could
do well in school, maybe I could be a paramedic, like you, and help people." Her tone
made that dream sound as faraway as the
moon.

"If that's what you want, I'm sure you
could. Let me talk to Brendan and see if

there's anything he can do, okay?" Brendan wanted to find some specific way to help the Ortiz family. This might be it.

Raindrops spattered against the window-pane, startling her. "Uh-oh. Looks like the storm is coming. Maybe you'd better run home."

Manuela jumped up. "My mother will be worried." She slid the book onto the high shelf that ran above the chairs. "I'll leave the book here, where it will be safe. Thank you, Terry."

She turned and darted out the door, running down the path toward the cement block building that was her temporary home.

There was no point in wondering what the girl had meant about leaving her book here so it would be safe. Maybe she just hadn't wanted to risk getting it wet.

Now she was the one who'd better hurry. The narrow road that twisted its way to the clinic was barely passable at the best of times. During a hard rain, it would be down-right dangerous.

She started through her checklist for clos-ing up the clinic, trying not to listen to the spatter of rain on the tin roof. Just a few more things, and she could leave.

The sound of a car engine distracted her. She wasn't expecting any of her volunteers at this hour. But it was Jake who hurried through the door, the shoulders of his navy windbreaker sparkling with raindrops.

"No customers?" He lifted his eyebrows.

Are you checking up on me, Jake? Despite the fact that their relationship had eased in recent days, it was impossible not to think that.

"It's been a quiet afternoon, so I sent Manuela home. I was just trying to get out myself before the storm hit." She picked up the clipboard. "Do you want to see today's records?"

He moved toward her, slipping the wet jacket off and tossing it over the desk chair. "Anything unusual?" He glanced quickly through the entries.

"Nothing much." Lightning cracked, and her nerves seemed to jump in response. "The road gets pretty bad in a storm, so maybe we should go—"

Another lightning crack, a boom of thunder, and the skies opened up. Rain poured down, thundering on the tin roof so loudly that it deafened her until her ears adjusted to the sound. Water streamed down the windows and turned the trees to a deep, iridescent green. The dirt clearing in front of the clinic changed in moments to glistening mud.

Rain and wind rattled the screen door, and Jake hurried to close the heavy inner door. He gave her a rueful look. "Sorry. If I hadn't interrupted you, you might have gotten out before this hit."

"Or I might have been sliding off the hill into the gully about now." She shrugged. "I'm afraid we're stuck for the moment."

"Sorry," he said again. "That wasn't my intent in stopping by. Is there any coffee left in the pot?"

She nodded, starting toward it, but he got there first and poured his own.

"Some for you?" He lifted the pot, looking at her questioningly.

For a moment, she couldn't seem to respond. In jeans and a blue polo shirt, his hair ruffled from the rain, Jake looked far too approachable for her peace of mind. Concentrate, she ordered herself fiercely. Don't act like some sort of medical groupie.

"No, thanks." Thank goodness her voice sounded casual. "I drink too much of that stuff when I'm on duty."

He nodded, taking a mouthful and making

a face. "Every first responder I've ever known has been the same."

"I'd argue at that sweeping statement, but I'm afraid you're right. If my partner had his way, we'd stop for coffee and doughnuts after every call."

A gust of wind sent rain clattering against the window. Something—a branch, maybe—hit the roof with a crash. She shivered and rubbed her arms, despite the fact that it wasn't really cold.

Jake crossed the room to her, leaning against the desk next to her, and his nearness had her nerves standing at attention. "Are you cold?"

"No. Just never too fond of being out in the middle of nowhere in a storm." She took a breath. Maybe she could turn the fact of being stuck here to good account. "Speaking of paramedics, Manuela told me this afternoon that she'd like to become one. I'd love to clear the way to get the training for her, when she's old enough."

Jake frowned at the muddy liquid in his mug and set it down on the desk. "She's a bright girl. Maybe she ought to aim higher than that."

For a moment, she couldn't respond at all.

Really, she didn't need to worry about feeling too attracted to him, since he managed to make her furious on a regular basis. She shoved herself away from the desk.

"Aim higher? Meaning that paramedics are at the bottom of the totem pole, as far as you're concerned."

"That's not exactly what I said."

He wouldn't think of apologizing, of course.

"Paramedics are on the front lines in medical emergencies. We go into situations other professionals never dream of, and we help people at the time of their greatest crisis." She shouldn't have to defend her profession to Jake, of all people.

Suddenly it hit her, like a blow to the stomach. The words Jake had spoken in the aftermath of Meredith's death seemed to ring in her ears. "Or maybe it's just me you don't want Manuela to emulate. Maybe you think she shouldn't aim to follow a poor excuse for a medical professional like me."

Jake could only stare at Terry. This storm between them had blown up more suddenly than the one that battered the building from outside. Could he possibly pretend he didn't know what she was talking about?

He put the cup aside, the coffee turning to acid in his stomach. No. He couldn't ignore this. He owed Terry more than that.

"Did I say that to you?" It took an effort to keep his gaze on hers.

"Yes. Don't you remember?" She'd taken a few steps away from him, and she stood braced, her hands tensed into fists as if ready for a fight.

"I remember saying some things I shouldn't have when I—" he stopped, swallowed "—when I realized Meredith was dead."

Pain flickered in her face. "You meant what you said. That she might have lived if a more experienced crew had responded to the call."

He shoved his hand through his hair. His head was starting to pound with the effort of revisiting those memories. "I don't know what I meant, Terry. You must have had patients' families lash out at you before this. It may not be pretty, but it happens."

"It's a lot more serious when a doctor does the lashing out." Her eyes flickered. "I've been through worse things than that inquiry, but not many."

He shook his head, his throat tightening. "You shouldn't have had to go through that. I know. But it was all right. Your team was cleared. You didn't suffer any consequences from it."

Her eyes widened. "No consequences? Only that it sent me scurrying back to Suffolk with my tail between my legs. But I'm sure that's what you intended."

Had he intended that? He'd just known he hadn't wanted to see her again in his hospital. But then, it hadn't stayed his hospital for long, had it?

"I'm sorry." He had to force the words out. "It wasn't fair to you. I know." The words he'd never said to anyone hovered on his lips, wanting to be released.

"Then why?" Her face twisted, and he realized that she was still hurting. "Why did you blame us? It wasn't our fault."

"No." He knew then he'd have to say it. Terry was the one person in the world he couldn't pretend to about this. "It wasn't your fault Meredith died. It was mine."

The words seemed to echo in the shocked silence between them. There was no sound but the drumming of the rain. That, and his own ragged breathing.

"Why?" The word sounded strangled. "Why was it your fault?"

He rubbed the back of his neck, where the tension was building. It didn't help. "You deserve to hear this, don't you? You're the one who was caught in the fallout of my mistakes. What did you know about Meredith?"

"Just what everyone knew. That she was a Main Line socialite. That she was crazy about you. That you two were going to be married."

He shook his head. There it was again—he'd never understood how that misperception had flown through the hospital. "We weren't. I dated her, yes. My sister had known her at school, had introduced us. But it was never that serious between us."

"Everyone said it was." Terry watched him, eyes serious, as if weighing his words for truth.

"The notorious hospital grapevine, in other words." He leaned back against the desk, trying to relax the tension that rode him. "That's really a reliable source."

Something flared in her gaze. "It wasn't my only source. She—Meredith—she said that, the first time we were called to her apartment. That we should take her to General, because her fiancé was a resident there."

He was smothering again, caught in the lies Meredith had spun around them. "Terry, I'm asking you to believe me. I never asked Meredith to marry me. I never had anything more than a brief, casual relationship with her."

"Then why did she say that?"

She wasn't going to believe him unless he told her everything, and he wasn't sure he could. He shook his head slowly.

"Look, I'm still not sure how it happened. We went out a few times. I enjoyed it. Going out with her was a link to my old world, a break from the hospital. But it didn't take long to figure out that there was no future for us. She was completely uninterested in everything that was important to me—my work, my patients, my future. I knew I had to break it off before it got serious."

"She thought it was already serious," Terry said.

It wasn't much, but it was a faint indication that she might understand. "She didn't listen to me. She kept calling me, even at the hospital. I couldn't seem to make her understand."

He remembered, too well, how his discomfort had given way to irritation and then finally to a yawning fear that Meredith would never accept the truth.

"One night she called." Every instant of that time was engraved on his memory. "She said she couldn't live without me. That she'd taken an overdose of sleeping pills. She was calling to say goodbye."

In the stillness, he heard Terry's breath catch. "Had she really taken an overdose?"

"I was sure she had. I rushed over there, raced her to the emergency room, terrified of not being in time. They pumped the drugs out of her, suggested counseling, which she refused. She said she'd been depressed, foolish, she was all right now. I believed her, probably because I wanted to."

He couldn't easily forgive himself for his stupidity. If he'd insisted on counseling, tried to be her friend... But he hadn't.

"I thought she was all right. Until it happened again. And again. And finally the doctor who treated her broke all the rules out of his pity for me and told me she'd never taken enough to kill herself. Enough to make herself sick. Not enough to kill."

"I'm sorry." Terry's voice was very soft. "Sorry for her. Sorry for you."

Tears shimmered in her eyes, and the

warmth that was Terry seemed to reach out and touch him.

"You must have known some of it," he said, trying to keep the pain and shame out of his voice. "You answered the calls a couple of times."

"Yes. But the last time—"

"The last time I was in a meeting. I'd turned my cell phone off. And she'd taken a different medication, one it turned out she was allergic to. By the time your team got there, by the time I knew, it was too late." His throat was so tight he didn't think he could say much more, but one thing had to be said. "It wasn't your fault, Terry. It wouldn't have made any difference who answered that call. The only fault was mine."

Her heart was breaking for him. Terry moved closer, wanting to comfort him, afraid she was the one person who never could. The pain in his voice, his face, was indescribable. The cool, detached, unfeeling man felt only too much.

"It wasn't your fault, Jake. Honestly. You can't blame yourself for turning off your cell phone when you were in a meeting. If you'd known, you'd have gone."

"Would I?" The words sounded bitter, echoing in the quiet room. The rain had subsided to a gentle patter, making a soft background to their voices. "You have more faith in me than I have in myself if you believe that. Maybe I didn't want to get any more of those calls. Maybe I wouldn't have answered even if I'd gotten it."

She knew the answer to that one, even if she couldn't make this better for him. "Yes. You would have."

He blinked, probably at the conviction in her voice. "How do you know that? I'm not sure myself."

"Anyone who knows you would know. Think about it. Not even your worst enemy could accuse you of neglecting a patient, any patient. No matter what. You might have been angry. You might have wanted to be rid of the complications she'd brought into your life. But you would have gone."

"I wish I could be sure." He stared down at his hands—those talented, capable, surgeon's hands. "That keeps me awake at night sometimes."

"It shouldn't." She tried to project all her confidence into her words. "Maybe you can blame yourself for not handling the situation better, but you can't blame yourself for that. You would have gone."

He sent a fleeting glance toward her, and she thought she read hope there. It twisted her heart. She'd thought him so sure, so confident, so fortunate. And all the time he'd been suffering.

"Thank you, Terry." His voice was grave. "It means something to hear you say that."

For a long moment they stood looking at each other, and her breath seemed to stop. They'd come so close to each other in the past few moments. It seemed the barriers between them were gone.

That was an illusion, she told herself desperately. Just as it was an illusion that he was looking at her with a warmth she'd never seen from him before.

Slowly, very slowly, he reached out and touched her hair, pushing a wayward strand back behind her ear with as much concentration as he'd give to a complicated bit of surgery. Her breath seemed to have stopped completely, but her heart was thrumming in her ears.

His fingertips brushed her cheek, warming where they touched. His eyes darkened.

She had to do something, say something.

But she couldn't. She could only watch as his face grew nearer and nearer until his lips touched hers.

He didn't attempt to draw her into an embrace. There was nothing but the light pressure of his palm cradling her face, his lips gentle and undemanding on hers.

But there was longing behind that kiss; she knew it and felt the same yearning in herself. Careful, careful. But she couldn't seem to pull away.

He did, finally, drawing back a fraction of an inch, so that she still felt his breath against her lips. His fingertips drew a line down her cheek. And then he stepped away, something rueful in his eyes.

"I shouldn't have done that."

The words were a wake-up call. She shouldn't have, either. She moved back a cautious step, trying to gather whatever shreds she had left of self-possession.

"I—yes, I mean, it wasn't your fault, but it—it probably wasn't a good idea. We have to work together."

It didn't mean anything to you, Jake. And I'm afraid it meant too much to me.

"Besides, you don't like me very much, remember?" His voice had a teasing gentle-

ness that seemed to turn her spine to
marshmallow.

"I don't—" Maybe she'd better be careful
not to give too much away. "I don't dislike
you. Now that I understand what happened..."

The sentence died away, because she saw
the difference in Jake's face as she spoke.
He seemed to tighten, withdrawing from her,
as if moving back behind the shield of the
perfect, impersonal surgeon again.

"I'd rather no one else knew about that."

Now it was her turn to stiffen. Did he really
know so little of her as to think she'd blab
that around?

"I certainly won't say anything." The words
sounded just as tight and stiff as she felt.

The moment when they'd stood so close,
lips touching, understanding each other
without words—it might never have happened. Maybe as far as Jake was concerned, it hadn't.

Well, if that's what he wanted, she could
pretend, too. But she couldn't fool herself.
He'd kissed her, and her heart was never
going to be the same.

Chapter Nine

The next day, Terry turned down the pleasant residential street where Mary Kate and
her two children lived, trying to focus on
anything except that interlude with Jake.
Think about her sister, putting up that
bright, impervious facade to hide her grief.
Think about the clothes Shawna and Michael had outgrown, that Mary Kate wanted
to give the children at the migrant camp.
Don't think about Jake.

Well, that certainly wasn't the way to forget, by telling herself to do so. That just
brought it surging to the forefront of her
mind. She slowed to allow a group of boys
tossing a football to clear the tree-lined
street. In another week they'd be in school,
and this block would be silent and deserted

during the day except for a few mothers with strollers.

She bit her lip. Poor Jake. Whoever would have expected her to think that of him, the man she'd thought had everything? Instead, he was carrying a burden of guilt that was nearly crushing him.

What she'd told him was true, if he could only accept it. To think that he wouldn't have answered Meredith's call was ridiculous. No one who knew him in a professional capacity would believe he wouldn't fight to the end of his strength for a patient.

As for what prompted that fight—well, there she wasn't so sure. She'd heard one of the E.R. docs talking once, after having been asked to scrub in on a surgery Jake was performing on a patient they'd treated in the E.R.

"You have to hand it to Landsdowne, like him or not," he'd said. "It wasn't just his skill that saved that patient. It was his will. He wasn't going to let her slip away on his table." Then he'd added, "It'd be a reflection on him if she died. That's what he'd think."

Had that anonymous doc been right? She wasn't sure, but that had certainly been the overall impression he'd left at the hospital—

that of a brilliant surgeon who'd taken so much pride in his skill that it was an affront if a patient died.

He wouldn't have let Meredith die, not if he could have saved her. As for the rest of it—well, maybe he hadn't handled the situation as well as he could have. She could well imagine his impatience with Meredith. Still, he couldn't possibly have anticipated the situation going so very wrong.

She pulled slowly into Mary Kate's driveway, watching for abandoned bikes and roller skates. So he probably hadn't handled Meredith as well as he might have. Hadn't seen that she got the help she needed. On the other hand, he hadn't been a relative, just an acquaintance. There were limits to what he could do. And doctors could be just as blind as the next person to psychiatric problems in those closest to them.

Brendan would have handled it differently, but Brendan had unique gifts. She got out of the car, shutting the door and cutting across the grass toward the front door of the white ranch. Mary Kate's coneflowers and chrysanthemums made a splash of yellow and orange against the siding.

Brendan would say that people were given

different gifts so that they could come to-gether in the body of Christ and do the work Christ had commissioned. Probably it was wrong to wish her own gifts, or Jake's, had been different. But if she had a bit of Jake's detachment, she might be able to stop feel-ing a pain in her heart every time she thought of that kiss.

She knocked and opened the door simul-taneously, calling out. "Mary Kate? Kids? Anyone here?"

Her sister hurried into the living room from the hall that led to the bedrooms, her arms filled with two large cardboard boxes, her hair disheveled. "Don't shout, Terry. I'm here."

"Sorry." She went to take one of the boxes and realized that Mary Kate's eyes were red and swollen. For a moment, she couldn't speak. "Where do you want this?"

She was relieved to hear her voice coming out normally. Mary Kate never showed her grief to her little sister. Should she say something or ignore it?

Mary Kate took the decision out of her hands, plopping the box on the dining table and wiping her eyes with the back of her hands. "I climbed up in the attic for these. The dust up there made my eyes water."

She yanked one of the boxes open. "Let's see what's in here."

So they were supposed to ignore it. She couldn't help but think there were other things besides the kids' outgrown clothes in the attic—things related to Kenny that might have broken through Mary Kate's iron self-control.

"These were Michael's." Mary Kate was stacking small pairs of jeans and T-shirts on the table. "Do you think they'll fit any of the kids at the camp?"

"They'd be great." She smoothed out a blue shirt decorated with trucks and bull-dozers. "This would at least fit Juan Ortiz and I'm sure plenty of others."

"That's the family with the daughter you were talking about at the picnic, isn't it?" Mary Kate paused, hands on the pile of clothing. "Was Jake able to do anything about the girl?"

"Jake?" Mary Kate's casual use of his name startled her, and for a moment she couldn't respond. She gathered her scattered wits. It wouldn't do to let her sister know she had any feelings for him. "Yes. He gave Manuela a job at the clinic. She's done very well there. We're hoping the family can stay through the fall, so she can get in some regular school time."

"Sounds like a nice guy, going to that trouble for her." The comment was accompanied by a sidelong glance from Mary Kate's bright blue eyes.

She swallowed. "He's nice enough." She felt the betraying flush come up in her cheeks and ducked her head, hoping Mary Kate didn't notice.

"Terry!" Mary Kate swung to face her. "Are you involved with him?"

Obviously that hope had been futile. "No, I'm not involved. We work together, that's all."

"You don't blush at the mention of a man just because you work with him. Come on, out with it." Her voice had that familiar, I'm-the-big-sister, commanding tone.

"There's nothing to tell," she said. "Do you want me to take all these things?"

Mary Kate pushed the clothes out of her hands impatiently. "Quit trying to avoid the subject. I know something's going on. Why won't you be honest with me?"

Her Flanagan temper, never far away, flared at that. "Maybe for the same reason you're not honest with me about your feelings."

"What are you talking about?" Mary Kate's face whitened, her freckles standing out against her fair skin.

"You." Maybe it was time this came out. "You put up this ridiculous, shiny barrier that no one can get through, making the rest of us pretend that everything is just fine. Well, it's not—don't you think I know that?"

Mary Kate's face was dead white now, her eyes blazing. "Of course it's not! Do you think I don't think about Kenny a thousand times every day? And at night—" Her voice broke, tears welling over.

"Oh, honey, I'm so sorry." She reached for Mary Kate, aghast at what her well-meaning meddling had done. "I'm sorry. I know how much you're hurting."

"No, you don't!" Mary Kate shoved her hands away so hard she went back a step. "I pray you never do." She grabbed the boxes, thrusting everything inside and shoving them into Terry's arms. "Take all of it."

"Mary Kate—"

A decisive shake of the head stopped her. "Leave it, okay? I have to deal with this my way. Now just go."

She'd made a mess of things. What on earth had made her think she could help her sister? When it came to out-of-control emotions, she couldn't even help herself.

Jake tried to concentrate on the charts he was reviewing, but the headache that pressed on his temples and clamped the back of his neck made focusing difficult. Giving up, he slid them back into the chart rack and headed for the break room. The E.R. was late-afternoon still, the only patient a nursing home resident who was being transferred upstairs. The staff could spare him, and caffeine might help his head.

Maybe the headache was the aftermath of yesterday's mistakes. He should never have let things go so far with Terry. He'd blurted out far more than he'd intended about his own affairs. He'd never told anyone that much about what happened with Meredith. Never. His head pounded in time with his footsteps on the tiled floor. It was his burden to carry.

Her confession that she'd fled Philadelphia, considering herself a failure even after the inquiry had cleared her, had shaken him. He should have talked to her about that, tried to draw her out and repair some of the damage he'd done.

Instead, he'd just soaked up all that warmth and empathy she provided so selflessly and given her nothing. And then he'd compounded his mistakes by kissing her. Any one of her brothers would probably be happy to give him the punch in the jaw he richly deserved.

He shoved open the swinging door to the break room, stepped inside—and there she was. Terry turned from the coffeepot, mug in her hand, her cheeks brightening at the sight of him. It was too late to retreat now. Maybe, if his head would just stop pounding so much, he could try to make amends.

"Jake—Dr. Landsdowne." She gestured toward the cup. "Harriet said I could help myself to coffee. I mean—"

"It's okay, Terry." He managed a smile. "So far, the budget axe hasn't fallen on our coffee fund. Help yourself. Did you and Jeff bring the nursing home patient in?"

"Our last run of the shift." She took a sip of the coffee. "I have to confess, this is better than the coffee we've been making at the clinic. My mother took one taste and insisted she's bringing in a new coffeemaker. And some decent coffee."

"It certainly couldn't hurt." He gulped,

feeling a touch of relief the instant the hot liquid hit. "Is she at the clinic today?"

Terry nodded. "She was also taking some more books for Manuela. That kid must be a speed reader, and in a second language, no less."

"She's a bright girl." He needed to say something to her about the previous day, but his brain seemed fogged. "Listen, Terry, about yesterday—"

"Please, don't." Anything that had seemed relaxed about her manner toward him vanished in an instant. "It's fine. Really. It's forgotten."

She thought he was talking about that kiss. Oddly enough, that was the one thing that had happened between them that he didn't regret.

"I just wanted you to know I think you're a fine paramedic. I've been saying all the wrong things about that lately. We've worked together long enough that I don't doubt your skill or your devotion."

She flushed, but this time he thought it was with pleasure. "Thank you. I'm sure you'll still have to put me in my place from time to time."

He managed a smile, but the buzzing in

his head was so loud he didn't think he could say a word. He put the mug down, rocking it so badly that coffee sloshed onto the table.

"Jake?" Terry grasped his arm, her grip firm. "You're sick." She put her hand on his cheek and then jerked it away. "You're burning up. You shouldn't be working in this condition. Why didn't you say anything?"

"It's nothing." It wasn't nothing. He knew what it was, but no one else must know.

"You have a fever. You can't treat patients. I'll call Harriet."

"No!" He grabbed her hand. "Don't. You're right. I shouldn't be here. I'll go home."

"Let her check you out."

He tightened his grip, his head spinning. "Nobody can know. I have to get home. My meds are there. But nobody can know." He tried to push himself erect, but the walls were wavering oddly. "I'll go."

Terry slid his arm across her shoulders, bracing his body with hers, and he was surprised at the strength of her. "Not by yourself," she said firmly. "I'll drive your car for you."

He tried to concentrate. "You can't leave work—"

"My shift is over. Jeff will take the rig back to the firehouse."

He couldn't do this. He couldn't let Terry, of all people, see how weak he was. Panic flooded through him, giving the momentary illusion of strength. He couldn't let anyone know. He had to pull it together long enough to get to his car, get home.

"You don't have to drive me." He tried to put some energy into the words. She'd never release him if she guessed how bad he was.

"I'm not letting you get behind the wheel of a car in this condition, so get used to the idea. If you don't want me to take you, fine." He heard the hurt in her voice. "Just give me the name of someone else I can call for you."

He couldn't. That was the barren truth. There was no one else in Suffolk that he could call to help him.

He closed his eyes for a moment. *Please. Help me.* When he opened them, he still felt like passing out. And Terry still watched him with anxiety clouding those clear green eyes.

Maybe God wasn't answering him. Or maybe that's why Terry was here at just this moment.

"All right," he muttered, trying to shrug out of his lab coat.

Terry moved quickly, pulling it off and hanging it on one of the hooks. He picked up the phone, dialing Harriet.

"I think I'm coming down with a cold." He rushed the words out. "Can you hold the fort if I go home early?"

"Of course." Her cool, professional tone didn't allow her to sound pleased. "Do you want me to have a look at you?"

"No. Thanks. I'll be fine." He clicked off. She'd think him rude, but that was better than having her know the truth.

No, it seemed that Terry was the one person destined to know the truth about him. Well, if she'd ever nursed a secret longing to see him at his worst, at his weakest, she was certainly getting her chance today.

Terry wanted to turn around a half-dozen times during the drive to Jake's condo and take him straight back to the E.R. If he were anyone else, she'd have continued to try and get him to see a doctor. But Jake was the doc, and whatever was going on, it was obviously familiar to him. Supposedly he knew how to handle it. Still, she wasn't about to leave him alone until she was sure he'd be all right, whether he liked it or not.

Not was most probably the answer to that. Well, she'd deal with it when the time came.

The address he'd given her was in a condo development down near the river—town houses, for the most part, that had been sold to young families and a few single young professionals. She frowned, weaving her way through the older residential streets that surrounded it. Funny that she hadn't even thought about where Jake lived. She only associated him with the hospital and the clinic.

She glanced at him. He'd surprised her by managing to walk out of the hospital without hanging on to her, but how was she going to get him into the house? He leaned back against the headrest, eyes closed, his skin clammy and gray.

"We're almost there. What number did you say it was?"

He roused himself to open his eyes. "It's 1142. In the next block, the end unit on the right."

The buildings had brick facing on the lower level with white siding on the second floors. Jake's door was a glossy burgundy,

and rosebushes, still putting out a few blossoms, flanked a front porch just large
enough for two wicker chairs. The geraniums in hanging pots surprised her—she
wouldn't have expected him to take an interest in plant care. But maybe the condos
had a gardener to deal with such chores.

She mentally measured the distance from
curb to front door. "Is there a way to get
closer? A back entrance?" She was used to
hauling limp bodies, but moving Jake without help would be a chore.

"No." He sat up straighter. "I can manage.
Just let me off here."

"Right. And watch you collapse on the
sidewalk."

She slid out of the car, shaking her head.
Was it just Jake? No, probably her brothers
would be just as irritated at showing weakness in front of her.

She reached the passenger door as he
opened it. As she suspected, he had an unpleasant surprise when he tried to get out. It
took a couple of uncomfortable, sweating
moments before he was standing on the
walk, leaning on her, both of them breathing
hard.

She took a firm grip on his arm, slung

across her shoulder, and gripped his waist with her other arm. "Okay. Let's just take it slow."

"Don't have to talk to me as if I'm one of your patients," he muttered.

"Wouldn't dream of it." She piloted him toward the door, his weight seeming to get heavier with each step. "But I am used to dealing with people who don't know what's good for them."

His only response to that was a grunt. He was probably trying as hard as she was just to stay upright.

Finally they reached the porch. She gave a sigh of relief and propped him against one of the chairs. "Key?"

He fumbled in his pocket and drew out a key ring. "I can do—" The keys slid through his fingers and bounced, jingling, on the brick porch.

"Please," she said. "You can't even hold them, let alone get the key in the lock. If any of your neighbors are watching, they're probably sure you're drunk."

His mouth twitched, as if in the beginning of a smile. "'Good people, we are not drunk, as you might suppose,'" he quoted.

It startled her to hear Peter's words on the

day of Pentecost coming from Jake's mouth. She wouldn't have supposed he knew the Bible that well.

That was certainly a sanctimonious thought. *Sorry, Father.*

"Well, it's not nine o'clock in the morning, either." She swung the door open. "Come on, let's get you inside."

She piloted him in, spotted a comfortable-looking black leather sofa, and steered him to it. He slid onto it and tilted his head back, breathing heavily. Worry edged along her nerves. Was she doing the right thing by not calling Harriet?

"Tell me where your meds are, and I'll get them," she said abruptly, hating the feeling of being kept in the dark, the possibility of making a mistake because of his stubbornness.

He shook his head slowly, rolling it back and forth against the leather. "I can manage. You can leave—"

"No way. Look, Jake, I've only gone along with you this far because you're a doctor and I hope you know what you're doing. But either you let me give you the meds right now, or I'm calling Dr. Getz."

His glare was a feeble effort, and he must

have realized that. He closed his eyes. "Upstairs medicine cabinet. Chloroquinine."

Chloroquinine. So that was it. Malaria. He'd obviously contracted it in Africa and was having a relapse.

She frowned. "I don't know much about malaria, but isn't there a drug that prevents relapses?"

He nodded. "But only if you're fortunate enough to tolerate it. Are you going?"

"Right."

She went quickly up the staircase, running her hand along the satiny finish of the railing. The stairway was lined with framed color photos of African scenes, obviously personal to Jake. She shot a quick glance across what she could see of the living area. No family pictures. His relationship, or lack of one, with his family wasn't any of her business.

The bathroom was black-and-white tile with an Art Deco feel. She glanced quickly through the shelves of the medicine cabinet. The chloroquinine was the only prescription med there. She grabbed it, filled the bathroom cup with water and hurried back down, mind busy with the implications of Jake's illness.

He didn't want anyone to know, that much was clear. Did that mean he hadn't told anyone from the hospital when they'd hired him?

When she reached Jake, he'd slid down to a lying position on the sofa, head against the wide arm. She slipped her hand under his head to lift it, seeing the muscles of his neck work as he swallowed the pill.

"Okay," he muttered. "You can—"

"If you tell me to leave again, I might hit you," she warned.

The ghost of a smile flickered on his lips. "I'm too weak to fight back."

"I'll get a blanket and pillow for you." She straightened, but as she did, he caught her hand. His felt hot and dry. "What is it? Do you want something else?"

He shook his head slowly, as if even that took an effort. "Just thinking," he murmured. "If you wanted something to use against me, you have it now."

"Why, for goodness' sake? You're sick. That's not criminal. Unless you didn't tell them when they hired you—" She hated to think that.

"Not that." His voice faded to a whisper. "Just failure. Failure." He slid into sleep.

Chapter Ten

"Thanks, Seth. And tell Mom thanks, too."
Terry kept her voice low as she closed the
door of Jake's condo behind her brother.

She probably didn't need to be so careful.
Jake had been asleep for three solid hours,
and he didn't look as if anything short of a
thunderclap would disturb him.

Her mother had sent Seth over to deliver
a couple of quarts of homemade chicken
soup—her remedy for everything from the
sniffles to a broken heart. She hadn't told
Mom what was wrong with Jake, but surely
chicken soup couldn't hurt.

She paused on her way to the kitchen to
put her hand on Jake's forehead. She didn't
need a thermometer to tell her he was still
burning with fever. So how long did she take

responsibility for him without calling in another doctor?

She could call Harriet. They were friends—surely she could ask for advice, couldn't she?

But she knew the answer to that. Jake didn't want Harriet to know. He'd made that very clear.

Please, Father, guide me. I'm not sure what to do, and I don't want to make a mistake.

That seemed to be her theme song for the past few years. I don't want to make a mistake.

Trying to push away the sensation of helplessness, she took the soup to the kitchen. After a moment's hesitation, she rummaged through the cabinets until she found a saucepan and dumped a quart of chicken soup into it. Maybe by the time it had heated, Jake would be stirring.

She put the soup on low and went back to the living room, drawn to check on him again, even though it seemed unlikely that anything would have changed in the past three minutes. She settled into the overstuffed leather chair opposite the couch, studying Jake's face.

Pale, with the faintest dark stubble beginning to show. The sharp lines of his features seemed less aggressive in sleep, his mouth softer. His head turned a little, as if he searched for a cooler spot on the pillow.

But even as she thought that, a shiver went through him. She got up quickly, grabbing the extra blanket she'd found in the linen closet. Chills and fever. She'd spent a few minutes on Jake's computer, trying to become an instant expert on malaria. He had the fever, now he was going to battle the chills.

She tucked the blanket around him. "It's okay, Jake. I know you're cold."

His eyes struggled to open, so dark the blue was almost midnight. He frowned at her, as if trying to identify who she was and why she was here.

"Terry. What—" The words were interrupted by a spasm of chills that set his teeth chattering.

"It's okay," she said again. "You took your pills about two hours ago, and you've been asleep. Is there anything else I can do to make you more comfortable?"

A shudder shook him. "Another blanket."

"Right." She ran up the stairs, pulled the

comforter off his bed, and hurried back down again. *Lord, please let me be doing the right thing.*

She tossed the comforter over him, tucking it around his body. He nodded, as if to thank her.

"My mother sent over some chicken soup. I have it warm on the stove. Do you think you could eat some?"

Weak as he was, he managed a glare. "You told her."

"Just that you're sick, not what the problem is. She always figures chicken soup couldn't hurt. How about it?"

He nodded. "Worth a try." The words were interrupted by another round of teeth-rattling chills.

It hurt to watch him. She hurried out to the kitchen and ladled soup into a mug. It might be easier for him to sip it than to try and use a spoon, and he probably wouldn't let her feed him. Everyone said doctors were the worst patients.

She knelt next to him and held the mug to his lips. "Just try a sip," she coaxed.

He managed to get a few mouthfuls down before the next chill hit. Was it wishful thinking, or were the chills a little less violent?

"Better now," he murmured. His eyes closed, his lashes dark against his pallor.

"That's quite a souvenir you brought back from Africa." She set the mug on the lamp table, close at hand. "Does this happen often?"

A frown set three sharp vertical lines between his brows. "I thought I'd had the last episode." His eyes snapped open. "Dr. Getz knows about it, if that's what you're wondering."

There wasn't much she could say in answer to that, since she had been wondering. "But you don't want anyone else to know."

"I don't want to give the rumor factory any fresh ammunition. My position at the hospital is precarious enough already." His mouth set stubbornly.

At least he wasn't shaking any longer. She offered him the mug. He took it and downed about half of it before slumping back against the pillows again, exhausted.

"You know your business best, I guess. But I think most people would find your work in Africa impressive, especially when it came at such a price."

He focused on her, frowning. "You mean the malaria?"

"Well, that, too. But I was thinking about giving up your residency, the plans you'd made for your future—"

His mouth twisted. "You and Getz, you're the same. Attributing noble motives to me. Believe me, it wasn't all that noble. I went to the mission field because no one else wanted me."

She could only stare at him. "But your residency—"

"I was allowed to resign, allowed to cover it up with talk of health problems."

"I didn't know."

His head moved restlessly again. "The truth was that after Meredith's death I couldn't cope. I started second-guessing myself. I was no good to anyone. If I hadn't resigned, they'd have dropped me from the program." He bit the words off as if they tasted vile.

"I'm sorry." Jake always seemed so sure of himself. She'd have expected him to ignore everyone else's opinion, but maybe his own sense of guilt had whispered that they were right. "If you didn't want to go to the mission, surely there were other options.

Your father must have so many connections."

His jaw clenched. "Connections? Yes, he has those. But he wouldn't use them. He wouldn't even recommend me when people he knew called him, thinking they'd give me a chance because I was his son."

"I don't understand. Surely he wanted to help you." Her parents would sacrifice anything to help one of their own.

"I'd failed. That reflected on him." He said the words evenly, but she could hear the pain he suppressed. "I didn't have what it took, letting myself get emotionally involved, showing weakness. He cut me off, as if he'd never had a son."

She tried to absorb it, to understand it, but she couldn't. She could never understand someone who'd behave that way to his own child.

"I'm sorry." Her hand closed over his, feeling the tension that gripped him. "I don't know what to say."

"You want to make it better?" A faint thread of mockery traced the words. "No one can make this better. All I can do is make it on my own. That's why I went to Somalia. Because they'd take me, and because I knew I'd be so busy there that I wouldn't have time to think."

"You did good work there. No matter why you went, you can't lose sight of the good you did."

He nodded slowly, meeting her gaze, his very serious. "In the midst of all that pain and turmoil, I met people who carried their own center of peace with them. It was a life-changing experience to work with them. For the first time, I took my focus off myself and turned my life over to God."

"I'm glad," she said simply, her throat tight with unshed tears.

His head moved restlessly on the pillow. "I thought I was doing what God wanted, but then the malaria hit, and they sent me home. Is that what God had planned for me, Terry? If you have an answer, give it to me, because I don't understand."

"If I had all the answers, I wouldn't struggle every day with my own doubts and fears. But I know one thing—God has the answers for you. You have to stop telling yourself you failed. Malaria is an illness, not a personal weakness."

He shook his head. His eyes closed, as if he'd talked himself into exhaustion. She stayed where she was, kneeling next to him, holding his hand, as he drifted into sleep.

He needs so much to do good work, Father. Please, let him see that he's punishing himself unnecessarily. Let him find his path.

Because if he didn't—she didn't want to think about what might become of Jake if he lost this position. So she'd keep his secret, and she'd do her best to help him.

And if her own heart got bruised in the process? Well, she'd just have to deal with that as best she could.

Jake struggled awake. Why was he on the sofa? He shoved away the blankets that muffled him, and memory came flooding back. He put his hand to his head, feeling the perspiration that streaked his hair.

Another relapse, just when he'd thought he was past all that. He gritted his teeth and pushed to an upright position. He was as weak as a newborn kitten, but at least the fever was gone. By morning, he'd be able to go back to work as if nothing had happened.

China clinked in the kitchen, reminding him that he had bigger problems than going back to work in the morning. Terry. He hadn't dreamed it. Terry had brought him home, had stayed with him. He had a hazy memory of her strong, capable hands tucking blankets around him.

He'd depended on her. Worse, he'd talked to her, spilling out things he'd never told a living soul. He'd trusted her with his future.

Terry was trustworthy. The thought had a feel of bedrock truth about it. Still, how reliable was his judgment? He'd certainly made a string of mistakes when it came to dealing with the emotional side of his life.

He heard her light step, and Terry came quickly through the doorway to the kitchen. She checked a moment at the sight of him sitting up and then came toward him.

"You may live after all." Her palm was cool against his forehead. "The fever's gone."

"That seems to be the pattern." He tried to keep his tone light. "Headache, fever, chills and eventually I sleep it off."

She eyed him critically. "But you still look as if a light breeze would knock you over. Could you manage some soup and toast?"

"You don't need to nurse me, Terry. I'm over the worst of it." And he didn't want to depend on her any longer. The longer she stayed, the greater the risk he'd do or say something he'd regret.

Her smile flashed, lighting her face. "I'm a paramedic, remember? You just get emergency care from me."

"No TLC?" Keep it light. They were colleagues, nothing more.

"No, but my mother would never forgive me if I left without feeding you again. That's her answer to life's problems—lots of love and a good meal."

"Sounds like a pretty good recipe to me." He leaned back, knowing if he tried to get up he'd fall on his face. "Okay, soup and toast, but only if you have some, too." He glanced toward the window. Dark outside, and Terry had turned on the lamps. "You must have missed your supper."

"No problem." She turned back to the kitchen. "You get used to eating at odd times when you work shifts."

This might be one of the coziest meals of his life, sitting side by side with Terry on the couch, plates on the coffee table, eating soup and buttered toast. Finally he leaned back, tired but with the relieved conviction that this relapse was over. Maybe the last one. Optimism buoyed him. He'd escaped again, and no one but Terry knew.

His gaze rested on her as she scooped up the last spoonful of soup. Her hair was ruffled, and any makeup she might have worn had long since vanished. The paramedic khaki pants and navy shirt looked as if they'd been slept in. She was the best thing he'd seen in a long time.

"Terry."

She turned her head, smiling at him. "What?"

"Just—thanks." It seemed a small return.

She shrugged, looking embarrassed. "Mom supplied the chicken soup."

"Not just for the food. For everything. I seem to recall being pretty rude to you when you were trying to help me."

Her eyebrows lifted. "Would it surprise you to learn that patients are often rude to paramedics?"

"No. But I'm not just a patient."

She was perched on the edge of the sofa, and he wanted her closer. He circled her wrist with his fingers, feeling her pulse accelerate at his touch.

"They do say doctors make the worst patients." The words came out with a breath-less quality.

"We do. All the more reason for me to apologize." He leaned toward her, his native caution warring with the longing he felt to hold her close.

"Forget it." Her voice had gone soft, and she turned more fully toward him. "Call it professional courtesy, or—"

The rest of the words were lost when his lips found hers. He shouldn't. But she was here. He cared for her. Her arms slid around him, her lips soft against his, and a wave of tenderness swept through him. He wanted to hold her, to go on holding her, to feel her warmth and caring and know that it was for him.

She drew back finally, a smile trembling on her lips. "I thought we weren't going to do that again." The words were a bare whisper, for his ears only.

"I don't think I promised that, did I?" He slid his arm around her, drawing her close so that her head rested on his shoulder. "I'm glad you're here, Terry. Glad you were the one in the break room when I walked in to-day."

"Me, too." Her head moved slightly against

his shoulder. "I do think you shouldn't worry so much about people knowing, though. They'd consider malaria a badge of honor after the work you did."

"Maybe, but I can't afford to take the risk. And I'm not sure I did anything that admirable."

"Jake—"

He shook his head. He didn't want her looking at him as if he'd done something heroic. "Just let it go. Please."

Concern for him darkened her eyes. "What is it? Were you trying to make up for Meredith's death by saving other people?"

The question hit him right in the gut. That was exactly what he'd been trying to do in Somalia. His mouth twisted.

"If it was, I failed. I turned into a patient myself instead of saving others. Maybe God was telling me that nothing I did was enough to make up for what I didn't do for Meredith."

"Jake, you can't think that. You did good work there, and you're doing good work now. You can't blame yourself—"

"Yes. I can." He shook his head, hating the pity he saw in her face. "Don't. This is something you can't make better. Nobody can."

He'd made a mistake, letting Terry get so close, letting her pity him. His father had been right about him. He'd let emotions cloud his judgment again. He should have realized he didn't have anything to offer Terry.

There wasn't a future for their relationship, but he couldn't push her away. Selfish, but he just couldn't do it.

"Are you sure they're going to like ham and scalloped potatoes?" Terry glanced across the church kitchen at her mother, who was putting the final touches to an immense tossed salad. Gelatin salads already chilled in the refrigerator.

"I asked Manuela, and she said that would be great." Her mother smiled. "Let's face it, Terry. We couldn't have put together a meal of Mexican food they'd even recognize."

"I guess you're right."

Inviting people from the migrant camps to the church for a home-cooked meal had been Mom's idea, and she'd marshaled her troops like a general. Volunteers had worked through the afternoon, and even now were setting the tables in Fellowship Hall. The aroma of baked ham was nearly irresistible.

"I invited Jake." Mom wedged the last salad into the refrigerator. "Do you think he'll come?"

"I'm not sure," she hedged. "He might not be able to get away from the hospital in time."

In fact, she wasn't sure of a lot about Jake right now, even though her lips curved into an automatic smile at the thought of him. She had it bad, all right. And she just didn't know if he felt the same.

He'd regretted confiding so much in her the night he'd been sick. She was convinced of that. If she tried to bring up the subject, he'd tense, so she'd stopped trying.

Still, he seemed to want to spend time with her. They'd even gone out on what she supposed was their first official date—dinner out after closing the clinic down the previous night. He'd steered the conversation away from anything personal, but his goodnight kiss certainly hadn't been impersonal.

She turned to check the status of the scalloped potato casseroles, hoping Mom would think her cheeks were pink from the oven's heat. She didn't want to talk about Jake, because she couldn't be sure there was anything in their relationship.

She probably shouldn't have said what she had about his motives, and yet it seemed so clear to her. How many lives did he think he had to save to make up for failing Meredith? He'd never think he'd done enough. And as long as he couldn't forgive himself, he couldn't accept God's forgiveness.

She closed the oven door. Maybe Brendan had an answer for that one. She didn't.

Mom folded a tea towel neatly on the rack. "Speaking of Manuela, Brendan told me he tried to speak to Matthew Dixon, but ended up talking to Andy instead. Andy promised to do what he could to see that the Ortiz family stays through the apple harvest, at least."

"I wish he'd hurry up with it. School started yesterday, but none of the migrant children from the Dixon camp went. I know Manuela is wild to go."

If the Ortiz family left in another week, they might never see Manuela again. The family would follow the harvest, and who knew what would happen to them then? Her heart hurt at the thought of never seeing Manuela again.

"I know." Mom's smooth brow wrinkled. "Your father and I have been talking about it. If there's no other way to help them, we'd like to offer to have Manuela stay with us and go to school. I don't know how her family would react, or what the legalities would be, but we'd like to try."

"You'd be willing to do that?" Silly question, really. Mom was noted for taking in strays. Dad grumbled sometimes, but he was secretly proud of her open heart.

"Of course." Her mother smiled. "We're used to having those bedrooms filled. In fact, we might be getting a full house for a while. I had a letter yesterday from your cousin Fiona. She'd like to come to see us."

"Fiona?" For a moment she was too stunned to say more. "But—Dad hasn't had any contact with her father in thirty years."

The breach between her husband and his younger brother was a grief to Mom, Terry knew. She'd struggled to maintain some contact, even though Michael Flanagan had settled in California years ago. Terry knew her cousins existed, but she'd never even met them.

"All the more reason why we should welcome Michael's daughter to our home," her mother said tartly. "It's time to put this foolishness behind us."

"Does Dad think so?"

"Not yet. But I'm working on him." She glanced through the pass-through window to Fellowship Hall. "Look, Jake did come."

Everything else slid to the back of Terry's mind as she saw Jake's tall figure sauntering toward them, pausing to greet the workers who'd finished setting the tables and now sat in a circle, chatting.

He reached them, his smile deepening as he looked at Terry. "Hi, Terry. Siobhan. What's for supper?"

"Can't you smell it? Baked ham."

"And you're just in time," her mother said. She glanced at the clock over the range. "Goodness, look at the clock. The food's about ready. They should be here by now. Brendan sent the bus for them ages ago."

Jake frowned. "You know, it would be like the crew chief to keep them working late tonight, just out of spite. I think I'll call Andy Dixon and see if he knows what's going on." He pulled out his cell phone and flipped it open.

It felt good to know Jake was on her side in this, at least. She studied him as he talked, liking the strength in his face, the determination in his jaw. Funny, he no longer seemed to have that superior look she'd told herself she disliked so much. Or maybe he hadn't changed, but her way of looking at him had.

He hung up after several minutes, shaking his head. "That's exactly what happened. Andy intervened, and they're getting on the bus now."

"Thank goodness you thought of calling." Siobhan beamed at him. "Otherwise we'd have been sitting here letting the food dry out." She clapped her hands to get the attention of her helpers. "They're on their way, ladies. Let's get the ham sliced and the biscuits baked."

In a moment the kitchen was a hive of activity, and Terry was swept into it, relegated to putting salads out on the long serving table. By the time she had a chance to look up, their guests were filing into Fellowship Hall, a little quiet and uncomfortable at first, but relaxing when they saw familiar faces from the clinic.

In the bustle of serving, she lost track of

Jake, but when things calmed down, she scanned the room, finding him in the corner, deep in conversation with Andy. They certainly owed Andy a vote of thanks for intervening in the crew chief's troublemaking. Now, if he'd done as he promised and talked to his father about having the Ortiz family stay, they'd really owe him.

She pulled off the apron her mother had insisted she wear over her khaki slacks and crossed the room to them. Andy's pleasant face broke into a smile when he saw her.

"Well, do I get an extra slice of pie for my efforts?"

"As much as you can eat. We can't thank you enough."

He shrugged. "I'm just glad Jake called. I'm afraid it was a case of the crew chief trying to enforce his authority at your expense."

"It worked out," Jake said. "That's the important thing."

"What about our other problem?" It certainly couldn't hurt to prod Andy a little. "Have you talked to your father about letting the Ortiz family stay through the apple harvest?"

Andy's smile disappeared, and she knew

what he was going to say before the words were out. "I'm sorry, Terry. I tried, but Dad has been impossible lately. As soon as I got the words out, he started ranting about do-gooders trying to interfere with how he runs his own farm."

"But didn't you explain that we're only trying to help Manuela have a chance at some stable schooling?" She tried to ignore the frown Jake was directing at her, the one that told her not to make waves.

"Honestly, Terry, it wouldn't have done any good to keep pushing him then. I'll try to bring it up again, I promise."

"Thank you," Jake said quickly. "That's all we can ask."

Well, that might be all Jake wanted to ask, but it wasn't enough for her. She'd give Andy another day or two to come through for them, but if that didn't work, she'd see Matthew Dixon herself, no matter how much Jake disapproved.

Chapter Eleven

Jake didn't like to admit what it said about his feelings that he was lingering near the emergency room admissions desk just because he knew Terry's unit was coming in with a nursing home transfer. The admissions clerk would handle sending the patient to the lab for tests. There was no reason for the Director of Emergency Services to be here, except that he wanted to see Terry's bright smile.

He pulled a chart from the rack and scanned it. Busywork, the rational side of his mind mocked him. You're trying to look busy so no one will know you're waiting here for Terry, like a high-school kid lingering near his sweetheart's locker.

Not a sweetheart, he assured himself. He didn't have a sophomoric crush on Terry. He enjoyed her company. That didn't have to mean anything serious for either of them.

For the first time in a long while, he had a sense of cautious optimism about the future. The thought startled him. He felt as if he were taking the first steps toward a normal life, and he couldn't deny that Terry had something to do with that.

Terry, and the mix of attraction, affection and caring he felt at just the sight of her as she and her partner moved a patient on a gurney toward the glass doors. Terry leaned over the gurney as she pushed, her face lit with that warm, caring smile, assuring her patient that everything was all right.

Even though he was prepared for it, the rush of pure pleasure he felt as she came toward him startled him with its strength. He tried to put on his usual professional demeanor as they neared.

"Good morning. Do you have a patient for us?" He'd like to believe Terry's smile was a bit warmer when it was aimed at him.

"Good morning, Dr. Landsdowne." Her tone was perfectly sedate, as if he hadn't kissed her good night at her door the previous night when he'd driven her home after the supper at church. "Mr. Atkins is just scheduled for some routine blood work, that's all."

"I'll check him in," Terry's partner offered. "No problem." He shoved the gurney over to the admissions clerk.

Just how much did Terry's partner know about them? He shoved that thought to the back of his mind. There wasn't really anything to know, was there?

"I hope your mother is taking it easy today, after everything she did yesterday to put on that dinner. Will you be having leftover ham for the rest of the week?"

"Mom doesn't know the meaning of taking it easy. And you don't have to worry about the food—she packaged up all the leftovers and took them out to the migrant camp."

"It was a big success—" The buzz of his beeper cut off his words. He checked it and frowned. "Dr. Getz. Excuse me."

He moved quickly to the phone on the desk and dialed the chief of staff's extension. The clerk was at the far end of the counter, dealing with the patient's paperwork. No one but Terry was close enough to hear. Maybe his optimism about the way things were going was misplaced. Why did the chief want him?

"Landsdowne, I'm glad I caught you." At least Getz didn't sound as if he'd called with a complaint. "Your father is here to see you. You can use my office to talk. Just come right up." He clicked off, leaving Jake staring at the phone.

Jake fumbled the receiver back on the phone, turning toward Terry without even thinking about the instant need to confide in her. "He says my father is here to see me."

Her gaze rested on his face. "Do you want to see him?"

"No!" The response was automatic. "Why would I? He's the one who cut me off." He reached for the phone. "I'll tell Getz to say I'm not available."

She stopped the movement of his hand with hers. "Don't, Jake. You don't want to put Dr. Getz in the middle of your quarrel with your father."

"It's not a quarrel." But she had a point. He shouldn't involve the chief of staff in a personal matter. It seemed his father had already done that.

"Still—"

"I know." He clasped her hand, grateful that she was here. "You're right. I'll have to speak to my father myself and make it clear there's nothing else to say."

Her eyebrows lifted. "Are you sure? I mean, he wouldn't be here if he didn't want to talk to you. His coming here must mean his attitude toward you has changed."

"You don't know my father. Once he's made up his mind, nothing changes it."

"He said things in anger. Everyone does that." She leaned toward him, intent in her desire to make things better. That was Terry, always trying to make things better.

"You're seeing the world through your family's rose-colored glasses." He thought perhaps a bit enviously of Joe Flanagan's obvious pride in his children, of Siobhan's overflowing love. "My family isn't like yours."

"Maybe so, but you still have to see him. You know that." Her hand clasped his persuasively. "If you don't hear him out, someday you'll regret it. Maybe not now, but someday. You don't want that hanging on your conscience."

"Your conscience is tenderer than mine." He smiled wryly. "But you're probably right. I have to see him. And he can't say anything that will matter to me any longer, in any event."

He hoped. Still, he didn't really have a choice, did he? Terry was right. He had to do this.

"Ready to head back?" Jeff paused at the corner of the desk, lifting his eyebrows at her. His expression suggested that he knew exactly why she lingered there and was trying to imply that he didn't.

She glanced at her watch. "As long as we don't have any calls, why don't we just wait for Mr. Atkins to be ready to go back?"

"Sure, save us a trip. Want to get some lunch?"

"I'm not hungry right now. You go ahead." Did he buy that? Well, it didn't matter. Jeff might suspect, but he wouldn't gossip.

He nodded and ambled down the pale green corridor toward the hospital cafeteria.

She shouldn't hang around here, waiting for Jake to come back. That implied that she thought he should tell her what was going on with his father.

She bent over the counter, concentrating on filling out the run sheet. Routine, nothing but routine. It didn't keep her from thinking about Jake.

Lord, please be with Jake right now. His

relationship with his father is beyond my understanding, but You know all about it. Jake has given his life to You. Please guide him now.

She didn't know what else to pray for. There was nothing simple or easy to understand about Jake, or about her feelings for him, for that matter. She leaned against the counter, gaze absently fixed on the bowl of yellow chrysanthemums that decorated it.

Yellow mums for fall. The season was moving on. Jake had been in Suffolk for a month now. Did he feel that he was fitting in, finding a home here? Or did he carry that restless, rootless feeling inside him?

She had to face facts. Until he'd resolved his feelings about failing Meredith, Jake wouldn't be free to love anyone else. Not that she was thinking about love in connection with him. She backed away from that quickly.

If she were thinking that—her mind drifted to her brothers, all happily married now. To her parents. There were plenty of examples of God-centered, solid, happy marriages in her family. That was what she wanted for herself. She wouldn't make the mistake of letting herself fall in love with someone who couldn't make that kind of commitment.

She was still standing there, frowning at the run sheet as if it held the secret of the universe, when the elevator doors swished open. Jake stalked out, and one look at his face told her the meeting with his father hadn't gone well.

"Jake—"

He shot a glance toward the receptionist, shook his head and took her arm. "Let's go in the lounge." He piloted her quickly toward the staff lounge, and she could feel the depth of his anger through the taut fingers that gripped her elbow.

As soon as the door closed behind them, Jake released her. He stalked across the room, looking as if he'd like to punch his fist into the wall, then turned back toward her.

"Tell me what happened."

Jake had to talk to someone, or he was going to explode. She already knew about his situation with his father. If he talked to her about it, it would only be because she was the one person who knew. Nothing more.

He turned away, planting both fists on the table, looking down. Tension was written in every line of his body. He looked as if he'd fly apart at any moment.

"Please, Jake," she said softly. "Talk to me. What did he say?"

He straightened, running his hand through his hair as if that would help him put his thoughts together. "Nothing I shouldn't have expected." He shook his head. "Oh, it started out well enough. After all, the fact that he was here showed he'd at least been interested enough to keep tabs on where I am."

"That's good, isn't it?" There was nothing in that to account for the anger that radiated from Jake in waves.

His mouth twisted. "You'd think so. Sounds like something any father might do. But he went a bit further. He got in touch with Getz and asked him if he found my work satisfactory." He sounded as if he were quoting. "Satisfactory! As if that's the best that could be expected from me."

"Whatever your father's motives, I'm sure Dr. Getz gave a good report about you." She was feeling her way, not sure what would ease the pain she sensed beneath the anger. Her heart hurt for him.

"Yes. He did. That's why my father came to see me." His hands flexed, then drew tight, the knuckles white. "Since my work has been satisfactory, he's decided to give me another chance. According to him, I'm wasting my talent here. I'm to give up my work, go back to Boston and take up the neurosurgery residency he's managed to wangle for me."

Go back to Boston. For a moment she faced the prospect of life without Jake. It looked bleak. She took a breath. This wasn't about her. It was about Jake.

"That's what you've always wanted, isn't it?"

"Yes. No. I'm not sure anymore what I want." He pressed his knuckles against his forehead. "One thing I know—I don't want my father telling me what to do. Not anymore."

"Jake—" This is about Jake, remember? Not about you. "Look, it sounds as if he went about talking to you all wrong, but maybe you should still think about it. Don't throw away an opportunity because you're angry with him."

"That's not it." He tried, and failed, to smile, and then came quickly back across the room to clasp her hands in his. "I don't know whether neurosurgery is what I want anymore, but even if it is, I don't think I'm willing to pay the price my father asks." His fingers tightened on hers, robbing her of the ability to breathe. "Thank you, Terry. For caring."

Caring. Her heart was too full to speak, and she couldn't kid herself any longer. What she felt for Jake wasn't caring, or friendship, or sympathy. It was love.

She was in love with him, whether there was any future in that or not.

Terry was supposed to be on her way to the clinic, but no one needed to know that she planned to make a stop first. She turned down the lane that led to the Dixon farmhouse. She could only hope she'd find Matthew Dixon at home, preferably alone.

Depending on Andy to intercede with his father didn't seem to be getting them any- where. Each day that passed made it more difficult for Manuela to start school. She hadn't been much help to Jake the previous day, but maybe she could accomplish something for Manuela if she could talk to Mr. Dixon.

He might think of her as Joe Flanagan's little girl, but he respected her father. Maybe he'd listen to her when he wouldn't listen to his son. Fathers and sons sometimes didn't respect each other's opinions—she only had to look at Jake's relationship with his father to see that.

Her heart clenched for him. Was Jake giving up something he'd regret later? That was what she feared. It would break her heart if he left, but if he stayed and felt he'd settled for second best, that would be worse.

She couldn't help but wonder if that interview with his father was as bad as Jake felt. Had his father really intended to denigrate Jake's accomplishments, or was Jake reading something into it out of his past pain? She didn't know, and she probably never would.

She pulled to a stop in front of the farmhouse. She'd been so preoccupied with thoughts of Jake that she hadn't rehearsed what she was going to say to Mr. Dixon. Well, maybe that was just as well.

Please, Lord. I believe I'm doing Your will in this. So please, speak through me.

She didn't see Andy's car anywhere. Maybe she'd be fortunate enough to find him out. Andy's protectiveness toward his father might be admirable, but in this case, she could do without it.

She went quickly to the screen door and rapped, the weathered door rattling under her assault. She paused for a moment, hand on that door. Had someone called out?

"Come in." The voice, sounding querulous, came from upstairs. "Come here and help me."

Nobody ever had to say "help me" twice to her. Terry yanked open the screen door and hurried across the hall and up the stairs. "Mr. Dixon? Are you all right?"

"In here." Dixon stood in the doorway of a bedroom, barefoot, his white hair ruffled. "Who are you?"

"Terry Flanagan, Mr. Dixon." He looked upset, but not ill. "You remember me. Joe Flanagan's girl."

"'Course I remember you." His voice was testy. "Just can't see you without my glasses, that's all. Fool boy is supposed to leave them on the nightstand so I can find them, and he didn't. Can't even get my shoes on without them."

"Suppose I have a look around for them?" She moved past him into the bedroom.

Dark, heavy furniture, the relics of an earlier age. Light-blocking shades were pulled down at the windows, making the interior of the room cavelike.

No wonder he couldn't find his glasses. She practically had to grope her way across the room to the window in order to flip up the shades, letting sunlight flood the room. Mr. Dixon blinked, like an owl exposed to the light.

"Those glasses have to be here somewhere. Use your eyes, girl. Find them." His bark sounded more assured now.

"Yes, sir." The glasses were probably right on the nightstand where Andy was supposed to leave them. But she checked the nightstand and then the floor around it without finding them.

"Well, where are they?"

Dixon took a step toward her, his hand out in front of him as if feeling for any obstacles, and she realized how little he could see without his glasses. A wave of pity swept through her. How terrible it must be, to feel so helpless.

"Not on the nightstand, but I'll find them in a minute or two, I'm sure." She checked the bed first, to be sure they hadn't become tangled with the covers, and then began working her way around the room. The glasses finally turned up on the mantel over the disused fireplace, tucked behind a framed picture of Matthew Dixon and his wife on their wedding day.

"Here they are. They were on the mantel."

He slid them on and peered at her, blue eyes sharp. "He hid them, that's what he did. Doesn't like me getting around on my own."

"I'm sure Andy wouldn't do that." She found a pair of black lace-up shoes in the closet and helped him put on socks and shoes.

He stood, grasping her shoulder for a moment. "You're a good girl. I'm going downstairs now."

She slipped around to his side, ready to grab him if he seemed tottery, but he went down the stairs as spryly as a younger man.

"Come on into the kitchen. I need some coffee. You can tell me what you want." He headed briskly to the kitchen, confident now, a complete change from the helpless soul he'd been a few minutes before.

He poured two mugs of coffee from the modern coffeemaker that looked out of place on the worn wooden counter and shoved one toward her. She took a sip of coffee strong enough to make her hair stand on end. Dixon downed his with every indication of enjoyment.

"Now then." The coffee seemed to complete his transformation. He stood erect, looking at her questioningly. "What was it you wanted?"

"It's about the Ortiz family—from the migrant worker camp. Their daughter has been helping us at the clinic, and we'd like to see her have a chance to attend school here for a while. If you could hire her father to stay through the apple harvest—"

But he was already shaking his head. "It's none of my concern. That's taken care of by the crew chief."

"You're the employer, Mr. Dixon. Surely, if you said you wanted them to stay, the crew chief would go along with you." She was losing him already, the rapport she'd thought she'd built slipping away.

His face tightened. "Why are you bothering me with this? The farm workers aren't any of your concern."

"They have to be somebody's concern."

She felt her temper slipping and tried to grasp control.

"You and your do-gooders." His face reddened. "I should have known better than to agree to that clinic."

"They need the clinic. They need better housing, too. You should be ashamed of the conditions they're living in." So much for controlling her temper. She'd end up regretting this, but somebody had to confront him about his treatment of the workers.

He slammed his cup down on the table so hard it was a wonder it didn't smash to pieces. "You're out of line, young woman. My workers have everything they need. My son sees to that."

"That's not what Andy—"

He didn't let her finish. "I'll thank you to get out of my house and mind your own business."

"Taking care of other people is everyone's business."

"Out!" His face was so red that she was afraid to pursue it any further.

She turned toward the door. "Please. Just think about it." She didn't dare say more. She went quickly down the hall and out of the house.

It wasn't until she was driving down the lane that she realized she was shaking, her hands trembling so that she had to grip the wheel to steer.

She'd failed. She never should have thought she could deal with Dixon herself. She'd just made the whole thing worse.

And if Dixon complained to Jake, or worse, to the hospital board, she might have created more trouble than any of them could handle.

Chapter Twelve

Terry rubbed the polishing rag along the chrome trim of the rig. The firehouse was quiet, with most on-duty personnel upstairs having lunch. The quiet suited her. She and Jeff had decided the rig needed a thorough cleaning, and the routine chore combined with the quiet soothed her.

Jeff was inside the rig, taking inventory of their supplies. His tuneless whistle was part of the background to her thoughts. Unfortunately, letting her mind stray from how many inches of chrome she had to polish was a good recipe for disturbing her mood.

She was certainly better off here than trying to intercede on Manuela's behalf. She'd messed that up thoroughly when she'd tried to talk to Dixon about her.

Her polishing cloth slowed its circular

movements. She'd been waiting for the shoe to drop for over twenty-four hours— waiting for an irate call from Jake or a stern one from the hospital board. So far, nothing had happened. Apparently Mr. Dixon hadn't complained about her. Yet.

Ripping off a paper towel, she wiped down the headlight, running the towel into the seam. Odd, what Dixon had said about letting Andy handle everything to do with the migrant worker housing. That hadn't been the impression Andy gave.

Maybe the truth lay somewhere in be-tween. Perhaps the elder Dixon gave Andy the work, but without the authority to make any changes. Fathers and sons seemed to have far more complicated relationships than mothers and daughters, from what she could see.

She might never really know the answer. Andy didn't have any reason to confide in her, even if he did claim friendship from kin-dergarten.

And as far as confiding was concerned, she had some of that to do. She ought to have told Brendan what happened with Dixon. Maybe he could come up with some other way to help the Ortiz family.

And she ought to tell Jake, as well. Her throat tightened at the thought of forcing those words out. He would not be happy with her. He'd warned her to tread cautiously with Dixon, and she'd plunged in as if everything depended on her.

If Dixon decided to complain, she'd put the work of the clinic in jeopardy. And even if he didn't, her actions might mean that he wouldn't agree to allow the clinic access to his workers next year.

Jake felt that any complaint about the clinic could reflect on him. She found it hard to believe that the board would refuse him a permanent contract based on her mistakes, but what mattered was what Jake believed. She had to confess to him, and the sooner, the better.

"Are you Ms. Flanagan?"

She straightened so sharply she nearly cracked her head on the rearview mirror. She had been so deep in thought that she hadn't heard the woman approach, although those high heels must have made noise on the concrete floor.

Fashionable, expensive heels, matching an equally expensive leather bag. A lightweight gray suit that echoed perfectly coiffed gray hair. This was not the sort of person one expected to find in the firehouse.

"I'm Terry Flanagan. May I help you?"

The woman let her gaze drift over Terry from head to foot, and Terry found herself squaring her shoulders. Okay, maybe she didn't look like a fashion plate in her paramedic uniform, with a cleaning rag in her hand. She didn't intend to.

"I'm Lila Landsdowne. Is there someplace we can speak? In private." She frowned at Jeff, whose startled face had appeared in the window above her.

Lila Landsdowne. Jake's mother—she had to be. Terry's stomach tied itself into knots. This couldn't be good. What did Jake's mother want with her?

"Well—" She looked around, finding nothing suitable for a private talk in the engine room. Besides, she wasn't sure she wanted a private talk with Jake's mother. Did he know she was here?

Jeff slid out of the rig. "I'll go up and have lunch, Ter. I'll make sure nobody comes down to bother you." He gave Mrs. Landsdowne an awkward nod and hurried toward the stairs.

The woman let her gaze follow him until he

was out of sight. Then she turned back to Terry, one silvery eyebrow lifted.

She was not going to let the woman intimidate her. This was her place. She managed a smile. "We'll be private enough here. I'm afraid there's no place to sit, unless you'd like to get into the rig."

A pained expression crossed Mrs. Landsdowne's face. "No. This will do. I understand you're a friend of my son's."

"Did Jake tell you that?" This visit seemed odd, to say the least.

"No." Her lips tightened, lines showing beneath perfect makeup. "I haven't spoken to Jacob in some time."

"Then how—"

"Really, Ms. Flanagan, we're wasting time. I make it my business to know what my son is doing. I know about your relationship." She looked as if the words left a bad taste in her mouth.

"Jake and I are friends," Terry said carefully. "That's all."

"If that's true, I'm sure you'll see the wisdom of doing what I ask."

"What would that be?"

"I want you to encourage him to come back to Boston, where he belongs, and take up the position his father has arranged for him."

Terry could only stare at her for a moment. Mrs. Landsdowne looked at her with, apparently, every expectation that Terry would accede to anything she wanted.

"I'm sorry. I can't do that."

"Can't?" She looked as if no one had ever said the word to her before.

"It's Jake's decision, not mine. It's none of my business." She had no doubt that Jake would agree with that sentiment.

"Don't play games with me." Her voice sharpened. "I've been told you have influence over Jacob. I'm asking you to use it."

Her patience was fraying. "Your source is wrong. And if I did have influence over him, I wouldn't use it."

The woman blinked. Her lips pressed together for an instant, and then she produced something that might be a smile. "I suppose I'm approaching this all wrong. I didn't mean to offend you."

Oh yes, you did, she thought, and was instantly ashamed. She owed Mrs. Landsdowne courtesy, if nothing else. "I'm not offended. There's just nothing I can do."

"I suppose you know that Jacob's father

tried to talk to him about this." She shook her head. "Really, I should have known those two couldn't talk without putting each other's back up."

"I wouldn't know about that."

"No, of course you don't know Jacob's family, his background." She gave an indulgent smile. "Jacob and his father are too alike. Both of them so gifted, so intense. Naturally they disagree, but really, they belong together."

She was out of her depth, and she knew it. She could hardly argue that she knew Jake better than his family. She could only say what she believed to be true. "Jake doesn't seem to think so."

"He's hurt, poor boy. He's had a difficult time, you must know that." She reached out to grasp Terry's hand. "Now he has a chance to put all that behind him and take his rightful place—the only place where he can use his talents to the fullest."

"I don't—"

"Now, don't say no." She pressed her hand persuasively. "You must understand, Ms. Flanagan. My husband is not a well man. He needs Jacob to return, but he's too proud to tell him that. You'll tell him, won't you? You don't have to try and persuade him of anything. Just tell him what I said."

She had a sense of being swept away on a riptide. "Why don't you tell him yourself?"

"It'll be better coming from you." She patted her hand and turned away. "You're his friend. I know you don't want Jake to spend his life regretting that he didn't respond when his father needed him. I know you'll do the right thing."

She turned and walked away before Terry could come up with a single thing to say.

Because there wasn't anything to say. She watched the outside door close behind Jacob's mother. If Jake's father was seriously ill—well, she couldn't take the responsibility of keeping that from him. But somehow she doubted that their friendship was going to survive everything she had to tell him.

Jake tossed the remains of his frozen dinner into the trash and wandered into the living room. In his first days in Suffolk, he'd welcomed the privacy and isolation of his evenings off. The condo was his sanctuary. Now he felt oddly restless, and he thought he knew the cause.

Terry. He glanced toward the telephone.

He hadn't seen her in two days, and her absence made a bigger hole in his life than he'd have imagined possible.

She'd tried so hard to help him over that business with his father. He felt his jaw tighten at the thought of his father's visit, and he had to deliberately relax it. Terry hadn't understood their relationship. Well, how could she, growing up with the family she had? She probably didn't know how lucky she was.

Still, he appreciated the fact that she'd tried, the fact that she'd cared. Terry, with that warm, open heart of hers, was proving to be a force to be reckoned with in his life.

In spite of his determination to concentrate on nothing but his job, she'd drawn him in—into the clinic, into her caring about Manuela's future, even into her family. Knowing her had even made him more aware of his relationship with God. Who would guess that one little red-haired whirlwind could have such an effect?

He was actually reaching for the telephone when the doorbell chimed. Somehow, even before he swung the door open, he knew who he'd see.

Terry had changed from her uniform into a

denim skirt and sunny yellow top, with a sweater slung over her shoulders against the evening cool, a reminder that fall was on its way.

"How did you manage that?" He gestured her in and closed the door. "I was just thinking of you, and here you are."

"I hope you don't mind." Her fingers twisted the sleeve end of her sweater. "I wanted to talk to you, and I thought it would be better away from the hospital."

"Sounds serious." But he didn't feel serious, not when just looking at her brought a smile to his lips.

She frowned, as if considering. "I'm not sure how serious it is. I have a couple of things to tell you, and I don't think you're going to like either of them."

She looked like a guilty kid, standing in front of the principal's desk. He'd never minded inspiring a little fear in his subordinates, but somehow he didn't want Terry looking at him that way.

"Let's sit down and have it out, whatever it is." He led her to the sofa and sat down next to her. "Come on. Spill it."

She folded her hands in her lap, took a

deep breath and met his gaze. "Your mother came to see me today at the firehouse."

He couldn't do anything but stare at her. "My mother. Are you sure?" He knew how ridiculous that was as soon as he said the words.

But at least it made her smile a little. "Late fifties, silver hair, better dressed than anyone who's ever come into the firehouse, I'd guess. You have her eyes, don't you?"

"I suppose so." The collision of what he'd considered two separate worlds boggled the mind. Still, since his father had failed, it was reasonable to expect his mother to try. That was how they always worked. But... "Why did she come to see you? How does she even know about you?"

Terry shrugged, clearly uncomfortable. "I don't know. I asked her how she knew we were friends, and she just said that naturally she kept tabs on her son."

"I don't know what's natural about it. They cut me out of their lives pretty thoroughly when I disappointed them." Anger smoldered along his veins. Who in Suffolk could be his mother's source of information? Dr. Getz?

"I tried to get out of talking to her. Really I

did. She just wouldn't take no for an answer."

Her distress touched him, and he put his hand over hers. "It's not your fault. I know what my mother is like. If she wanted to say something, you wouldn't be able to stop her." He managed a smile. "You're too well-brought-up to be outright rude, and even that wouldn't stop her."

"I still didn't like it. Feeling as if we were talking about you behind your back."

"What did she want?" He thought he already knew.

"She wanted me to persuade you to accept your father's offer."

"How did she think you could do that?"

Terry shook her head, obviously distressed. "I don't know. I told her no, of course."

"But you're here."

"I couldn't keep it from you. She said that you and your father always disagree, but it's just because you're so alike."

"Alike? I used to think so. Now I know that's the exact opposite of what I want to be." Once the words were out, he looked at them in astonishment. He'd never thought of his feelings toward his father in just that way.

Terry's face was somber. "She said—well, she implied—that your father is seriously ill. That he really needs you to come home, but was too proud to tell you."

"Terry—" How did he explain this to her? People like his parents were out of her realm. "They've been doing this my whole life. They each have their own way of getting me to do what they want. This is just another example of that."

"How can you be sure?" She clasped his hand in both of hers. "What if he really is sick? You can't just ignore it, even if you decide you can't do what he wants."

Her passion touched him. "Why does it matter so much to you?"

"Because I don't want you to do something you'll regret later."

"I know." He brushed her cheek with his fingertips, seeing the flood of warm color where they touched. "But why does it matter to you?"

It probably wasn't fair to put her on the spot that way—to ask for a declaration of caring from her before he was ready to do the same.

She met his gaze steadily. "Because I care about you. I want what's best for you."

"Terry—" His voice choked a little. "I don't deserve that kind of caring."

A smile trembled on her lips. "I can't help it."

He pressed his palm against her cheek, letting the silk of her hair flow across his fingers. She was so warm, so giving, and he was drawn to her as a freezing man seeks the fire.

He lowered his lips toward hers, and even while telling himself that he shouldn't, he kissed her. Her lips were soft and sweet against his. She leaned into his kiss with such trust and tenderness that his doubts slid away as if they'd never been.

She pulled back, so suddenly that his hand still touched her cheek. She shook her head, eyes troubled, soft curls moving against his hand. "I can't."

Easy—take it easy. "Why? We're both free, aren't we?"

"It's not that." She drew away from him, running a hand through her tousled hair. "It's just—you're not going to feel like kissing me when you've heard the rest of it."

Somehow he doubted that anything could take away his longing to hold her. "Maybe you'd better tell me, whatever it is. Did you agree to kidnap me and ship me back to my mother?"

She didn't smile in response. "I went to see Matthew Dixon."

"Dixon—I thought we were going to let Andy handle that."

"Andy hasn't done anything. I'm not sure he ever would." Her eyes brimmed with sudden tears. "I'm sorry. Dad always says I rush in where angels fear to tread. I thought I could make him see how important it is to Manuela that her parents stay."

"It doesn't sound as if you succeeded." There was little point in getting angry with Terry. She'd only done what was in her nature to do. He couldn't accept the fullness of her loving heart for himself and deny it to others.

"At first he seemed glad I was there." She frowned. "It was rather odd, as a matter of fact. He was alone upstairs, and he couldn't find his glasses. Apparently he can't see well enough even to get around the house without them."

"And you helped him." Of course.

She nodded. "He acted as if Andy had hidden his glasses on purpose. But then he turned around and insisted Andy was in charge of the migrant farm workers, and he refused to interfere."

"And he was angry at your interference." Angry enough to complain to the board?

"That was yesterday afternoon. Surely if he was going to make a complaint, he'd have done it by now." Terry obviously knew what his immediate thought would be.

"Let's hope so." He squeezed her hand. "Don't look so upset. If necessary, I'll talk to Dr. Getz about it. He has influence with the board and with Dixon."

"You're not angry?"

"No." Surprisingly, he wasn't. He stood, pulling her up with him. "But I think maybe you'd better go. Being alone with you here isn't the greatest thing for my self-control."

Her dimples showed. "Or mine." She started toward the door, then turned back just as she reached it. "I'm sorry if I've made things more difficult for you."

"It's okay."

She studied his face, as if to be sure he was telling the truth. "You will call your mother, won't you? Just talk to her."

If he didn't, Terry would take the burden of that on herself. "I'll call. I promise." But he wouldn't promise to believe everything he heard.

"Good night."

He wouldn't cross the room to her, because if he did, he'd end up kissing her again. "Good night, Terry. Don't worry so much. Everything is going to work out."

But when the door had closed behind her, his smile slid away. *Everything is going to work out.* He just wished he could believe that.

Terry smiled at the six-year-old who'd come to the clinic for a colorful bandage on a scraped knee. "There you go, buddy. Next time look before you run."

The little boy flashed a smile when Manuela translated the words. *"Muchas gracias,"* he said, and trotted happily toward the door.

Manuela shook her head disapprovingly, the single braid of her hair bouncing against her shoulders. She'd started wearing her hair that way after commenting on the braid Terry usually wore when working.

"He did not need to bother you with that. He just wants to show off to his friends that he was treated at the clinic."

"That's fine." Terry soaped her hands thoroughly. "That's what we want, you see. To have all the children feel comfortable about coming to us."

"I see. I did not think of that. But most of us will leave in a few days. There probably won't be a clinic at the next camp." She didn't ask the obvious question, but it was there in her dark eyes.

Terry dried her hands slowly, buying time. She hated to have to tell Manuela the truth, but the girl had a right to know. It was her future, after all.

"I'm sorry, Manuela." She touched her shoulder lightly. "I talked to Mr. Dixon myself, but I didn't have any success in getting him to agree to keep your father on. I wish I had better news for you."

The girl's eyes went bright with tears, but she didn't let them spill over. "It's all right." She lifted her head, as if trying to say that it didn't matter. "I knew it was too much to hope."

Terry's heart twisted. It shouldn't be too much to hope that a smart girl would have a chance at an education. Manuela was such a hard worker. She deserved better than bouncing from camp to camp for the next

few months, falling further and further behind in her schoolwork.

"I know most of the crew will be going to
North Carolina next, and then working their
way south." There was no way of knowing
what Manuela would think of Mom's idea
without asking her. That was the first step,
in any event. "If it were possible for you to
stay here without your family to attend
school until they go back to Mexico, would
you want to do it?"

Hope flared in Manuela's face, but she
seemed to force herself to tamp it down.
"How could that be? Would the government
let me stay with someone else? Who would
I stay with?"

"I don't know about the legal situation. My
cousin Brendan is working on finding that
out. But if it is allowed, my parents would invite you to stay with us and go to school, if
you wanted to."

"I would want, yes. But my mother—I
don't know how she would get along without me to help her. And my father depends
on me to speak English for him."

She was obviously torn, and Terry could
only honor her for thinking of her family's
needs first, instead of her own desires. For

that matter, she felt torn, too, not knowing whether what she was suggesting for Manuela was the right thing.

Please, Father, guide both of us to make the right choices.

"You'd have to decide that. Talk to them about it, too. But until we know if it's legally possible, maybe you should wait."

Manuela nodded. Maybe she was thinking that this, too, was an impossible dream.

"Whether this works out or not, I want you to know that you have friends here who want to help you. Will you believe that?"

Tears glistened in her eyes again. "I will. Thank you."

Before she could say more, the clinic door opened. The way her nerve endings jumped to attention told her it was Jake almost before she looked. He stopped at the registration desk, greeting the volunteers, before sauntering casually in her direction.

No, not so casually. She could detect tension in the way he moved, in the fine lines around his mouth. She waited until he'd spoken briefly to Manuela, until the girl moved away to help someone else.

"Is something wrong?"

Please, don't let this be a problem that I

caused. Maybe that's selfish, but I don't want to be a source of trouble for Jake. I want to help him.

"Not wrong, exactly."

He took the schedule of volunteers from its hook on the wall and seemed to be studying it, but she could see that his mind was preoccupied. Obviously he didn't want to appear to be having a private conversation with her during clinic hours. She began tidying up the first aid supplies.

"But not right, either?" she asked quietly.

He frowned down at the clipboard in his hand. "I talked with my mother. My father has been having some heart symptoms. Nothing as serious as she implied to you, but certainly he should slow down. He keeps a surgery schedule that would tire a man half his age."

It was a struggle to keep her voice even, ensuring that the anxiety she felt didn't show in her voice. "I suppose she asked you to come back to Boston."

He nodded. "That was the crux of it. The startling thing was that my father came on the phone and actually apologized for his manner the last time we talked. My father never apologizes."

"Maybe discovering that he's not made of steel had a humbling effect on him." She had to think of what was best for Jake, not of her longing to have him stay. "I guess he realizes that he needs you."

Jake's lips tightened. "He doesn't need me. Any bright young neurosurgeon would be delighted to come into his practice. He wants me because he's always wanted to build a dynasty."

Her heart hurt for him. He was still wounded over his family's rejection of him when he needed them most. No wonder he found it hard to consider going back now.

"You can't be sure of his motives. I know your relationship has been painful, but maybe he really does regret his actions."

Don't go, Jake. That was what she really wanted to say. Don't go. Stay here, with me.

"I don't know." Jake's frown deepened, setting harsh lines in his face. "I'm trying to be fair to them, but it's not easy. This whole Christian forgiveness thing is a tough one."

"I know." Maybe you have to forgive yourself, first. She wanted to say it, but she feared his reaction. "What did you tell them?"

"I said I'd think about it." He shot her a

look that was baffled, almost angry. "How am I supposed to know what to do? I turned my life and my career over to God, but He doesn't seem to be providing any answers."

"He will." She believed that with all her heart. "Pray and wait. He'll make it clear, in His time."

And if Jake decided that he was going back to Boston? She wouldn't attempt to prevent him. She'd find some way to say goodbye with a smile, even though her heart would be breaking.

Chapter Thirteen

The conversation with his parents still lurked uneasily in the back of Jake's mind the next day. Surprisingly, he no longer felt the anger with them that he'd battled for months. That was a good thing, even though he had no intention of taking up his father's offer.

Or did he? The delicate dance of the operating room still had its appeal, but he wasn't sure whether he'd wanted it because it was his special gift or because it had been drummed into him from the time he could talk.

That visit of his mother's to Terry still seemed odd to him. His mother had skillfully evaded his questions on the subject, leaving him no wiser than before he'd talked to her. There was no link between the Beacon Hill house and Suffolk, or at least that's what he'd thought when he'd come here.

Ahead of him in the hospital corridor, he spotted Sam Getz's portly figure turning into the doctors' lounge. Links, connections— well, there was one, if you looked at it that way. Dr. Getz had known his father, years ago.

Acting on impulse, he turned toward the lounge. Maybe Dr. Getz would say what his mother had not. Getz could, he supposed, have told his parents about Terry, although he couldn't imagine a reason why he would. Surely, as far as Getz was concerned, his only relationship with Terry was that of supervisor at the clinic.

And what is your relationship with Terry? The voice in the back of his mind pricked him. The truth was that he didn't know the answer to that question. But whatever he felt for her, it was complicating the decisions he made about his future.

Without Terry's prodding, he might never have called his mother. And she'd been right—if he hadn't made that effort, he'd have regretted it someday. Now, no matter what decision he ultimately made, he'd know he'd at least tried to mend the breach between them.

He reached the lounge door and paused, hand on the knob. His father would probably say he was letting his emotions cloud his judgment again. Maybe so, but he wanted to know what had led his mother to Terry Flanagan.

The door opened with a faint swish, and Dr. Getz glanced toward him from the counter where he stood, stirring his coffee. His round face broke into a smile.

"Jake, I hoped I'd run into you today. There's something I want to ask you."

"Of course, Dr. Getz." He crossed the room, wondering if he could possibly stomach yet another cup of coffee today. Maybe not. At least Getz didn't look as if he were the bearer of bad news. "What is it?"

Getz leaned against the counter, mug held between his hands. "I was wondering about your father. I understand he's been having some health problems."

Now how had he heard that? "Nothing serious, sir, but thank you for asking. How did you happen to hear about it?"

The older man shrugged. "The medical grapevine is alive and well. And more active than ever, thanks to the Internet. I happened to be e-mailing back and forth with the person who's trying to set up a med school class reunion. She mentioned it. Seems she'd heard that you were going into practice with him, since he's not well."

And that was probably what the chief of staff really wanted to know. *Are you going to leave us?*

"My father did make that suggestion," he said carefully. He couldn't lie to the man, but he didn't want to burn any bridges in Suffolk. "I told him that I'm happy here. I don't have any plans to change my career path at the moment."

"Well, good." Getz beamed. "I don't want to lose you, either. It can be hard to find someone who has the gifts we need and settles so easily into small town life."

"Suffolk's a good place." *Just ask him. He's not going to take offense.* "Speaking of the grapevine, I wondered if you happened to say anything to my father about Terry Flanagan."

Getz's gaze slid away from his, and he actually looked embarrassed. "I hope I didn't speak out of turn. Truth to tell, I find your father a bit hard to talk to, and I was trying to make conversation. Was that a problem?"

"Not at all. I just didn't want my parents to get the wrong idea about our relationship."

"I don't think I implied anything but friendship. I'm pleased that you've made friends with the Flanagan family. They're good people."

"Yes, they are." So Getz had probably mentioned Terry, his father had repeated it to his mother, and she'd added two and two and come up with sixteen, afraid he was getting involved with someone she'd consider inappropriate.

"You know..." Getz began and then stopped. He shook his head. "I've been debating all day about whether to mention something to you. But I guess maybe you should know."

He tensed. Had Dixon been stirring up trouble?

"Something about the clinic?"

"No, no, nothing to do with that. Well, the fact is, there are rumors circulating around the hospital. Rumors about why you left Philadelphia."

For a moment he was speechless. That

was the last thing he'd expected to hear. "I—what are they saying about me?"

Getz flushed. "Talking about your relationship with the young woman who died. Now, you were perfectly honest with me when we hired you, and I know you weren't to blame. But you know what hospital grapevines are like."

He knew only too well. His memories of just how bad it had been in Philadelphia were still strong in his mind. He'd hated the feeling that everyone was talking about him, feeling as if he were enmeshed in a sticky spiderweb of innuendo and half-truth, impossible to fight.

"I thought I'd be free of that here."

Getz put a fatherly hand on his shoulder. "I understand, but you can't let it get you down. I've tried to scotch any rumors I've heard, but that just means they'll be careful not to talk in front of me. The best thing you can do is ignore it."

That was good advice, but probably impossible to take. Still, what could he do? He couldn't go around telling his side of the story to half the hospital, the way he'd told it to Terry.

Terry. Terry was the only person in Suffolk who knew about his past.

Terry pushed Michael on the swing at the park, smiling when his face broke into a wide grin. "Okay, you need to pump now if you want to go higher. Do it the way Shawna does." She nodded toward Michael's big sister, who'd already pumped high enough to take Terry's breath away.

"It's more fun when you push me," Michael complained, but he struggled manfully to match his sister's height.

Terry took a few steps back, watching them. She'd been surprised when Mary Kate called and asked her to pick the kids up from school and keep them busy for an hour or so. Mary Kate didn't often ask for help.

Not only had she asked, she'd actually admitted, to her kid sister, of all people, that she was feeling low today and didn't want Mom to know.

Perhaps her talk with Mary Kate hadn't been so futile after all. If her big sis could admit she needed help once in a while, maybe they could move to a more equal relationship.

"Hey, Aunt Terry, look who's coming!"

If it was Mary Kate, coming to check up on her— But it wasn't. Instead, she saw Jake coming across the grass toward them. Her heart gave that little jolt it always did when she saw him, but today it was muted by apprehension. Was he planning to tell her that he'd decided to accept his father's offer?

"Hi, Shawna. Michael. Are you trying to see how high you can go?"

He actually remembered their names, even though he'd only met them once, as far as she knew. She sensed something distracted behind the smile he turned on the kids.

"They're trying to give their aunt a heart attack, that's what they're doing," she said. She grabbed Michael's swing. "Okay, you two. Go join the crowd on the sliding board for a while."

Michael frowned, but when Shawna hopped nimbly off her swing and darted toward the sliding board, red curls bouncing, he followed her. She watched them run, reminded again of their loss. Michael had been especially close to his father, and his usual sunny disposition had undergone a change since Kenny's death.

"They're cute kids." Jake seemed to be watching them, too. "How is your sister doing?"

"Not bad. She was feeling a bit down today, so she asked me to pick up the kids. She never wants them to see her cry."

"It must be tough."

He sounded sympathetic, but she sensed that his mind was elsewhere.

They might as well get this over with, whatever it was. She swung to face him. The place where they stood, under the shade of an oak tree behind the swings, was as private a spot as any, despite the running children and the mothers with strollers over near the sandbox.

"What is it, Jake? I can see that something's wrong."

He didn't bother to deny it. "I had a little chat with Dr. Getz this afternoon."

Apprehension made her fingers clench. "Was it Dixon? Did he complain about me?"

"No. It wasn't that."

He stopped, frowning, and she had the sense that he'd moved away from her. His guard was up in a way she hadn't seen in weeks. The rapport she'd felt recently, even when they were arguing about something, had vanished. She was suddenly chilled, despite the warmth of the day.

"What is it, then? Did Getz call you in about something else?" Just tell me, please.

"He didn't call me in. I saw him going in the lounge, and I caught up with him. I wanted to know if he was the one who told my parents about you."

It took a moment to adjust her thoughts, so much had happened since that odd interview with Jake's mother at the firehouse.

"What difference does it make how they found out about me? I told your mother that I wouldn't attempt to influence you."

His mouth set. "I don't like the idea that someone's spying on me. Talking about you to them."

Why, Jake? Are you ashamed of our relationship? She didn't need him to tell her that she wasn't the kind of woman they wanted for their only son.

"I wasn't bothered by it." That wasn't quite true, but she didn't know what else to say. She could hardly tell him that she didn't appreciate his mother looking down on her.

"I was. I don't like the idea of my mother going to my friends behind my back."

"What did Dr. Getz say?"

"He admitted that he probably mentioned you and your family to my father when he was here. I'm sure my mother filled in the rest of the blanks without any trouble."

She still didn't understand why it bothered him so much. She tried to imagine her mother going to one of her friends in an attempt to manipulate her, but the image just made her smile.

"That wasn't the worst of it." Jake's voice hardened. "Dr. Getz told me something else. He said that rumors are making the rounds of the hospital."

He made it sound so dire.

"If people are talking about our friendship—" she began.

"Not that." His tone dismissed their friendship as if it were of no importance. "Rumors about Meredith's death. Rumors blaming me for it."

Her breath caught. It was so unexpected that she couldn't speak for a moment. "Jake, I'm so sorry." Tears filled her eyes, and she blinked them back. "I don't understand. How could that have happened? I thought no one here knew about that except Dr. Getz, and he certainly wouldn't have said anything."

"No. He wouldn't."

"But then how—"

"One other person knew." His face was very still. "You knew, Terry."

It was as if he'd struck her. "You can't believe that I'd do that."

"I don't want to believe it."

"Don't you?" Anger came to her rescue, holding the pain at bay for the moment, at least. "You look as if you do."

"I don't." To do him credit, making the accusation did seem to cause him pain—pain that he held behind that stony mask he wore. "But I can't argue with the facts. You were the only one who knew. Now everyone knows. What am I supposed to believe?"

The anger seeped away too quickly, leaving only the hurt. "I don't know, Jake. I think you might trust me as a friend, if nothing else." Her mind winced away from the kisses they'd shared. "But I guess I'd be wrong, wouldn't I?"

She could only turn away, trying to keep him from seeing how much he'd hurt her. He stood for another moment, but he didn't speak. And then he walked quickly away.

* * *

"Here you go." Terry forced a smile when Mary Kate opened the door. "Two kids, safe and sound."

Mary Kate hugged them, and only the very observant could detect the faint redness around her eyes. The dusting of flour on her jeans and the scent of baking said she must have worked through her sorrow. "Did you have fun with Aunt Terry?"

"I went down the big slide," Shawna announced. "And we saw Dr. Jake, too. He came to talk to Aunt Terry."

Mary Kate sent a questioning glance her way, seeming to register all the things Terry had no intention of saying to her. "Okay, you guys." She gave the children a little shove toward the kitchen. "Milk and oatmeal cookies are on the table."

"Oatmeal cookies!" They shouted it in chorus and raced for the kitchen, immediately beginning an argument over whose cookies were bigger.

"Good luck." Terry turned. The only thing she wanted right now was to be alone and lick her wounds.

Her sister grabbed her arm. "Not so fast. What's wrong?"

"Nothing." She tried to pull free.

Mary Kate just tightened her grasp. "Don't kid me, Ter. I've had too much practice trying to hide my feelings not to know when you're doing it. Besides, you helped me. Give me a chance to return the favor."

She let Mary Kate pull her inside. "There's nothing you can do." She grimaced. "Nothing I can do, either."

"Jake, I guess, from what the kids said."

She nodded, blinking away the tears that wanted to fill her eyes. "You know, I really thought we were getting someplace. I thought—" She stopped, shrugged. "Well, it doesn't matter, because I was wrong."

Mary Kate put a comforting arm around her shoulder. "Are you sure? Judging by the way I've seen him look at you, he has feelings for you."

"Feelings, maybe. But not enough to trust me." Bitterness left an acrid taste in her mouth. "He found out rumors are circulating around the hospital about him. About something that happened in Philadelphia that he thinks only I know. So of course he jumped to the conclusion that I gossiped about him."

"Well, that's just plain stupid. Anyone who knows you knows you can be trusted."

Mary Kate's anger was heartening.

"I guess he doesn't know me, then." She shook her head. "Thanks for listening, M.K., but there's nothing anybody can do about it. I just thought—" The tears welled again, silencing her.

"You love him."

She nodded. "Dumb, huh?"

"He's the one who's dumb." Mary Kate's tone grew brisk, so that she almost sounded like Mom. "But don't you tell me you can't do anything. You've never admitted in your life that there was a problem you can't do anything about."

"This is different."

Her sister gave her a little shake. "Come on, you know better than that. You wouldn't put up with anyone else being unjustly accused. Why would you take it for yourself?"

She blinked at Mary Kate's vehemence. "You know what? You're right." She gave her sister a quick kiss on the cheek. "I'm going to the hospital right now, and I'm not leaving until I know who started this stupid rumor."

"Good for you." Mary Kate smiled. "Now that's our Terry talking."

Propelled by a wave of righteous indignation, she started for the car. She'd find out whose fault this was, and she'd give that person a piece of her mind.

It was nearly two hours later when she trudged down the hallway toward the E.R. She'd been over half the hospital, it seemed, questioning people, tracing the garbled story from one person to another, trying to do damage control as she went.

But it was no good. Once started, a rumor was like a stubborn weed that sent up new sprouts each time you cut one down. She couldn't reveal the things Jake had confided in her, and there was just enough of a seed of truth to make it impossible to fight without revealing everything.

She'd done what she set out to do. She'd tracked the story down to its source, but knowing wasn't giving her any pleasure.

Harriet was on duty in the E.R. She stood in the hallway, conferring with a nurse, but when she saw Terry she handed over the chart she held and started toward her.

"Hi. I didn't expect to see you back here today. I thought you were off duty."

"I am. How about a cup of coffee?" She

tried to manage a smile, but it was no good. She couldn't, not knowing what she did.

Harriet blinked at her tone, and then she led the way into the break room—empty, thank goodness. The door swung shut behind them.

"What's wrong?" Harriet frowned at her. "I can see there's something. Is it the clinic?"

"No." Her throat went tight. What if she were wrong—but she wasn't. "Why did you do it, Harriet? Why did you tell people about Jake and what happened in Philadelphia?"

For a moment Harriet just stared at her, and she knew their friendship was on the line. If Harriet denied it...

Finally Harriet shook her head, her gaze sliding away. Her shoulders slumped under the white lab coat. "How did you find out it was me?"

It took an effort to swallow. "I just kept asking people. Every trail led back to you. Why? And how did you even know about it?"

She shrugged, still not looking at Terry. "Our medical world isn't that big, is it? I knew someone who'd been an intern at the hospital when Landsdowne was there. I gave him a call. He was only too happy to pass along what everyone said about why Landsdowne left."

"Gossip." She wished she had enough energy to be angry with Harriet. "You know as well as anyone that the story probably got added to and embellished by everyone who repeated it. Why would you do such a thing?"

"Why would you defend him?" Harriet's anger flared. "I thought you disliked having him here. That's certainly what you said when he came."

She had to be careful. She couldn't violate Jake's privacy, even to clear him. "We had our problems, yes. But that doesn't mean I'd set out to sabotage him. Why, Harriet? That's what I don't get. Why did you go to all that trouble to hurt him?"

Harriet's hands tightened into fists. "Why? Because I should have gotten that job, not some outsider brought in just because Getz went to med school with his father. It's not fair. The old boys' network wins every time."

This, at least, she could clear up. "You're wrong, Harriet. That's not why Getz wanted him. I heard him myself. He chose Jake because he admired his work in Somalia. Maybe that's not the reason he should have hired someone, but it didn't have anything to do with his father's influence." Despair swept over her. She was losing her friend. "If someone had told me you'd do this, I wouldn't have believed it. Not of you."

For a moment longer Harriet stared at her, angry. Then, slowly, her expression changed. She put her hand up to her forehead, shielding her eyes. The hand shook a little.

"When you put it that way, I guess I don't believe it of myself." Her hand dropped, and she faced Terry, tears sparkling in her eyes. "You're right. I've been telling myself I was justified, but—" Her mouth twisted. "I'm sorry. What can I do to make it right?"

That was a question that didn't seem to have much of an answer. "I suppose you can try to tell people that the story was just gossip, but I don't suppose it will do much good."

She was suddenly tired, too tired to go on struggling with this. No matter what Harriet did now, even if she went to Jake and confessed—it didn't really matter. The bottom line was that he hadn't trusted her, and the relationship she'd thought they had was nothing but a sham.

Chapter Fourteen

Jake managed a smile for the small girl he'd just immunized and nodded to Manuela. "Make sure the mother understands that the vitamins are not candy. She's to give each child one each day, and keep the bottles where they can't get them."

Thanks to the generosity of Brendan's church, when the migrant families left tomorrow, each child would have a two-month supply of vitamins, in addition to having their immunizations up to date. And thanks to Manuela, he didn't have to worry about making a mistake with the instructions.

So far, he'd managed to spend over an hour at the clinic without crossing paths with Terry. She had her own station across the room, helping to give well-baby checkups, and she was probably just as happy to avoid him.

He'd spend the past two days at the hospital trying to ignore the whispered conversations that cut off abruptly when he walked by. It wasn't easy.

He could just imagine what his father would do in this situation, not that that would ever happen. His father would blithely ignore the talk, confident as always in his own judgment, not swayed by what anyone else thought or said.

As for him—well, once again he'd let his emotions get in the way of his good judgment. He'd let his feelings for Terry override his self-control, and look where that had gotten him.

Almost without willing it, he glanced toward her. She was smiling at a baby who reached, entranced, for a red curl that had come loose from her braid. Just as quickly, he looked away, his heart twisting. Terry probably hadn't spilled his secret deliberately, but the result had been the same.

The whispers followed him, and sooner or later they'd reach the hospital board. Dr. Getz had interviewed him—Dr. Getz had heard the whole story and hired him anyway. But if the board started demanding answers—well, maybe he should accept his father's offer before this whole thing exploded in his face.

Manuela ushered over the next mother and child and began translating his questions carefully. Manuela was another source of regret. All their efforts seemed to have come to nothing. She'd leave tomorrow with her family. The Flanagan family had declared their intention of staying in touch with her, but how realistic was that?

A shadow fell across the shaft of sunlight from the open door. He looked up to see Brendan Flanagan hurrying toward him, a broad smile on his face.

"Jake, I have news." He glanced at Manuela and then at the child, sitting in his mother's lap. "I won't interrupt, but once you're free, will you meet me in the back room?"

"Of course." Judging by Brendan's cheerful expression, this wasn't about the gossip that was circulating through the hospital. At least, he hoped not.

Brendan nodded and started across the room, stopping to talk to everyone he met. Their clients were used to the pastor by now, and they tried very politely not to smile at his fractured Spanish.

Jake smiled at Manuela. "It's a good thing I have you to translate for me, and not Pastor Brendan. He'd probably tell the mother to put the vitamins in her baby's ear."

Manuela managed a smile, but her sorrow still showed, like a cloud darkening the sun. The poor kid wanted an education so much, and she saw it slipping out of reach.

He'd like to believe she'd be able to go to school at the next migrant camp, but that seemed a futile wish. He'd like to encourage her, but he wouldn't be much good at that right now.

He glanced around while she gave the instructions to the young mother. "It looks as if we're about finished for the day. I'm going back to speak to Pastor Brendan. Will you clean up for me?"

"It is my pleasure," she said, patting the baby's head.

Those weren't just words, he knew. Manuela so obviously enjoyed every moment of her work at the clinic, even the routine cleaning that others might try to avoid.

I know I don't deserve any happy endings, but shouldn't Manuela have her chance?

He went quickly through the door to the back room of the clinic, stopping short when he saw Terry. Brendan grinned at him. "Come on in. I've got some news that will knock your socks off."

"Just tell us." Terry fidgeted, not glancing toward him. "Stop teasing."

Brendan shook his head. "Don't you remember that patience is one of the fruits of the Spirit, kid?"

"It's not one I've managed to grow yet, so unless you want the proof of that—"

"Okay, okay." Brendan held up both hands, as if to fend her off. "Thanks to my lovely and talented wife, who did all the research, we've done the thing. Manuela can stay with Joe and Siobhan and attend school, at least until her family is ready to go back to Mexico."

Terry's face lit up like a Christmas tree, and she threw her arms around her cousin. "Brendan, I could kiss you. That's wonderful news. And tell Claire we really owe her for this."

"That is good news." He felt out of place in the midst of all this Flanagan family rejoicing. He hadn't contributed much to the cause except a few dollars out of his pocket. "Shall I bring Manuela in?"

"Let me do it." Terry darted past him. "I can't wait to see her face."

Brendan looked at him and shrugged. "Terry's the excitable one of the family. Can you tell?"

He nodded. Obviously Brendan didn't know that there was anything wrong between him and Terry, even though he felt as if the chill in the air was advertising it to the world.

Terry was back in a moment, propelling Manuela, who looked half-frightened.

"What is it? Have I done something wrong?"

"Of course not." Terry hugged her. "We just have good news." She nodded to Brendan.

"At least we think it is good news." Brendan's calm tone must have reassured Manuela. "If you want to, and if your parents agree, we've arranged for you to stay with Terry and her parents and go to school here. Would you like that?"

"Stay?" For a moment there was no expression at all on her face.

"Until your parents go back to Mexico, at least. What do you think?"

Her gaze sought out Jake's. "Dr. Jake? This is true?"

"Pastor Brendan has made all the arrangements. It's true."

Maybe, when she heard it from him, she thought it was safe to believe. The expression on her face was sunshine, breaking through to light a cloudy day.

"I can stay," she repeated, swinging toward Terry and grabbing her arms. "I can stay!"

"You sure can." Terry enveloped her in a hug, all the love in that warm heart of hers shining in her eyes. Over Manuela's shoulder, her gaze met his. Met, and nearly knocked him off his feet.

Terry. His heart felt as if it was twisted in a vise. He wanted to believe she hadn't let him down. He hadn't realized until this moment how much he wanted to believe that.

Manuela wiped tears from her cheeks. "I must go and tell my parents. I must ask my father for permission." She hesitated. "I will finish cleaning up first."

"No, you won't." He smiled at her, forcing himself to look at her, not Terry. "We can muddle through without you this once. Go."

She nodded, smiling through her tears, and darted toward the door.

He didn't dare look at Terry, because he didn't know what she might read in his eyes. Or what he might read in hers.

At least, if nothing else, Manuela was getting her happy ending.

When Jake finally finished congratulating Brendan and went back into the clinic's work area, Terry sagged against the nearest counter. She hadn't realized how hard it would be to go on pretending everything was fine when Jake was around.

She caught Brendan looking at her and straightened. "I guess I'd better get back to work."

"That can wait a minute." Brendan came to lean against the counter next to her, putting his arm across her shoulders. "Come on, give. What's wrong between you and Jake?"

She pressed her fingers against her forehead, trying to will away the dull ache that throbbed at her temples. "It shows, huh?"

"It does to me." His grasp tightened. "Can I help?"

"I don't think anyone can fix this one." She

managed a ghost of a smile. "Even me. Jake believes I broke a confidence."

"Well, if he believes that, he doesn't know you very well, does he?"

"I thought he did." Her voice quivered, and she tried to swallow the lump in her throat.

"I'm sorry, Ter. I wish I could make it better."

She nodded. "It's just—I've been trying to follow God's leading. It's hard to understand why things work out the way they do sometimes."

"I know." His voice roughened, and he pressed a light kiss against her temple. "I know."

A pang of regret went through her. Brendan, of all people, knew how that was. He and Claire had been trying for a baby since their wedding, and that prayer hadn't been answered.

"So what do you do when you don't see any chance that things are going to turn out the way you hoped and prayed?"

"I guess I just keep trying to run the race." His smile flickered. "Here comes the minister, quoting scripture. 'Since we are surrounded by so great a cloud of witnesses, let us lay aside every weight, and the sin which so easily ensnares us, and let us run with endurance the race that is set before us.' Some days that's just more of a challenge than others. And some days I just want to lie down by the side of the track."

She had to smile at the wry tone. "Right." She went on tiptoe to kiss his cheek. "I knew there was some good reason we have a minister in the family. Thanks, Bren."

"Any time."

She took a deep breath. Okay, on to the next thing. She marched back out to the clinic.

The last few stragglers had gone through while she'd been in the back, and the remaining volunteers were packing up, getting ready to leave. She felt a pang of regret. Most of the workers would be on their way south tomorrow, and the clinic would remain open only three days a week to serve those who stayed. The project was drawing to a close. They'd done a good job, and seeing it end was bittersweet.

Gradually, the volunteers filed out, followed by Brendan, until only she and Jake were left.

She cleared her throat. "There's not much

else to do. I can handle it, if you want to leave. I'm staying until Manuela comes back anyway, so we can talk about getting her moved to the house."

He nodded, sliding some forms into the file cabinet, but he didn't seem in any hurry to leave. "That's a nice thing your folks are doing."

"It's always open house at the Flanagans. I've gotten used to coming home and finding that someone has moved in for a while." She smiled. "The latest is my cousin Fiona. Dad's still protesting that one, but Mom's already invited her to come."

"It'll be good for Manuela, having you around as a role model."

That startled her. She swung to face him. "If I'd really spread rumors about you, I'd hardly be a good role model for anyone, would I?"

He just stared at her, the width of the room between them. "Did you?"

"No." Did he believe her? And would it make any difference if he did?

His brows drew together. "I want to accept that. It's just that I don't see how anyone else could know."

Believe me, Jake. For your sake, if not for

mine. "You've said yourself what a small world the medical community is, and Philadelphia isn't that far away. Is it so hard to believe that someone else in Suffolk might have connections there?"

He considered that for a long moment, his eyes grave. "You know who it is, don't you?"

"I can't answer that without breaking someone else's confidence."

His mouth tightened, but finally he nodded. "Fair enough. I guess I owe you an apology. When I saw you with Manuela— well, I just knew you didn't have it in you to do something like that. I should have known the moment I heard about it. I'm sorry, Terry. That was a poor repayment for everything you've done."

She let out a breath she hadn't realized she'd been holding. It took a struggle to keep her voice even, but she didn't want him to guess at the happiness that bubbled through her. "It's all right. I'm just glad we're friends again."

A smile lit his grave expression. "Same here. There's something I'd like to tell you." He turned away, as if he didn't want to look at her when he said the words. "I'm thinking of accepting my father's offer and going back to Boston."

At some level, she'd thought she was prepared for that. But she wasn't. It was slicing her heart into little pieces. She swallowed, trying to loosen tight muscles enough to speak. "Whatever you decide, I wish you—"

Her words cut off when the screen door slammed. Manuela stood there, breathing hard, hand pressed to her diaphragm.

"Manuela? What is it? What's wrong?" Apprehension clawed at her.

"My father." Manuela gasped the words. "I can't. My father won't allow it. He won't let me stay."

"Oh, Manuela." Her heart twisted as she put her arm around the girl's shoulders. Manuela shook with suppressed sobs. "I'm so sorry. Why doesn't he want to? Maybe if we talked to him, it would make a difference."

Manuela shook her head, crying too much to say anything coherent. Terry looked at Jake over the girl's bent head, seeing the sorrow there.

"We did it all wrong," she said. "We should have gone to the family first. We have to go and talk to him."

Jake took Manuela by the shoulders. "Crying isn't going to help." His tone was brisk. "Let's talk this over and see what we can do."

Terry glared at him. That was taking detachment a little too far, wasn't it? Still, it seemed to be working. Manuela choked back her sobs and wiped her cheeks with her hands, looking at Jake obediently.

"That's better." He grabbed a tissue from the box on the desk and handed it to her. "Now, let's figure out what we should do. Did your father give any reason for telling you no?"

Manuela sniffed a little. "He doesn't trust outsiders. He thinks we'll only be safe if we're with him."

"Well, maybe we can find a way of reassuring him."

"We'll go over right now—" Terry began, but Jake shook his head at her.

"This may work out better if we have someone else to translate for us. I'll see if I can reach Maria Esteban." He pulled out his cell phone and began to flip through the list of volunteers that was posted over the desk.

It made sense, she supposed, to recruit

the volunteer nurse who spoke fluent Spanish, but she didn't want to wait. The need to do something pulsed through her. She couldn't let Manuela's chance slip away if there was anything she could do.

She tried to comfort the girl while listening to Jake's side of a short conversation. He flipped the phone closed, frowning a little.

"Maria will be glad to help, but she doesn't have transportation. I'll have to run into town and get her. Maybe you should come along."

She suspected he was thinking that he didn't want her to do anything rash. "I'll walk over with Manuela and meet you at the camp. All right?"

Jake looked a little doubtful, but he nodded. He gave Manuela an encouraging smile. "Don't give up yet. We may still be able to work this out."

He turned and went quickly out of the clinic to his car. Manuela looked as if she'd begin to cry again once he was gone, so Terry handed her a stack of sheets. "Put these in the closet for me, please. I'll just lock the medication in my car and then we'll go."

There were a few more things to do, but

she could deal with them later. She shoved the drug box into her trunk for safety and slipped her cell phone in her pocket.

"Okay. Let's go."

Manuela followed her silently toward the path that skirted the hillside, leading toward the housing facility. It was so quiet here; no one would guess that on the far side of the rounded, wooded mountain, there was a busy interstate, leading out to the wider world. Sometimes she felt as if they were cocooned in their little world.

If she didn't do something, Manuela would be leaving this world, going on to the unknown—to another migrant camp where she might or might not find a welcome.

Are we wrong, Lord, to try and keep her here for a while? I know it might be hard for her to be away from her family, but she has such a thirst for knowledge. It seems wrong to deny her this chance.

She glanced at the girl. Manuela walked with her head down, her gaze fixed on her feet. All of her bright confidence seemed to have fled, leaving her lost and resigned to whatever life might hand her.

"It's going to be all right." She spoke as

much to reassure herself as Manuela. "You'll see."

Manuela just shook her head, her black braids swinging.

The poor kid—what must she be feeling? They'd held out to her the promise of a path toward the education she longed for, and now that hope had been dashed.

They emerged from the trees and approached the cement block buildings. A quick glance showed Terry that Jake and the translator hadn't arrived yet, but Mel Jordan, the crew chief, swung around at their approach, staring at them with narrowed eyes.

"What are you doing here?" He shot a look from her to Manuela. "Haven't you caused enough trouble?"

Temper, temper. Her mother was always telling her she had to learn to control herself. She forced a smile to her face. "I'm here to talk with Manuela's parents."

"They don't want to talk to you. They don't like interfering outsiders."

"I'll let them tell me that." She moved to go around him, but he stepped into her path.

She'd dealt with recalcitrant patients and

violent drunks on duty. She wouldn't be intimidated by him. "Please get out of my
way."

"How are you going to make me?"

The sound of a car engine answered him.
Terry looked up to see Jake's car pulling into
the graveled lot in front of the dorms, and a
wave of relief went through her.

"I don't think I'll have to."

Jordan shot a balked, annoyed look at the
car and then turned and stalked away.

Jake got out and came toward her, followed by Maria. "Trouble?" He frowned, as
if to say he couldn't trust her alone for more
than a minute at a time.

"Not now." She smiled at the nurse.
"Thanks for coming out, Maria."

"My pleasure." Maria shoved a lock of
dark hair back from her face. She must have
come straight from work, because she wore
hospital scrubs. "Manuela is a dear. I'm
happy to help."

"Let's get this done," Jake said briskly.
"Manuela, will you come in with us?"

Manuela shook her head, taking a step
back. "My father—he would not change his
mind in front of me."

"Okay." Terry squeezed her hand, understanding. Manuela's culture was different from that of the typical American teenager.

Terry followed Jake and Maria into the large, square room, which had been filled with the aroma of cooking the last time she'd been here. Today it looked dusty and deserted. Deserted, except for one person—Manuela's father sat at one of the rickety wooden tables, as if waiting for them.

Terry took a breath, suddenly shaky. *Please, Lord.*

Jake took the lead, and she was happy to let him. With Maria translating, he told Mr. Ortiz what their plans were—how happy they'd be to have Manuela stay with them so she could go to school. That they'd bring her to meet them when it was time for the family to return to Mexico. That they'd make sure she was safe and happy.

And she knew it was no good. She might not understand the words Maria spoke to him, but she understood his response. No. No matter what Maria said to him, the answer was the same. No.

Maria finally turned back to them, shaking her head. "I'm sorry. It's no good. He doesn't trust us, and I suppose he can't be blamed for that. He says Manuela is needed to help her mother. He fears that if she stays, even for a couple of months, she won't want to go back."

Manuela's father rose, shoving his chair back. His face stoic, he turned and stalked into the back room.

"That's it then." Jake's face was bleak. "We'd better tell Manuela."

"What's wrong with you? We can't give up that easily." Her fists clenched. Didn't Jake see how important this was?

"There's nothing we can do." It almost sounded as if he pitied her. "We've tried everything possible."

"Not everything." Her mind scrambled to come up with some other solution. "Maybe if we took them to see my parents, he'd see that we don't mean any harm. Or maybe Mr. Dixon could speak to him. He might listen to him."

"No." The pity was eaten up by what sounded like frustration. "Give it up, Terry. It's over, and you'll only make it harder for Manuela if you keep holding out false hope."

She wanted to argue, but his words hit

home. Her throat tightened. "I'm afraid we've already done that."

He gripped her shoulder for a moment, his touch conveying sympathy and support. "Do you want me to tell her?"

"No. I will." This had been her idea. She'd have to accept the responsibility for this failure.

"I have to drive Maria back to town. Are you going to be all right?"

She nodded, her throat too tight to speak. Manuela would leave, to be lost in the stream of migrant workers. And it looked as if Jake would leave, too. She was going to be all right, but she'd be a long time filling the hole they'd left in her heart.

She followed Jake and Maria outside and watched while they drove away. Then she looked around for Manuela.

There was no sight of her, but the sound of childish voices led her around the side of the building. Juan, Manuela's little brother, was playing with a couple of older children.

She squatted next to him. "Hey, Juan. Where's Manuela?" The boy's English had improved immensely in the past few weeks. Surely he could understand that.

For a moment, Juan's face was stolid, as

expressionless as his father's had been, as if he were a little old man, inured to the blows of life. Then his face puckered.

"She go." He pointed toward the narrow logging road that led over the mountain, towards the interstate. "She go up there when she wants to be by herself." His face puckered. "I want her to come back."

Chapter Fifteen

She wanted her to come back, too. Terry's heart hurt at the thought of the girl alone someplace in the woods, crying. "When Dr. Jake comes back, tell him where I went. Okay?" She gestured to herself and to the path, hoping he understood. Then she started up the trail.

She glanced at her watch. Nearly four. At least, in early September, she wasn't going to run out of daylight anytime soon. She hadn't attempted to find out from Juan how long Manuela had been gone. The little boy's English wouldn't have been up to that. In any event, they hadn't spent more than twenty minutes with Mr. Ortiz.

Poor Manuela. She must have guessed how their interview with her father would go. So she was running off and hiding, like an injured animal. She was only sixteen and acting on emotion, not common sense. She depended on the adults in her life for that, and they seemed to be letting her down.

Please, Lord. Manuela is out there alone, and I have to reach her. Please, lead me to her, and give me the right words to say to her when I find her.

The hill grew steeper, and the logging road disintegrated to a shallow wash filled with last year's dead leaves. Manuela had gone up here before. There should be nothing to worry about, but fear was chilling her, as if to warn her.

The signal strength flickered from one bar to none. She punched in the number, but it went straight to Jake's voice mail. Static crackled in her ear.

"Manuela's disappeared. Juan says she goes up into the woods to be alone. I've gone after her." She hesitated, not wanting to sound irrational. "Please come. I need you."

She flipped the phone closed, feeling marginally better, and focused on forcing her aching legs up the trail. Afternoon sunlight, slanting through the trees, gave the woods an almost golden glow. The sumac bushes that grew along the trail had already donned their fall color. Autumn was on its way, summer slipping imperceptibly away.

She stopped, pressing her hand against her side, catching her breath. She listened, but no sound broke the silence except the faint twittering of birds. It couldn't be far to the crest of the ridge. Surely Manuela wouldn't go farther than that.

"Manuela! Manuela, can you hear me? It's Terry."

Nothing. Maybe she'd heard and didn't want to answer. She probably thought Terry had already failed her.

The taste of that failure filled Terry's mouth. Manuela was right. Terry had held out a promise to her that she hadn't been able to fulfill.

Please, Father. I want so much to make up for this. Let me find a way to help her now.

It was harder and harder to climb. Terry scrambled to the slight ridge along the side of the log drag. The footing was firmer there, but rocky and treacherous with the tangle of tree roots that forced their way to the surface.

She slowed for a moment, trying to orient herself. Ahead was the top of the ridge. It would slope down fairly quickly on the other side. She couldn't believe Manuela would go that far.

"Manuela! Come on, if you can hear me, let me know." Again nothing. Maybe Manuela had gone back to the camp already, and she was foolishly overreacting.

Terry's breath caught. Was that the cry of a bird? It almost sounded—

"Help! Help me!"

Manuela! Terry charged toward the sound, heart thumping. "Manuela, where are you? I'm coming. Keep calling out."

"Help..."

The voice seemed fainter, but it gave Terry enough direction. She cut to the right, scrambling as fast as she could up the increasingly rocky slope. Another wordless sob sent her hurtling ahead.

She stopped, heart pounding, grabbing the rough trunk of a hemlock tree. Beyond the tree, a ravine cut through the ridge top, as sharp as a knife slice. Clutching the tree, she leaned forward, scanning the steep tumble of rocks and gravel. A few small trees grew out at odd angles from the wall of the ravine.

At the bottom—her breath caught. At the

bottom lay a small crumpled figure. The instinct that sent her here was true.

"Manuela, it's all right. I'm coming." *Please, God. Let her be all right.*

She forced herself to concentrate. She had to look at this as a professional, as if the victim were a stranger, not a girl she'd come to care for. Anything else invited hasty decisions and increased the chance of making a mistake.

She yanked out her cell phone, but as soon as she glanced at it, she knew she was on her own. No signal. No help. Just her skill and caring.

Quickly she assessed the scene. If she attempted to climb down directly above the girl, she'd risk sending a shower of rocks and gravel right down on her. She'd have to take a slower, more roundabout route.

"Manuela, I'm on my way down. How are you? Talk to me." Was she conscious? She had to get to her, stabilize her, then find some way of getting help.

A low moan was the only answer. Adrenaline pumping, Terry hurried her pace—scramble down a few feet, stop and assess the next step, then go on. She had no equip-

ment with her, just her hands and her knowledge.

"Come on, Manuela, talk to me."

She was close enough to see the twisted
way the girl sprawled. That leg was probably fractured.

"It hurts."

Relief spread through her at the sound of
Manuela's voice. Praise God, she wasn't
unconscious.

"I know it hurts, honey." She slid down the
last few feet, picking up an assortment of
scrapes and scratches, and raced across
the rough ground to drop to her knees next
to the girl. "You're going to be okay. I'm here
now."

Manuela didn't attempt to move, but her
gaze focused on Terry's face and clung
there. "You came."

"Of course I came."

She kept her voice calm even as her heart
twisted. Quickly she assessed the damage.
No bleeding, and Manuela was conscious,
but her breathing was shallow, her pulse
rapid. Her first instinct was to immobilize
the spine, but she had nothing to work with.

"Tell me where it hurts."

"My leg." Manuela gasped the words. "And

my chest." She gestured slightly toward her ribs on the right side.

"How about your head?"

"It's okay."

She moved her hands lightly over the small body, feeling helpless without her usual equipment. Still, it was her knowledge and skill Manuela needed now. The right leg was definitely fractured, but she was more concerned with the ribs. Probably a fracture there, as well, and in a place where it could so easily puncture a lung.

She touched the girl's face gently. "You're going to be all right. Believe me. I'm going to immobilize your leg, and then I'll have to go for help."

Manuela's eyes widened, and she grasped Terry's arm. "Don't leave me."

"Honey, I wouldn't if I had any choice. But I need help getting you out of here safely, and my cell phone isn't working this deep in the woods. There's nothing else to do. You trust me, don't you?"

The girl's gaze clung to hers. Slowly, she nodded.

Am I doing the right thing? Please, Lord, show me. I don't want to leave her alone, but I don't see what else I can do.

"Okay, then." She squeezed Manuela's hand. "All you have to do is stay perfectly still. Right?"

"Right." The ghost of a smile crossed her face.

Terry's heart clenched again. Manuela was a fighter. She wouldn't give up easily, no matter how hard the battle.

It took a few minutes to immobilize the girl as best she could, using broken branches and strips torn from the tail of her shirt. And all the while her brain was ticking away the moments from finding the victim to getting her to the hospital. Too many minutes. Manuela needed more care than she could provide in this situation.

From now on, Father, I'm not going any-place without a decent first aid kit.

When she'd done everything she could, she hesitated for a moment, then bent and kissed Manuela's forehead. "Be a brave girl, and I'll be back before you know it. God be with you."

"And with you," Manuela whispered.

Terry had to force herself to let go. No choices, she reminded herself. Manuela needed help, and she had to bring it. It would take time to get a unit here, more time to maneuver a gurney into the ravine and out again. That had to be done while they still had daylight to work by.

Jake, I wish you were here.

She turned toward the hill and began to climb, as quickly as possible. Trying to climb away from the doubt that pursued her.

Was she doing the right thing? Had she exhausted every other option? Even when she knew she had no other choice, the habit of self-questioning had burned so deeply that she couldn't shake it off.

She grabbed a drooping branch of the hemlock and used it to pull herself up the last few yards. She hesitated, still hanging on, and looked down at Manuela. The girl looked so small, lying there. Pain gripped her heart.

Lord, this is my fault. If I hadn't encouraged her, it never would have happened. She'd be safe with her family.

She took a breath, pinned a smile to her face, and waved down at the girl. Regrets couldn't help Manuela now. Only action could.

"Remember, stay very still. I'll be back before you know it."

Manuela wiggled her fingers.

That was the image she'd carry with her. Terry turned and scrambled down toward the trail. Not images of failure. The image of a brave girl who relied on her. Trusted her. She wouldn't let her down.

She slithered down the last few yards of rocky slope and landed on the low ridge of ground that bordered the logging trail. Her feet found balance and she began to hurry, afraid to run where the ground was still so rough. If she fell and became immobilized, who would help Manuela then?

You would fail her. That insidious voice whispered in the back of her mind. You would fail again.

She tried to ignore it, but the doubt began to creep through her. She hit a patch of dead leaves, slid and fetched up against the trunk of an oak tree, breathing hard and clutching it.

You're okay. She tried to still her frazzled nerves. Don't think about how near you came to falling. Just do the job that is set in front of you.

She scrambled down a few more yards, searching for solid ground beneath her feet. Once she reached that, she could begin to run. But her breath was coming in gasps, and her leg muscles had begun to shake from the exertion.

Please, Lord. Please. I have to get help.

The words Brendan had spoken earlier seemed to form in her mind, as if in answer to her frenzied prayer.

Since we are surrounded by so great a cloud of witnesses, let us lay aside every weight, and the sin which so easily ensnares us, and let us run with endurance the race that is set before us.

She knew, only too well, the weight of self-doubt that hampered her, and the sin of giving in to that, setting snares for her feet. But she was not alone. She was never truly alone. Calm flowed through her in a cleansing wave.

She took a breath, feeling the weight roll off her, and hastened her steps, gaining sureness with every stride. The ground became firmer under her feet, and she began to jog, then to run, the trees hurrying past as she kept her eyes on the goal and her mind on her Lord.

Down past the growth of pines and hemlocks that crowned the top of the hill, past the maples and oaks, the thick patches of rhododendron and mountain laurel, the sumacs lifted their bronze torches high as if to show her the way.

Her breath came hard now, but her legs felt strong. She could run all day if she had to. She could do it.

But she didn't have to, because there was Jake, coming up through the trees toward her. And, blessing of blessings, he carried her med kit with him.

He started to run when he saw her, and she slithered down through the fallen leaves to bump into him. He grabbed her, holding her securely.

"Did you find her? Is she all right?"

"She fell." She gasped out the words. "No head or spine injury that I could detect, but a leg fracture and possible rib fractures. I stabilized as best I could, but we've got to get back to her. Thank God you brought the kit."

"You sounded so upset—it seemed like a good idea. If you go on down for help—"

"You might not find her without my help." If she'd lost consciousness. Terry didn't want to say the words, but Jake knew what she meant. She yanked out her cell phone and saw, to her relief, that she finally had a signal.

It took only seconds to call in the accident, setting the mechanism in motion for the rescue effort. They wouldn't be able to bring the unit up that logging trail, but the department had an ATV for situations just like this one.

"Straight up the logging trail toward the ridge. We'll mark the point at which you have to leave the trail." Her shirt was taking a beating, but she could sacrifice a little more. "Watch for a yellow streamer where you have to veer off to the right."

She ended the call, knowing she was ending contact with her lifeline. But it didn't seem to matter. Jake was with her, and the Lord was guiding both of them.

Jake leaned against a tree, catching his breath while Terry tied a strip of fabric from her shirt to the branch of a shrub overhanging the trail they'd been on. He felt like sliding right down to the ground, but Terry looked as if she could go on forever. And she'd already been up and down this mountainside. He'd admired her before, but never quite so much as he did at this moment.

If only—but what did he have to offer her? An uncertain future with a man who couldn't trust his own feelings?

"This way." Terry forged ahead.

He followed. All he could do now was concentrate on Manuela. Get her stabilized, get her to the hospital. That was all either of them could do.

Terry moved between two trees and suddenly seemed to disappear. Heart in his throat, he reached the trees and found her climbing down at an angle into a ravine he hadn't even guessed was there. She looked up, her gaze meeting his, and jerked her head toward the ravine floor.

Manuela. The girl lay very still, and he couldn't tell from here whether she was conscious or not. He slung the kit over his shoulder and started down in Terry's path.

"We can't go straight, or we'd send rocks down on her." Terry moved as surely as if she did this every day. "Manuela, we're coming."

He heard the tension in her voice, felt it echo through him.

Father, I haven't asked much lately. I've felt so separated from You. Please, be with us now. Guide us to save this child.

Then he was too busy climbing to think of anything but getting down the steep slope in one piece. Finally he and Terry rushed to Manuela.

Her eyes flickered open. "You came," she whispered. "I knew." She stopped, gasping for breath. "Hurts."

He already had a stethoscope out, but he knew what he was going to find even before he listened. Decreased breath sounds on one side—just what he'd suspect with a pneumothorax.

His gaze met Terry's, and he nodded.

"What has happened?" Manuela gasped the words. "I can't breathe."

"It's okay, honey." Terry's voice was sure and soothing. She smoothed hair away from the girl's face. "You have a broken rib, and it's causing your lung to collapse. They'll be able to fix it when we get you to the hospital."

He shook his head, frustrated at the limited supplies at their command. "How long?" He looked at Terry. She was the expert at this aspect of care. "How long until the team reaches us, gets her out, gets back to the hospital?"

Her eyes darkened with fear. "Probably

close to an hour for them to reach us. Another hour to get her out safely and get to the E.R."

"That's too long." He began to sift through the med kit, automatically double-checking what they had to work with. "We can't wait."

"You're going to put in a chest tube."

He lifted his eyebrows at her tone. "You don't agree?"

"It's not that." She lowered her voice. "What about the clinic rules? Morley will have a fit when he learns you've done a procedure like that out here."

For just a moment he hesitated. Some analytical part of his mind, that part of him that was like his father, weighed and measured the risks and benefits—not just to the patient, but to him and his career.

Then he looked at Terry, watching him, ready to do whatever he wanted to assist him. At Manuela, lying helpless, looking at him to take care of her.

There really wasn't anything to measure at all. A sense of freedom washed over him. "We're doing it." He smiled at Manuela. "Hang on, sweetheart. We're not going to let you down."

Chapter Sixteen

Terry hesitated in the hallway outside the waiting room. Manuela's family was inside, waiting for word from the doctors who were treating her. It shouldn't be long. Manuela was going to be fine—she was sure of that. God had held her in His hand today.

By the time the rescue team had arrived, Jake had successfully inserted the chest tube. Manuela was breathing easier, and they'd splinted the leg and had her ready for transport. Terry had been so proud of the firefighters and paramedics as they'd brought the stretcher down into the ravine, loaded Manuela and taken her back up as gently as if they'd lifted fragile china.

Everything had gone exactly as it should. Still, she hesitated to face Manuela's parents. What must they think of her? It had been her interference that had brought Manuela to this place.

She couldn't be a coward about it. She'd go in and try to comfort them while they waited. Even from outside the door, she could hear the murmur of Maria's voice. The nurse had been with the Ortiz family, translating, from the moment she'd heard what happened.

The elevator doors at the end of the hall swished open. Perhaps Jake—

But it wasn't Jake who stepped off the elevator. It was Matthew Dixon.

She stared at him blankly. What was he doing here? Surely not checking on Manuela—he'd exhibited little enough caring for his workers to this point.

Dixon stalked down the hall to her and stopped, fixing her with that intimidating glare. "You're here, are you? I guessed you would be."

"I'm waiting to hear how Manuela is. They should be ready to take her to a room soon."

He nodded shortly. "Heard about it. Heard about how you're the one who found her, too. You did a fine job."

"Thank you." That was surprising praise from him.

"Something else I have to say to you." White brows drew down over his fierce blue eyes. "I didn't believe you. What you said about the housing. You want to know why I didn't believe you?"

She nodded.

"Because I put my son in charge of renovating the housing months before the crews arrived. I turned that over to him, along with a lot of other things that had to be done, after I had a bad turn with my heart back in the spring." His face was bleak and old. "Turns out I shouldn't have trusted him. My own son, and he was salting the money away for himself instead of using it the way I ordered."

"I'm so sorry." But not, she realized, totally surprised at some level. Maybe she'd always recognized something lacking in Andy's character. She put her hand on Dixon's arm. "I really am. If there's anything I can do—"

He covered her hand with his. "Nothing. I made a mistake, keeping Andy here, thinking he'd want to take over the operation once I couldn't run it anymore. It'll be better for him to be on his own for a while. Maybe give him time to do some growing up." He fixed a pleading gaze on her. "That's what he needs, don't you think?"

Her heart hurt for him. Maybe he had made mistakes in raising his son, but he didn't deserve this betrayal. "You're probably right." She patted his hand. "Do you want to go in with me to see Manuela's parents?"

He hesitated for an instant and then squared his shoulders, nodding. She knew exactly how reluctant and guilty he felt, because she felt the same. Together they approached the waiting room.

Mr. and Mrs. Ortiz looked up simultaneously when they appeared, faces questioning. Juan sat on a chair in the corner, completely absorbed in the cartoon program someone had put on the video player for him.

"No news yet," Terry said quickly. "Maria, please assure them that she was stable when we brought her in."

"I already have, but I will again." Maria spoke quickly to the parents.

Terry cleared her throat. "There's something else I have to say, if you'll translate for me. I'm so very sorry. I realize my responsibility in all this. It was my idea to offer Manuela the opportunity to stay for a few months to attend school. I didn't realize her family would refuse, or how badly Manuela would take it—"

"*¿Que?*" Manuela's mother interrupted the soft flow of Maria's voice. She turned on her husband, letting loose a torrent of words that battered at him. He began shaking his head, obviously trying to explain something, but she didn't seem to want to hear it.

Maria blinked, looking from the agitated parents to Terry and Matthew Dixon. "Apparently, Mr. Ortiz never talked to his wife about your offer. She seems to have some pretty strong feelings about it herself. She wants Manuela to have her chance at a good education."

Hope flickered through Terry. If only something good could come out of this. *Please, God.*

Maria paused for a moment, listening to the rapid exchanges between the parents. "He's arguing that it's not safe to leave a young girl here with strangers, no matter how nice they may seem."

"Wait one minute." Matthew Dixon stalked

across the waiting room and came to a halt in front of the upset parents. "This girl that's hurt is the one you talked to me about?"

Terry nodded. The situation had spun out of her control. She could only watch and wonder where it would go next.

"You." He barked the word at Maria. "Tell them that I have a permanent job for them, if they want to stay. A decent place to live, too. I could use both of them, if Mrs. Ortiz is willing to look after the house and Mr. Ortiz wants farm work. Tell them." His face tightened. "I've got a bit of making up to do. That's a good first step, if they agree."

Terry held her breath, but she didn't have to wait until Maria had translated their answer to know what it was. The expressions on their faces told her only too clearly. They would stay. Manuela would have her happy ending.

She blinked back tears. Manuela deserved it, and she wouldn't allow even a whimper of self-pity to ask why she couldn't have the same.

Jake paused in the doorway to the patient room. Manuela, leg encased in plaster, lay propped up in bed, still on oxygen, but looking much better. Her skin had not quite returned to its rosy glow. Still, the contented smile that touched her lips and the happiness in her eyes more than made up for that.

Her parents sat on either side of her bed, talking to her softly. Terry was bending over Juan, showing him a book, but she looked up as if she knew he was there.

She rose quickly, coming toward him. "Come in, please. You're the hero of the hour. I know Manuela's parents want to thank you."

"You're the one they should thank." He pressed her hand, longing to tell her what he felt, but not daring to venture there. "You're the one who ran up and down that mountainside twice today. Feeling a little sore?"

"By tomorrow I will." She grimaced. "But don't you dare tell anyone I admitted it. Paramedics are supposed to be tough."

"I wouldn't dream of it."

Tough? Well, Terry was tough in the professional way she needed to be, but in every other way she was more tender and warmhearted than anyone he'd ever met. And he couldn't tell her so.

The parents, roused by their soft conversation, came toward him, beaming, their gratitude overflowing in words he couldn't understand. Still, they didn't need translation, did they?

He nodded, smiled and felt relieved when Terry's parents, her sister, Mary Kate and Pastor Brendan came in. Their arrival took the pressure off him—the pressure to accept gratitude for something he'd actually hesitated to do.

"They don't understand the risk you took." Terry's soft words reminded him that she seemed to have developed the ability to sense his thoughts.

He managed a smile and resisted the impulse to pull her against him and bury his face in her bright hair. "They don't ever need to know." He shrugged. "As for the risk—well, it may have made my decision for me, in a way."

Something that could have been pain darkened her eyes. "That's not fair. Surely you're not going to let Mr. Morley force you out for doing something you know was medically necessary."

Her caring moved him more than he could say. "Don't make a crusade out of me, Terry.

I don't need rescuing." Quickly, before he could let her see too much, he moved out into the hall. "Tell Manuela I'll stop back to see her before she goes to sleep."

She nodded, accepting the rebuff, and turned back to the group around the bed.

He started down the hallway, not sure where he was going, just away from Terry. Around the first corner, he saw the hospital administrator, William Morley, coming straight toward him, purpose in every step.

So here it came, the end to his time in Suffolk. Now that he faced losing it, he recognized how much he had come to love this place, this job, these people. It wasn't just Terry, despite her importance to him.

This work was satisfying in a way that neurosurgery had never been. That had been nerve-racking, challenging, a personal triumph when he succeeded. But here— here he focused on the people—both the patients and the team. He loved this. And he was going to lose it.

"Dr. Landsdowne." Morley's tone didn't leave much doubt as to his agenda. "I can hardly believe what I've been told. You deliberately flouted the rules we set down for the clinic. I would not have believed it of you."

The self-righteousness in the man's tone set his teeth on edge. He'd had some brief thought of apologizing, of trying to justify what he'd done, of promising never to break the rules again, but that wouldn't be true to himself or to what God demanded of him.

"What wouldn't you believe, Mr. Morley? That I would put the patient's welfare above your petty regulations?"

Morley went red, then white. "Petty? You'll see how petty my regulations are. You've broken hospital rules, doctor, and your contract is hereby terminated."

"Well, now, what's all this?" Sam Getz's booming voice exploded the tension in the hallway into a million pieces. "Who's talking about termination?"

Morley stiffened. "This isn't the place to have this discussion."

"Seems to me you're the one who started it here." Getz's gaze had a hint of steel.

"Dr. Landsdowne has broken the rules that were clearly established and agreed upon for the clinic's operation, undertaking a risky procedure out in the woods, setting the hospital up for the possibility of a lawsuit—"

"Nonsense!"

The edge in Getz's voice sent Morley back a step.

"Really, Dr. Getz, I think you'll allow that hospital administration is my province."

"Supervising medical staff is mine, and I wouldn't give a nickel for any doctor who'd let rules come before saving a child's life." Ignoring the administrator, Dr. Getz focused on Jake. "I don't see any need in prolonging this probationary period. You're the man for the job here, and I've got the votes on the board to make it official. What do you say?"

"Yes." *Thank You, Lord.* "I say yes."

Terry was aware of Jake the instant he came in the patient's room. She'd lingered after the others had gone. Because she wanted to see him again? Probably.

He stopped just inside the door, letting it swing behind him. She slid off the faux leather chair and went to him, her sneakers making little sound on the tile floor.

"She's asleep," she whispered. "Her mother is coming back after she gets Juan to bed, so I thought I'd stay for a while."

"Taking care of other people, as always."

"I guess so." In the illumination provided

by the night-light on Manuela's bed, she could see his face, but she wasn't sure of the expression in his eyes. "Is anything—did something happen?" Maybe she didn't have the right to ask, but she had to.

"Everything has happened." He shook his head. "I can hardly believe it. Morley was actually in the middle of firing me when Dr. Getz walked up and offered me the job permanently. Said he wouldn't give a nickel for a doctor who'd put rules before a child's life."

Happiness rippled through her. For him, she told herself. Not for her. "I'm so glad. I can just hear Sam Getz saying that. But what about your father, and the residency he arranged for you? I thought that was what you wanted."

"Maybe it was, once." In the dimness, his expression was inward, as if he still tried to understand himself. "You know, despite what happened between my father and me, I was still trying to apply his standards to my life. Trying to be the impersonal surgeon who never gets emotionally involved. Can you believe that?"

If Jake saw that, he'd come a long way. "I

guess we're all affected by what our parents think."

"Don't get me wrong. I'm glad we're at least speaking to each other again, even if we'll never have the kind of relationship you have with your folks." He smiled suddenly, his face lighting. "But that's not the kind of doctor I want to be. What I've been doing here has been far more satisfying than that residency could ever be. This is what God intended for me all along."

Her heart was thudding so loudly it was a wonder he couldn't hear it. "That's wonderful. For you and for the patients you'll care for here."

"Just the patients?" His voice went very soft, and he brushed her cheek with his fingertips. "What about you, Terry? You must know how I feel. I'm not going to let my father's standards rule my personal life, either. Are you willing to give our love a chance?"

Now her heart was too full to allow for speech. She looked into his face, seeing the barriers swept away, the love shining unguarded in his eyes.

"Yes. Oh, yes." She stepped forward, feeling his arms close around her.

She didn't have to struggle any longer,

constantly worrying about whether she'd done her best. She just had to do what she'd done out in the woods when Manuela's life was at stake—run the race God had set out for her, relying on Him, thankful that God had given her Jake to run life's race with her.

* * * * *

Dear Reader,

Thank you for picking up this latest book in the story of the Flanagan family. I hope you enjoyed visiting with old friends and meeting new ones.

I knew Terry should have a story of her own since the moment she walked onto the pages of *Hero in Her Heart,* and I'm glad she finally has the chance. It was difficult to find the right hero for her, but I think Jake Landsdowne fills the bill. Someone as strong as she is needed an equally strong hero!

The plight of migrant farm workers in this country is a very real one, as they are often totally dependent on the crew chiefs who bring them in—a situation ripe for exploitation. Churches have been at the forefront of ensuring decent treatment for them, as Pastor Brendan's church does in this story.

I hope you'll let me know how you felt about this story. I'd love to hear from you, and you can write to me at Steeple Hill Books, 233 Broadway, Suite 1001, New

York, NY 10279, e-mail me at marta@martaperry.com or visit me on the Web at www.martaperry.com. Please come back for the next Flanagan story, *Restless Hearts,* coming in March 2007.

Blessings,

Marta Perry

QUESTIONS FOR DISCUSSION

1. What qualities in Terry make her a good paramedic? Do you think she could be as effective without those innate qualities?

2. Jake feels as if this position is his last chance. How do you feel about his need to succeed? Do you approve of everything he does to achieve that?

3. Terry says to Manuela, "Once you've learned something, nobody can take that away. It will go with you wherever you are." Have you found that to be true in your life? How?

4. Terry finds she's envious that Jake thought of a way to help Manuela that she didn't. How have you shown similar feelings? In what circumstances?

5. Siobhan quotes the verse that says we are called for the good works God has already prepared for us. How have you found yourself led to the people and situations God has prepared for you?

6. Jake says he thought he was doing God's will in Africa, but then he contracted malaria and had to be sent home. How did God work in Jake's life in spite of that? How has God surprised you with the way in which He has used you?

7. As long as Jake couldn't forgive himself, he couldn't accept God's forgiveness. Why do you think forgiveness is such a difficult issue for so many Christians?

8. When she thinks of her future, Terry wants a God-centered, happy marriage. How important is it to put God at the center of a marriage? What happens when people don't?

9. Jake faces a dilemma—to do what he thinks is right at the risk of losing his job. How have you faced the difference between what the world expects and what God expects? How did you resolve it?

10. It can be difficult for people from another culture to adjust to a new society. Was staying the right decision for the Ortiz family? Why or why not?

Restless Hearts

Restless Hearts
Marta Perry

DOUBLEDAY LARGE PRINT HOME LIBRARY EDITION

Steeple
Hill®

Published by Steeple Hill Books™

This Large Print Edition, prepared especially for
Doubleday Large Print Home Library, contains
the complete, unabridged text of the original
Publisher's Edition.

STEEPLE HILL BOOKS

Steeple
Hill®

ISBN-13: 978-0-7394-8848-5

RESTLESS HEARTS

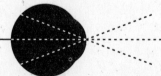

This Large Print Book carries the
Seal of Approval of N.A.V.H.

And we know that in all things,
God works for the good of those who love him,
who have been called according to
His purpose.

—*Romans* 8:28

This story is dedicated to my granddaughter, Estella Terese Johnson, with much love from Grammy. And, as always, to Brian.

Chapter One

She was lost in the wilds of Pennsylvania. Fiona Flanagan peered through her windshield, trying to decipher which of the narrow roads the tilted signpost pointed to. Maybe this wasn't really the wilds, but the only living creature she'd encountered in the last fifteen minutes was the brown-and-white cow that stared mournfully at her from its pasture next to the road.

Clearly the cow wasn't going to help. She frowned down at the map drawn by one of her numerous Flanagan cousins, and decided that squiggly line probably meant she should turn right.

She could always phone her cousin Gabe, but she shrank from having to admit she couldn't follow a few simple directions. Both he and his wife had volunteered to drive her or to get one of his siblings to drive her, but she'd insisted she could do this herself.

The truth was that she'd spent the past two weeks feeling overwhelmed by the open friendliness offered by these relatives she'd never met before. She'd spent so many years feeling like an outsider in her father's house that she didn't know how to take this quick acceptance.

The pastures on either side of the road gave way to fields of cornstalks, yellow and brown in October. Maybe that was a sign that she was approaching civilization. Or not. She could find her way around her native San Francisco blindfolded, but the Pennsylvania countryside was another story.

The road rounded a bend and there, quite suddenly, was a cluster of houses and buildings that had to be the elusive hamlet she'd been seeking. Crossroads, the village was called, and it literally was a crossroads, a collection of dwellings grown up around the point at which two of the narrow blacktop roads crossed.

Relieved, she slowed the car, searching for something that might be a For Sale sign. The real estate agent with whom she'd begun her search had deserted her when he couldn't interest her in any of the sterile, bland, modern buildings he'd shown her on the outskirts of the busy small city of Suffolk. But she didn't want suburban, she wanted the country. She had a vision of her practice as a nurse-midwife in a small community where she'd find a place to call home.

Through the gathering dusk she could see the glow of house lights in the next block. But most of the village's few businesses were already closed. She drove by a one-pump service station, open, and a minuscule post office, closed. The Penn Dutch Diner had a few lights on, but only five cars graced its parking lot.

The Crossroads General Store, also closed, sat comfortably on her right, boasting a display of harness and tack in one window and an arrangement of what had to be genuine Amish quilts in the other. And there, next to it, was the sign she'd searched for: For Sale.

She drew up in front of the house. It had probably once been a charming Victorian, but now it sagged sadly, as if ashamed of such signs of neglect as cracked windows and peeling paint. But it had a wide, welcoming front porch, with windows on either side of the door, and a second floor that could become a cozy apartment above her practice.

For the first time in days of searching, excitement bubbled along her nerves. This might be it. If she squinted, she could picture the porch bright with autumn flowers in window boxes, a calico cat curled in the seat of a wicker rocker, and a neat brass plate beside the front door: Fiona Flanagan, Nurse-Midwife.

Home. The word echoed in her mind, setting up a sweet resonance. *Home.*

She slid out of the car, taking the penlight from her bag. Tomorrow she could get the key from the reluctant real estate agent, but she'd at least get a glimpse inside in the meantime. She hurried up the three steps to the porch, avoiding a nasty gap in the boards, and approached the window on the left.

The feeble gleam of the penlight combined with the dirt on the window to thwart her ability to see inside. She rubbed furiously at the glass with a tissue. At a minimum she needed a waiting room, office and exam room, and if—

"What do you think you're doing?" A gruff voice barked out the question, and the beam of a powerful light hit her like a blow, freezing her in place. "Well? Turn around and let me see you."

Heart thudding, she turned slowly, the penlight falling from suddenly nerveless fingers. "I was just I-looking."

Great. She sounded guilty even to herself.

The tall, broad silhouette loomed to enormous proportions with the torchlight in her eyes. She caught a glimpse of some metallic official insignia on the car that was pulled up in front of hers.

The man must have realized that the light was blinding her because he lowered the beam fractionally. "Come down off the porch."

She scrabbled for the wandering penlight, grabbed it and hurried down the steps to the street, trying to pull herself together. Really, she was overreacting. The man couldn't be as big and menacing as she was imagining.

But at ground level with him, she realized that her imagination wasn't really that far off. He must have stood well over six feet, with a solid bulk that suggested he was as immovable as one of the nearby hills. In the dim light, she made out a craggy face that looked as if it had been carved from rock. A badge glinted on his chest.

She rushed to explain. "Really, I didn't mean any harm. I understand this building is for sale, and I just wanted to have a quick look. I can come back tomorrow with the real estate agent."

She turned toward her car. Somehow, without giving the impression that the mountain had moved, the man managed to be between her and the vehicle.

Her heart began to pound against her ribs. She was alone in a strange place, with a man who was equally strange, and her cell phone was in her handbag, which lay unhelpfully on the front seat of the car she couldn't reach.

"Not so fast," he rumbled. "Let's see some identification, please."

At least she thought he said please—that slow rumble was a little difficult to distinguish. She could make out the insignia on his badge now, and her heart sank.

Crossroads Township Police. Why couldn't she have fallen into the hands of a nice, professional State Trooper, instead of a village cop who probably had an innate suspicion of strangers?

"My driver's license is in my car," she pointed out.

Wordlessly, he stood back for her to pass him and then followed her closely enough to open the door before she could reach the handle. She grabbed her wallet, pulling out the California driver's license and handing it to him.

"Ca-li-for-ni-a." He seemed to pronounce all of the syllables separately.

"Yes, California." Nerves edged her voice. "Is that a problem, Officer?"

She snapped her mouth shut before she could say anything else. Don't make him angry. Never argue with a man who's wearing a large badge on his chest.

"Could be."

She blinked. She almost thought there was a thread of humor in the words.

He handed the ID back. "What brings you to Crossroads Township, Ms. Flanagan?"

"I'm looking for a house to buy. Someone from the real estate office mentioned this place. I got a little lost, or I'd have been here earlier."

She shifted her weight uneasily from one

foot to the other as she said the words. That steady stare made her nervous. He couldn't really detain her for looking in a window, could he?

She looked up, considering saying that, and reconsidered at the sight of a pair of intense blue eyes in a stolid face made up entirely of planes. Don't say anything to antagonize him.

"I see." He invested the two words with a world of doubt. "You have anyone locally who can vouch for you?"

Finally she realized what she should have sooner. Of course she had someone to vouch for her. She had a whole raft of cousins. Family. Not a word that usually had much warmth for her, but maybe now—

Ted Rittenhouse saw the relief that flooded the woman's face. She'd obviously come up with a solution she thought would satisfy him.

"I'm staying with a cousin, Gabe Flanagan." She was so relieved that the words tripped over each other. She snatched a cell phone from her bag. "Look, you can call him. He'll vouch for me. Here's my cell phone. You can use it."

"Seems to me I've heard of those newfan-gled gadgets," he said dryly, pulling his own cell phone from his uniform pocket. "You have his number?"

Even in the dim light provided by the dome lamp of her car, he could see the color that flooded her fair skin at that. He assessed her while he punched in the number she gave him. Slim, erect, with a mane of strawberry-blond hair pulled back from a heart-shaped face.

A pair of intelligent gray eyes met his directly, in spite of the embarrassment that heightened her color. Something about the cut of her tan slacks and corduroy jacket suggested a bit more sophistication than was usually found in Crossroads Township, where the standard attire was jeans, except for the Plain People.

"Mr. Flanagan? This is Ted Rittenhouse, Crossroads Township Police. I've got a young lady here who says she's staying with you. Fiona Flanagan, her name is."

"Fiona? She's my cousin." Quick concern filled the man's voice, wiping away some of Ted Rittenhouse's suspicion. Potential housebreakers didn't usually come equipped with respectable-sounding relatives. "Has she had a car accident? What's wrong?"

"Nothing wrong. She maybe got a little lost is all. I'll guide her back to your place all right." The Pennsylvania Dutch cadence, wiped from his voice during his years in the city, had come back the instant he'd moved back home to Crossroads. "If you'll just give me directions...."

As Flanagan gave him the directions, Ted realized he knew exactly where that farm was. The next township over, but he knew most of the back roads and landmarks in the county, even if that area wasn't his jurisdiction. Somehow you never forget the land that meant home when you were a kid. Maybe that was especially true of a place like this, where the same families had owned farms for generations.

When he slid the phone back in his pocket, he realized Ms. Flanagan was watching him with wariness in those clear eyes.

"It's not necessary for you to guide me anywhere. I can get back to my cousin's on my own."

"No problem at all. It's not out of my way. I'll guide you there."

"I'd prefer to go alone." She enunciated

the words as if he was a dumb hick who couldn't understand.

Well, fair enough. In her eyes, he probably was. But he wasn't going to let her just disappear, not until that last faint suspicion was cleared up. As the law in the township, he was responsible and he took it seriously.

"Sorry, ma'am. You heard me tell your cousin I'd guide you home, and I'm not about to let you get lost. Again."

For a moment longer she glared at him, sensing he was poking mild fun at her. Then she jerked a nod, as if to admit defeat, and rounded her car to slide into the driver's seat.

He paused, flashing the light around the old Landers place and then over Ruth Moser's general store next door. Be a good thing if someone bought the Landers place. It had been standing empty too long. But Ruth wouldn't appreciate it if someone up and put a phony Pennsylvania Dutch tourist trap right next to her shop.

Course he didn't know what the Flanagan woman had in mind for the building. He didn't think anyone who dressed like she did would sell plastic Amish dolls made in some third world country.

No sign of life in the general store, and everything looked locked up tight. He'd advised Ruth to put in an alarm system, but so far she hadn't listened. Folks liked to think this was still the quiet countryside it had been fifty years ago, but that wasn't so.

He walked back to the patrol car and slid in. Vandalism, petty crime, the theft of some handmade Amish quilts out at Moses Schmidt's place... Even Crossroads Township had its share of crime. And when he'd pinned this badge on, he'd made a vow to protect and to serve.

A familiar pang went through him at the thought. He pulled out, watching the rearview mirror to be sure the Flanagan woman pulled out behind him. He thought he'd made the right choice in coming back home after the trouble in Chicago, but maybe a man could never know until the end of his life if he'd been following God's leading or his own inclinations.

As it was, there were those he loved who'd never understand his choices. Thank the Lord, they were willing to love him anyway.

At least he'd been coming back to something he knew when he'd come here. What on earth would bring a woman like Fiona Flanagan to buy a place here? The address on her driver's license was San Francisco. Did she have some pie-in-the-sky dream of rural bliss? If so, she'd no doubt be disappointed.

He'd frightened her when he'd accosted her so abruptly, and he was sorry for that. All he'd seen had been a dark figure at the window of the empty house, and he'd reacted automatically. Still, she'd recovered soon enough, ready to flare up at him in an instant.

There was the gate to the Flanagan farm. When he saw the fanciful sign with its cavorting animals, recollection began to come. He'd heard about this place—they trained service animals for the disabled. If she really belonged here, Ms. Flanagan was probably all right.

She tooted her horn, as if to say that he could leave her now. Instead, he turned into the lane and drove up to the house. It was full dark, and it wouldn't hurt to see the woman safely into her cousin's hands.

The farmhouse door opened the moment his lights flashed across the windows, and a man waited outside by the time he came to a stop. The other car drew up under the willow tree with a little spurting of gravel, as if the driver's temper were not quite under control.

He got out, leaving the motor running as he took the hand the man extended. "I'm Ted Rittenhouse."

"Good to meet you. Gabe Flanagan." Flanagan turned to his cousin, who came toward them reluctantly, probably too polite to just walk away from him. "Fiona, we were getting a little worried when you weren't back by dark. I'm glad you ran into someone who could help you get home."

She managed a smile, but he suspected she was gritting her teeth. "Officer Rittenhouse was very helpful."

"It was my pleasure, ma'am." He would have tipped his hat, but he'd left it in the car. "I hope you'll stop by and see me if you ever come to Crossroads again. I'd be glad to be of help to you."

"I'm sure that won't be necessary. Thank you for leading me back." She hesitated a moment, and then she held out her hand.

Surprised, he took it. It felt small but strong in his. "Good night, Ms. Flanagan."

"Good night." She might have wanted to

add "good riddance," but either manners or common sense kept a slight smile on her face. She turned and walked toward the house, her back very straight.

Fiona crossed the guest bedroom at Gabe and Nolie's farmhouse a few days later, charmed again by the curve of the sleigh bed and the colorful patchwork quilt. Maybe she'd have something like that in her new house. Her house, officially, as of ten o'clock this morning.

She had to admit she'd hesitated about buying the place in Crossroads after her experience there the other night. But the house was irresistible, and, in the clear light of day, she had to admit the police officer was just doing his duty.

Besides, the lure of the place overrode everything else. *Home,* it kept saying to her. *Home.*

Crossroads, she'd learned, was a fairly large area, encompassing several small villages on the outskirts of Suffolk, as well as farmland. Surely a township police officer like Ted Rittenhouse would be too busy with his other duties to bother about her. Or to annoy her.

She picked up her jacket and slipped it on. October had abruptly turned chilly, at least for the day. Still, anyone who'd grown up in San Francisco was used to changeable weather. That wouldn't bother her.

She paused at the dresser, letting her fingers slip across the painted surface of the rectangular wooden box she'd brought with her across the country. It was all she had of the mother she'd never known. How much had that influenced her decision to come here? She wasn't sure, and she didn't like not being sure about something so important. When her advisor in the nurse-midwife program had mentioned that his part of Pennsylvania had a growing need for midwives, something had lit up inside her. Some instinct had said that here she'd find what she was looking for, even if she didn't quite know what it was.

"That's a replica of a dower chest," Nolie spoke from the doorway. "It's lovely. Did you buy it here?"

Fiona smiled at her hostess. With her fresh-scrubbed face, blond hair pulled back in a ponytail, jeans and flannel shirt, Nolie Flanagan looked more like a teenager than a busy wife and mother, as well as an accomplished trainer of service animals for the disabled.

"I brought it with me. It was my mother's." She hoped the shadow she felt when she said the words didn't show in her voice. "I hate to show my ignorance, but what is a dower chest?"

Nolie came closer, tracing the stiff, painted tulips with their green leaves, fat little hearts and yellow stars in circles that decorated the box. "A traditional dower chest is much larger than this—like a cedar chest—for Pennsylvania Dutch girls to store the linens they make in preparation for their wedding. This smaller one was probably for a child to keep her treasures in."

It hadn't occurred to her that Nolie would be a source of information, but her Aunt Siobhan had said that Nolie's family had lived on this farm for generations. "When you say Pennsylvania Dutch, do you mean Amish?"

Nolie leaned against the dresser, apparently willing to be distracted from whatever chores called her. "The Amish are Pennsylvania Dutch, but not all Pennsylvania Dutch are Amish." She grinned. "Confusing, I know. And to add to the confusion, we aren't really

Dutch at all. We're of German descent. William Penn welcomed the early German immigrants, including the Amish. They've held on to their identity better than most because of their religious beliefs."

"It can't be easy, trying to resist the pressures of the modern world."

"No. There are always those who leave the community, like your mother."

Fiona blinked. "I didn't realize you knew about her."

Distress showed in Nolie's blue eyes. "I'm sorry—I didn't pry, honestly. Siobhan mentioned it, when she told us you were coming."

Her Aunt Siobhan and Uncle Joe knew about her mother, probably more than she did, of course. During the week she'd spent in their house she'd wondered if they'd talk about her mother, or about the reason her father hadn't spoken to his brother in over twenty-five years. But they hadn't, and Fiona was too accustomed to not rocking the boat to mention it herself. In any case, the breach between brothers meant they'd know little of what happened after her parents left.

"It's all right. I don't know much about her myself. She died shortly after I was born."

"I'm sorry," Nolie said again. "But your father must have spoken of her."

"No." She transferred her gaze to the chest, because that was easier than looking into Nolie's candid eyes. "My father couldn't take care of me—I was in foster care for years. By the time I went to live with him, he'd remarried."

And he hadn't particularly wanted reminders of that early mistake. She wouldn't say that. She wasn't looking for pity, and she'd already said more than she'd intended.

Nolie's hand closed over hers, startling her, and she repressed the urge to pull away. "I know what that's like. I was in foster care, too. And with a great-aunt who didn't want me. It can be tough to get past that sometimes."

Fiona's throat tightened in response, but the habit of denial was too ingrained. She used the movement of picking up her handbag to draw away.

"It was a long time ago. I don't think much about it now." At least, she tried not to.

Nolie made some noncommittal sound that might have been doubt or agreement, but she didn't push. "I suppose you'll want to look up your mother's family, too, now that you're here."

Fiona shook her head. She'd been over this and over it, and she was sure she'd made the right decision. "I don't plan to do that. It's not the same thing as coming to see the Flanagan family. Aunt Siobhan always tried to keep in touch, and I knew she'd be glad to see me."

"But they probably—"

"No." That sounded too curt. She'd have to explain, at least a little. "My mother's family never made any effort to contact me. The one time my father spoke to me about it, he said they'd rejected my mother for marrying him. It's hardly likely they'd want to see me."

"You can't be sure of that." Nolie's face was troubled. "I'd be glad to help you find them. Or maybe that police officer you met could help."

"No. Thanks anyway." She forced a smile. "I appreciate it, but I've made my decision. I don't want to find them."

Because they rejected your mother? The small voice in the back of her mind was persistent. Or because you're afraid they might reject you?

"If that's what you want—" Nolie began, but her words were interrupted by a wail from downstairs. "Uh-oh." She smiled. "Sounds like trouble. That music video keeps her happy for a half hour, but then only Mommy will do. All my years of taking care of animals didn't prepare me for the demands of one small human."

"And you love it." Fiona picked up her corduroy jacket and handbag. "Go ahead, take care of little Siobhan. I'm fine, really."

Nolie nodded. "If you ever want to talk—"

"Thanks. I'm okay."

The wails soared in pitch, and Nolie spun and trotted down the steps. "Mommy's coming. It's all right."

Fiona followed more slowly. The maternal love in Nolie's face was practically incandescent. Seeing that when it happened for the first time was one of the best rewards of being a midwife. Once her practice got on its feet, she'd have that opportunity again and again.

She was off to take possession of her new house, the first step toward her new life.

Lord, please bless this new beginning. Help me not to dwell on the difficulties of the past, but only on the promises of the future.

Chapter Two

When no one answered his knock at the old Landers house, Ted pulled open the screen door and stepped into the hallway, glancing around. Come to think of it, he'd have to start calling this the Flanagan place. Or Flanagan clinic, maybe. Rumor had it she was starting a midwife practice here.

Whatever she was doing, Ms. Flanagan really shouldn't leave her door standing open that way. Then he noticed that the latch had come loose when he pulled on the screen door, probably one of hundreds of little things to be fixed.

"Ms. Flanagan?"

The two large rooms on either side of the central hallway were empty, except for a few odds and ends of furniture left by the last inhabitants. He could see what attracted the woman to the house—under the dust and neglect were beautiful hardwood floors, and the rooms were graciously pro-portioned, with bay windows looking out toward the street.

"Hello, is anyone here?"

A muffled call answered him from some-where upstairs. Taking that for an invitation, he started up the staircase, running his hand along the curving banister. An oval stained-glass window on the landing sent a pattern of color onto the faded linoleum someone had been foolish enough to put over those beautiful stairs.

Sunlight poured through the tall window at one end of the center of the second floor landing. He paused, blinking at the sight of a rickety stepladder under what had to be the opening to the attic. A pair of sneakered feet balanced on the very top. Nothing else was visible of Fiona but a pair of trim legs in dust-streaked jeans.

The stepladder wobbled dangerously, and he grabbed it, steadying it with both hands. "What on earth are you doing up there? Try-ing to break a leg?"

As soon as the words were out, he real-ized that was more or less what he'd said that first night when he'd spotted her. Now, at least, she owned the house, but that was no excuse for endangering herself.

Fiona poked her head down from the dark rectangle of the attic opening, looking disheveled and annoyed. "What are you doing here?"

"At the moment, I'm keeping this ladder from collapsing under you."

"It's perfectly fine." Her weight shifted, and the ladder swayed.

He raised an eyebrow. "You want me to let go?"

Her lips clamped together. "No." She seemed to force the word out. Then, hands braced on the edge of the opening, she started lowering herself.

He caught her elbows and lifted her the rest of the way to the floor. The stepladder, relieved, collapsed in a heap on the dusty floorboards.

For a moment Fiona looked as if she'd like to kick the recalcitrant ladder, but then she managed a rueful smile. "Much as I hate to admit it, it looks as if you're right."

"I'll find something sturdy to stand on and close that for you. No problem."

"I'd say I don't need help, but that would

just convince you I'm totally irrational." The smile warmed a bit, and her eyebrows lifted. "Did you come for something in particular?"

"Just being neighborly," he said mildly. He glanced around, spotting a solid-looking chair in the nearest room, and hauled it over. Fiona wouldn't be able to reach the ceiling from it, but he could.

He climbed onto the chair, reached up and eased the hatch back into place. It set off a puff of dust as it settled into its groove. He stepped back to the floor.

Fiona, apparently aware of how dirty she was, attempted to transfer the dust from her hands to her jeans, not looking at him. "Thank you."

"Any time."

That fierce independence of hers amused him, but it also made him wonder what was behind it. If she couldn't accept a little nosy neighborliness, she'd never fit in here. He'd had to get used to that again when he came back.

She straightened. "I'm glad this isn't an official call. As you can see, I'm rather busy just now."

"Looking over your new purchase from top to bottom," he agreed. The girls he'd grown up with had had plenty of spirit, giving as good as they got, but Fiona was different. Defensive, almost, and the cop part of his mind wondered what she had to be defensive about.

"It's a beautiful house, really. It's just been neglected." Her smile flickered, and he thought her pride of ownership was getting the better of her wariness with him. "Once I have the renovations done, you won't know it's the same place."

"What do you have in mind to do?" He was happy to keep her talking about the house, because it seemed to put her at ease. Since she was moving in, she was part of his responsibility, and he liked to stay on friendly terms with folks.

"My living quarters will be up here." She gestured. "At first I thought I'd have to install a kitchen on this floor, but there's actually a back staircase that leads down to the current kitchen, so I can just use that."

"A remnant from the days when people had servants, I guess. What happens downstairs?"

"The old parlor will make a perfect waiting room." She started down the steps, gesturing as she talked, and he followed. "The other rooms will have to be partitioned to make an exam room and an office, maybe space for classes. The birthing clinic where I worked in San Francisco ran a lot of childbirth classes, but I don't know how much demand there will be here."

He shrugged, coming down the last step to stand beside her in the hall. "You may be surprised. Plenty of women among the Plain People prefer home births and might enjoy the classes. You should be able to build a good practice, if you stay."

"If?" Her eyebrows shot up at his words. "I'm not going to all this trouble with the intent of leaving. Why would you say that?"

He shrugged. "You wouldn't wonder if you knew how this state has been losing medical personnel to other places. We've seen too much coming and going, mostly going, to take anything for granted. Folks just start to rely on someone and then find they've moved on to greener pastures."

Especially city-bred people like you, he thought but didn't say.

"I'm not going anywhere." She stroked the intricate carving of the newel post. "This place is going to be my home."

Her voice actually trembled with emotion

on the last word, touching him, making him want to know what lay behind that emotion, but he didn't figure he had the right.

He was here because it was his duty to protect and serve all the residents of his township, he reminded himself. Not because he had a personal interest in a woman like Fiona Flanagan, with her quick tongue and urban manners.

"Well, if that's what you plan to do with the house, I guess you're going to need someone to do the carpentry work, won't you?"

She nodded. "Is there any chance you might be able to recommend someone?"

"There are a couple of possibilities among the Amish carpenters, it being fall and the harvest is in. I'll see what I can do."

"Amish," she repeated, and he couldn't tell what emotion tightened her face for an instant.

"They're good carpenters, and this is an Amish community. I'd think you'd want an introduction to them."

"Yes, of course, that would be perfect." Whatever the emotion had been, it was gone. "Do you think they'd be able to start soon?"

She looked up at him with such appeal

that for a moment he'd do most anything to keep that hope shining in her eyes.

"I'll see if I can get hold of Mose Stetler. Maybe he can come over today or tomorrow."

"Thank you so much." All her wariness was washed away by enthusiasm. "Thank you."

"No problem." He took a reluctant step toward the door. "I'll see what I can do."

And while he was at it, he'd best give himself a good talking to. Fiona's blend of urban sophistication and innocent enthusiasm was a heady mixture, but he couldn't afford to be intrigued by a woman like her. If he ever decided to risk himself on love again, it would be with a nice, ordinary woman who understood the balancing act between two worlds that he maintained every day of his life.

By midafternoon, Fiona had finished cleaning the room intended for her bedroom and even hung some clothes in the closet. It wasn't going to take much more than elbow grease and a little furniture to make her upstairs apartment livable. Now, if Ted came through on his promise to contact the carpenters, she could actually have an opening day in sight.

She'd already gone through the arduous process necessary to get her certification in order, and she'd contacted several obstetricians and the hospital in Suffolk, as well as a birthing center in the city that could use her services on a part-time basis until she got her practice on its feet. Now all that remained was to complete the office and find some clients.

Nolie, who knew the area well, had advised her to build word of mouth by meeting as many people as possible, and she might as well start on that today. After a shower and a change of clothes, she went outside, hesitating for a moment on the porch. She'd much rather be judged on her professional expertise than her personality, but if she planned to build her own practice, this had to be done.

Taking a deep breath and straightening her jacket, she headed for the general store. She'd already noticed how busy it was, and since it was right next door, it was a logical place to start.

The sign on the front door read Ruth Moser, Proprietor. Maybe Ruth would be the friendly type of neighbor who'd let her post her business card where people would see it. Another deep breath was necessary, and then she opened the door and stepped inside.

The store was bigger than she'd thought from the outside—extending back into almost cavernous depths where aisles were stocked with what she supposed were farming supplies, as well as hardware and tools she couldn't begin to identify. The front part of the store carried groceries, and through an archway she glimpsed what must have been the tourist section—quilts, rag rugs, cloth dolls with blank faces—all the souvenirs a visitor to Pennsylvania Dutch country might want to take home.

"Welcome." The woman who came toward her wore a print dress with an apron over it. A white prayer cap was perched on abundant gray hair pulled back into a bun. Her smile echoed the welcome. "I'll spare you the usual Penn Dutch spiel. You're not a tourist." She held out her hand. "I'm Ruth Moser."

Fiona found her hand caught in a grip as strong as a man's. "I'm Fiona Flanagan. I just bought the house next door."

"And you're a nurse-midwife," Ruth finished for her. "We already know that about you, we do. Hard to keep any secrets in a place like Crossroads, believe me."

The woman's smile was contagious. Bright blue eyes in a weathered face inspected Fiona, but it was a friendly inspection that she didn't find intimidating.

"I guess I don't need the explanation I'd planned to give you then, do I?"

"Ach, well, you'll have to forgive us. Folks who live in an area like this all know each other so well that an incomer is a nine days' wonder. Everyone in the township knows about the new midwife, and welcome news it is. The closest Amish midwife is nearly twenty miles away, and folks out here don't like going clear into Suffolk, either."

"I'm certainly glad to hear that." This was going better than she'd imagined. "I'd hoped you might be willing to post one of my business cards where your customers would see it."

"Give me a whole stack of them, and I'll pass them on to anyone who might be thinking of babies," Ruth said promptly.

"That's wonderful." She pulled a handful

from the side pocket of her bag. "I'll bring some more over later, if you can use them."

"Sure thing." Ruth took the cards and slipped them into an apron pocket. "I suppose Ted Rittenhouse told you how short of medical help we are around here, unless we want to go into Suffolk."

Why would she suppose anything of the kind? "Ted Rittenhouse?"

Ruth seemed oblivious to the edge in her voice. "Ted certainly is a nice fellow. Born and bred in the township, and glad we were to have him come back home again after that time in Chicago. You like him, don't you?"

"I—I thought he was very helpful. When I got lost, I mean, the first time I came to see the house."

"Helpful, yes. Kind, too. Why, I've known that boy since he was running around barefoot. There's not a mean bone in his body."

"Yes, well—I'm sure that's true." And why on earth did the woman think she needed to know that? "Do you mind if I look around your store?"

"I'll show you around myself. Not exactly busy on a weekday in the fall, though weekends we still get the rush of tourists trampling through, oohing and aahing over the Amish and blocking the roads every time they spot a buggy. Still, their money helps keep me afloat."

"You seem to carry just about everything anyone could want in here." A cooler marked Night Crawlers sat next to a rack filled with the latest celebrity magazines.

"That's why it's a general store." Ruth looked around with satisfaction at her domain. Apparently she felt the same way about her store as Fiona did about her practice. "I have something for everyone from the Amish farmers to the senior citizen bus tours. No good Pennsylvania Dutchman ever turned down profit."

Fiona glanced at the woman's print dress. "You're not Amish, I take it?"

"Mennonite. First cousins to the Amish, you bet." She brushed the full skirt. "You can tell by the clothes. You'll soon get onto it." The bell on the door tinkled, and she gestured toward the archway. "I'll just get that. Go on through and check out the other section. I've got some lovely quilts and handmade chests if you're looking to furnish your house local."

She hadn't thought of that, but obviously

it would be good public relations to buy some of what she needed locally. She walked through the archway. The rag rugs would be beautiful against the hardwood once the floors were cleaned and polished. And—

She rounded the end of the aisle and lost her train of thought. The back part of this area was a large, well-lit workroom. Finished quilts lined the walls, their colors and patterns striking.

Two Amish women bent over a quilt frame, apparently putting the finishing touches to a quilt whose vibrant colors glowed against their dark, plain dresses. Another sat at a treadle sewing machine. All three glanced at her briefly and then lowered their eyes, as if it were impolite to stare.

But she was the one who was being impolite, unable to tear her gaze away. Was that what her mother would have looked like now, if she hadn't run away, if she hadn't died? Dark dress, dark apron, hair parted in the center and pulled back beneath a white cap, seeming to belong in another century?

"Looks like plenty of work is being done in here." The voice from behind startled her into an involuntary movement. Ted nodded coolly and strolled past her to lean over the quilt on the frame.

"Another Double Wedding Ring? Haven't you made enough of those in the last year, Em?"

The woman he spoke to surprised Fiona by laughing up at him in what could only be described as a flirtatious way. "That's what the English want, Ted Rittenhouse. You know that well, you do."

"Well, give the customers what they want, I suppose." He nodded toward Fiona, apparently not noticing that she stood frozen to the spot. "You meet the new midwife who's setting up next door, did you?"

Apparently now that he had, in effect, introduced her, it was all right to stare. Three pairs of eyes fixed on her as Ted mentioned the women's names: Emma Brandt, Barbara Stoller, Sarah Bauman. Emma was probably in her thirties, although it was difficult to judge, and the other two probably in their sixties.

Fiona nodded, trying to get past the unexpected shock she'd felt at the sight of them. These were people who might introduce her to prospective clients in the Amish community, so she'd better try to make a decent impression.

"It's a pleasure to meet you. The quilt is wonderful. I didn't realize you actually made them here."

"Ruth says the tourists like to see the work done." Emma seemed to be the spokeswoman for the group. "We do special orders for folks, too."

"That's great." Fiona knew how stupid she sounded, but she couldn't seem to help herself. She'd assumed all Amish women were cloistered at home, taking care of their families, instead of out earning money. How much more didn't she know about her mother's people?

Ted strolled back toward her. "Could I have a moment of your time? I'll walk out with you."

She nodded, saying goodbye to the quilters, and preceded him toward the exit. When the door closed, its bell tinkling, he spoke before she could get a word out.

"I'd say if you want to have an Amish clientele for that practice of yours, you'll have to stop looking at them like they're animals in the zoo."

"I didn't!" But she probably had. "I was

just surprised, that's all. I didn't realize any-one was back there." How did the man al-ways manage to put her in the wrong?

"Uh-huh." He managed to infuse the syl-lables with such doubt that her embarrass-ment was swallowed up in anger. She cer-tainly wasn't going to tell him what had precipitated her behavior.

"Excuse me. I have things to do." She turned, but he stopped her with a hand on her arm.

"Don't you even want to know what I had to tell you?"

She gritted her teeth. Be polite, Fiona. "Of course. What is it?"

"The carpenters will be coming around in an hour or so. Try to get over your feelings about the Amish before then, will you?"

Before she could respond, he walked off across the street.

"Well, it's not exactly what I expected." Fiona cradled the cell phone against her ear with one hand and continued scrubbing the kitchen sink with the other. She might have to rub all the enamel off to get it clean.

"Better or worse?" Tracy Wilton, her clos-est friend from midwife training, sounded as if she were in the next room instead of three thousand miles away. "You could always come back, you know. They haven't filled your job here yet."

"I'm not sure whether it's better or worse, but it's definitely different." She thought of Ted's obvious doubt that she'd stick it out. "I'm staying, though. I'll make it work."

"I bet you will. Listen, if your practice gets too big for one person, just give me a call. Especially if you've found any great-looking men among those Pennsylvania Dutch farmers of yours."

Fiona pushed an image of Ted Rittenhouse from her mind. "I'm not looking for any. Trust me. Getting my practice up and running is enough to occupy me for the moment. All I'm worried about right now is whether my money will hold out that long."

A rap sounded on the front door, and she headed into the hallway. "Listen, Tracy, someone's here. I'll give you a call later, okay?"

"Okay. Take care."

Fiona snapped off the phone as she swung the door open and saw what appeared to be a whole congregation of Amish men in black trousers and dark shirts filling her porch. She blinked against the late-afternoon sunlight and realized there were only four, surveying her silently.

What on earth?—and then she realized they had to be the carpenters Ted had said he'd send. The oldest man, his beard a snowy white, nodded gravely.

"I am Mose Stetler. Ted Rittenhouse said as how you are wanting some carpentry work done. Said you needed it in a hurry."

"Yes, he told me he'd talked to you. I'm Fiona Flanagan." She nodded to the men and held the door wide. "Please, come in. I'm glad you were able to come so soon."

And a little surprised Ted hadn't told them to forget about coming after their exchange earlier.

"Oh, we had to." He jerked his head toward the youngest of the men, hardly more than a boy, with rounded cheeks above a rather straggly beard. "Young Aaron, here, he'll be needing your services before long, won't you, Aaron?"

The boy blushed, his prominent ears reddening. "My Susie..." He stopped, apparently embarrassed to actually say that his wife was expecting.

"Well, then, all the more reason to get my

practice up and running. But I'll be happy to talk to your wife anytime, even if my office isn't ready." She started to say the woman could phone her, and then realized that she couldn't. "Just have her send a message if she'd like to talk."

He bobbed his head, flushing when one of the other men said something to him in what sounded like German. She didn't understand the words, but the teasing was obvious.

"So, now." Mr. Stetler rubbed callused palms together. "You show me what you want done, and I will figure out a price." His eyes twinkled. "A fair price. You're one of us, after all."

She blinked. Surely he couldn't be referring to her mother. No one knew except the Flanagans. "One of you?"

"A resident, not a tourist," he explained. Apparently tourists were fair game, but not someone who planned to live here.

She showed them over the downstairs, explaining what she needed. Mose made several helpful suggestions for the arrangement that she hadn't thought of.

Finally he took out a stub of pencil and a scrap of paper and figured a price. She looked at the paper with a sense of relief. It was high, but she'd known it would be, with the cost of materials, and it was well within her budget.

"Fine. We have a deal. When can you start?"

Stetler beamed. "Right away. We do some measurements now, and then be back here at eight o'clock tomorrow morning."

"Excellent."

By the time they'd finished up the measurements and were heading out the door, they were on a first-name basis, even with Aaron, the shy expectant father. She was just assuring him that he wasn't going to feel a thing when one of the other men said something that made them all double over with laughter.

"He said unless Aaron's wife hits him for getting her into that predicament."

Somehow she wasn't surprised to see Ted Rittenhouse standing by the porch, one large boot propped against the front step and a grin on his face.

"I'll protect him," Fiona shot back, her gaze challenging his. She'd let him see that she was getting along perfectly well with his Amish friends.

Ted nudged at the step with his boot.

"Hey, Mose, you'd best put fixing this step at the top of your list."

Mose nodded gravely. "Before you put your big foot through it, yes." For some reason, everyone thought that was funny, and they all trooped off, laughing, toward the wagon and its patiently waiting horse.

She was very aware of Ted, standing silent beside her. When he didn't speak, she realized there was something she had to say. She turned toward him, and found him watching her.

"Thank you very much for sending Mose and his crew over. I'm so relieved to have the project underway."

"They'll do a good job for you. And they'll be honest about the price, too."

She nodded. "I'm sure they will." She hesitated, and then decided she'd better say the rest of what she'd been thinking. "You know, I thought maybe you'd change your mind and tell them not to come."

He looked surprised. "Why would I do that?"

"Well, you weren't exactly happy with me earlier."

"That doesn't mean I'd make things difficult for you. Maybe you have something to learn about folks around here."

Those words might have been said snidely, but she couldn't detect anything other than genuine concern in his voice. Concern, and perhaps even kindness.

"Maybe so." She struggled to speak over the sudden lump in her throat. "This move is a big change in my life. I know I have to adjust some of my attitudes if I'm going to make a go of it here."

His lips twitched in a slight smile. "You'll be fine. You have something to offer. Just give yourself a chance. And give us one, too."

The gentleness in his voice drew her. She looked up to find his intense gaze so focused on her face that it seemed to generate warmth. She couldn't look away, couldn't even seem to draw breath. Was it the afternoon sunlight dazzling her eyes, or was it the man?

And then he took a step back. It was hard to tell with that stolid face of his, but she had a feeling he felt just as shocked as she did.

Chapter Three

Her mother's box now sat on her brand-new dresser in her own bedroom in the house in Crossroads. Fiona touched it, smiling a little at the sound of hammering from down-stairs.

She'd moved in yesterday, in spite of Nolie and Gabe's repeated urging to stay with them until the work was completely finished. Much as she'd appreciated their kindness, she'd given in to the need to be here, on the spot, supervising the renovations.

She had a bedroom and a kitchen—at the moment she didn't need anything else. Once she'd found time to paint the room that was going to be her living room, to say nothing of getting some furniture in it, she'd be ready to entertain. She could invite her Flanagan cousins over.

The past few days had been busy ones, notable only for the absence of one person. Ted hadn't dropped by again. Maybe he was occupied with township business. Or maybe he'd been as shocked by that moment of rapport as she had been.

In any event, it was fine that he hadn't been around. She'd been able to write the incident off as nothing—just a random flare of attraction that she could quickly forget. She had nothing in common with a man like Ted Rittenhouse, and even if she'd wanted it, she had no time in her life for romance.

Making a success of her practice had to be the only thing on her mind now, and she'd already made a good start. An invitation had been relayed by Aaron from his wife and had resulted in her first visit to an Amish home.

The simple, painted interior with its large, square rooms and handmade furniture had charmed her. When she'd commented on the beauty of a hand-carved wooden rocking chair, young Susie had shrugged off the compliment, saying the chair was "for use, not for pretty."

She'd been surprised to find Susie already in her thirty-fourth week, but she learned that the couple had only recently returned to the family farm after living in an Amish community in Ohio where Aaron was apprenticed to a master carpenter. Susie was healthy, happy and eagerly looking forward to the birth, and especially to having her baby at home. Fiona had come away with a sense of satisfaction that she would provide the kind of birthing experience the couple wanted.

And happy that she was wanted and needed—she couldn't deny that. It was a step toward belonging. And another step might be—

She lifted the lid on the box, her fingers touching the perfectly matched corners. Here was all she had of the mother she'd never known. An Amish cap and apron, put away never to be worn again. A white baby gown, edged with delicate embroidery. And the patches for a quilt, each one sewn with stitches so tiny they were practically invisible.

She carried the pieces to the spool bed which was her latest purchase and spread them out, not sure how they were intended to fit together. Each piece was a rectangle composed of smaller square and rectangular pieces in rich, solid colors. The deep pink shade that predominated made her wonder if her mother might have intended the quilt for a daughter. If so, she'd never know.

But she could have the quilt. She didn't have the skill to put it together, but the quilters at Ruth's store did. She could imagine it gracing her bed, symbolizing her ties to her new community.

She gathered the pieces, slipped them into a bag and went quickly down the steps, greeting the carpenters, amazed as always by how much they'd accomplished. The rooms were taking shape before her eyes, and her dream was closer to reality every day.

She hurried over to the general store, eager now to set this project in motion. Ruth looked up when the bell tinkled, but she was busy with a customer, so Fiona waved and went on through to the workroom. Emma Brandt greeted her with a smile, while two older women she hadn't seen before glanced up, nodded and bent over the quilt frame again.

"Emma, I'd like to show you something." She approached the quilt frame slowly. It wasn't too late to change her mind, but Emma was nodding. Waiting.

"Yes?"

For a moment her hand held the bag shut. This would be the first time she'd shown the quilt squares to anyone, and she felt an odd reluctance to have them out of her possession. Shaking the emotion off, she drew out the fabric squares.

"I have these quilt pieces, and I wondered if you'd be able to put them together for me."

Emma pushed her glasses into place and took them, turning them slowly in her capable hands. "A log cabin design," she said. "The colors are lovely. This will make a fine quilt for your new bed."

She was getting used to the fact that everyone seemed to know everything about her. It seemed the rumor mill was always grinding in Crossroads. Emma could probably tell her where she'd bought the bed and how much she'd paid for it.

"That's what I thought, although I don't even know how the squares fit together."

She may as well admit her ignorance up front.

Emma quickly moved some of the blocks together. "The traditional manner would be to arrange them like this, so that the darker colors make diagonal lines across the surface."

The quilt seemed to come to life under her hands, and Fiona could visualize it on her bed. Maybe she could find curtains in one of the solid colors.

"That would be perfect. Do you have time to finish it for me?"

"I'm sure we can." Emma picked up one of the pieces, examining it closely. "The workmanship is very fine, uh-huh. Did you make it yourself?"

Fiona shook her head. "It's all I can do to sew a button on. These were given to me. I was told that my mother made them."

"Ah." Emma's look of sympathy said she understood. "Then very special the quilt will be for you."

"Yes." She willed away the lump in her throat. "It will be very special."

One of the older women rose from the quilting frame. She walked toward them, her faded blue eyes magnified by the thick glasses she wore. She reached for the quilt pieces, turning them over in work-worn hands.

Emma said something in the low German that Fiona had learned was the common tongue of the Amish. For a moment the older woman stood frozen. Then she said something that made Emma give an audible gasp.

Their expressions startled Fiona. "Emma, is something wrong?"

Emma shook her head, not looking up. Then, so quickly Fiona hardly understood what was happening, all three women folded up their work and scurried away without a word.

By evening, Fiona was feeling thoroughly exasperated with all things Amish. Ruth had had no explanation for what happened and seemed as mystified by the women's behavior as Fiona. She'd promised to talk to Emma and try to smooth things over as soon as she could.

But that hadn't been the worst of it. The carpenters had left for lunch as usual, but they hadn't come back. They hadn't sent word, either. They were just gone, with tools left lying where they'd put them down.

Clearly she'd offended someone, but how, she didn't know. She'd have been happy to apologize for whatever it was, but since she couldn't get in touch with any of them that was impossible.

She walked slowly from one unfinished room to another. What if they didn't come back? Panic touched her. Would she be able to find someone else to finish the work? She pulled her cardigan tighter around her. She'd had her share of feeling isolated and helpless in her life, and she didn't like the sensation.

A knock on the door came as a relief. At last, maybe someone was coming to explain. She yanked the door open to find Ted on her porch, frowning down at her.

"We have to talk," he said.

She nodded, stood back for him to enter, and gestured down the hall. "Come back to the kitchen. It's the only finished room downstairs."

She followed him down the hallway, his tall frame blocking out the dim light she had left on in the office. Reaching the kitchen, she switched the light on and the room sprang to life.

Originally it had been one of those huge, inconvenient rooms that had probably given the cook fallen arches, but at some point it had been renovated. Now the stove, sink and refrigerator made a convenient work triangle, and her few dishes were arranged in the closest of the glass-fronted cabinets.

She started to offer Ted a seat, but he'd already planted large fists on the round pine table. And he didn't look as if he planned to sit down and relax any time soon. He wore jeans and a blue sweater that made his eyes even bluer, but from the way he leaned toward her, he didn't seem any less intimidating than when he wore the uniform.

He didn't need to glare at her as if she'd committed a cardinal sin. A little flare of anger warmed her.

"You may as well stop looking at me that way. I've obviously made a mistake and offended someone, but I don't have the slightest idea what I've done." She folded her arms.

Ted's face was at its most wooden. "Why didn't you tell me you were Hannah Stolzfus's daughter?"

For a moment she could only stare at him. How could he— "How do you know that? I didn't tell anyone here."

"It's true, then? You're actually her child?" The passion in his voice reverberated through the room.

She hugged herself tighter as if to shield herself from him. "Not that it's any of your business, but yes, my mother's name was Hannah Stolzfus. She died shortly after I was born, so I never knew her, but I've seen the birth certificate. That was her name."

His jaw seemed to harden, if that was possible. "Why did you come here?"

She looked at him blankly. "You already know why I came here. To open my practice. What on earth is going on? Why did those women walk out of Ruth's today after they saw my quilt pieces? Why did the carpenters leave?"

"You really don't understand, do you?" Frustration edged his tone.

"Understand what?" She had plenty of her own frustration to go around. "Why is everyone talking in riddles?"

"All right. No riddles." His hands pressed against the table so hard it might collapse under his weight. "Just straightforward English words. Emma Brandt is the younger sister of Hannah Stolzfus. And the older woman who looked at those quilt pieces and recognized them is her mother, Louise Stolzfus."

Her mother, Louise Stolzfus. My grandmother. She could say the words in her head, but not out loud. She tried to stop the inward shaking that she couldn't let him see.

"I didn't know." She spaced the words out clearly. "Don't you understand? I had no idea anyone would recognize those quilt pieces. No idea that Emma Brandt was any relation to my mother. No idea that my mother's family was even still around here."

Ted obviously wasn't convinced. He straightened, folding his arms. "Do you expect me to believe that?"

"I don't expect anything of you!" She snapped the words and immediately regretted it. Getting angry at Ted wouldn't help matters any.

Please, Lord, help me deal with this—with him—in the right way.

"Look, I'm sorry." She thrust her hand into her hair, shoving it back from her face. "Can't we talk about this sensibly, instead of sniping at each other?"

His eyes were watchful, but he jerked a reluctant nod. "All right. Talk."

She frowned, trying to get her mind around everything he'd said. "Are you sure about this? Emma is surely too young to be my mother's sister. Maybe it's a different family altogether."

Some of the harshness seemed to go out of his face. "I'm sure. Amish families are often spread out over a lot of years. Hannah was the eldest, fifteen years older than Emma, who is the youngest."

"I see." She had to admit he seemed sure of his facts. "Even if what you say is true, I'm not sure what all the fuss is about. I'm sorry for startling them with the quilt, and obviously I'll get someone else to finish it for me."

"And you think that will resolve the problem?" He looked at her as if she were a creature from another planet.

The anger flickered again, but under it was a desolation she wouldn't give in to.

"I don't know what else I can do or say. I didn't come here looking for my mother's family, and I don't particularly want anything to do with them. Maybe we can just chalk it up to an unfortunate coincidence and get on with our lives."

Ted had to remind himself that a city-bred creature like Fiona had no idea what she was talking about when it came to family relationships in a place like Crossroads. He'd pity her, if her coming wasn't creating such a problem for people he cared about, people he had to protect.

"Did you actually think you could come here and not run into your mother's family? Why else would you pick Crossroads Township to settle in, if not to find them?"

She shrugged, hugging her slim frame as if she needed protection from him. Her face was very pale, but her gray eyes blazed with life. With anger, probably aimed at him.

"I came to this area because it had a need for nurse-midwives, that's why. And because I wanted to get to know the Flanagans, my father's relatives. I didn't have any ulterior motives, and I certainly have no desire to intrude on my mother's family."

"Why not?" He shot the question at her. "You admit you came to get to know your father's family. Why not your mother's?"

Her lips tightened into a firm line. She was

probably thinking this wasn't his business, but he intended to know the truth if he had to stand here all night.

"Because they rejected her." The words burst out of her. "My mother. They turned away from her because she married an outsider. Why would I want a relationship with them now? They haven't bothered about me all these years."

"That's not how it was." He remembered all he'd heard, all he'd known. "She's the one who left. She deserted them, not the other way around, and they've never recovered from that."

"How do you know so much about it?" Suspicion edged her tone.

Emma had only been three when her sister left, but she'd remembered how her mother had aged overnight, how all the happiness seemed to go out of the house with Hannah. And he remembered how she'd cried in his arms when she'd told him she couldn't do the same thing to her parents that her sister had done.

He stiffened. Some things Fiona didn't have the right to know, especially that.

"It's a small community," he said. "I don't think you realize how small. I've been a friend of the family for a long time. I know how much the Stolzfus family grieved when Hannah left. I don't want to see them hurt again."

"I don't want to hurt them. I don't want to have anything to do with them." She thrust her hands through her reddish-blond mane as if she'd pull it out in her frustration. "Can't you just accept that?"

He watched her steadily, trying to read the truth in those gray eyes. Did she really believe what she was saying?

"No," he said slowly. "I can't accept that. How can I, when all of your actions have brought you to a place where you're bound to run into them? You say it's not intentional, and maybe that's so. But the results are the same, and people I care about are already hurting as a result."

"I'm sorry." She stood very straight, facing him, her face pale and set. "Sorry if this hurts them, and sorry you don't believe me. But they rejected my mother, and—"

"Will you stop saying that?" He took a step toward her, as if his very nearness might convince her to believe him. "They did not turn her away."

Her face was like stone. "I read about the

Amish, once I was old enough to understand that's what my mother had been. I
read about how they shun people who don't
do what they're supposed to."

"That proves the old saying, doesn't it?"
He sighed in frustration. Did he have to give
the woman a crash course in what it meant
to be Amish? "'A little learning is a dangerous thing.' It's true that someone might be
separated from the congregation to help
him see the error of his ways, but that
doesn't apply in this case."

"What do you mean?" Doubt flickered in
her face.

"Hannah was seventeen when she left, not
yet a baptized member of the church, so she
didn't break any vows by what she did. I'm
sure her parents didn't approve of her
choice, but if she'd stayed, they would have
made peace with it. They never had the
chance. If she'd come back, anytime, they
probably would have welcomed her."

Fiona shook her head stubbornly. "How
can you say that? They never attempted to
get in touch with her after she left. And after
she died, they never tried to find me. My
whole life, I've never heard a word from
them."

Her pain reached out and grabbed his heart, and for a moment he couldn't speak. The urge to comfort her was so strong he had to fight it back. He could pity her, yes, but his loyalties lay elsewhere.

"Fiona, what makes you think they knew you existed?"

He saw that hit her, saw the doubt and pain in her eyes, and thought he'd be a long time regretting that he'd put it there. But it had to be done. This was a bad situation, and an impulsive act on her part could make it even worse.

He shook his head. "I'm sorry," he said again. "Could be you think I'm interfering, and maybe I am. But the best thing you can do now is to stay away from the family. You don't begin to understand them, and you can't judge them by your California standards. Just leave them alone, before you cause each other more pain than you can bear."

Chapter Four

Twenty-four hours had passed since that difficult confrontation with Ted, and Fiona still hadn't shaken off the feelings it had brought on. She dried the few dishes that sat in the dish drainer, glancing out the kitchen window as she did so.

It was dusk already. Yellow light glowed from the windows of the few houses behind hers, partially obscured by the trees, looking distant and lonely. If she'd been looking for privacy when she came here, she'd certainly found it.

In more ways than one, it seemed. The carpenters hadn't turned up again today, and when she'd gone to the store to speak to Ruth about it, she found that the quilters were missing as well.

Ruth had been sympathetic, but her only

advice had been to be patient. Sooner or later, the situation would resolve itself. Until then, there was no point in pressing.

She could admire the older woman's patience, but not emulate it. The need to get on with things drove her to pace across the kitchen and back again.

Lord, I don't know what to do. Was Ted right about me? Did I really come here because I wanted to be accepted by my mother's family? If so, it looks as if Your answer to that is no. Please, guide me now.

She blinked back unaccustomed tears, appalled at herself. There was little point in crying over something that had been over and done with before she was born. She couldn't influence it now.

"And we know that in all things, God works for the good of those who love Him, who have been called according to His purpose."

The verse from Romans had always resonated in her heart, but how did she even know that God had called her here? She'd told herself she was following God's leading for her life when she'd made the decision, but if Ted was right about her, maybe she'd only been following her own unconscious desires.

She hung the dish towel on the wooden rack, aligning it as neatly as if that were the most important thing in the world right now. Well, maybe not important, but at least it was something she could control, unlike everything else that had happened lately.

A noise from the unpaved drive that ran behind the house startled her, sending her pulse beating a little more rapidly. Someone was there, but she didn't expect anyone. She went quickly to the door, pulling aside the lace curtain that screened the glass panel so she could peer out.

If a UFO had landed, she couldn't have been more surprised. An Amish buggy had pulled up next to the back step. The horse dropped its head to nibble at the sparse grass. A slim girl in a black cape slid down, turning to say something to the person who held the reins. In a moment he was down, too, and both of them headed toward the door.

They stepped into the pool of light from the lamp above the door. Young, both of them, probably not more than sixteen. She'd never seen either of them before.

She took a breath. If the Amish community intended to tell her to leave, they certainly wouldn't send two teenagers. She opened the door.

"Hello. I'm Fiona Flanagan. Are you looking for me?"

"Yes, we come to see you." The girl, who apparently was the spokesperson, gave a short nod, her dark bonnet bobbing. She had a pretty, heart-shaped face, a pert, turned-up nose and a pair of lively blue eyes. "I am Rachel Stolzfus. We are cousins."

"Cousins?" For a moment she could only gape at the girl, and then she stepped back, holding the door wide. "Please, come in. I'm sorry, did you say you are my cousin?"

"Cousin, yes." The girl, Rachel, came in and then spun toward her, her black cape swinging out. "This is my friend Jonah Felder."

The boy nodded, flushed to the tips of his ears. He entered, but stood just inside the door, as if ready to bolt back out in an instant.

"I'm happy to meet both of you." And more than a little puzzled. "Won't you sit down?" She gestured toward the straight-backed kitchen chairs. "I'm afraid the rest of the house isn't ready for visitors."

Rachel shook her head at the offer of seats. "We cannot stay long. We are on our way home from visiting Jonah's parents."

She took off her bonnet, though, revealing corn-silk blond hair parted in the center and pulled back into a knot that was covered by a prayer cap.

"But I had to stop and see my new cousin." Her eyes sparkled. "I wanted to be the first, except for Aunt Emma and my grandmother."

Something tightened inside Fiona at that. Her grandmother hadn't even wanted to look at her, much less speak to her. Still, that wasn't Rachel's fault.

"I'm glad you did, but I wouldn't want you to get into any trouble."

"No one will guess that we stopped here." She darted a glance toward Jonah, as if commanding his silence. Her black cape swung open, revealing the deep rose of the dress she wore beneath.

Fiona's heart clenched. "Your dress is the same shade as the rose in my quilt pieces."

Rachel brushed the full skirt with her hand. "Maybe my aunt Hannah had a dress like this. It's only after joining the church that women wear the dark colors. When a garment has no further use, it is cut up for quilting."

"I see." She did see, in a way. A picture of the mother she'd never known was beginning to form in her mind—a smiling girl whose rose dress brought out the roses in her cheeks. "Tell me, how are we related?"

"My father, Daniel, was younger brother to your mother, Hannah." Rachel beamed. "We are cousins. So you see, it is right for me to call on you."

It sounded as if she were trying to convince herself. "Is that what your parents would say?" The last thing she needed was to cause a fight over encouraging Rachel's teenage rebellion.

Rachel shrugged. "Not exactly. Everyone is waiting for my grandfather to decide how we should act. But I didn't want to wait."

Anger spurted up at Rachel's description of the family's reaction. Rachel's grandfather—her grandfather, too—would decide whether the rest of the family should speak to her. She'd told herself she didn't want anything to do with them, so why did that hurt?

"Rachel, I appreciate your coming to see me, but I don't want to get you into trouble. Maybe you should go."

Jonah shuffled his feet. "Ja, Rachel. It is time we were home."

Rachel tossed her head. "Some things I can decide for myself. Besides, Ted Rittenhouse is your friend, and he is an old friend to my family, too. He and my aunt Emma courted when they were young, they did."

That was a tidbit of information about Ted she'd have to consider later.

"I'm happy you came, but maybe you should get on home. It'll be night soon." The thought of them out on a dark highway in that buggy sent a chill down Fiona's spine. That couldn't be safe. "I hope we'll meet again."

A loud rap on the door put a period to her words. Rachel grabbed Jonah's hand, and both of them looked as if they'd been caught raiding the pantry.

Somehow, even through the curtain, there was no mistaking that tall, broad figure. She gave them a reassuring smile and opened the door. It was Ted, of course.

"I wasn't expecting you." That was an

understatement. Ted had a way of showing up at the most inconvenient times.

"No, I guess not." Ted stepped inside, not waiting for an invitation. "And you two weren't expecting me either, I'll bargain."

He frowned at the two teenagers, but instead of looking intimidated, as Fiona anticipated, Rachel gave him a saucy smile. "Not expecting, no. But we are not doing anything wrong, Mr. Policeman."

"Your parents might not agree to that."

Rachel pouted, obviously sure of her relationship with him. "You won't tell. Everyone knows the kinds of things you got up to when you were our age."

Was that actually a twinkle in Ted's steely blue eyes? "I might have to arrest you for blackmailing an officer of the law, Miss Rachel."

"We were on our way out." Jonah tugged at Rachel's sleeve. "I will see Rachel safe home, I will."

Rachel let herself be led to the door. "I will see you again, Cousin Fiona. Soon."

"I'll look forward to it."

She tried to ignore the disapproving look Ted sent her way. This was not any of his business, no matter how much he might think otherwise.

She went to the door to see them off, and Ted followed the teens outside. "You have your lights and reflectors on properly, Jonah?"

The boy nodded, climbing up to the buggy. Fiona watched from the doorway as Ted walked around to the back of the buggy, apparently double-checking the orange reflective triangle and the blinking red warning light that must have worked off some sort of battery when Jonah flipped it on.

"All right, then." He came back around and smacked the horse on its rump. "Get along home, you two."

Fiona heard Rachel giggle as Jonah slapped the reins, and the buggy moved slowly off toward the road. Regret slid through her. Would Rachel come back? It hardly seemed likely if her parents heard about this little visit.

She stepped out onto the back stoop. "You won't tell Rachel's parents about this, will you? She didn't mean any harm."

"No. I won't." He planted one foot on the low step and leaned against the railing. The soft glow from the light over the door caught them in its small circle, picking up glints of gold in Ted's thick brown hair. "And you don't need to tell me this wasn't your idea. I know full well it was Rachel's."

At least he didn't sound angry, with the kids or with her. "I was—well, astonished. I didn't realize Amish kids had that much freedom."

"The rumspringa," he said. "I suppose you don't know about that."

She folded her arms across her chest, drawing her sweater close around her.

"Tell me about it."

"It's a time when Amish teenagers get to taste the outside world, generally when they're between sixteen and twenty. Sowing wild oats, I suppose you might say. A time when they go courting, too."

It flashed through her mind, then, what Rachel had said about Ted courting her aunt. Flashed through, and was quickly dismissed. She didn't know him well enough to ask him about his personal life, even though he didn't hesitate to intrude in hers.

"They seem too young for that."

He shrugged. "They'll probably be married by the time they're in their early twenties.

But before they are baptized into the church, they have the chance to explore the world a little. It's a way to make sure the Amish life is really what they want."

"So it wasn't that bad—Rachel coming to see me?"

He frowned. "That's another thing altogether. If her parents forbade her to see you, she shouldn't disobey. And they wouldn't appreciate your encouraging her."

"I didn't. How could I possibly encourage it? I had no idea who she was until she explained the connection. She was just curious about me. Haven't you ever been curious?"

His gaze rested on her for a long moment, and her breath seemed to catch in her throat at the warmth in his eyes.

"Yes, I have been curious." For a moment she almost thought he'd add, *about you.* "But I am not sixteen. Or Amish."

"You just said her parents gave her more freedom now." She rushed the words. It was safer to keep the conversation on Rachel, not on Ted, because otherwise she might read too much into the way he was looking at her.

"That doesn't mean they don't worry about

her. About the influence of English people on her."

"English?"

"World people. Those who are not Amish." His expression lightened. "The world calls the Amish Pennsylvania Dutch, when they're really German. So the Amish call all outsiders English."

"People like me." She got it, finally. "You mean they wouldn't want her to be around me because they're afraid of the influence I might have on her." She straightened. "That's so far-fetched it's ridiculous."

"Is it?" He looked at her steadily, and that stolid face of his didn't give anything away. The growing darkness pressed around them, reminding her of that first night, trapped in the beam of his flashlight.

"Yes." The word came out defiantly. She wouldn't let him intimidate her into saying she'd turn Rachel away from her door, if that's what he had in mind.

"You're forgetting." His voice was quiet, but there was suppressed emotion in his intent eyes. "But they haven't. It was during her rumspringa that Hannah met your father. She turned her back on everything that was important to her. They never saw her again."

She took an involuntary step away from him, trying to frame a response through the chaos his words set off in her mind. But Ted turned and disappeared into the darkness.

"And today they all reappeared without a word of explanation." Fiona glanced across the front seat of Nolie's battered old station wagon.

Nolie lifted her hands from the wheel for a second. "I can't explain it. And there's probably no use in asking. The Amish don't generally explain to outsiders their reasons for doing things."

"I've gathered that." Fiona's mind flickered to that disturbing conversation with Ted after Rachel's visit.

If Ted was trying to help her understand, he wasn't doing a very good job of it. Maybe his own emotions were getting in the way. After what Rachel had said about Ted courting her aunt, she could understand why he'd have strong feelings on the subject.

But she wasn't going to discuss that with Nolie. "Anyway, I was glad to see the carpenters back at work today. And for Ruth's sake, I was happy to see the quilters back in the general store. I'd hate to cause problems for her."

Nolie nodded. "I've heard about her store. I understand she gets orders from all over the country for those handmade quilts." She glanced toward the back of the station wagon, piled high with packages. "Speaking of buying and selling, we did pretty well today, didn't we?"

"We did. I can't thank you enough. I'd never have found all those outlets alone." Thanks to Nolie's expertise, she'd found most of the curtains and linens she needed for the house and her practice at bargain prices.

"It was fun." Nolie shot her an amused glance. "Much more fun than shopping with Gabe, believe me. All he ever says is, 'It looks fine. Are you done now?'"

"I can imagine." She smiled, but a thread of worry still laced through her mind. "I just hope I'm going to need all these things. What if the Amish decide not to use my services? That would really make a dent in my practice."

"That's not going to happen," Nolie said comfortingly. "But even if it did, I'm sure there are plenty of other moms who'd choose to have midwife care. And you still have your work at the birthing center in Suffolk, too."

"Only two days a week." That was all the birthing center needed of her. At first she'd been delighted. Affiliating with them gave her the backup she needed while allowing her the time to build her own practice. Now that two-day-a-week paycheck was starting to look pretty small.

"I wouldn't worry too much." Nolie hesitated for a moment. "You know, I've felt from the beginning that God had a specific purpose in bringing you here. I hope you don't mind my saying that."

"No, not at all." A lump formed in her throat. "It's what I've felt, too. But sometimes it's hard to see how it's working out."

Nolie smiled. "Walk by faith, not by sight. That's all any of us can do." She pulled up in front of Fiona's house. "Can I help you carry the packages in?"

"I'll get them. I know you're eager to get home to Gabe and the baby." She leaned across the seat to give Nolie a quick hug. "Thanks. For more than just the shopping."

"Anytime." Nolie's return hug was warm. "What are cousins for?"

Fiona unloaded her purchases onto the porch and waved as Nolie drove away. She and Nolie had moved from being unknown relatives to being friends, and that was certainly a blessing for this day.

She carried one load inside, startled to hear the sound of hammers from the office. She'd thought the carpenters had gone for the day. Dropping the packages at the foot of the stairs, she headed for the office.

And stopped dead in the doorway. One man, Amish by his clothing, knelt to hammer a shelf into place. The person holding the shelf was Ted.

"I didn't realize you were still here."

They both looked up at the sound of her voice, two pairs of nearly identical blue eyes staring at her. Then Ted rose, dusting off his hands.

"Jacob stayed to finish up the shelves." He darted a quick glance around the office. "He thought you might want to start putting things in here."

"That's very thoughtful." Her voice sounded stilted, but she couldn't seem to help it. "Are you helping him?"

What are you doing here? That was what she wanted to say, but she'd already created enough waves in this small community without starting a fresh argument with its only full-time police officer.

The carpenter stood, putting his hammer into a wooden toolbox. "Not so much help," he said, his eyes twinkling. "Ted is good enough for holding things while I work, but if I turned him loose with a hammer, you might be finding your books sliding off the shelf."

Ted's face relaxed in a smile. "If that's so, then you're to blame. You taught me whatever I know about carpentry." He looked at Fiona, and she caught the slight wariness in his eyes. "This is Jacob Rittenhouse. My brother."

She could only hope the shock she felt wasn't reflected in her face. She managed what she hoped was a credible smile. "It's nice to meet you, Jacob. You've done a wonderful job on those shelves."

He ducked his head gravely. "They will be useful."

She'd already noticed that the Amish responded that way. They stressed the usefulness of an object, but the shelves really

were a work of art, each rounded edge finished perfectly by hand.

"It's obvious that nothing will slide off any
shelves that you make."

He didn't respond to that, as if to recognize the compliment could be construed
as bragging. "I will be on my way, now." He
started toward the door, pausing long
enough to say something in dialect to Ted.

Ted grinned, clapping him on the shoulder,
and answered in kind. Then he turned to
her, apparently feeling the byplay needed an
explanation. "He's warning me not to touch
his tools. He's been saying that to me since
I was three."

"Because you dropped the bow saw
down the well and we were half the day getting it out again." Jacob settled his straw
hat more firmly on his head. "You will come
to dinner one night soon."

"Soon." Ted followed him out to the porch,
saying a few more words she couldn't
understand.

Fiona stood where she was, trying to wrap
her mind around this. Ted Rittenhouse had
been born Amish, obviously. Just as obviously, he was one no longer. How did that fit
into the warnings he'd given her about not

seeking any relationship with her mother's family?

The screen door creaked. Ted stopped with the door half open. "May I come back in for a moment?"

She nodded. What would he do if she asked the questions that were battering at her mind? Walk away again? That seemed to be his usual response.

"That's really your brother?" The words were out before she had time to censor them. But why should she? He was the one who'd opened the subject of his family background, just by being here with Jacob.

"Yes."

"Just yes? You didn't come back in to satisfy my curiosity?"

"No." His brows drew together. "I came back because I wanted to apologize. What I said about your parents, after Rachel left—I shouldn't have. It wasn't my place to say anything about them."

"I agree. It wasn't." She stared at him, trying to understand what had driven this apology.

"I'm sorry. Can't you just accept that and let it go?" Exasperation edged his voice, and she was tempted to tell him that he wasn't really very good at apologizing.

"No, I can't." She took a breath. Maybe it wasn't wise, but this had to be said. "Because how you react to me has an effect on my acceptance here. And it's really not fair if you're prejudiced against me because my mother left the Amish community, when it's clear that you did exactly the same thing."

Chapter Five

Ted stood where he was for a moment, fighting the urge to turn and walk right out the door. And an almost equally strong urge to take Fiona by the shoulders and make her listen to common sense about dealing with people she didn't understand.

But he couldn't do either of those things. He couldn't walk away, because he was honest enough to recognize the truth in what she said. And he couldn't touch her, because—well, it was better if he didn't explore the possibility of touching her.

She was right in one sense. His attitude toward her was tainted by his past. Neither of them could help that. Maybe that meant she had the right to know a bit more of the truth, if for no other reason than to keep her from stumbling around and causing more trouble by asking the wrong person.

Fiona still waited, her arms folded, face closed off to him. She had that rare ability to wait, her silence demanding answers.

He moved closer, resting his hand on the carved newel post. The smooth grain of the oak felt warm under his fingers. "The builders did some fine work in this house. Jacob's work will be up to theirs."

"I know." She gave a short nod. "I've seen your brother's skill."

"You want to know." He shrugged. "I guess it's inevitable. Why does Jacob Rittenhouse, Amish carpenter, have a brother who's a police officer?"

Her hands, which had been pressing stiffly against the sides of her navy slacks, relaxed a bit. "It does seem an odd combination."

"I guess it does." He smoothed his palm over the smooth round ball that topped the newel post. The carpenter was long dead, probably, but his craftsmanship lived on. "Folks here in Crossroads know all about me."

"But an outsider like me doesn't."

He studied her for a moment. That almost-red hair came from her Irish relatives, probably. But her skin was the same creamy ivory as Rachel's, and those clear gray eyes turned up here and there in the Stolzfus family and their kin.

"You're not really an outsider, are you? Like it or not, you have ties here." He shrugged. "It's not a very exciting story. You might be bored."

Her mouth softened, and she took a step toward him. "I won't be bored."

"Well, then." How to explain this so that Fiona, who'd probably always had every choice in the world, would understand? "I grew up on a farm not far from here. My brother Daniel and his family run it now." He smiled. "If you want to know what I was like, just go out and look at Daniel's kids—barefoot towheads learning how to care for the stock and harrow the fields. That was me."

"But you weren't just like them. Or you wouldn't be wearing this." She was close enough now to reach out and touch the police patch on his sleeve.

"My mother always said I was born asking why. I suppose that was the first sign. By the time I was a teenager, I was always restless." Maybe he still was, still trying to be sure of his place in the world. "Didn't you ever feel that, even with a warm, loving family behind you?"

Some emotion he couldn't identify crossed her face and was gone. "Not exactly." She shook her head. "We were talking about you, not me."

What was there in his comment to raise her hackles? He didn't know, but he wanted to.

"I was the kid who was always looking over the pasture fence, wondering what was on the outside."

She nodded, gray eyes thoughtful. "I can see that. But why a cop, of all things?"

"That was Bill's fault." He smiled. "Bill Brinks. State Trooper assigned to this area. He had a soft spot for the Amish kids. He'd follow the buggies home on dark nights, when maybe someone had been having a wild rumspringa."

"Someone like you, for instance?" Her lips curved.

"Guilty," he said, trying not to imagine how those lips would feel against his. "My mother says I gave her more gray hairs than all my brothers put together."

Her eyebrows lifted. "I can imagine that."

"Anyway, Bill went from being an interfering nuisance to being a mentor. My family liked him, but they didn't like where my friendship with him was leading me. Away from them. I suppose your family would have felt the same in that situation." He said it deliberately, watching for her reaction this time.

The reaction was there, quick but unmistakable. Odd. He could guess what kind of family life the Flanagans he'd met would have—warm, loving, nosy, interfering. Like Amish Irish. But apparently that wasn't what Fiona's family life had been like.

"So you left home to become a cop."

He nodded. "I left the community before I was baptized into the church, so I wasn't breaking any vows by the actions I took."

Should he remind her that her mother had done the same? Maybe not. She didn't need the reminder.

"You didn't go into the state police, like your friend," she said.

"I was too young, then, and I wanted to see a little of the world. I went to Chicago, worked, finished my education, eventually went to the police academy there."

She looked at him with a bit of skepticism in her face, as if trying to picture him as a big-city cop and having trouble doing so.

"Obviously you didn't stay. What made you decide to leave?"

Everything in him hardened against her at that. No one here would tell her, and he wouldn't, either. "Just got to longing for the rural life again. So here I am."

"And they welcomed you back."

No wonder she sounded skeptical. The Stolzfus family hadn't exactly welcomed her.

"They did. They don't understand my choice, and they have a lot of trouble seeing me wear a gun, but they accept me." He took a step closer to her, close enough to see the tiny blue highlights in the gray of her eyes. "You see, I know how much pain it causes an Amish family when a child leaves. I know, because I did it."

Her gaze evaded his. "But—children do leave home. It's natural, isn't it?"

"It's natural for the world. Not for the Amish."

Her head came up. "It's not my fault that my mother made the choice she did."

"I know that. They do, too. All I'm saying is—"

What was he saying? What did he hope to gain by telling his story to this outsider?

But she wasn't an outsider, not really. And

she was hurting. He could see beyond her brave facade. He knew she was hurting, probably more than she wanted to admit.

"Just be patient." He forced a smile. "Maybe, in time, your mother's family will come to terms with Hannah's choice, like mine did."

Her eyebrows lifted. "Didn't you leave a little something out of your story?"

"I left a lot out." His mind flickered to the pain of those last months in Chicago, and he pushed the thought away. "Most of it pretty boring."

"What about your relationship with my aunt Emma? That's kind of pertinent, isn't it?"

"Rachel told you." He traded annoyance for resignation. Young Rachel bubbled on like a brook, and there was no changing that.

She nodded. "I thought maybe—" She stopped, as if reluctant to voice what she thought.

"You thought my attitude toward you was affected by my courting Emma." He shrugged. "Well, maybe it was, but not in the way you think."

"You don't know what I think." She rushed the words.

He couldn't suppress a smile, thinking of Fiona's younger self. "I was sixteen, maybe seventeen. Emma was the same. She was my first love."

"They say you never forget your first love," she said.

"They say?" He raised an eyebrow. "What about you? Have you forgotten your first love?"

A faint flush bloomed like a rose. "We weren't talking about me." Her eyes slid away from his.

Well. That was an interesting response from a woman her age, he'd think.

"I guess we weren't. Well, I was already planning on leaving, and like any young fool in love, I wanted Emma to say she'd go with me."

"She refused to leave her family?"

"She refused. Smartest thing she could have done. We weren't anywhere near ready for marriage." He'd still rushed away in anger and hurt. "But we didn't see that then, and she stayed because of her mother."

Fiona instinctively moved her hands, as if to push him away. He met her gaze and held it.

"She'd been a small child at the time,

but she remembered what happened when Hannah left. She remembered that their mother seemed to turn into an old woman overnight. She remembered the pain that she felt nearly killed her mother. And she wouldn't go with me, because she couldn't subject her parents to that pain again."

Fiona's face whitened, her gray eyes looking very dark. "It wasn't my fault." It was a whisper.

"No, it wasn't." Sympathy for her flooded him. "I'm not saying it to hurt you, Fiona. I'm not blaming you for anything that happened to Emma and me. It was for the best. She has a happy marriage, and I have the career I want. We're friends. But the family—well, now you know how they were hurt when your mother left."

"Now I know," she repeated, looking as if the words were acid in her mouth.

"Just tread carefully where the family is concerned. For your sake, as well as theirs."

He touched her then, gripping her shoulder in what he meant to be an encouraging gesture. He wasn't ready for the warmth that surged through him from that touch. It was as if they were connected by a current that flowed back and forth between them, binding them together.

He let go, his mind scrambling for something coherent to say. There wasn't anything. But it was very clear that Fiona wasn't the only one who'd better be careful.

"Aunt Siobhan, that sandwich tray is beautiful." Fiona shook her head at the array of food that her Flanagan relatives were piling on her kitchen table and counters. "This is too much. I didn't expect you to do all this."

Her aunt paused in the act of sorting cookies onto a serving tray, glancing at her with something like surprise in the deep-blue eyes that were so like Gabe's. "Well, of course we want to help, Fiona. That's what family is for."

Something grabbed Fiona's heart, making her momentarily speechless. Maybe Aunt Siobhan realized it, because she left the cookies and came to give Fiona a quick hug, her movements as light and supple as a girl's.

"We love being part of your open house, dear." She pressed her cheek against Fiona's. "You wouldn't take that away from us, would you?"

"Just be happy the men aren't here." Mary Kate, Aunt Siobhan's older daughter, pushed her way through the screen door, balancing a large white box filled with cupcakes. "You don't know how they can eat. There'd be nothing left for your prospective mothers."

"It won't just be moms," Fiona said. She took the box, sliding it onto the counter. "Although I'm hoping for a good turnout of possible clients." And praying. "I've invited the whole township, it seems. You never know who might be in a position to refer a pregnant woman."

"Good business," Mary Kate said approvingly, running a hand through curls so deep a red they were almost mahogany. Those came from the Flanagan side of the family, and Mary Kate's two kids had inherited the red curls, too.

"It was nice of you to come. I hope you didn't have to hire a sitter." She said the words tentatively, knowing Mary Kate's husband had died about a year earlier, not sure how she managed with two young children, and a burgeoning career as a physical therapist.

"The kids are busy pestering Grandpa this afternoon." Mary Kate smiled. "And I'm happy to have some girl-time, even if I'm not a prospective client."

Something seemed to shadow Mary Kate's face at that. Regret, perhaps? She was still young, still capable of falling in love again, having more children.

The door swung again, and Nolie came in with Terry, the younger Flanagan daughter who'd followed her father and brothers into firefighting but had gone on to become a paramedic. The kitchen was suddenly filled with laughter and female voices, and a warmth she hadn't known she was missing flooded Fiona.

This was how a kitchen should be. Filled with the pleasure that came of working together with family—of having people who accepted her and shared her aims just because they were hers.

Even if they didn't approve, as in Ted's case. His family accepted him back, even though they could never accept the gun and badge he wore.

"Have you seen Ted Rittenhouse lately?" Nolie asked, as if she'd been reading her thoughts.

"Not in a few days, at least not to talk to." Ten days, but who was counting? She'd thought he might turn up again to help Jacob with the carpentry, but he hadn't, and that job was finished now.

"He seems like a nice guy, from what Gabe said." Nolie filled a tray with cupcakes. She paused, pulling one from the tray and handing it to Mary Kate. "This one looks as if someone's little finger got into the icing."

"I guess you'll have to eat it, Mary Kate." Fiona could only be glad that Mary Kate's child's indiscretion took the conversation away from the subject of Ted.

The others began teasing Mary Kate about her having to eat any cakes with fingerprints, and Fiona escaped with a tray into what she'd begun calling the "group room," where she hoped she might eventually hold birthing classes. At the moment, it had two long, covered tables—one for food, the other divided between a coffee and tea station and rows of booklets and materials about midwifery to give out to anyone who was interested.

The questions about Ted had unsettled her, and she tried to push them away. Ted's social life was no concern of hers. She had no idea what he did during his free hours.

He might be going out on dates every night of the week, for all she knew.

Not with her. After that revelation about the end of his relationship with Emma, she understood his attitude toward her a lot better. But the attraction was there—they both recognized that, even if they had no intention of admitting it.

Her mother's actions had, however inadvertently, ruined his love for Emma. Maybe it was just as well, maybe they'd been too young, maybe it would have ended as unhappily as her parents' marriage had. Still, he had to find her a reminder.

She'd known he found her presence painful for his friends. Now she realized that it might be painful personally, as well. No one could blame him for steering clear of her. No one.

"Your first visitors are gathering on the porch." Aunt Siobhan hurried in, followed by the others, bearing more trays of food. "Go on, dear, and welcome them. We'll see that everything is set up properly here."

Fiona nodded. She should thank them again, but a flock of butterflies seemed to be fluttering around her stomach, and her throat had closed. Pinning a smile to her face, she hurried to the door to open it officially for the first time.

An hour later she was taking a breather after having given her hundredth introductory spiel when Nolie shoved an oatmeal cookie into her hand.

"Relax and eat something. Enjoy." She grinned. "You're a success."

"I guess so." She looked around at the rooms, still crowded with people. "Are you sure they're not just here for the free refreshments?"

"Look at them. Every person is holding some of your brochures. If they're not going to be clients themselves, they'll tell someone else. It may take time and patience, but this is going to work."

"Patience is a given in the midwifery field. Babies seldom arrive when expected." She glanced around again. There were several young women who might be in need of her services, but none in Amish garb. "I'd hoped for some sign of acceptance from the Amish today."

Nolie poked her. "Well, then, you have it. Look who's coming in."

Pleasure flooded Fiona, and she hurried

toward the three women in the doorway—
Susie, Aaron's wife, obviously blooming
with pregnancy, along with two other young
Amish women. Ridiculous, to be so elated
at the sight of them.

"Susie, I'm so happy you're here."

"I wanted to see your office, even though
my baby will be born at home." Susie patted her rounded belly, and then she nodded
to the young woman on her left. "This is my
friend, Miriam Hostetler. She wants you to
deliver her baby. And her sister, Elizabeth.
Elizabeth's father planted a whole row of
celery in the garden this year, so we think a
wedding will be announced soon." Fiona
looked at her, puzzled. Celery?

The younger woman blushed, nodding.
Miriam said something to her and then
smiled at Fiona. "Celery is an important part
of the wedding feast. We say you can tell
when a daughter will be married by the
amount of celery in the garden."

"Well, I'm happy to meet both of you.
Miriam, if you'd like to make an appointment, I can come to your home, or you can
meet me here." She gestured toward the
door to the meeting room. "Why don't you

go in and have some refreshments now, and we'll talk later."

They nodded, moving off in a group. She couldn't control the elation that bubbled through her. This day was a success, wasn't it?

She glanced toward the door, saw who stood there, and swallowed hard. She really shouldn't feel that rush of pleasure at the sight of Ted's tall figure. He hovered awkwardly on the doorstep, as if unsure of his welcome.

She smiled at him. "Please, come in. The open house is for everyone, not just expectant mothers."

He stepped inside, holding out something in a soft cloth. "I brought you a little housewarming gift. Sorry it's not wrapped fancy, like some of those."

He glanced at the hall table that overflowed with everything from homemade jelly to houseplants.

"You didn't need to bring anything." She took the bundle, her fingers brushing his as she did. "I didn't expect gifts from anyone."

"Folks around here like to say welcome," he said. "Open it."

She opened the cloth, exposing what it

hid. The plaque was of wood, not brass, but otherwise it was exactly as she'd envisioned it that first night when she'd looked at the house: Fiona Flanagan, Nurse-Midwife.

Her throat choked. "Thank you." She managed to stammer the words. "And thank Jacob." For surely this delicate carving must have come from him.

"Jacob just supervised," he said. "In spite of what my brother might say, I did the work." His fingers brushed hers again. "Welcome to Crossroads, Fiona."

"Thank you." She didn't dare look up at him, because she didn't want him to see the silly tears in her eyes.

He glanced over her shoulder, as if sensing her feelings and trying to spare her embarrassment. "I see Susie brought you some prospective clients."

She nodded, clearing her throat so that she could speak normally. "Only three Amish turned up, but plenty of other people."

"Well, it's a start." His fingers touched hers again as he took the sign. "Would you like me to go and put this up for you?"

"Yes. Thank you." As he said, it was a start.

*　*　*

The auction sign was large, handmade and decorated with a bunch of balloons so that no one could miss the proper turn. Fiona turned her car onto the narrow dirt lane that led between cornfields toward, presumably, the site where she hoped to pick up a few pieces of furniture she needed for the house.

The corn had been left standing in the field. She'd learned enough in her weeks here to know that was unusual. Most of the corn had long since been cut for silage to feed the animals over the winter. Only here did the stalks stand, brown and sere, look-ing abandoned.

She shook her head. Silly to be thinking such mournful thoughts. Perhaps the farmer and his wife had retired to a well-earned rest in Florida or some other sunbelt state, and the proceeds from the sale of things they'd left behind would pay for new furni-ture for a bright sunroom or a boat to putter along a warm bay.

She emerged from the cornfields to a busy sight. People thronged over the lawn be-tween house and barn, talking, laughing, acting as if this event was a party. The auctioneer stood beneath a canopy ringed by lawn chairs, already filled. It was probably smart, auction-goers bringing their own chairs with them.

She pulled into a row of cars in a stubbly field and parked, trying to douse a surge of apprehension. She didn't look like any more of an outsider than the yuppie couple climbing out of their big SUV next to her. And if any of her mother's family happened to be here—well, she'd cope with that if it happened.

In the week since the open house, things had settled down to what might be her new normal. Several clients had come to engage her services, including Susie's friend, Miriam Hostetler. Ruth's quilters were back at work, including Emma, but she'd regretfully put the pieces of her mother's quilt away again. Somehow she didn't have the heart to ask anyone else to finish the quilt after what had happened.

She slid out of the car, grabbed her bag and headed for the center of activity. She could hear the auctioneer's chant from here, and she pushed her way through the throng. It would be nice to see someone she knew, although the odds of that probably weren't great. The auction had certainly attracted a mob of people—farmers mixed with smart, young well-dressed couples who'd probably come out from Suffolk for a Saturday of antiquing, together with a scattering of Mennonite and Amish.

Her stomach churned. She looked around, trying to see if any of her mother's family was there. It had to happen sooner or later.

Not today, Lord. Please. I'm not ready.

How often had she said that? She knew, perfectly well, that she'd spent much of her life withdrawing from the chance of emotional hurt. She even knew why. The problem was finding the courage to change.

I know I said I'd be different when I came here, Father. I'll try not to be a turtle, hiding in my shell. I will. I just don't want to face them today.

And what about Ted? Did she want to face him? He'd stopped by the house twice during the week, casually—so casually, in fact, that she couldn't decide whether the visits were a gesture of friendship or what he saw as his duty, checking up on the new resident.

She'd reached the edge of the crowd around the auctioneer, and she peered past bodies to get a look at what he was selling. Farm equipment, apparently. Maybe she'd have time to look over the furniture before he got that far.

She glanced across the crowd. The furniture seemed to be set out on the dry grass on the far side. She took a step in that direction and then stopped. That slim figure, surely, was Emma Brandt, bending over to inspect a marble-topped nightstand.

Without even thinking about it, she turned and walked in the opposite direction, ending up on the edge of the crowd. She faced a garden with pumpkins and winter squash that showed orange and green among the vines.

"Looking for a nice pie pumpkin?"

She knew it was Ted without looking. She turned, managing a smile. There was no point in letting him know she was such a coward.

"Miriam Hostetler told me about the celery in Amish gardens. I was just thinking there's none planted here."

He smiled, face relaxed. He wasn't in uniform today, but his broad shoulders filled out the plaid shirt he wore with jeans and a denim jacket. "Old man Henderson wasn't

Amish, and he wasn't marrying off any daughters this November, that's for sure."

"November?"

He nodded. "It'll soon be here. November is the traditional month for Amish weddings, after the harvest is in and before the snow flies. Maybe Miriam told you that they don't announce the wedding until a few weeks ahead, but if a man plants a lot of celery, it means he's thinking of a wedding feast."

"That's what Miriam said."

A silence fell between them, but it seemed a comfortable one. Maybe Ted had gotten past his worries about her presence here. It would be nice to think they could be friends.

Just friends, the cautious side of her added quickly. Just friends.

Suddenly the silence didn't feel so comfortable. "Are you planning to bid on anything today?" she asked.

He shook his head. "Probably not, but I can never resist the lure of an auction. You never know what treasure you might find. How about you?"

"I thought I might pick up a piece of furniture or two for the house. I can't bid on anything very big, or I won't be able to haul it."

He gave her a quizzical look. "The furniture is over on the other side of the tent."

"I know. Unfortunately, so is my aunt Emma. Maybe my grandmother."

She hadn't been able to identify any of the other black-caped figures from this distance, their bonnets and capes making them as anonymous as she'd thought she'd be in this crowd.

"I see." He glanced across the crowd, his height letting him see easily over the heads of most people. "It looks like most of the Stolzfus and Brandt families are here today."

She tried, and failed, to read any emotion in his voice. "Do you think I should leave?"

She could see that he didn't like being put on the spot with the question. She wasn't sure how to read him—his expression didn't change with the question. But she knew. Maybe his square jaw got a little squarer, or maybe she was developing way too much insight where Ted Rittenhouse was concerned.

"No," he said finally. Reluctantly, she thought. "If you're going to live here, they'll have to come to some way of dealing with your presence."

His concern, as always, was for them, not her, but at least he seemed to recognize that they needed to adjust, too.

"There's no 'if' about it. I'm here to stay."

He gave a short nod. "There's your answer, then."

And you regret it, don't you? Maybe she'd better get away from him before she said something like that aloud to him, instead of in the privacy of her mind.

She pulled her corduroy jacket a little closer around her. "I'm going to find some hot coffee. Will you excuse me?" She didn't wait for an answer, but started across the short, crisp grass to the food stand she'd spotted near the barn.

He didn't follow her. Well, she hadn't expected him to. He'd made it clear from the beginning whose side he was on in this standoff with her mother's family. She needn't imagine he'd change because of some vagrant bits of attraction between them.

By the time she reached the food stand, she'd managed to let go of whatever irritation she felt toward Ted and refocused her attention on what she hoped to buy today. A nightstand would be nice, and she could fit that in the back of the car. She tried to picture how it would look in her bedroom, next to the new bed.

The steaming hot chocolate smelled even better than coffee, and she took a large cup. One sip sent warmth surging through her, chasing away the late-October chill.

She'd just started back around the barn when she heard the sound of rushing feet behind her. Before she could turn they'd raced past her—three or four teenage boys, brushing so close they jostled the cup, splashing hot chocolate over her hand. Judging by the muffled laughter she heard as they disappeared around the barn, that was what they'd intended.

Annoyed, she fumbled in her bag for a tissue to mop the chocolate from her hand and wrist. A splash had hit the sleeve of her jacket, but it wasn't bad. The boys had judged it nicely. They'd bumped her just enough to bother her, but not enough that she'd go seek out the law.

The odd thing was that, although three of the four had been typically clad in jeans and expensive sneakers, their jackets emblazoned with the emblem of the local high school, one, slighter and smaller, had been

Amish. That was a strange combination, she would think.

Now she had a soggy tissue, but there was a large plastic trash bin at the corner of the barn. She dropped the tissue in. Well, no harm done. She rounded the corner, still feeling distracted after the odd encounter, barely looking where she was going, and stopped, face-to-face with her aunt Emma and her grandmother.

For an instant they froze, too, obviously just as shocked as she was. Then, with a quick movement, her grandmother turned her face away, the brim of the black bonnet effectively hiding her face. Emma did the same. And they walked off.

Fiona stood stock-still. The spray of hot chocolate had been nothing compared to this. She felt as if she'd just been doused with an entire bucketful of ice water. If she'd wondered how they'd react to seeing her, she certainly knew now.

Chapter Six

Fiona was straightening the exam room after her last appointment of the day when she heard the bell jingle over the front door. Maybe a new client? She walked quickly through to the reception room. Standing uncertainly near the door was Rachel Stolzfus, and behind her was a young Amish boy.

For an instant Fiona felt as she had the previous Saturday at the auction—first icily frozen, and then scalded with hot embarrassment at the public snub. She forced her emotions under control. These were two kids, hardly responsible for what their elders had done.

"Rachel. How nice to see you." She had to tread carefully. "But I suspect you shouldn't be here."

Rachel's pink cheeks turned even pinker,

but she shook her head, her bonnet ties fluttering. "No, it is all right, Cousin Fiona. Really." She pulled the boy forward. "This is my little brother, Levi. He is almost thirteen."

Levi looked like every other Amish boy she'd seen—blond hair in a bowl cut under his cap, round blue eyes that stared at her solemnly, rosy cheeks, and clothes that were a smaller replica of what his father would wear. He looked younger than the average twelve-year-old, but that was probably the inevitable difference in clothes and hairstyle.

"Hi, Levi. It's good to meet you." Fiona smiled at them.

He nodded, not speaking, and his gaze swept around the room, taking in the braided rug on the floor, the straight-backed, padded chairs, racks of mother-to-be magazines and the small television that played quietly in the corner.

Well, maybe it was better not to give him too much attention. Levi was obviously shy of his strange new cousin, and Rachel had probably dragged him along on this visit. Fiona turned back to the girl.

"Are you sure you should be here? I don't want to get you into any trouble."

But Rachel was already shaking her head again. "Aunt Emma brought us with her. She has some work to do at Ruth's. She told us she would be busy for an hour, and we should find something to do. She knew we would come here." Rachel beamed. "So, you see, it makes no trouble."

In other words, Emma had given the kids tacit approval to do what she wouldn't. Or couldn't. Fiona wasn't sure how she felt about that, but again, she couldn't take that out on the kids.

She slipped out of her lab coat and hung it on the coatrack. "Come back to the kitchen. I think it's about time for a snack."

Levi glanced from the television to Rachel. She shook her head.

"Levi would like to stay here and watch the television, if that's all right, while we have a sit-down talk."

"That's fine." She didn't suppose a half hour of daytime television could do him much harm, and the game show that was on seemed fairly innocuous.

She led the way back to the kitchen, taking a mental inventory of her snack provisions. Probably not much there that would appeal to them.

"How about a peanut butter and jelly sandwich?" She glanced at Rachel. "I haven't had a chance to get to the store lately."

"Levi would love it." Rachel took her bonnet off and patted her hair. "Maybe you and I would share one?"

"That sounds good."

Fiona got the makings out quickly, slicing the loaf of brown bread that one of today's clients had brought and getting out the peanut butter and a jar of strawberry preserves Miriam had given her. One thing about working here—she certainly wasn't going to starve, with all the gifts of food that were being pressed on her.

Rachel took the plate with one sandwich from her hand. "I will take it to Levi."

Wondering a bit, Fiona looked after the girl as she slipped out of the kitchen. It seemed fairly obvious that Rachel wanted a private talk. But about what?

Rachel was back quickly, sliding into the chair opposite Fiona at the round kitchen table. Her spotless apron and deep cherry-colored dress seemed to fit well with the simple aspect of the pine table.

"This is nice, Cousin Fiona."

"Yes, it is." *And what is on your agenda, Rachel?*

Rachel stared down at the sandwich, not eating it. "Cousin Fiona, will you tell me something?"

"If I can," she replied, wary of promising anything she might not be able to deliver.

Rachel's gaze met hers. "Will you tell me how your mother died?"

For a moment Fiona couldn't speak. That was certainly the last question she'd expected from her young cousin. She swallowed hard.

"Doesn't the family know that?"

Rachel shook her head. "Only that she is dead. That was all my grandfather ever heard about her after she left Crossroads."

She blinked. "But he could have found out more. If he'd wanted to know."

Bitterness twisted. *He could have found out about me, that was what she really wanted to say.*

"That is not the Amish way, you see. Accept what happens as God's will. Don't question. That is our belief."

"But you do question, don't you, Rachel?" She'd glimpsed a bright, inquiring mind in this young cousin.

Rachel shrugged. "I try not to. But I see our grandmother's sorrow, and I wonder if it might have been eased if she'd known more."

"Maybe you're right." She took a breath to release the tightness in her throat. "My father only ever told me that my mother died after I was born. When I was old enough, I found out more for myself."

"You needed to know," Rachel said.

She nodded, trying to frame the words. This was harder than she'd thought. "Apparently she never adjusted to being away from here. She was sad, crying a lot. After I was born, she developed an infection while she was still in the hospital. The doctor I spoke with said that she just seemed to give up. I guess she didn't want to live."

Even for me, the little voice in the back of her mind said. Even for me.

Rachel's warm, strong fingers wrapped around hers. "I'm sorry. Sorry that you never knew her. That your father had all the care of you."

She shook her head. "My father couldn't take care of me. He put me in foster care."

"Foster care." Rachel frowned. "That is

when a relative takes care of the children if the parents can't."

Maybe in Rachel's world that was what happened. "We didn't have any relatives in California. I was placed with strangers, not family."

Judging from Rachel's expression, that concept was beyond her understanding. Her blue eyes were wide, protesting.

"I was well taken care of," she went on quickly. "After my father remarried, I went to live with him."

"And then you were happy." Rachel obviously wanted a happy ending to the story. "You have brothers and sisters, a real family of your own."

The innocent words hurt, but she wouldn't let Rachel see that. "One brother, two sisters. They're quite a bit younger than I."

Rachel nodded sagely. "I know what that is like. Levi, he wishes to follow me everywhere, as if it is time for his rumspringa, not mine."

Fiona smiled, relieved the subject had moved away from her parents. "He probably envies you."

"He must wait until he is older." Rachel sounded severe. "He doesn't yet have good judgment to make decisions." Her smile sparkled suddenly. "Tell me about college. You went to college, yes?"

"Yes. I went to college to study nursing. And after that, to become a midwife. It was hard work, but fun, too."

"You lived in a dormitory, with other girls, and went out on dates." Rachel happily constructed the life she thought Fiona should have had. "And you have traveled?"

She opened her mouth to talk about her summer at a mission in South America and closed it again, remembering Ted's misgivings about exposing Rachel to the outer world. It wasn't her place to make Rachel long for a different life, even if it might seem natural to her.

Natural to her, yes. But would such a life really be any happier? She didn't know the answer to that.

"A little," she said evasively. "Mostly I studied. And then I worked at a birthing clinic in San Francisco before I came here."

Rachel nodded. "I understand. You became a midwife because of what happened to Hannah."

"I—I don't know." She didn't. She'd have said she barely thought of the mother she'd never known, but maybe the longing had been lurking in her heart all the time. "Tell me, is our grandmother all right?"

Rachel gazed down at the table. "I think she is. But I heard my father and mother talk of the time after Hannah left, when she lay on her bed and cried until my grandfather took her to the special doctor in Suffolk and she had to be in the hospital for a long time."

Here was something she hadn't imagined. So, her grandmother had had a depression severe enough to require hospitalization. Maybe their grandfather feared that Fiona's appearance might cause a recurrence.

Rachel glanced at the clock over the stove and exclaimed something in German, jumping to her feet. "We are past our time. We must meet Aunt Emma."

She whirled, enveloping Fiona in a quick, hard hug before rushing out to the other room and calling Levi's name.

Fiona followed, but they were already out the door by the time she got there. She stared absently at the cartoon on the television and the empty plate on the coffee table.

Rachel had come looking for answers to satisfy her own curiosity about what must seem to her a family secret. She'd left Fiona with enough food for thought to last her a good long time.

Late-afternoon sunlight gave the main street of Crossroads a golden haze. In the distance, Ted could smell a faint whiff of burning leaves, a sure sign of autumn. Crossroads seemed to doze on weekday afternoons, but the weekend would bring its influx of tourists.

And its share of traffic issues. If he was lucky, the only problem would be a fender bender caused by some fool driver gawking at an Amish buggy instead of watching where he was going.

Ted turned into the minuscule office that was all the township could afford for its small police force. If he weren't lucky, the weekend would see more thefts or vandalism. So far the problem had been more annoying than serious, but it rankled that he hadn't been able to lay his hands on the culprits yet. He was here to protect, and he didn't like failure.

At least Fiona no longer seemed to need his help. He didn't begrudge any single moment he'd spent with her, but it was probably best for both of them not to let their friendship become any more than what it was. There were too many complications inherent in that sort of relationship.

He flipped briefly through the report filed by one of his part-time officers. Jerry Fuller aspired to be a big-city detective, and his reports managed to make a lost cat sound like a major felony.

He hadn't seen Fiona since the auction, but he'd heard this and that. Her practice was picking up, apparently, although the Amish hadn't yet fully accepted her. Maybe somebody should have warned her that building a clientele among the Amish took a decade or two.

And her relationship with the Stolzfus family probably complicated matters for her, with people unwilling to take sides between her and her grandparents. He regretted that, but there was nothing he could do. It was past time for him to back off.

He'd just poured himself a mug of coffee when he heard the door open. He swung around to see Fiona standing there, lingering in the doorway as if unsure of her welcome.

He'd have to do something about that

rush of pleasure he felt at the sight of her. "Fiona. Come in. Can I help you with something?"

"So this is where you hang out." She glanced around the tiny office, as if interested in the crumbling cork bulletin board that bore community notices and the white board that listed staff assignments. "If you turn around too fast, you'll trip over yourself."

The way she evaded his question told him she did, indeed, want something—something she was reluctant to bring up. Well, that was okay. Plenty of people who came in here just needed a bit of patience to bring out their troubles.

"That's why I try not to make any sudden moves." He gestured toward his one and only visitor's chair. "Would you like a cup of coffee?"

"No, thanks." She drifted to the white board. "Just how big is the Crossroads police force? I guess a resident like me ought to know that."

"You're looking at the full-time force." He perched on the edge of his desk, bringing himself to her level. "I have two part-time officers now, and usually we add another one in the summer. No dispatcher—if someone calls after I go off-duty, the call comes right to my cell phone."

"In other words, you're never really off duty." She sat, finally, her back very straight.

He shrugged. "That's how I like it."

"It's very different from Chicago." Her gaze slid away from his, as if she regretted expressing so much interest. "You mentioned you'd started in police work there."

"Yes." That came out more abruptly than he meant it to. He didn't care to discuss with Fiona, of all people, why he'd left the Chicago force. "Crossroads police work is different. I suppose it looks like a hayseed operation to you."

Her clear gray eyes widened. "Not at all. I'm impressed that you can manage everything you have to handle. It can't be an accident that this is the most peaceful place I've ever lived."

"Usually." He shrugged, trying not to feel too pleased at her praise. "I wish I could say nothing ever happened here, but then the township wouldn't need me."

"Is there a crime wave going on?" She said it as if the idea were absurd.

He shrugged. "Right now the only press-

ing cases are a missing dog and a few incidents of vandalism. The dog will probably
find his own way home, but I'd love to lay
my hands on the vandals before they grad-
uate to something more ambitious than
knocking over outhouses."

"I guess I'm lucky I don't have an out-
house." A smile curved her lips at the
thought.

He tried to ignore the effect of that smile.
"Maybe you're not worried about an out-
house, but you didn't come here just to
chat. Not that I don't enjoy it."

The smile slid away. "Yes." She clasped
her hands in her lap. "At the auction last
Saturday—something happened."

He leaned toward her, elbow on his knee.
"Tell me."

"Some boys had jostled me, spilling my
hot chocolate. Otherwise I might have been
watching where I was going more closely.
As it was, I nearly walked into Emma and
my grandmother." She took a breath, as if it
were difficult to say. "They both turned their
heads and walked off as if I weren't even
there."

"I'm sorry." He kept the words gentle,
sensing the pain the event had caused even

though she didn't exactly admit it. "But your grandmother—"

"I know." She looked up, her gaze zoning in on his face. "Rachel came to see me. With, apparently, Emma's tacit approval. She told me about my grandmother's illness."

Was she blaming him for not telling her? He couldn't be sure.

"The family never talks about it," he said.

"Are they ashamed of emotional illness?" Her gray eyes flashed.

"Not ashamed, exactly." How to explain this to an outsider like her? "The Amish way is to accept what happens to you as God's will. Your grandmother wasn't able to accept Hannah's leaving. It took some time for the family to realize that her reaction needed medical intervention."

Pain shadowed Fiona's face. "Rachel said she was hospitalized for a long time."

He nodded, wondering whether she was hurting for her grandmother, her mother or herself. "I don't remember it, but I guess so. I'm sure that's why they're all trying so hard to protect her now."

"You think it's wrong for me to want to see them." Her gaze challenged him.

"Not wrong," he said carefully. "I just think it might be unwise. You have to be cautious."

She surged out of her chair so suddenly that the movement startled him. "Be cautious. Be patient. That's all anyone will say to me."

He rose, playing for time, trying to decide what to say to her. "That's the Amish way."

Her hand slashed, seeming to reject that. "It's just prolonging the agony. Maybe I ought to go out to the farm and confront them."

"No." He hurt for her, even as he worried about the family. "Fiona, you can't do that. If you force the issue, you may never get what you want."

"You don't know what I want." The fire in her was so intense he could feel it. "I'm not sure I do."

He shook his head. "You want to talk to them. Your grandparents. To resolve your feelings."

For a moment longer she glared at him. Then her shoulders sagged, and she shook her head. "I suppose. I've started feeling that I'll never come to terms with the past until I do."

Her eyes met his, and he could see what she was going to ask before the words were out of her mouth.

"Please, Ted. Will you help me? Will you convince them to see me?"

There it was—the straightforward appeal for his help that he'd hoped wouldn't come. He'd never found it easy to say no to someone who needed him. And sometimes it was downright impossible.

He ran his fingers through his hair, wishing he had some magical answer that would make everyone happy. There wasn't one.

"Fiona Flanagan, I knew you were trouble the moment I saw you."

She surveyed him gravely. "Is that a yes or a no?"

"It's a maybe." He shook his head at the hope in her face. He didn't want to respond to that hope. Didn't want to start feeling responsible for her. But it was probably already way too late for that. "Don't build on it too much. But I'll try to think of a way I can help you."

Taking the black bag that contained everything she needed for a routine prenatal visit, Fiona slid from the car. The Hostetler farm didn't look quite as prosperous as some she'd seen, but Susie's friend, Miriam, had mentioned that she and her husband had just managed to buy it a few months earlier, from an elderly, non-Amish farmer who'd let the place go in recent years.

They'd have a struggle to get the place up to Amish standards, perhaps, but given the price of farmland in the area, they'd been lucky to buy. According to Ruth, many young Amish had left for areas farther north because they couldn't afford land here. Ironic that the presence of the Amish had created the tourism that now threatened their very existence.

Miriam came out onto the porch to greet her, bobbing her head with what seemed a nervous smile. She had the round, rosy cheeks and bright blue eyes of a china doll, but the tension was new since Fiona had met her. Still, first pregnancies could do that—each step in the process could bring up new concerns.

"It's good to see you, Miriam." She smiled reassuringly. "How are you feeling?"

"Fine. I am fine." Miriam gestured to the door. "Please, come in. We must talk."

That worried look wasn't the usual reaction to a prenatal visit, but maybe the young woman had some fears she wanted to be sure she brought up. Fiona followed her into a spotless, sparsely furnished living room.

"Is something worrying you?" Fiona said. "You can talk to me about anything." She set the bag down on the shining wooden floor.

Miriam's cheeks flushed. "It is not that. I wish—I must tell you that I cannot continue to be your patient."

For a moment Fiona could only stare at her. "But I thought we had agreed. If there's some problem with my fee—"

"No, no. It is not that." She paused, fingers twisting together, obviously reluctant to say whatever it was. "It is just that my husband's father, he is second cousin to John Stolzfus. And he thinks—"

She stopped, unwilling or unable to say anything else.

She didn't need to say more. Fiona didn't know whether to laugh or cry.

"Did my grandfather ask you not to see me?"

"Not exactly." Miriam pressed her lips together, shaking her head. "I am sorry. But it would be better if you left now."

She had to take a deep breath and remind herself that the young woman wasn't responsible for this. Miriam would give in to the others' wishes, because that was the Amish way. Fiona managed a smile as she picked up the bag she wasn't going to need.

"It's all right, Miriam. I know it's not your fault." She patted the young woman's arm. "Really. If there's ever anything I can do for you, just let me know."

Miriam nodded, cheeks scarlet.

There wasn't anything else to say, was there? Fiona kept a faint smile on her lips until she got out the door, though it probably looked more like a grimace. Then she stopped, staring.

Her car still sat where she'd left it, but behind it was the township's black patrol car. Ted leaned against the driver's-side door, but at the sight of her, he pushed away and came toward her.

"Are you following me around?"

The words were snapped in a way Ted didn't deserve. After all, he wasn't to blame, but he was male and he was handy. She stamped down the steps toward her car.

He blinked, but that was the only sign of surprise. His face wasn't made for expressing much emotion, but she'd still learned to read him fairly well.

"No. I'm not following you. Should I have been?"

She tossed her bag into the back seat of the car. "Sorry." She bit off the word. "I shouldn't take my feelings out on you."

"Feel free." He planted one large hand on the door frame. "But you might tell me first what has you so upset."

She'd probably explode if she didn't. "I've just lost a client. Miriam's husband would prefer she didn't see me. And guess why— because his father is my grandfather's second cousin."

"I'm sorry." He shook his head slowly. "I guess this is small consolation, but it's only one client, after all."

She frowned at him, narrowing her eyes against the sun's glare. Around them, fertile fields stretched toward the line of low hills, and a herd of black-and-white cows munched grass in a nearby pasture. It was a tranquil scene, but she didn't feel very peaceful at the moment.

"Clients aren't exactly falling out of the trees for me right now. I can't afford to lose even one. And how many more might I lose if my grandfather has his way?"

Ted studied her with those calm blue eyes that were nearly as placid as the cows' in the face of her annoyance. "Look, you don't know that this was John Stolzfus's idea. It's entirely possible that Miriam's father-in-law is guessing at that, or just wants to stay un-involved. It doesn't mean your grandfather is trying to undermine your practice."

"Doesn't it?" She stared at him bleakly. He didn't understand. Her bank account was dwindling steadily, and if her practice didn't pick up soon, the likelihood of it surviving a year wasn't very good. "If his influence keeps prospective clients away, it won't really matter whether he told them to stay away or not."

"I'm sure you're tired of hearing this, but you have to give it time. Nothing moves quickly among the Amish." His smile was cautious. "It took two years for the bishop to decide it was all right for an Amish business to have a telephone. Rotary dial, of course."

He obviously hoped to lighten her mood, but it wasn't working.

"Maybe my initial reaction was the right one. Maybe I should just go out and talk to them."

"Don't." He moved then, so quickly that it seemed his casual attitude was just a pose. His fingers closed around her wrist, as if to emphasize his warning. His hand was warm and strong, and she could feel her pulse accelerate against it.

He must have felt it, too. Almost without her will, her gaze lifted to his. His blue eyes darkened as his pupils dilated, and a current flowed back and forth between them where their skin touched.

They stood motionless, caught in the moment. His muscles tightened, as if he'd pull her against him. She should pull away, but something seemed to push her toward him. The faintest of movements would have her in his arms...

He shook his head, as if surfacing from under water. "I'm sorry." He let go of her wrist slowly. "I know I can't tell you what to do."

He seemed to have trouble getting back to the conversation. She understood. Her heart was beating so loudly she could barely concentrate.

"It's all right." Her voice sounded husky, and she cleared her throat. "You're trying to be fair to everyone. But I just don't know what else to do."

"Maybe there's another way." He shook his head again, as if still trying to clear it. "I wasn't following you today, but I was trying to find you. Ruth mentioned she thought you were coming out here. I talked to Emma." There was the faintest hesitation in his voice as he said her name. "She asked me to tell you she'd like to stop and see you tonight."

Her breath caught. "Did she say why?"

"No, but that's a good sign, isn't it?"

He so obviously wanted to make things right for everyone that it touched her. The big, tough cop had a heart like a marshmallow.

"Maybe." She couldn't allow herself to hope. It wasn't safe to risk her happiness on other people. They so often let her down. She'd learned that before she'd learned to walk. "I guess I won't know until I see her, will I? Did she say what time?"

He shook his head. "Probably whenever she can get free after supper."

"Or when she can make some excuse." It was ridiculous to think that her own aunt had to sneak around in order to visit her.

"At least she's coming." His fingers brushed hers lightly, setting up a tingling that rushed across her skin. "Be happy with that for now. All right?"

"All right." Her fingers brushed his again, in spite of herself. "I'll try."

The flicker of hope she felt startled her. She'd better be more careful. If she spent too much time with Ted, she might actually start to believe in all those old-fashioned things he so obviously valued—things like family loyalty and happily ever after.

Chapter Seven

By the time she'd wiped the sink for the third time, Fiona had to admit that she was nervous about this impending meeting with her aunt. She glanced out the kitchen window. It was fully dark now, and loneliness seemed to close in on the house as the light went. Surely, if Emma was really coming, she'd be here by now.

Ted had said she would come, and she trusted him. That thought gave her pause. She did trust him. Quite aside from the attraction that flared each time they were together, she liked and trusted him. If he said Emma would be here, then she would.

Crossing quickly to the stove, she turned the gas on under the teakettle. She would treat this visit like a friendly social call, and maybe that's what it would be.

She leaned against the counter, waiting for the kettle to boil, her mind drifting back to those moments with Ted outside Miriam's house. She'd expect, if she were being honest, that it would be that surge of attraction that demanded her attention. Oddly enough, as powerful as that attraction had been, she found herself returning again and again to the sense of concern that had flowed from Ted.

He had cared that she was hurting. His sympathy had been the real thing, not some facile expression. He wanted to make things right for her, and that was stronger than any mere attraction could have been.

Her fingers curled against the edge of the countertop. Other people here cared about what happened to her—the Flanagans, maybe even Ruth and Susie. And she'd let them in—she'd started feeling for them in return.

That wasn't her way. She'd learned as a child that the best way to protect herself was not to open herself. Then it didn't hurt so much to be shipped off to another foster home at a moment's notice, or to sense that she was the outsider in her father's house.

The old ways of protecting herself didn't

seem to be working since she'd come here, but she didn't know how else to respond. Apprehension shivered through her. What if she opened herself up to these people and got kicked in the teeth for her trouble? How would she deal with that?

A knock stopped the downward spiral of her emotions. Rubbing her palms against her jeans, she went to open the door.

Emma gave a quick glance back over her shoulder as she stepped inside, but nothing was in the alley between the buildings but her buggy.

"Fiona, I am happy to see you." She shed her bonnet and cloak, revealing the simple dark dress and apron she always wore. "I am sorry if you have been waiting too long."

"Not at all." Fiona hung the cloak over the back of a chair. The kettle whistled, and she turned to pull it off the burner. "Will you have a cup of tea? Peppermint or Earl Grey?"

"Peppermint, that sounds good."

Fiona poured the tea, then lifted the tray on which she had the mugs ready, along with a small plate of poppyseed bread that Ruth had brought over earlier. "Let's go upstairs to my living room."

She'd half expected Emma to protest that

she couldn't stay long, since that seemed to be the pattern with any Amish visitors, but Emma nodded. She followed Fiona up the back staircase, her long dress rustling.

"This is nice, having the stairs that come right down to your kitchen. Saves time and steps, ja?"

"Yes, it does." She led the way into the living room, where the lamps were already on, bathing the room in their soft glow. "I haven't quite finished with the painting up here yet, but the room is livable, at least."

She was nervous, and that was making her babble. What had brought Emma here tonight? Surely she risked getting into trouble with her parents if they found out.

Emma sat on the sofa, looking around with frank curiosity as she picked up the steaming mug. "This is very nice." She fingered the afghan that was draped over the back of the sofa. "This is Elsie Schuler's work."

Fiona had to smile, despite the tension that skittered along her skin. "If I'd known how recognizable handwork is to you, I probably wouldn't have shown you my mother's quilt pieces."

"The quilt squares." Emma gave a quick,

characteristic nod. "I would like to see again."

That startled her. She'd have thought Emma would be happy to forget about them.

Fiona crossed to the bookcase and picked up the small dower chest, carrying it across to Emma. "Maybe you recognize the box, as well."

Emma took it, holding it at eye level for a moment, her eyes bright. "I know it. Our papa, he made one for each of the girls. Mine will go to my daughter one day." She sat the box in her lap, her fingers caressing it. "He made these with much love."

For Hannah, Fiona reminded herself. Not for the granddaughter he didn't want to know. Still, that love seemed to show in the precise corners and delicate painting, even after all this time.

Emma opened the lid carefully and lifted out the quilt pieces. She saw what was underneath and hesitated for a moment before picking up the cap and apron. Her eyes flickered. "So many years. I miss her still, my big sister."

Fiona's heart clenched. "I didn't think about that. I'm sorry."

"It is not your fault. The memories are

good ones." She fingered the delicate baby gown. "She made this for you."

"I suppose she did." Tears stung her eyes, and she blinked them back. "Why did you want to see the quilt patches again?"

Hannah set the box on the coffee table and turned the fabric squares over in her hands. "If you still want, I will make the quilt for you."

"Yes, of course I want. But your mother—"

"I will do it at Ruth's. No one will say anything to my mother about it." Her gaze met Fiona's and slipped away. "You understand, about her illness."

"I know that you're trying to protect her. I don't want to do anything to upset that." Her heart twisted at the thought that her grandmother had to be protected from her existence.

"She won't know," Emma repeated. She smoothed the squares with gentle fingers. "When I was very young, I had a doll, and a tiny cradle my father had made. Hannah— she was one of the grown-ups to me, because she was so much older. But she made a little quilt for the doll cradle." Her smile was soft. "So I will piece the quilt for you, and think of her."

Fiona's throat was too tight for words. She reached toward Emma, barely knowing that she was doing it, and Emma clasped her hand in a hard grip. Fiona couldn't be sure whether the tears that splashed on their hands were hers or Emma's, but they were melting the shell that protected her heart.

Much later that night, Fiona sat cross-legged on her bed, the dower chest open in front of her. Carefully she folded the tiny baby dress and tucked it inside, then the apron, and finally the cap.

She closed the lid, letting her fingers stroke the painted designs. Her grandfather had made this for his firstborn child. It didn't take a lot of imagination to picture the love in his face—after all, she'd seen fathers catching their first glimpse of a son or daughter.

Her heart was so full her chest seemed to ache with it. Another image filled her mind. Her mother, a blond, rosy-cheeked teen-ager, sat making a doll quilt for her little sister, sewing love into every stitch.

Had she felt that love when she'd sewn the tiny dress for her unborn child? Or had it been overshadowed by her sense of being a stranger in a strange land?

Tears spilled over onto her cheeks, and she wiped them away with her fingers. It was too late now, wasn't it, to cry for her mother? Too long for something she'd never known?

Through the blur of tears, she saw her past more clearly than she ever had. When she'd gone to live with her father and her stepmother, she'd known that they didn't welcome questions about her mother. If she'd been a different kind of child, the kind who demanded answers, perhaps things would have turned out differently.

She swung off the bed in a quick movement and put the dower chest on her dresser. She was being foolish, crying over something that was long past. She'd go to bed, and things would look better in the morning.

But even when she'd turned off the lights and curled up in bed, her busy mind wouldn't shut down. She stared at the ceiling, where a faint light reflected from Ruth's store next door, facing the thought that had nibbled at the edges of her mind for days.

Her father hadn't had to put her in foster

care with strangers. He could have sent her back to Pennsylvania after her mother died, even if he hadn't wanted to return himself.

The Flanagans would have taken her in, no matter what the quarrel was between her father and her uncle Joe. She'd seen enough of their warm, open hearts to know that.

And her mother's family? Her heart twisted. Would they have taken her in or turned their backs? She didn't know. Maybe she'd never know.

Lord... Her prayer choked on a sob. *I've held back all my life, always afraid of rejection if I got too close. Maybe I've even done the same thing with You. I can't seem to do that any longer, but I'm afraid to change. What if I can't? Please, help me see the way.*

She wiped the tears away again, too tired to get up and do something, too restless to seek refuge in sleep. She stared at the ceiling, trying to sense an answer in her heart. *What...*

Something crossed the rectangle of reflected light on the ceiling. She blinked. What had that been? A bird, maybe, flying between the two buildings—would that cause a shadow like that?

She lay still, watching. In a moment, another shadow crossed the pattern of light, and tension skittered along her skin. That was no bird, or anything else that had reason to be between the buildings or in Ruth's store at this hour of the night. That was a human shape.

Ruth, coming in to do some work? She turned cautiously, as if someone might hear her, looking at the bedside clock. It was hardly likely to be Ruth out and about, not at nearly two in the morning.

She slid out of bed, her bare toes curling into the rag rug, and shivered as she reached for the robe that lay across the footboard. Pulling it around herself, she padded silently toward the window. No one could see her, surely, as long as she didn't turn the light on.

Still, she stood to the side of the window, cold with tension, and peered out cautiously. There was the nearest window of Ruth's store—it was the window of the workroom, where the quilts were. If someone were there on legitimate business, they'd put on a light, wouldn't they? The soft glow was that of the dim light Ruth always left burning in the back room, visible only from the side or the back of the store.

She stood, undecided, clutching the curtain with one hand, her feet cold on the floorboards. She leaned forward, pressing her face against the pane. Her eyes must be growing accustomed to the faint light, because she could make out objects in the narrow passageway between Ruth's store and her house—the old-fashioned rain barrel that stood beneath Ruth's downspout, some boards the carpenters had leaned against the wall.

And a figure. He was mostly in shadow, but she saw the slight movement. On its heels came a sound, the faintest tinkle of breaking glass. Barely audible, it shrilled an alarm in Fiona's mind. The police—she had to call the police.

Afraid to turn on a light, she felt her way across the room and snatched her cell phone from the dresser, taking comfort from its glow. Even as she punched in 911, she remembered what Ted had said. Night calls went directly to him. The thought was oddly reassuring.

"Crossroads police, Ted Rittenhouse here."

She pressed the phone against her ear. "This is Fiona." She kept her voice low. She'd heard the glass break. Could they hear her? "Someone is in Ruth's store. I can see them moving around, and there's a person in the alleyway between her place and mine."

"Stay where you are." His voice was crisp, authoritative. "Are you upstairs? Are your doors locked?"

"Yes. But the store—they're in the quilt room."

"I'm on my way. Don't come out of your house until I tell you it's safe. And don't hang up."

She could hear the sound of the car's motor through the cell phone and realized that he was, literally, on his way.

"Don't worry about me. I'm fine. But all those quilts—"

"Better a quilt than you." He sounded grim. "I'm almost there."

She slid along the wall to the window. "I'm at the upstairs window." A crash interrupted her words, and she realized she was shaking at the violence that implied. In the city it would have sickened but not shocked her— here in this peaceful place it was obscene. "They've knocked something over."

Several things happened at once. She heard, faintly, the sound of a car. The lookout, if that's what he was, must have heard it, too. He moved, rapping sharply at the window frame.

"They've heard you." She rushed the words, as if that would make a difference. "They're coming out the side window, three of them, dark clothes, I can't make out their features. Running toward the back of the building. The other one, the lookout, he's running, too."

Ted muttered something, and then the wail of his siren shattered the night air. Too late now to worry about alerting the intruders. She shoved the window up, leaning out in hope of getting a better view of them.

Their figures were silhouetted briefly as they skirted the light cast by her back porch lamp. Teenagers, she'd guess, by their size and the way they moved. The first three had hoods up, turning them into featureless shapes. The last one—

She pulled back inside so sharply that she struck her head on the window frame, seeing stars for a moment. She sank down on the floor, rubbing her head, the cell phone dropping in her lap.

The last figure—she couldn't be mistaken. The dark clothes, the shape of the hat, the cut of the trousers—it had been someone in Amish garb.

Ted walked toward Fiona's back door, frustration tightening every muscle. He'd been close, so close. Closer than he'd ever been to catching or at least identifying the vandals, thanks to Fiona, but they'd slipped away again.

He glanced toward the dark patch of woods behind the store. Were they back there someplace, watching him? Common sense said they'd headed straight for home, but he couldn't shake off the thought. What kind of cop couldn't outwit a few teenagers?

No use feeling sorry for his circumstances, because they were his choice. He wasn't a big-city cop anymore, with plenty of backup and a forensic team. He was only one man, and they'd had just enough of a head start to elude him. He could only hope that Fiona had seen something that would help him identify them.

He rapped on the door, frowning at the glass window in it. Very nice to see who was out here, but also very easy for someone to break.

Fiona swung the door open, eyes widening at his expression. "What is it? What's wrong?"

"Nothing. I was just thinking that you should have something more secure for a back door—either a solid door or wire mesh over the window."

She stood back to let him enter the brightly lit kitchen. A kettle steamed gently on the stove, and the windowsills were bright with pots of yellow mums. "I thought this was a safe place to live."

"So did I." He pulled out his notebook and flipped it open. "Tell me exactly what you saw."

"What about Ruth's store? Have you told her? Did they damage the quilts?"

It was tempting to answer her, to get into a conversation between friends about what had happened, but he couldn't. He needed to get a statement from her as close time wise to the incident as possible so it wouldn't be contaminated in any way by his outside information.

"Concentrate on what you saw and heard." That sounded more abrupt than it needed to. "Please, Fiona. It's important to go over it before you forget."

"I'm not likely to forget." Her voice was tart. She picked up the mug of tea that sat on the table and held it between her hands, as if she needed its warmth. "I couldn't get to sleep, because—well, that doesn't matter."

Because of that visit from Emma? He longed to ask her, but that too would be sidetracking.

She clutched the mug a little more tightly. "The light that Ruth leaves on in the store reflects on my bedroom ceiling. I saw a shadow move across it." She frowned, as if trying to be sure she got it exactly right. "I waited a couple of minutes, thinking maybe it was a bird flying between the buildings, but then I saw it again and knew it was a person. I went to the window."

"Is it possible they could see you?" The last thing either of them needed was for the vandals to target her next.

She shook her head. "I was careful to stay back and leave the lights off." She shut her eyes briefly, as if to visualize what she'd seen. "There were people moving in the store. And there was one outside in the alley, in the shadow of the building."

"People? What kind of people? How

many?" His frustration put an edge to his voice.

Her lips tightened. "I'm telling you what I saw then. That was when I called you."

He was ticking her off, apparently. He regretted it, but duty came first. If he'd gotten here a little sooner—but he knew that was impossible. "Did you get a better look at them at any point?"

"The one outside, the lookout, must have heard your car. He said something to them, but I couldn't hear what. Then they all bailed out the window and started running down the alleyway between the buildings."

She came to a stop, but he sensed that there was more. "Your back porch light was on?"

She nodded, glancing toward it.

"Then you must have seen something when they ran past."

"Not much." Her tone was guarded. "The three who had been inside the store ran past first." She frowned a little, shaking her head. "I couldn't get a good look—it happened so fast. They all wore jeans and dark sweatshirts or maybe jackets with the hoods pulled up. Judging by their size and the way they moved, I'd guess they were teenagers, but I can't swear to that." She shrugged. "I'm sorry I can't be more help."

She was holding something back. He knew it, and it angered him.

"This is no time to be evasive. What else did you see? Come on, Fiona, out with it."

"Or what? You'll lock me up?"

"Or you'll be withholding evidence in a criminal case," he replied evenly. "And I know you don't want to do that."

She lifted a hand to her forehead, shoving her hair back, the fight going out of her. "No. Of course not. It's just that I—" She shook her head.

"Whatever it is, it's my job to figure out. Is it something about the fourth boy?"

She nodded. "He was several steps behind the others. When he passed the light I could see—not his face, but his clothing. He was wearing Amish clothing."

It was like a punch to the stomach. For a moment he couldn't say anything at all. Then he shook his head violently. "You must be wrong."

"I know what I saw." Her eyes flashed. "The hat, the dark jacket and pants—believe me, I'd like to be mistaken, but I'm not."

The pain behind her words convinced him. "It's just—" He shrugged, not knowing what to say. "It's unheard of, that's all. Even during their rumspringa, when they have more freedom to try things, Amish youngsters don't get up to criminal mischief, especially not with English teens."

Fiona rubbed the back of her neck tiredly. "I wish I hadn't seen it. But maybe it was some kind of a prank—a kid dressed up in Amish clothing, hoping to throw the blame on them."

"Possible, I suppose, if these kids are cleverer than I've been giving them credit for." Dread was building in him. Balancing between two worlds wasn't an easy thing at the best of times. If he had to arrest an Amish kid, he'd be landing in no-man's-land. "Look, are you sure—?"

"Do you think I like this any better than you do?" Fiona had to be at the end of her rope. "What do you think it will do to my practice with the Amish if word gets out that I'm accusing one of them?" She paled. "Please—this doesn't have to be public, does it? Maybe you can forget who told you."

He stiffened. "I have to do my duty, no matter how little I like it."

"I'm not asking you to break any laws." Her eyes darkened. "But does doing my duty as a citizen have to cost me a big share of my practice? The Amish community is already wary of me."

"I hope not." He shook his head, suddenly bone-tired. "I won't be making anything public while I'm conducting an investigation, but if it comes to an arrest, I can't promise you anything."

She gave a short nod, seeming to pull back into herself. "All right. I guess I can't expect anything else."

His duty stood like a barrier between them, and she must know it as well as he did. Unfortunately, there wasn't a thing he could do about it.

Chapter Eight

"This is going to look terrific." Nolie ran her paint roller over the wall of Fiona's living room, then stood back to admire the effect of the light moss green. "I love to paint. It makes everything look so fresh and new."

"You've come to the right place, then." Fiona divided her smile between Nolie and Aunt Siobhan, both clad in jeans and T-shirts, bandanas protecting their hair. "I can't tell you how much I appreciate your help."

And your support. She wanted to add that, but was still reluctant to expose how much they all meant to her.

"It's a pleasure." Aunt Siobhan, looking as young as one of her daughters in the casual clothes, swept a brush along the wood-work. "And besides, it gives us a chance to catch up with you. How is the practice going? Is it building the way you expected?"

Fiona frowned, watching the dingy tone of the wall disappear with a sweep of the roller. "I'm not sure just what I expected. I'm getting by, so far." She wouldn't tell them how slim her bank account had become. "But the Amish should be a large part of a nurse-midwife practice in this area, and so far that's not happening."

Siobhan's concerned expression seemed to say that she read what wasn't spoken. "You know that you can come to us if you need anything, don't you?"

Her throat tightened. She still wasn't used to the open-handed, open-hearted way these relatives had accepted her. "Thank you, but it hasn't come to that yet."

"Is this reluctance of theirs because of your mother's family? Have you had a chance to talk with them yet?" Nolie's roller moved in time with her question, efficient as always. No wonder she was able to juggle her family and her life-altering work so smoothly.

"I've talked with an aunt and a cousin," she said. "So far my grandparents haven't been willing to see me."

Distress filled Siobhan's eyes. "I'm sorry. That just seems so heartless—"

"It's not that," she said quickly. "I thought that at first, but it seems my grandmother ended up hospitalized with severe depression after my mother left. They're trying to protect her, not hurt me."

"Even so, it affects your livelihood," Nolie said. "It's so unfair."

And now she had that business with the vandals to add to her potential problems. At least according to Ruth, they'd been scared off before they'd done more than tip over a display stand. Even Ruth didn't know her involvement. Ted had said he'd keep her part quiet for the time being, but he clearly wouldn't bend any regulations for her. She'd come up against that rigid cop mentality of his a couple of times, and she didn't like it.

"Is something else wrong?" Siobhan's words were soft, but they pierced Fiona's heart. Her aunt Siobhan just saw much too clearly.

The longing to pour all her worries into her aunt's sympathetic ear almost overwhelmed her. Almost, but not quite. The old habit of holding back, not rocking the boat, was too strong to be overcome that easily.

"No, nothing." She managed a smile. "I guess I just didn't realize how much of an effect my mother's decision would have on me."

"Ripples in a pond," Siobhan said. "We can never know how many people will be affected by the things we do. It wasn't just your mother's decision, you know. Your father's actions caused their own set of problems."

"You mean with his brother?" Was she finally going to learn what the breach between Uncle Joe and her father was all about?

Siobhan's eyes were touched with sadness. "It was a terrible quarrel, terrible. Joe was as much to blame as his brother. He should have known you don't dissuade someone from falling in love by shouting at him."

Her throat tightened. "You mean their breach was caused by my mother?"

Siobhan caught her hand and held it firmly. "No, don't think that. It certainly wasn't your mother's fault. They fell in love, and the only way Michael could see to deal with the situation was by taking her away. Of course Joe thought they were too young, that Michael was ruining her life, and that he wasn't thinking it through. All that was true enough, but not what Michael wanted to hear.

"I'm so sorry that they've never made it up." Ripples in a pond, indeed.

"Well, what Joe never wanted to admit was that he'd always pictured Michael going into the fire service, as he and their other brother did. That rankled, when Michael was ready to throw that away. And then it turned into plain old Flanagan stubbornness, with neither of them willing to make the first move."

"Flanagans are famous for their stubbornness," Nolie said, bending to put her roller down on the tray. "But this seems over the top, even for a Flanagan."

"Of course it does." Siobhan's tone went brisk with what sounded like exasperation. "The sad part is that say what he will, that stubborn husband of mine will never really be right spiritually until he's forgiven his brother and himself for this foolish quarrel."

"I suppose my being here has only made it worse." Everywhere she turned, it seemed Fiona found more problems generated by her presence.

Siobhan's eyes widened. "If you think that, then I'm telling this all wrong. If not for that stupid quarrel, we'd have known earlier about your mother's death and maybe have been able to help. Your being here is finally making Joe take a long look at his behavior. Mind, I'm not saying he'll jump right in with an apology, but I think he's ready to mend things if your father is." She looked at Fiona expectantly.

Fiona felt helpless. "I don't know," she said. "Really, I don't. My father never talked about his brother, just as he never talked about my mother. I have no idea how he'd react if Uncle Joe called him."

"How did he react to your coming here?" Siobhan asked.

"He didn't like it." She could only hope her voice didn't betray how difficult that had been. She still cringed when she thought of that icy scene. "And it seems unanimous. My grandparents don't like it, either."

Or Ted. But she wasn't going to say that.

Siobhan gave her a hug, heedless of their paint-daubed clothes. "Well, it's not unanimous, because we love having you here. And it will work out with the others, too. You'll see." She kissed Fiona's cheek. "I'm praying for you. God will bring good out of this situation. I know it."

Siobhan's words still comforted her that evening as she turned off the light in the office. She'd sat there after supper, going over the records on her patients, organizing her files. The work comforted her, as Aunt Siobhan's words did. It affirmed who she was.

The difficult moment came when she'd turned off the lights and walked up the stairs, as she was doing now. This was the lonely time, she had to admit it. Crossroads was so quiet at night, the house incredibly still. Of course she'd rather have it that way than have the excitement of the break-in at Ruth's store.

She was bending over to take a magazine from the basket next to her chair when the phone rang. It was rare enough to hear it that the sound startled her. She picked it up.

"Fiona Flanagan."

"Fiona, I'm glad I caught you." Ted's voice crackled in her ear, and she caught the wail of a siren in the background. "Miriam Hostetler and her husband have been in an ac-

cident—a car hit their buggy. The paramedics are on their way, but she's asking
for you. Will you come?"

"Of course." A silent prayer for the young
woman and her husband filled her mind.
"How bad is it?"

"I'd have said not too serious, but she's
scared and shaken up and worried about
the baby. We're on the road you took to
their farm the other day—about three miles
past the Amish schoolhouse."

"I'm on my way." She hung up, snatched
her handbag and raced down the stairs to
pick up her medical kit as she rushed to the
car.

She spun out onto the road, mentally re-
hearsing the way to the farm. It would take
just minutes to get there, just time enough
to consider the possibilities. It was highly
unlikely for an accident to harm the baby at
this early stage, as well protected as it was,
but she'd learned to listen to the mother's
intuition. If Miriam thought something was
wrong, she had to take that into account.

*Lord, You're seeing what's going on far
better than I could. Please, be with Your ser-
vant Miriam now. Protect and comfort her.*

It seemed she'd barely finished the prayer

when she spotted the revolving lights on Ted's patrol car. The paramedic unit was on scene, too, and she grabbed her bag and rushed toward it, thanking God that the EMTs had gotten here so quickly. Miriam could use help from all of them.

The black buggy, smashed almost beyond recognition, lay on its side in the ditch, its battery-operated rear lantern still blinking. The big new sedan that had hit it, in comparison, looked barely touched, and she swallowed back anger at the unfairness of it all.

Ted met her at the rear of the unit. He grabbed her and swung her up next to the stretcher. "Let me have your keys," he murmured. "I'll see to your car."

She nodded, handing them over.

"Here's Fiona, Miriam. Just like you asked." The heartiness of his voice didn't quite mask his concern.

"Hi, Miriam." She kept her voice calm, even as her mind raced, considering possibilities. "How do you feel?"

Miriam's legs moved restlessly, and she turned her head from side to side, but she didn't speak.

Miriam lay on the stretcher, the paramedic

opposite Fiona bending over her. Only one paramedic in the Suffolk Fire Department had those bright-red curls—her cousin, Terry.

"Terry. I'm glad it's you. How is she?"

Terry's blue eyes were dark with concern. "Bumps and bruises, mainly. Shaken and scared." She straightened, turning her head and lowering her voice. "She's holding her belly, terrified for the baby. We'd best take her in, I think. Maybe you'll have better luck than I have at reassuring her."

Nodding, Fiona edged past her in the narrow confines of the unit to take Terry's place at the side of the stretcher. She knelt, clasping Miriam's hand. The girl was pale, her blue eyes wide with shock, as she clung to Fiona's hand.

"Miriam, I'm here. We're going to take good care of you. We want to take you into the hospital. Is that okay?"

"If you say so," Miriam whispered. "My Jacob, is he all right?"

Fiona glanced toward Terry, who nodded as she closed the rear doors.

"He's fine," Terry said. "One of the officers is going to drive him to the hospital, while Fiona and I stay here with you."

Miriam nodded. She was pale, sweating, and her hand kept going to her abdomen. "My baby," she murmured, her voice fading as if she didn't want to ask the question.

Fiona looked up at Terry again. "Vitals?"

"Everything okay, but—" Terry shook her head. Obviously her instincts, like Fiona's, told her something more was wrong. "See if you can get her to talk to you."

Fiona held Miriam's hand between both of hers. "Miriam, you have to tell us what's wrong, so we can help you. It's all right. Honestly."

Tears spilled over on the girl's ashen cheeks. "Cramps," she whispered. "I kept having them today. I'm afraid for the baby. That's where we were going. I told Jacob he must take me to you."

Her heart clutched. Cramping happened sometimes early in pregnancy with no ill effect, but she didn't like it, not combined with the accident and the way Miriam acted.

"Okay, I'm just going to have a quick look. You hold on. We'll be at the hospital soon." She maneuvered to the foot of the stretcher as Terry slapped the door that led to the cab of the unit.

"Hit the siren, Jeff."

The van accelerated, swaying a little, as the siren started to wail. Fiona pushed Miriam's dark skirt aside, moving gently, and saw what she feared she'd see.

Her gaze met Terry's over the patient, and it was as if they could read each other's thoughts. The siren's wail was like a mournful cry, echoing the pain in her heart.

Ted stalked down the hospital corridor. Ironic. He'd ended up bringing the driver of the car to the same hospital where Miriam was being treated, but in his case it was for a blood alcohol test. A salesman, the driver had been out celebrating a big sale and decided to take a shortcut back to Suffolk. He must have been ripping along the dark country road. The buggy hadn't had a chance.

Ted would never be able to prove the speed, of course, with no witnesses, but the lack of skid marks told the story, and the results of the blood alcohol test would seal the case.

Unfortunately, that wasn't going to ease the pain Miriam and her husband were feeling.

He rounded a corner, hesitated, and then

went forward. Miriam's and Jacob's parents waited, faces stoic, eyes bright with unshed tears. They must know what he'd just been told. Miriam had lost the baby.

"Joseph. Anna." Ted nodded toward the other set of parents, whom he didn't know as well as he did Jacob's family. "I'm very sorry."

"It is in God's hands," Joseph said. He clasped work-hardened hands together. His wife nodded, but Ted could feel her grief.

"Are you waiting to see Miriam?"

"The midwife is with her now." Joseph gestured slightly toward the door opposite them.

It stood ajar, and the tableau he saw made his breath catch. In the pool of light from a fixture above the bed, Fiona leaned forward, holding Miriam's hand, talking earnestly to her. Even in profile, he could see the warmth and caring that flowed from her toward the girl on the bed.

Jacob stood on the other side, head bent. Tears trickled into his beard, but he nodded, as if taking comfort from Fiona's words.

His throat tightened. Fiona had so much caring and devotion to give. This had to be tearing her up, too.

She moved, apparently catching sight of those who waited, and stood. She said something else, to the couple, and then bent to press her cheek against Miriam's before straightening and walking toward them.

She nodded to the parents, holding the door open so that they could file through. He heard Miriam give a soft cry at the sight of her mother, and the door swung shut, closing the family in, leaving him and Fiona alone in the hallway.

"Ted." Her voice trembled on the edge of tears. She wiped her eyes with her fingers. "I can't even begin to imagine—" She looked around blindly.

His heart twisted with pity. "Here." He grasped her arm and steered her toward a nearby door. "Let's go in the lounge."

Fortunately the room was empty. A lamp on the pale wood end table illuminated a hard-looking couch and a straight-backed chair. A few old magazines were strewn on a coffee table. He led her to the couch.

"Relax a minute. There's nothing else you can do for her now."

She sank down, covering her face with her hands. "There was nothing I could do at all.

Terry and I were right there, but we couldn't save the pregnancy."

Anger burned along his veins. "The accident—"

"The accident didn't cause the miscarriage." She looked up at him and shoved her hair back with her fingers. Her eyes were red, but she seemed under control. "It would be unlikely, since the baby's so well protected at this early stage. Miriam told me she was already having cramping. Jacob was bringing her to see me when the car hit them."

Her lips trembled, and she pressed them tightly together.

He sat down next to her. "I wish it could have had a happier outcome for them. And for you." That was as close as he could come to comforting her.

"I don't matter," she said quickly. "But Miriam—well, I tried to reassure her. The obstetrician from the birthing center will check her out as well, but I don't see any reason why she shouldn't have a successful pregnancy the next time."

"That's good news."

She nodded, but anger flickered in her eyes. "I hope it doesn't make things any easier for the driver. He can't be held responsible for the miscarriage, but he ought to spend time inside a cell for this."

"He'll be prosecuted, believe me." Almost without willing it, his hand had covered hers where it lay on the couch between them. "I have enough evidence, which is fortunate because Jacob and Miriam won't testify against him."

"Won't testify?" She turned a fiery gaze on him. "What do you mean?"

"Just that." He understood, but it didn't make his job any easier. "It's not the Amish way. They'll forgive, and they won't turn to the law. Even if they were actively being persecuted, they would leave rather than fight back. It's a matter of religious conviction with them."

The anger drained away from her expression, leaving her pale and tired looking. "I guess maybe I need to work a little harder on the forgiveness aspect of being a Christian. Right now I can only ask God why this happened."

His fingers curled around hers. "I don't think He minds a few honest questions. Or even a little honest anger. At least I hope not, or I'm in trouble."

"Is that part of why you left the Amish community?" She turned slightly toward him, and for the first time he felt as if the barriers between them had weakened.

"Among other things." He shook his head. "I can never leave entirely. It's a part of me, even though I can't live the life."

"You're doing a balancing act between two worlds." She said what he had often thought, and it moved and startled him that the understanding could come from someone he thought of as an outsider.

"That's it. Sometimes I feel as if I really am one of the 'world people.' And then I'll hear someone blaming the Amish for causing accidents by driving buggies on public roads—"

"That's ridiculous."

"Yes." He felt the conviction harden in him. "Driving under the influence caused tonight's accident, and justice will be done because that's the law, not because I know and care about the folks who were injured."

"You can't stop caring." Her hand turned so that their palms touched, their fingers entwining, and her warmth flowed through that touch.

"No, I can't." He barely murmured the words.

Something—her closeness, the silent room, the touch of her hand—was making him loosen the grip he kept on his emotions. His gaze met hers, and he felt as if he were drowning in the cool gray depths of her eyes. "Fiona—"

It was no good. Nothing rational would come out of his mouth. Instead, all he wanted to do was follow his instinct. And instinct meant touching the curve of her smooth cheek, tilting her face toward his, covering her lips with his.

For an instant she seemed to hold back. And then she leaned into the embrace, her hand moving on his arm in a gentle caress. Tenderness flooded through him, and for a dizzying moment he thought he'd be content to stay this way for hours.

Unfortunately, reason clamored to be heard. This was a public room, and someone could walk in at any moment. He pressed his cheek against hers and then reluctantly drew back.

"I guess this isn't the right place," he murmured.

She looked dazed for an instant. Then she

shook her head, as if needing to clear it, and managed to smile coolly, as if they hadn't just kissed each other senseless.

"I guess not." She rose, glancing around. "I must have left my bag in the ER. I'd better pick it up and head home."

He thought of touching her shoulder, but that probably wasn't a good idea, when it would just make him want to kiss her again. "You don't have your car here, remember? I had someone drive it back to your place. I'll drop you off."

There was a certain amount of wariness in the look she gave him, but she nodded. Well, he could understand that, because he felt the same. He needed to do some serious thinking before he let this relationship get any deeper.

But as he followed Fiona out into the hospital corridor, he knew he couldn't kid himself about one thing. He'd begun to care about her, maybe too much, and he couldn't do a thing about that.

Chapter Nine

Fiona stood in the afternoon sunshine on her porch, trying not to grin like an idiot as the latest of a flow of new patients climbed into the waiting black buggy. Five new patients in the past few days, and four of them were Amish.

Still smiling, she turned to look at the carved wooden sign beside her door: Fiona Flanagan, Nurse-Midwife. Was it her imagination, or did it glow a bit brighter today?

"Is something wrong with the sign?"

Ted's voice broke into her mood, but instead of shattering it, it just made her more optimistic. Cautious, but optimistic.

"Not at all. I was admiring it."

She turned to find him in that familiar posture, one foot planted on the step, his hand braced against the porch railing. He was in uniform, the light-gray shirt fitting snugly across his broad shoulders. The slant of sunlight brought out gold flecks in his brown hair. He looked good—good enough that she had to suppress the urge to put her arms around him.

She hadn't seen him for several days—not since that kiss at the hospital, in fact.

His gaze was focused on the sign, not on her. Did that imply that the memory made him uneasy or that he wanted to forget what had happened between them?

"It's not a bad piece of work, though I sound prideful when I say it."

"I take it 'prideful' is a no-no in the Amish world."

"You take it correctly." He smiled suddenly, the movement rearranging the hard planes of his face into something more approachable. "Although if polishing a buggy until it shines or stitching the most perfect quilt doesn't involve a tiny bit of pride, I'll eat my hat."

The smile nearly undid her, setting up ripples of warmth that had nothing to do with the sunshine. "I guess saying the words out loud is the problem." She flicked a bit of dust from the carved letters. "Actually, I was thinking that maybe the sign isn't so much a hope as a reality, the way things are going."

"New clients?" He leaned against the railing, apparently in no hurry to move on.

She couldn't suppress the grin. "Five of them, and four are Amish." She spread her hands wide. "I don't understand it. Really, I don't. And it's not just the new clients. In the past couple of days, people have suddenly started greeting me on the street as if I've been here for years. It's great, but a little unnerving."

She was looking to Ted for answers, she realized. Somehow she'd started depending on him for an interpretation of all the things she didn't understand in this new life of hers. Usually that realization would be a signal to run in the opposite direction, but she didn't feel like running.

His eyebrows lifted. "You honestly don't get it? It's because of Miriam."

"Miriam? But why? I didn't even succeed in saving her pregnancy."

Sorrow touched her, and the knowledge that no one could have done better didn't remove the sadness, although maybe it made it a little easier to bear.

He studied her face. "You've been out to the farm, I hear. How is she doing?"

"Physically, she's recovering nicely. Emotionally—" She could hear the frustration in her own voice. "I've tried to counsel her as I would any patient who's suffered a miscarriage."

"Is that a problem?"

She shrugged. "She's been reluctant to talk. I think her feelings are at war with accepting God's will. If she doesn't want to talk to me, that's fine, but she should talk to someone."

"Her sister's going to stay with her for a while. Maybe that will help." He smiled. "I know that was your suggestion. You aren't angry that Aaron told me that, are you? I mean with patient-doctor privilege and all…"

"I guess not." An answering smile tugged at her lips. "How do you know everything that happens?"

"Gossip," he said. "It's invaluable to a cop. I just wish it would turn up those vandals for me. So you shouldn't wonder about your five new patients. Everyone knows how kind you were."

"I only did what any midwife would do."

"Maybe so, but it was you. You were there

for her. You went out of your way to stay with her and comfort her. People admire that."

Some emotion crossed his stolid face, but it was gone again so quickly that she wasn't sure what it was. Do you admire that, Ted?

"Even so—" she began, but he stopped the words by touching her hand. For a moment she couldn't think clearly enough to say anything.

"Let people appreciate you." The normally low timbre of his voice went even deeper. "Don't turn away from that, Fiona."

Was he talking about the inhabitants of Crossroads? Or about himself? If she had the courage to ask him that, what would he say?

"Ted Rittenhouse, are you just going to stand there like a moonstruck calf or are you going to hitch my horse?" a female voice complained behind them.

Fiona spun around, heat rushing to her cheeks. Her cousin Rachel leaned forward on the buggy seat, reins in her hands, blue eyes sparkling. Neither of them had even heard the buggy approach.

Rachel looked from Fiona to Ted with a

satisfied smile, as if she enjoyed knowing she'd startled them.

Ted straightened, unhurried. "Since you ask so nicely, Miss Rachel, I'd be happy to give you a hand." He wrapped the line Rachel tossed him around the porch railing. The horse dropped its head and began munching the narrow strip of grass next to the steps.

"Rachel, it's nice to see you." And unexpected. She hadn't seen anything of her young cousin in days. "Can you come in?"

"I can stay only for a minute. I am on an errand." Rachel hopped down lightly from the high seat, ignoring the hand Ted held out to her. She came up the steps to Fiona, excitement dancing in her pert face.

Ted patted the mare's neck. "Just how fast were you coming down the road, young lady? Bessie's all sweated up."

Rachel made a face at him. "Not nearly so fast as the cars do."

For an instant Fiona saw the mangled buggy again, and heard Miriam's sobs. A shiver she couldn't control went through her. "You should be careful out on the road."

"I can be nothing but careful, with pokey old Bessie between the shafts." She caught

Fiona's hand. "You will never guess why I have come."

"If she won't guess, Rachel, you'd best come right out and tell her," Ted said. "It's not polite to tease."

Rachel's fingers tightened on hers. "Our grandfather has asked me to come to see you. You are invited to supper on Saturday evening. The whole family will be there. You'll come, won't you?"

She couldn't respond. An invitation to supper with her mother's family was the last thing she'd expected after weeks of being ignored.

"You will come, won't you?" Rachel repeated, worry darkening her blue eyes. "I said for sure you would come if we asked you. Please, Cousin Fiona."

How could she resist Rachel's enthusiasm? "Of course I'll come. I appreciate the invitation."

And even if she never saw them again after this one night, at least she'd have had a glimpse of what her mother had come from. Maybe that would ease the restlessness within her.

Rachel let out her breath in a whoosh of relief. "That is good. And Ted is invited, too,

so there will be someone else you know."
She gave Ted a teasing glance. "You won't
mind that, will you?"

Fiona paced across the waiting room Saturday evening, glancing out the bow windows for a glimpse of Ted. Were the dark
skirt and blazer she wore suitable for supper
with her mother's conservative Amish kin?
She hadn't any idea.

Up to this point, when she'd gone into an
Amish home, it had been in her professional
capacity, and she hadn't thought much of
what she wore. This evening was different.

She could have asked Ted's advice about
what to wear, but she'd been too embarrassed after that episode with Rachel—especially the girl's obvious enjoyment at
teasing her and Ted about their friendship.
Friendship, not relationship—she wouldn't
admit to anything serious. Not yet.

Did the entire township recognize the attraction they held for each other? If so, she
could just imagine the talk. She folded her
arms across her chest, hugging herself.

The familiar response welled up in her. Walk
away. Pretend it didn't happen. Pretend you
don't care. That way no one can hurt you.

But the old way of reacting wasn't working for her any longer. She actually felt like taking a risk—on Ted, on her mother's family— even knowing she could get hurt. Maybe God had led her to a situation where she had to change and where the reward for change might be greater than she'd ever dared to hope.

She glanced at her watch. Ted had said he'd pick her up, but no cars were in sight, only one Amish buggy coming down the road. It pulled to a stop in front of her steps. Ted held the reins.

This was the last thing she'd expected, and it took a moment to recognize the feeling in the pit of her stomach as apprehension. Grabbing her handbag, she went quickly out the door and down the steps.

Ted jumped down as she approached. Wearing dark pants and a light-blue shirt, he looked as if he'd dressed to blend in, if not to match. She straightened her jacket.

Was she only imagining it, or did his blue eyes soften when he looked at her?

"I hope you don't mind." He gestured toward the buggy. "I borrowed this from my brother. I thought you might enjoy seeing how your relatives travel."

She tried to block out the image of the overturned buggy. "That's nice of you."

"Sorry." He apparently understood what she didn't say. "That was stupid of me. After the accident—well, it will just take a few minutes to go back and get the car."

He started to turn, and she stopped him with a quick touch on the arm. At least, she intended it to be quick, but somehow her hand lingered at the sensation of warmth and strength under the smooth cotton of the shirtsleeve.

"Don't. It's all right." She pulled her hand away, confused by the rush of feelings. "You're right. I would like to experience riding in a buggy." She glanced up at the step. "Rachel hops up and down so handily that I didn't realize it was that high. In this skirt—"

"Not to worry." He grasped her waist, the movement taking her breath away. "I'll help you." He lifted her easily.

She grasped the edge of the seat and pulled herself into place, hoping he couldn't see the flush she was sure colored her cheeks. "Thank you."

He paused for a moment, hand braced against the buggy, looking up at her. "Are you sure this is okay?"

"Positive." She managed a smile. "I want to understand how my mother lived. I think it will help me make sense of who I am."

He nodded, then walked quickly around the back of the vehicle and swung himself up easily. He picked up the reins with a sureness that reminded her that this had been part of his life, too, for a long time.

Could he ever leave that fully behind? Not living here, certainly. She'd think, having made the decision, that he'd want to be as far as possible from reminders of what he'd given up. Or had he come back out of lingering feelings for Emma? He hadn't given her any sense of that when she'd seen them together.

He clucked to the horse, and they moved off. The swaying of the high seat sent her off balance. She grasped the seat with one hand and pulled her skirt down with the other.

"Don't worry," Ted said. "You're dressed fine."

"Really?" She was ashamed of her need for reassurance. "I don't want to offend anyone."

"You won't. They're used to being around the English."

The English. The outsider. Well, she knew that role. She could cope. But what was Ted thinking about this invitation?

She glanced at him. The setting sun brought out glints of gold in his hair, gilding his tanned skin. The ease with which his body moved to accommodate the shifts of the buggy, the strength of his hands, holding the reins—she felt her attraction for him growing with each—well, maybe she'd better get the conversation moving.

"Are you okay with this? I mean, you've tried so hard to protect my grandparents from being hurt by my presence."

He shrugged, frowning at the horse's back. "Maybe I was wrong to interfere. In any event, they've taken it out of my hands now."

It wasn't exactly a rousing vote of confidence, but it would have to do. "Have you heard anything about why they've changed their attitude?"

"I've always heard something, you know that." He smiled. "Apparently Emma and Rachel have been encouraging your grandmother to see you."

A frisson of apprehension slid down her spine. "I don't want to cause problems for her. What if seeing me brings back all her grief for her daughter?"

Ted grasped her hand firmly. "Don't over-analyze it, Fiona. She's asked for you. I don't see how you can do anything else but go."

The warmth from his hand traveled up her arm. "I guess I'm feeling protective of her, too."

He grinned. "There's a lot of that going around."

"You should know. I've never met anyone with a stronger protective sense." She swayed with the movement of the buggy, beginning to sense the rhythm of it.

"That's the police motto. To serve and protect." His tone was light, but there was a thread of something darker underneath it.

"People appreciate that," she said, wondering if appreciate was the right word.

His shoulders moved. "I guess. Amish folks might not exactly approve of my profession, but at least they trust me. And I know I can trust them."

Emotion colored the words; they reached out and clutched her heart. This was important to him, maybe the most important thing.

"Is that why you came back to Cross-roads? Because you could trust the people here?"

His eyes darkened, and for a moment she thought he'd tell her to mind her own business. Then he shrugged. "Maybe. Maybe I just realized I didn't belong in a big-city police force and never would."

"You were pretty young when you went there, weren't you?" She was feeling her way, trying to get at the source of all that suppressed emotion.

"Young. And naive." He gave a short laugh, but it didn't sound as if he found anything very humorous. "Talk about hayseed—I'm surprised I didn't literally have hay in my hair."

"That must have made it tough for you at the police academy." She tried to picture that young Amish farm boy thrown in with a bunch of tough cops. She couldn't quite reconcile that boy with the man he was now.

"I was the butt of every joke, believe me. I grew up in a hurry. I had to." He shrugged. "Things got better after a while. I still felt like a fish out of water, but I made some friends. It helped that I was doing what I really wanted to do." He glanced at her. "You know what that's like. If you're doing the work you know you're created to do, that makes up for a lot."

"Yes." Her voice choked a little. How was it that he seemed to see things in her that other people didn't, like the pain of trying to fit in? Maybe because he'd been through it, too. "So you started work as a Chicago cop."

"Saw things I'd never seen before, that's for sure." His jaw tightened. "Things I'd rather not see. Still, I had a good partner, an older cop who showed me the ropes. I'd have been lost without Steve."

"But something went wrong." She just seemed to know, the way he knew things about her. They turned into a lane, and she grasped the seat railing as she swayed against him. "What was it?"

The sun dipped below the horizon, painting the clouds with red and purple, as if it wanted to linger a bit longer.

"Went wrong. That's a nice way of putting it." His hands must have tightened on the reins, because the horse tossed its head. "We were in on a drug bust, a big one. Guess I was proud of my role in that. It seemed as if I was finally getting where I wanted to be."

He was silent for a moment, seeming to study the stubble of corn in the fields on either side of the road. She didn't speak, knowing there was more but afraid to push.

Finally he sighed. "Some of the drugs went missing. The investigation showed there weren't many people who'd had access to them. Internal Affairs got an anonymous tip that I was the one."

"But you—they couldn't accuse you on the basis of an anonymous tip."

"They didn't accuse me, exactly. I was suspended, pending investigation. It never occurred to me that anyone I knew could think I'd do something like that. I found out I was wrong. Everyone believed it. Even my partner." He paused. "Especially my partner." Bitterness laced the words.

"He was the one?" She barely breathed the words, her heart hurting for the pain and betrayal he'd suffered.

He nodded. "The truth came out, eventually. He was arrested. I was cleared. But it was never the same after that."

"The others must have tried to make things right with you."

"They did." He shrugged. "I couldn't blame them, I guess. But they hadn't trusted me, and I'd found out that I couldn't trust them."

"So you came home."

"I learned that trust was the one thing I couldn't live without. So I came home."

"As hard as it was," Fiona said softly. "It brought you back here, where you belong."

He didn't react for a moment, long enough for her to wish she'd said something else. Then he actually chuckled, putting his arm around her shoulders and drawing her closer against him. She could feel the laugh moving in his midsection.

"I never thought I'd say this, but you remind me of my brother Jacob."

She pictured the Amish carpenter. "I do?"

"The one and only time we talked about what happened to me in Chicago, he said pretty much the same thing. He said it reminded him of the story of Joseph."

She blinked. "You mean Joseph in the Old Testament? I guess he did have some grief over not being trusted."

"True, but that's not what my brother was thinking about. He reminded me that even when he was betrayed by those he'd loved, Joseph could still forgive. And he could say that even though they'd meant what they did for evil, God meant it for good." He snuggled her closer to his side. "I didn't see it that way at first, but I've come to think Jacob was right."

She nodded, thinking of her own favorite verse. "I try to believe that 'in all things, God works for the good of those who love Him.' Sometimes it's not easy."

"I know. But once I accepted that, I realized I was exactly where I was meant to be." He smiled. "Even if God did have to hit me upside the head with a two by four to get me here."

She thought about the implication of his words, warmed both by the strength of his body next to her and by his confiding in her. Their bodies swayed together with the movement of the buggy, and she wished the ride could go on forever.

It couldn't, of course. They were almost to the farmhouse, and she had to find a way through the difficult times ahead. Maybe, thanks to Ted, she was a little more ready to face them.

Chapter Ten

Ted drew into a spot in the lineup of buggies near the barn and slid down. It looked as if the whole Stolzfus extended family had already arrived and was waiting for them.

Maybe it would have been better if he'd brought the car. Somehow the buggy had a way of encouraging intimate conversation. That was the only explanation he could think of for having told Fiona all of that. He didn't normally talk about what had happened to him—hadn't, in fact, since he'd unburdened himself to his brother when he'd first come back to Crossroads.

He took his time fastening the horse to the hitching rail and walking around the buggy, trying to get a handle on this need to confide in someone he'd only known a month. After all, he'd known he could trust Jacob to tell people only what they needed to hear. Did he really trust Fiona that way?

Trust was a precious thing. He'd grown up taking it for granted, not knowing how valuable it was until he'd lost it. He'd have to guess that confiding in her said something about the feelings he was starting to have for Fiona.

He reached up to help her down from the high buggy seat. Her face was tight with apprehension, so he squeezed her hand. She had enough on her plate right now without adding him and his concerns to the mix.

Besides, the habit of caution was strong within him. He wouldn't do or say anything he might have cause to regret.

He held her hand a moment longer than he had to. "Are you ready to do this?"

She nodded, trying to smile and not quite succeeding. "You will give me a kick under the table if I make any bloopers, won't you?"

"You've got it." The impulse to continue holding her hand was strong, but he beat it back. "Don't worry. You'll be fine. And you already know Emma and Rachel. They'll help."

They walked together toward the kitchen door. Did she realize that in the country, family and friends always came and went by the back door? He'd given it some thought, but he wasn't going to lead Fiona to the front door, as if she were a stranger. She belonged, whether anyone wanted to admit it or not.

They'd barely reached the steps when the door was thrown open and Rachel was smiling at them. "You're here at last. And you came by buggy."

"I thought Fiona would enjoy it." He stood back to let Fiona enter first.

She hesitated for an instant before moving, but Rachel grabbed her hands and drew her inside.

"Ach, your hands are cold." Rachel frowned at him. "Ted, you should have warned her she might need mittens."

"Yes, ma'am, I should have. You'd make a good boss, Rachel, you know that?"

"Better than some I know." She put her arm around Fiona's waist. "Now you must meet the family. Don't worry about remembering everyone's name."

Ted ducked his head slightly, coming into the kitchen. The doorway hadn't been made for someone his height. Since he was behind Fiona, he got the full effect of all those

pairs of eyes focused on her. It was intimidating enough, and that was just the few
who were in the kitchen. Goodness knew
how many Stolzfus kin would eventually
gather around for the meal.

To her credit, Fiona didn't freeze. She
moved forward, greeting Emma with what
might have been relief in her voice at the
sight of a familiar face. He stood back, letting Emma take over introducing Fiona to
the other women.

Her grandmother, he noticed, wasn't yet
present. Was she still over in the daadi
haus, the cottage the older couple had retired to when eldest son Daniel had taken
over the farm? Was she perhaps regretting
this visit?

If Fiona wondered about her grandmother's absence, it didn't show, as she
politely greeted one woman after another.
The elder Stolzfus couple had had five
children—Hannah the eldest, Emma the
youngest, and the three boys sandwiched in
between, but the family had grown with
marriages and children and those children's
marriages until they'd probably sit down
close to thirty around the long tables.

He'd known them all his life, and he had a

tad of difficulty keeping all the young ones straight, but Fiona seemed to be doing a fine job of it. Because it meant so much to her, or because she was determined not to appear rude in front of all these unfamiliar family members? He wasn't sure.

The men, hearing all the fuss, began filing in to be introduced. He was just exchanging a few words about the winter wheat with Daniel when a silence fell over the crowded kitchen. John Stolzfus stood in the doorway, his tall frame bent a little with age, his beard snowy white below his weathered face.

For a moment he and Fiona stared at each other. Then he nodded gravely. "You are welcome in our house, Fiona."

"I'm pleased to be here," she answered, just as formally. "It was kind of you to invite me."

He turned toward Mary, Daniel's wife, with a question about supper. That seemed to break the tension, and a hum of conversation began again. Ted edged forward as unobtrusively as possible until he stood beside Fiona.

"So far, so good," he murmured.

She glanced at him. "Is it good?" He heard the fear in her voice.

"Plain folks are always a little formal with newcomers." That wasn't really an explanation, and he knew it. "Just give this a little time. It'll work out."

"I wish—"

Whatever she wished, he apparently wasn't going to hear it, as Mary directed everyone to the table except for her appointed helpers.

"In other words, she wants all non-essential personnel out of the kitchen." He touched Fiona's arm, nudging her toward the two long tables that had been set up to accommodate the crowd. "I hope you brought your appetite, because someone's sure to be disappointed if you don't try everything."

"Ach, don't listen to him," Emma said, whisking past them to deposit a steaming bowl of potatoes on the table. "Just be sure you have my cucumbers in sour cream. And don't forget to eat yourself full." Smiling, she scurried back toward the kitchen for another load.

He was holding out a chair for Fiona when he felt her fingers tighten on his arm. He looked up.

Her grandmother came toward the table, moving slowly. It wasn't until she reached the chair next to her husband that she glanced toward those gathering around the table. It felt to him as if each person held his or her breath.

Louise placed one hand on the table, leaning on it as she seemed to force herself to look at Fiona. The silence stretched. Even the children were still. Louise's lips trembled, her eyes filling with tears. Then she nodded and sat down heavily.

Fiona's fingers dug into his arm, and the tension zigzagged from her to him and back again. He sensed the battle going on inside her. Gently, he nudged her toward the chair.

She sat down, and he settled into the seat next to her. If all he could do to help her was be beside her, that was what he'd do.

The meal had begun with a long prayer in German and continued through a bewildering assortment of dishes to an array of pies and cakes for dessert. When Emma had said she should eat herself full, she hadn't been kidding. Fiona felt as if she'd split a seam in her jacket if she ate another bite.

Chicken, ham, chicken pot pie, pickled

beets, hot potato salad, molded salads... the food seemed endless. Some of the dishes she'd never tasted before, like the dried corn casserole, with its nutty flavor, and the relish her aunt called chow-chow, made, she said, with everything that was left in the garden at the end of the season. Obviously the Amish didn't like to let anything go to waste.

Fiona glanced at Ted, who had three different kinds of pie on his plate and was eating through them happily. The slice of dried apple pie she'd taken was delicious, but she couldn't possibly finish it.

Emma leaned over her chair and took the plate. "I will make you a basket to take home for tomorrow," she said.

Ted looked up at her. "What about me? Don't I get a basket?"

"You already had more than your share, you did." She cuffed him on the shoulder, gave him a sisterly smile and carried plates toward the kitchen.

Her grandfather's chair scraped as he stood, and he said something in the low German that was the home language for the Amish. Ted leaned closer to translate, his warm breath stirring her hair.

"The kids are scattering to do their chores, and the men will wander out of range of any dishwashing. It might be a good move if you offered to help in the kitchen." He looked at her rather tentatively, as if afraid she'd consider that comment a putdown.

"Of course I'll help." She slid her chair back. "You go smoke a pipe, or whatever the guy thing is."

He nodded and followed Fiona's uncles toward the front porch. She picked up a couple of serving bowls. In spite of her confident words, she still felt unsure of her welcome.

Ted paused at the door, glancing back, and gave her a smile and a thumbs-up sign. When she turned, her answering smile lingering on her lips, she found Emma watching the doorway where Ted had disappeared, her face unreadable.

Did Emma resent what she saw when she looked at the two of them? If Rachel was aware of their attraction, surely Emma would be, too. She might be remembering her first love, and how it had ended because of Fiona's mother.

Emma turned, saw Fiona watching her

and smiled, eyes twinkling. "That Ted, he is a good boy, ja?"

"Not a boy any longer."

"No, I forget." Emma put her arm companionably around Fiona's waist as they walked to the kitchen. "To me he is always the boy he was."

"The boy you loved?" She couldn't believe she'd actually said the words.

"We were sweethearts, ja, once upon a time. But our paths went different ways, and I have never regretted my choice." She handed Fiona a dish towel, seeming to take it for granted that she would help. "I would be very happy if you and he found yourselves on the same path."

"We're—we're just friends," she said quickly, taking the hot bowl Mary had just set in the dish drainer. "That's all." She rubbed the bowl vigorously, hoping her expression didn't give anything away.

Emma scraped plates into a bucket that sat next to the sink. "That's too bad, that is. It's time for Ted to settle down, don't you think?"

The question seemed to be addressed to the whole room, and a chorus of agreement answered her question. Cheeks burning, Fiona picked up another bowl.

"We won't tease you anymore," Sarah said. Daniel and Mary's eldest daughter was a slightly more mature version of Rachel, with her rosy cheeks and blond hair, but with round glasses that gave her a more serious air. "You and your coming-to-call friend want to take your time, ja?"

It was probably useless to say that Ted wasn't her coming-to-call friend, and she'd welcome anything that would get them off the subject. "Yes, that's right," she said, mentally apologizing to Ted for the evasion.

Sarah's intervention seemed to work, because the conversation steered away from her, bouncing around the kitchen from woman to woman in time with the clink of dishes. She sorted them out, finally, in the little breathing space it gave her.

Mary, Daniel's wife, was clearly in charge, a cheerful, buxom woman who seemed to relish her role as farmer's wife and who directed the household in a calm, firm manner. Was she what Hannah would have been, if she'd stayed?

There was Sarah, her eldest daughter, who taught in the Amish school, followed by a couple of boys, then Rachel, then young Levi, the baby of the family. The boys had headed for the barn to do evening chores, but the girls hung around, helping in the kitchen, joining in the cheerful conversation.

The wives of her mother's other two brothers were there, too—shy, quiet Anna and hearty Margaret, whose laugh bubbled like a flowing brook. Their daughters, hair in braids, were younger than Rachel, who seemed to enjoy bossing them around as they helped.

Would this have been her life if her father had sent her back to Hannah's family instead of putting her in foster care? Would she have been sweet and sassy, like Rachel, or would she have rebelled, like her mother?

She couldn't change the past, but she couldn't help wondering. She'd never want to give up her career, but still, she envied them this family warmth and the secure place they had in their world.

"Your practice, it goes well, does it?" Anna reached across her to put silverware in a drawer.

"It has been picking up. I've had a few long drives this week to some outlying farms."

"Ach, yes, you had best hope Margaret Beachey does not go into labor on a rainy night. Your automobile could get lost in the mud puddles in their lane."

"If she took the old road over the ridge—" Sarah began.

"She would never find it in the dark," Margaret said. "Better she tells Amos Beachey to fix his lane if he wants the midwife to make it to his wife in time."

Apparently Amos Beachey was known for being the only Amishman in the valley who didn't keep his farm in good order, so that led to one silly suggestion after another about how to solve the problem.

The only one who didn't join in the lively talk was her grandmother. Fiona glanced at her quickly, not wanting to be caught staring. Her grandmother seemed to be taking a very long time putting leftovers in the gas-powered refrigerator. Maybe she welcomed that as an excuse not to talk.

And maybe all the lively conversation the others provided was a screen to mask her grandmother's silence. Or a way of protecting her from the pain caused by Fiona's presence.

I don't want to hurt her. I just don't know what to do. Please—

The kitchen fell silent as abruptly as if someone had turned a switch. Her grandmother walked toward her. Fiona held her breath, not sure what was happening. Her grandmother reached out, almost tentatively, and touched her cheek.

"At first I thought there was nothing in you of my Hannah," she said slowly. "But I look into your eyes, and I see her there."

Fiona's throat went tight. "I never knew where my gray eyes came from, until I came here."

"It was right that you came." Her grandmother's cheeks glistened with tears, but she smiled. "When I first saw the quilt, I was afraid, but that was wrong."

"I'm sorry," she said quickly. "About bringing the quilt pieces to Ruth's that day. I didn't realize anyone would recognize them."

"It makes no matter." Her grandmother patted her cheek. "The quilt is a good thing. Emma will finish piecing it soon."

That brought a gasp from Emma. "You know about it?"

"Ja, I know. And when the quilt top is ready, we will have a quilting party. Fiona will come, and we will all finish her mother's quilt together. That is what is right."

She could only stand there like an idiot, trying to keep the tears from spilling over, her heart ready to burst.

The clop-clop of the horse's hooves echoed on the dark ribbon of road as Ted turned the buggy back toward Crossroads. Fiona hugged her jacket closer around her against the evening chill, but the cold air didn't really bother her. She was still warmed by her grandmother's hug when she'd said goodbye to everyone at the farm.

"Cold?" Ted reached behind the seat with his free hand and pulled out a plaid blanket, spreading it over her lap. "Is that better?"

"I'm fine." The happiness that bubbled up within her wanted to burst free. "I can't tell you what this evening meant to me."

She glanced back, watching as the yellow lights of the house disappeared behind a row of trees. She could see the reflection of the red battery-powered lantern as it blinked a soft good-night from the back of the buggy.

Ted's arm slid comfortably around her

shoulders. "I'm glad it worked out. I take it your grandmother finally talked to you."

"She did. She said I reminded her of my mother. No one ever said that to me before." Her throat got tight at the thought. "I guess I didn't realize how much I wanted to hear that."

"Hannah would be happy that her daughter and her mother are together."

That didn't seem to need an answer, and she just let the thought settle into her heart. Her mother would be happy. That was a good way of thinking about it, making her feel the strength of family connection, threading from mother to daughter through the generations.

Ted drew her a little closer, and she rested her head against his shoulder, enjoying the solid strength of him. Despite the chill, the night was perfect, with a nearly full moon riding low over the nearest ridge. The only sound was the clop of the horse's hooves, the creak of the buggy's wheels and the rustle of grass along the road as some night creature passed.

"Look," Ted said softly.

The buggy's lantern cast its yellow circle on a red fox that stood at the edge of the road, head high, nostrils quivering as it deciphered their scent. Then it was gone in a blur of scarlet, darting off into the shelter of the stubbly field.

"Beautiful." She tilted her head to look up into his face. "That's not something I'd ever see in San Francisco."

"I guess not. Do you miss it? The city, I mean."

"Not a bit." The realization startled her. "I thought I'd find it lonely here, but instead I feel as if I've come home."

"That's good." His face was so close to hers that she felt his breath, stirring the hair at her temple. "You've found family here, to make up for the ones you left behind."

He didn't understand about her family. He couldn't, because she'd never talked to him about it. Now the silence, the darkness, the sense that the two of them were alone in the world all combined to suggest she could tell him anything.

She paused for a heartbeat or two. "I've been wondering what my life would have been like if my father had sent me back here after my mother died, instead of putting me into foster care."

"Foster care?" He drew back a little,

searching her face in the dim light. "He didn't keep you?"

"He couldn't." Odd, to be defensive about her father's actions after all this time. "I mean, there he was alone in a strange city, his wife dead, no family to help him. It was the only thing he could do."

Even in the dim light, she could see his jaw tighten. "Sweetheart, I can think of plenty of other things he might have done— day care, a nanny, sent you back here, either to his family or Hannah's. Seems to me any of those things would have been better than giving you to strangers."

Sweetheart. The word echoed in her heart.

"I can't argue about that, because that's what I've been thinking, too. I did go back to live with him, eventually. After he remarried, when my stepmother was pregnant and decided to leave her job, then they took me home with them."

"Big of them."

The suppressed anger in Ted's voice caught her by surprise.

"I guess they did the best they could," she said carefully. Trying to be fair; she always tried to be fair. "It can't have been easy, adjusting to a six-year-old who'd been raised by other people. Once their children came along—well, they were a complete family without me."

"And you were on the outside, looking in."

Again she sensed his anger and was comforted that it was on her behalf. She looked up, finding his face only a breath away from hers, and for an instant lost track of what she was going to say.

"It's all right. It doesn't matter to me the way it used to." She thought about the scripture passage he'd mentioned earlier. "Maybe, in a way I haven't yet seen, God means it for good."

"You have family now. People to care about you." His voice went to a low rumble on the words. "That's good, isn't it?"

Yes, she did have that. Somehow she didn't want to confess to him that she was still wary of all those people who seemed to want to care about her, a little afraid of how she felt about them. That was cowardly, wasn't it?

"Fiona?" He touched her cheek gently, caressingly.

Her heart was beating so loudly that surely he could hear it. "Don't—don't you have to hang on to the reins with one hand, at least?"

"Nope." He smoothed her hair back, the touch of his fingers sending waves of awareness through her. "Sophie could take us home if I didn't touch the reins at all."

He was going to kiss her. That was what she wanted, wasn't it? So why did she feel as if she trembled on the edge of a precipice, ready to topple over in an instant?

Then his lips found hers, and she stopped thinking at all. Only feeling—feeling the tenderness of his kiss, the strength of his arms around her, the steady beat of his heart under her hand as she turned into his arms. There was a precipice, and she was falling, head over heels. Falling in love with him.

Chapter Eleven

He was going to see Fiona on business. Wasn't he? Ted walked past Ruth's store, aware of an urge to quicken his steps as he drew closer.

Sure he was. Never mind that he'd have found some excuse to seek her out anyway, after last night.

He hadn't been able to dismiss the memory of that kiss. That alone should have been enough to set the cautious habits of years on high alert. He hadn't felt this way since—well, maybe since the thrill of his first love.

Caution was probably a good idea. He and Fiona were very different, and she was struggling with who she was and where she belonged. Still, she wouldn't have kissed him the way she had unless she was interested.

So, he was combining business with pleasure. He had to talk to Fiona again about his continuing search for the vandals. He frowned. They'd struck again, probably at about the time he was taking the slow route back to Fiona's in the buggy.

The front of Fiona's house came into view. She'd planted bronze and yellow mums in pots along the porch recently. Every time he saw the place she seemed more settled. The sign he'd made for her looked good— as if it were where it belonged, too.

A buggy was drawn up to the front of the house. Well, what did he think—that she'd be sitting there waiting for him to come along? Naturally she'd be busy, with her practice increasing the way it was.

Aaron Yoder leaned against the buggy. The young man might have looked relaxed, but Ted detected the nervous strain in his shoulders and the way he rubbed his hand up and down his pant leg.

"Aaron." He braced one hand against the buggy. "Your Susie in seeing the midwife?"

Aaron nodded, swallowing. "Susie thinks it will be time soon."

"That's good news. I'm sure she's tired of waiting."

"Ja." He managed a smile. "Tired. She re-arranges the clothes for the little one a dozen times a day. She's had me move the cradle every five minutes, it seems."

"It'll be over soon." He clapped Aaron's shoulder. "Then she'll be too busy with the baby to think of anything else."

Even as he spoke, the door opened. Susie emerged, looking so pregnant it was a won-der she could move. Aaron sprang toward her to help her down the steps, glancing up at Fiona, who'd come onto the porch after Susie.

"It will be soon, ja?"

She smiled, her hand on Susie's back. "Soon, but not today. Probably not tomor-row, either, but you can never be sure. Ba-bies arrive when they want to, not when we want them to."

Susie smoothed her hand over her belly. "This one isn't listening to me, that's for sure, or he or she would already be here."

"Come back in a week, if nothing has hap-pened by then. Or send Aaron for me, any-time."

The expression on Fiona's face when she

watched the pregnant woman was something to see. It wasn't just the devotion to
her patient—Ted had seen that before. This
was a sense of pure pleasure, as if antici-
pating the birth gave her as much joy as it
gave the parents.

He helped Aaron maneuver his very pregnant wife up to the buggy seat. "Take good
care of her, Aaron."

"I will that." Aaron tucked a blanket
across Susie's knees, then clucked to the
mare, and they moved slowly off.

Ted turned toward Fiona. "You look as
happy as if she were related to you."

"Do I?" The smile lingered on her face. "I
guess I do feel that way about all of my
moms. It's such a joy, especially when
everything's going well and the parents are
so eager. But even when it's a difficult situation, there's still that pure joy of helping new
life into the world."

Each time he saw her, he found more
things to admire about this woman. "I don't
know much about midwives, but I'd say you
must be one of the best."

She smiled, shaking her head. "The people who trained me set a high standard.
Some of them were true pioneers in having

midwifery accepted by the medical estab-
lishment." She turned toward the house.
"Will you come in?"

"I think I'd better." He followed her up the
steps.

She turned a questioning look on him. "Is
this a professional call, then?"

"In part." He held the door open for her.
"I'd have come anyway, to tell you how
much I appreciated being with you last
night."

Her cheeks flooded with color as rosy as
the top she wore. "And I appreciated your
support, more than I can say." She gestured
toward the door to her office. "Come in
here. I don't expect any other patients this
afternoon."

He glanced around as he entered, taking
his time, taking it all in. His brother's book-
cases were filled with books now, except for
the ones closest to Fiona's desk, which carried neat stacks of pamphlets on childbirth.
The graceful windows that were the first
thing he'd noticed about the house were
filled now with potted geraniums on one
side and African violets on the other.

"Nice, very nice." Everything from the
flowers to the braided rug on the polished

floor to the comfortable padded visitor's chairs to the small fountain that gurgled on a side table seemed designed to set a nervous client at ease. It was a far cry from his utilitarian police station. "You've made this very welcoming."

"My Flanagan aunt and cousins helped." She sat down—not behind the desk, but in one of the pair of chairs, gesturing him to the other one. "Tell me what's going on. Is this about the vandals?"

He nodded. "They hit again last night, probably about the time we were on our way home."

If the reminder of that ride home had embarrassed her a few minutes earlier, she was probably determined not to show it again. "What happened?" Apprehension darkened her eyes. "I hope it wasn't too bad."

"It could have been, but luckily they were heard." He frowned absently at the twined strands of the braided rug. With a bit of luck, he hoped this business with the vandals would arrange itself as neatly. "They drove a vehicle through the fence out at Mose Stetler's place—you remember him, the Amish carpenter?"

"Of course. What happened?"

"I guess everyone's nerves have been on edge lately. Mose heard them and went running out. They'd ripped through what was left of the vegetable garden and were headed toward the barn." His jaw clenched. He could almost see the scene as Mose had described it. "Before he could reach them, they'd smashed a burning lantern into the hay he had stacked in the shed next to the barn."

Fiona's hands clasped, as if in prayer. "Is he all right? Did the barn catch fire?"

"He got there in time to beat it out. A couple of minutes later and he might have been too late." He thumped his palm on the chair's arm. "They're escalating. I've got to catch them before they hurt someone."

"I know." She leaned toward him, her face distressed. "I wish I could help more, but I've already told you everything I saw."

"One thing—maybe they're getting a little overconfident. They didn't bother with the dark sweatshirts this time. Mose caught a glimpse of a local high school jacket."

She drew in a breath, something startled and aware in her face.

"Fiona, what is it?" He swung toward her

so that their knees were almost touching. "What did you remember?"

"Not anything from the night Ruth's store was vandalized." She was shaking her head, as if to push a memory away. "It's nothing. It must have been a coincidence."

He clasped her hand firmly in his. "Tell me what it is. Let me decide if it's a coincidence."

"At the auction." Her gaze was troubled. "I think I might have mentioned it to you. There were four boys—they went running by, jostling me, on purpose, I thought. Three wore high school jackets, and the fourth was Amish."

The moment she'd said the words, Fiona regretted it. She could see by Ted's expression that he thought this meant something, but how could it? There were probably hundreds of teenage boys in the township, and running around was what kids did best.

"Did you recognize any of them?" That was his crisp cop's voice.

She shook her head. "I didn't know many people in town then. I certainly didn't know them."

"What about now? Picture them in your mind. Have you seen any of them since?"

She pulled her hand away from his, clasping them both in her lap. "It was just a glimpse. If I did see them now, I probably wouldn't recognize them."

"You're not trying." He leaned toward her, face intent. "Picture it happening again. What did you see?"

She closed her eyes briefly, hoping that would convince him that she was trying. "Blue jeans, high-school jackets. Those pricey sneakers all the kids seem to wear. I didn't really get a look at anyone's face—they went by too quickly."

"What about the Amish kid?"

Frustration gripped her. "I just saw him from the back. He looked like any Amish boy—dark clothes, fair hair under a black hat. It could have been anyone."

He leaned back in the chair, and she didn't care for the way he was studying her. "Maybe if you took a walk around the high school, you'd spot one of them."

"I couldn't possibly identify anyone. And even if somebody did look familiar, you can't arrest him on that." He wasn't leaning toward her any longer, but she still had the sense that he was pressuring her.

"I wouldn't be relying on that for an arrest,

but it might give me a lead. At the moment, I have nothing."

"You haven't told anyone that I reported the vandals in Ruth's store, have you? You said you'd keep it quiet. But if I went wandering around the high school, it wouldn't take people long to figure it out."

"You have a point." He frowned. "That would certainly alert them. I want to catch them, not just scare them off. Look, what about glancing through the school yearbook?"

"How could I possibly pick anyone out that way?" She wanted to shake him until he accepted that. "Even if I did, there's not a shred of evidence that the boys at the auction are the vandals."

"Maybe not, but it's odd, three high school boys ramming around the auction in the company of an Amish kid. That doesn't often happen."

"I still can't—"

"What's really going on here, Fiona?" Ted planted both hands on the arms of the chair. "You're stonewalling everything I suggest. I agree, this might be a wild-goose chase, but I have to do something. Don't you want to help?"

Her throat went tight. She hated arguing with him, hated feeling that she was letting him down, and she had a feeling he wasn't going to understand her reasons.

"Look, it's not that I don't want to help. It's just that I'm finally starting to feel as if I belong here. You of all people know how difficult it's been."

He tried to interrupt, but she swept on, riding a wave of determination not to lose what she'd found.

"If the Amish were practically ready to boycott me because I'm Hannah's daughter, what do you think they'll do if I turn in one of their kids for vandalism? And what about the rest of the community? They'd go right back to seeing me as an outsider, interfering in their business." Maybe that was selfish, but she risked losing everything she'd built here.

His jaw looked as hard as iron. "You can't let that keep you from doing your duty."

"It's not my duty. Maybe it's yours, but it's not mine." Why couldn't he see that she only wanted to live in peace?

He shoved himself out of the chair and stood for a moment, towering over her. Just looking at her. Finally he shook his head.

"I know how much you want to belong here. But if you're going to accept the advantages of belonging, I'd think you'd be willing to accept the responsibilities, too. I guess you're not."

He turned and walked out. She didn't call him back.

Fiona hung up the phone and walked slowly toward the hall, touching the lush blossoms of the geraniums on the windowsill as she passed them. Her office had turned out well, but now she couldn't think of that without remembering Ted admiring it. Somehow all of her thoughts of this place were tangled up with him.

And now with the disappointment he'd shown yesterday when she'd refused to help him.

Not refused, she corrected quickly. She couldn't help him. Didn't he understand that?

She knew perfectly well why she'd made that call to San Francisco. She'd needed to talk to her friend, to someone from that other life, who'd understand why she'd reacted the way she had to Ted's suggestion.

Tracy had been supportive, and while

Fiona was talking to her she'd felt perfectly justified. Unfortunately, once she'd hung up, all those rationalizations sounded hollow. Was she really refusing to take on the responsibility she should for her new community?

Frustrated with herself, and more than frustrated with Ted, she grabbed her handbag, making sure she had her cell phone, and went out the door, locking it behind her. She'd walk over to Ruth's store and have a chat. Maybe that would reassure her that she was doing the right thing, not risking what she had here.

The bell over the door jingled, seeming louder than normal, as she went inside the store. She glanced up at it, then at Ruth, who was coming toward her from the counter with a welcoming smile.

"Did you get a new bell?"

Ruth glanced at it, mouth quirking. "Sign of the times. Ted said I should be sure I could hear when someone came into the store." She shook her head. "I can remember when folks would come in, get what they wanted and leave the money on the counter. Now it's bells and alarm systems and not even trusting your neighbor."

"I'm sorry." Here was a different aspect—not a question of law but one of being able to trust. "Did you put in an alarm system after the vandals hit your store?"

Ruth nodded, smoothing her hair back under her cap. "Ja, I decided Ted was right about that. I was fortunate that it wasn't worse—maybe something scared them off before they could do too much damage. Or somebody." She gave Fiona a bright-eyed, questioning look.

Fiona struggled to hold a polite, interested expression. There'd probably be no harm in letting Ruth know she'd called the police, but how would she know how fast that would spread, or how other people would react?

"I'm glad you have protection now. That must make you feel safer."

"That's true, but still I'm sorry for the need of it." She sighed. "Used to be I knew every living soul in Crossroads Township. Now, with all the new folks coming in from goodness knows where, with goodness knows what kind of values—" She stopped, flushing slightly, and reached for Fiona's hand. "I didn't mean you, no. After all, you're one of us."

Fiona wanted to hold on to that sense of belonging without adding in that little smidgen of guilt that Ted had induced. It would be nice if she could get his voice, and his disappointment, out of her mind.

"Goodness, I'm forgetting myself. Your aunt is in the workroom. You're probably here to see her, not listen to me babble."

"It's always a pleasure to see Emma, but yes, I actually came to see how you're doing." Somehow she hadn't been able to form the habit of saying 'Aunt Emma,' probably because Emma seemed like a contemporary of hers, instead of her mother's.

She went through the archway, minding her step on the old wooden floor that sloped erratically between the two sections of the store. When she got past the display rack, Emma was already looking up, smiling, obviously having heard her voice.

"It is good that you are here today. I was hoping to show you this." With a flick of her wrist, she unfurled the quilt top over the counter.

Fiona let out an audible gasp as she approached, reaching out to touch the flowing colors. The rose centers of each square drew her with their beauty, but the thing that truly caught her eye was the way Emma had put the patches together, so that the dark and light colors created diagonal stripes across the quilt.

"It's so beautiful." She touched one of the dark lines, realizing that it seemed to disappear as she looked closely at each patch, forming an optical illusion. "I love the effect."

"Will keep you warm at night," Emma said, her face showing the pride in her work that she wouldn't say aloud. "This design is called Log Cabin with Straight Furrows, like the furrows of a new-plowed field."

"Is it done?" She stroked the fabrics, longing to see it on her bed right now.

"Not yet." Emma's smile suggested that she knew what Fiona was thinking. "I must put the borders along the sides, and then it will be ready to add the batting and the backing, and we will quilt it together."

"I'm not much of a seamstress." She hated to think of ruining the beautiful thing with her crooked stitches.

"It makes no matter," Emma said. "We will all help you. When we all work together on a quilt, it is…" she hesitated, as if searching for the right words. "It is like sewing love into the quilt. For you."

Her heart was too full to speak easily. "Thank you." Their hands met over the quilt her mother had begun for her. "It means a great deal to me."

"To us, too." Emma patted her hand. "You are one of us, now."

One of us. The words echoed in her heart. Ted's voice seemed to provide the counterpoint. *You have to accept the responsibilities of belonging, too.*

Little though she wanted to admit it, he might have a point.

Chapter Twelve

Ted shoved the budget report away, frustrated. How could he concentrate on figures when his thoughts were totally wrapped up with people—people he cared about, people who were hurting. Or who would be hurting, if he didn't do something.

He ran his hand through his hair, then rubbed the back of his neck, feeling the tension that had gathered there since that early-morning phone call. If he ignored it—

Let justice roll down like the waters, and righteousness like an ever-rolling stream. If he didn't pursue justice, he was betraying everything he believed.

He had to do his job, even when he hated it. Like Fiona, who hated the idea of doing something that could get someone in trouble.

But Fiona was a civilian. She had the luxury of standing back, if that was what she chose to do. He didn't.

He'd probably been too harsh with her, but the conflict that raged in her was too familiar for him to see clearly. He understood, too well, the cost of belonging. Maybe she was just beginning to find that out.

Getting up, he stretched, his hand bumping the wall. It reminded him of Fiona's comments the single time she'd been to his office. A shadow moved across the glass window in the office door. He looked, feeling the quickening of his pulse that he should have been getting used to by now. Apparently Fiona was about to pay her second visit.

She opened the door slowly. Her reluctance to enter was so strong he could feel it.

"Fiona. Come in."

She walked into the office, closing the door with far more care than it deserved. She apparently found looking at it preferable to looking at him.

He pulled the visitor's chair to a more welcoming angle. "What brings you to visit me?"

"I've been thinking." She cleared her throat. "About what you asked me to do. I still don't like it, but I've decided I should do as you asked and look at the high school yearbook."

"I see." The words came out slowly, but his mind was racing. What had changed her mind? It hadn't been anything he'd said—he'd messed up that conversation thoroughly. He gestured to the chair. "Please, have a seat."

She sat down, drawing her brown corduroy jacket around her. When she didn't speak, he knew he had to ask the question.

"What made you change your mind?"

She folded her hands in her lap, looking down at them. "Does it matter?"

He sat down on the corner of his desk, watching her. "Not to me as a cop, no. But to me as a friend—well, yes, it matters."

Her lips pressed tightly together. Maybe he'd made a mistake in pressing her. Or in referring to himself as a friend.

Finally she glanced up at him, her gray eyes troubled. "I've been thinking about what you said—about the responsibilities that come with belonging."

"And I've been thinking that maybe I crossed the line when I said that."

Her smile flickered. "Maybe. But perhaps I

needed to hear it." She shrugged, the movement restless. "Since I came to Crossroads, I've begun to realize that I've been looking for a place to belong all my life. But I haven't thought about what that might cost."

"It's not easy." His mind touched on the perennial sore spot—the knowledge of the pain he'd caused his family by his choices.

"No, I guess it's not." She sat up very straight, as if to underscore her decision. "Do you have that yearbook for me to look through?"

He nodded, reaching across the desk to pick it up and hand it to her. "Take your time. You're not accusing anyone of anything, remember."

She didn't look convinced, but she took the book with both hands. She began paging through it, scanning each page as carefully as if her happiness depended upon what she saw.

Watching her, he thought about the tidbit of new information that had come his way. He found himself wanting to share the burden with her, not only because she might help him rule it in or out, but because the load would be easier for him if he shared it.

But not easier for her, not by a long shot. The careful way she studied each page told him how conscientious she was, how concerned she was not to make a mistake.

The things she'd told him about her family life had shocked and saddened him. They'd also gone a long way toward explaining how guarded she was in some ways. She didn't want to risk the pain that could come from opening her heart.

She was just now beginning to take a step toward belonging. He didn't want to think about what it would do to her if that belonging were snatched away. If he asked her to help him further he was risking pain for her, to say nothing of endangering the fragile bond that had formed between them. Still, what choice did he have?

Her fingers touched a photo, and she drew in a deep breath and let it out. "I think this was one of the boys I saw at the auction." She shook her head. "Not just think. I'm sure."

"Okay." He moved to her side to look at the photo.

She glanced up at him. "I'm sorry, but I didn't realize until I saw the picture that I really could identify him. I guess I got a better look than I thought when he rounded the corner."

He looked at the photo, his heart sinking. "Jared Michaels. He's just sixteen, but he's already had a couple of brushes with trouble."

"You know him?"

"I know everyone, remember? Somehow, I'm not surprised you picked out Jared's picture."

"I can only say that he was one of the boys at the auction. There's no connection between the auction and the vandals."

"Unfortunately, there is a link. Someone came back to the site of the auction that night and trashed the things that hadn't sold. Stuff was left sitting outside, so that made it easier for them."

"You didn't tell me that before." She frowned at him.

"If you hadn't been able to identify anyone, there'd have been no need for you to know."

He thought she might flare up at that, but she just nodded, her eyes thoughtful. "You don't look especially happy at having the boy identified," Fiona said. "What trouble has he been in?"

"Nothing serious. And unfortunately nothing he was ever held responsible for. His mother claimed her son couldn't possibly have done anything wrong, and his father took a 'boys will be boys' attitude."

"You think they'll do the same with this?"

"I think I'd like to have a little proof before I actually tackle Jared."

"Well, I wish you success with it." She stood up, obviously ready to escape.

He held out his hand to stop her. "There's something else."

"I didn't see enough of the other boys to be able—"

"It's not that." He took a breath. This was going to hurt her, but he didn't see any way out of it. "I received an anonymous tip this morning, saying the caller knew who the Amish boy was who's running with the vandals."

Her eyes darkened, as if she were bracing herself for bad news.

"Who?"

"Rachel's brother. Levi Stolzfus."

"I just can't believe it." Fiona took the curtain rod from her Aunt Siobhan's hand and mounted the step stool to slip one end into its bracket.

"Can't believe Levi would do it, or can't believe anyone would say that about him?"

Siobhan held the other end of the rod, her hand keeping the drape from dragging on the floor of Fiona's living room. Not only had her aunt insisted she had the perfect drapes for the room, she'd even hemmed them to fit and then come to help Fiona hang them.

"Both, I guess." She stepped back down, moved the stool and climbed up to take care of the other side. "He's such a quiet boy—I haven't gotten to know him as well as I have Rachel. But even so, I just can't believe it of him."

Did she really know him well enough to say? That was the question that had haunted her since she'd stormed out of Ted's office.

"What is he, about thirteen?" Her aunt smoothed the folds of the drapes. "That's a difficult age. Boys can become secretive and very easily influenced by their peers."

"You sound as if you speak from experience."

Siobhan smiled. "After the crew I raised? You can believe I speak from experience.

What one of them didn't think of to do, the others did. And Ryan was the worst of the lot, always trying to outdo his older brothers with one outrageous trick after another."

"Well, now he's settled down to be a model husband and father, hasn't he?"

"That he has." Siobhan's face softened into a sweet smile. "I have to say that grand-children are a wonderful reward for having raised your children."

"I'm sure they are." Although she couldn't imagine her stepmother thinking it a good thing for anyone to call her "Grandma."

She stepped down from her perch, stroking the floral print fabric with pleasure. "These really are beautiful. The colors are almost like a watercolor painting. You're sure you didn't need them any longer?"

"My husband said that he'd get hay fever if he had to sleep in a room that looked like a flower garden any longer."

"So you let him have his way."

She waved a hand in the air. "It was a pleasure. And now you can enjoy them."

Her aunt smiled as if she really enjoyed giving something up to make her husband happy. Well, maybe that went along with the fact that Siobhan and Joe were as obviously in love as any newlyweds.

"I *will* enjoy them." Fiona carried the step stool to the next window. "To say nothing of appreciating your hard work in fixing them."

Curtains for her living room from one aunt; a quilt for her bed from another. She wasn't used to the sensation of having all these relatives wanting to help her.

"What did your friend think about the likelihood of young Levi being involved?"

Ted. Her friend. She wasn't sure that was how she would describe their relationship at this point.

"I don't think he liked it much, but of course he has to investigate. It's his job." That came out rather tartly, and her aunt seemed to notice.

"Yes, it *is* his job. He certainly couldn't show favoritism toward someone just because he knows them."

"I know that." She went back up on the step stool and took the second rod her aunt handed her. "But it is his job, not mine."

Aunt Siobhan raised her eyebrows. "Has someone suggested that it's yours?"

She fitted the rod end carefully in place.

"He keeps talking about the responsibility that comes with belonging, as if I should—"

She stopped. She really hadn't intended to say that much to anyone, although of course Aunt Siobhan was perfectly trustworthy.

"He wants you to do something." Siobhan took her hand as she clambered down. "And you don't want to."

"No. I don't." She may as well tell her aunt the rest of it. Surely Siobhan would agree with her. "He doesn't want to talk to Levi in any official way if he can help it. Not yet."

Her aunt nodded. "I can understand why he'd feel that way, given his friendship with the family."

"He wants *me* to do it." The words burst out of her. "Just because Rachel and Levi sometimes come to visit me, he thinks I can get him to admit it if he's involved."

"Is that how he put it? Try to get him to admit something?" Siobhan sounded doubtful.

"Well, not exactly." She was ashamed of herself for trying to make Ted's request sound worse than it was. "He just wants me to bring up the subject and see if Levi reacts. He seems to feel that if he is involved, he might be longing for someone to give him an opening to talk about it."

She looked at her aunt. The curtain fabric cascaded from her hands, making her look as if she held a bouquet of flowers.

"I don't want to be the one. Is that cowardly?"

"No one would think that." Siobhan's gaze was as loving as if she were counseling one of her own children. "But that's not really the point, is it? You don't want to feel as if you're betraying your family, just when you're starting to be accepted by them."

Everyone seemed to see that clearly. "That's not wrong, is it?"

"No, not wrong. But you know, if the boy is involved in these tricks, the sooner it ends, the better it will be for him. I can't imagine, from what you've said, that he's anything but a pawn for these older boys."

"If it's him." She still wasn't ready to concede that.

"If it's him," her aunt agreed. "Still, if it is, it would do him more harm not to stop him. What if they did something that hurt a person, instead of property? He could be held accountable, even if all he did was keep watch."

That sinking feeling was the recognition that she didn't have any choice in the matter. "So you think I should do this."

Siobhan stroked her shoulder gently. "I think you should pray about it and open your heart for God's answer. You'll know what to do when the time comes, I promise."

You'll know what to do when the time comes.

Aunt Siobhan's words sounded in Fiona's heart as she cleaned up after her last appointment the next day. Though they probably wouldn't recognize it, her aunt Siobhan and her aunt Emma were similar in many ways, especially in the fact that they were both strong women of God.

I want to be like them, Lord, but I don't feel very strong right now. Please guide me. Help me to find the answer.

She dropped a load of sheets into the washer in the kitchen and started it, finding its hum companionable in the quiet house. Even with patients, family and new friends, the house still sometimes felt lonely.

The clop of a horse's hooves alerted her, and she looked out the kitchen window to see Rachel halting her buggy next to the back steps. She wasn't alone. Levi sat beside her.

Panic gripped her. *Not now, Lord. I'm not ready yet.* She'd asked God to help her find the answer, and He'd immediately presented her with an opportunity to do just that, ready or not.

She dried her hands and reached the door just as her young cousins did. Rachel beamed at her. "We surprise you, ja?"

"Yes, you do. Come in, please."

"I must do some shopping at Ruth's for my mother." She gave Levi a little push toward Fiona. "Levi does not like shopping. Is all right if he watches the television?"

She could hardly imagine this was anything but God's answer to her prayer, with the opportunity to talk to Levi alone thrust at her.

"Of course." She touched Levi's shoulder lightly. "Go on in, Levi. I'll fix a snack for you."

He nodded, not speaking, and headed down the hall. She glanced at Rachel, who was frowning at the doorway through which her brother had gone.

"Is anything wrong?"

"N-no." Rachel didn't sound as confident as she usually did. "It's just that Levi has been quiet—more quiet than usual. Often I can worm it out if something bothers him, but not this time." She shook her head. "I will come back soon. Thank you, Cousin Fiona."

She stood for a few minutes after Rachel left, hands braced against the counter. *Please, Lord.*

She took a breath. She knew what she had to do. The question was, could she do it? Well, she had to try.

Quickly, she took out the peanut butter, bread and jelly. It might be easier to talk over a snack, assuming she could get the boy to talk at all.

She put the sandwiches on a tray, added two glasses of milk, and carried the tray through to the waiting room, where Levi sat cross-legged on the rug in front of the television, gaze rapt on the flickering images on the screen.

Sitting down next to him, she held out the tray.

"Ser gut." He gave her a shy smile that made him look about eight. He took a bite

of the sandwich, returning his attention to the television.

She couldn't possibly force a bite down her dry throat. Instead, she drained half a glass of milk.

Some cowardly part of her told her to get up, make an excuse and scurry back to the kitchen until Rachel returned. Don't get involved. That's safer. You can't get hurt that way.

But it was too late for that. She was already involved, and no matter what happened, she had to try.

She glanced at the television, looking for something to start the conversation. The show was typical cartoon fare, with plucky teen heroes battling monsters.

"I've never seen this one before. Is it good?"

Levi shrugged. "Is all right. Not as good as video games."

Something tightened inside her. "I've never played one of those. Do you like them?"

"You have to learn to control them." He gestured with his hands, as if working an imaginary control. "I learned fast."

That was so close to bragging that it took

her aback for an instant. Without noticing it, she'd become accustomed to the ingrained Amish modesty.

"You must have some English friends to teach you video games." Who are they, Levi? What trouble did they lead you into?

"I have some. There's nothing bad with that." His voice turned defensive. "You are English, and you are my cousin."

"That's true," she said slowly. *Do it.* "Unless those English friends want you to do something you know is wrong. Then it might be very bad."

Levi stared at her, blue eyes widening. Then he dropped the remains of his sandwich, scrambled to his feet and bolted for the door.

"Levi—"

But by the time she reached the door, he was gone.

She stood in the doorway for a moment, arguing with herself. He hadn't admitted anything, had he? There was nothing that she could really tell Ted—no evidence that Levi was involved with the vandals.

But she couldn't fool herself about this. Something had been very wrong about the way the boy reacted.

Her aunt Siobhan's words came back to her again. If Levi was involved, the best thing for him was to be caught quickly, before anything else happened. She couldn't hide her head in the sand. She had to call Ted.

She glared at the phone a few minutes later, frustrated. It was one thing to get her courage screwed up to do this, and another to be confronted with nothing but an automatic answering machine instead of Ted.

If she waited until later—but that was the coward's way out, and she couldn't take that any longer. The message tone sounded.

"Ted, it's Fiona. I just had a conversation with my cousin. I think we'd better talk as soon as possible."

There, it was done. Why was it that doing the right thing felt so much like being a traitor?

Chapter Thirteen

"Look, I'm really sorry I didn't get back to you last night."

Ted stood just inside Fiona's kitchen doorway, because she hadn't offered him a seat. Judging by how annoyed she looked with him, it was a wonder she'd even let him in the door.

"That's all right." She didn't sound as if it was all right, but at least she'd said the words. Fiona poured a mug of coffee and held it out to him.

"Thanks." The mug warmed his palms, but it didn't take away the chill in the atmosphere.

He couldn't be irritated in return, because he knew the strain on her face was his fault. By the time he'd finally retrieved his messages and heard Fiona's voice, he'd told himself it was too late to disturb her. And today had been completely jammed, so that it wasn't until late afternoon that he'd been able to get here.

If her pale face and heavy eyes were any indication, she probably spent the night worrying about her cousin. He longed to offer her sympathy and reassurance, but unfortunately that was in short supply right now.

"Sit down," she said abruptly, pulling out a seat at the kitchen table. "Please," she added, as if realizing how short that had been.

"Right." He sat down across the table from her.

"I'm sorry." She pushed the waves of thick hair back from her forehead. "I didn't get much sleep last night."

"No, neither did I."

Her eyes widened, as if she were startled and frightened. "Why? What happened?"

"You first." He gestured toward her. He was a cop in the middle of an investigation, and he'd best remember that. "What did Levi say?"

He thought she'd protest at that, but she just frowned down at the dark brew. "He didn't really *say* much. He let it slip that he's been hanging around with some English friends, and he was pretty defensive about it."

"He mention any names?" Tension knifed through him. If that boy was involved in what had happened last night, a lot of people were going to be hurting.

Fiona shook her head. "It was like talking to a clam. So then I said that having English friends wasn't a problem, unless they wanted him to do things he knew were wrong."

"What did he say?" His fingers tightened on the mug.

"Nothing." She refused to look at him. "He jumped up and ran out of the house."

Heaviness settled in his heart. "I guess that tells us what we need to know, then."

"Maybe not." Her head came up. "It could mean a lot of things other than his being involved with the vandals."

"I suppose it might, but that's not all there is to it. Not now."

Apprehension filled her eyes. "What is it? What happened?"

He frowned. "Look, some of what I'm going to tell you is public knowledge, or soon will be. Some of it is police business, but I'm telling you because you're in a position to help."

Was that all? He wasn't sure any longer.

"I understand." She clasped her hands together tightly. "Just tell me."

"They're getting careless. And dangerous. They set fire to a barn last night at Marvin Douglas's place. Like they tried to do at Mose's farm." The chill he'd felt when he heard the fire alarm went down his spine again. "That's the worst thing a farmer can face—a barn burning. Old Marv's dairy cows were inside the barn."

"Oh, no." Fiona's face had gone even whiter. "How bad was it?"

"Marv's seventy-five if he's a day. He got the cows out all right, but the barn's a total loss. And he had a heart attack watching it burn."

Fiona's breath caught, her hand going to her lips as if to hold back a cry. "Is he—"

"In the hospital, in coronary care. He's a tough old bird—says he's fine and wants to go home."

"Could he identify the boys?"

"He didn't get a close enough look, but the vehicle he spotted sounded enough like Jared's to give me cause to run over there.

I caught Jared and two of his buddies coming home—with empty beer bottles in the car and an empty kerosene can in the trunk."

"Not Levi?"

"No. But if he had been with them, they'd have dropped him off first."

"You sound as if you want him to be guilty." She flared up, eyes blazing.

For a fraction of a second he wanted to lash back. How dare she attack him, when he was doing the work he'd sworn to do?

The reaction seeped away when he recognized the pain in her face. She was trying to protect her cousin, trying desperately to believe he wouldn't do this.

"I don't want any such thing," he said evenly. "And I think you know that."

She put her hand up, seeming surprised to find a tear trickling down her cheek. "I'm sorry. I know you care about Levi. I shouldn't have said that."

"I want to help him, too, but the only way to do that is to find the truth."

"What happened to the other boys? Are they saying anything?"

"Nothing helpful." He frowned. "They haven't been charged yet. I'd like to produce a bit more hard evidence before I do that. Jared was pretty cocky, practically daring me to arrest him. Naturally his parents don't believe he'd do anything as serious as setting a fire."

She paled. "I understand how they feel. That's how I feel about Levi."

"Levi hasn't been in a string of malicious mischief incidents dating back three or four years. And he's not mouthing off to police officers."

"I take it you don't care much for Jared."

There was more truth to that than he wanted to admit. "He actually hinted around, as if he was trying to blackmail me."

"Blackmail you? That's ridiculous." She was quick to his defense, and it warmed him.

"Influence, maybe is a better term. He was careful not to admit anything, but he hinted that I'd be unhappy if I found that fourth vandal." Ted reached across the table to put his hand over Fiona's. "He implied that it was someone close to me. Like Levi."

The words echoed in the quiet room.

Fiona couldn't say anything for a long moment. She could only stare at Ted, her heart pounding in her ears. His fingers tightened over hers.

"Did you believe him?" Ted knew Levi far better than she did. If he thought Levi capable of—no, she just couldn't buy that. "Ted, you can't believe Levi would set fire to a barn knowing there were cows inside. Maybe some of the other things, but not that."

The stern planes of his face seemed to harden. "A week ago I'd have said it was impossible. But the evidence keeps piling up."

She shook her head helplessly. Unable to sit there any longer, she crossed to the counter, staring out the window at the setting sun.

She heard the scrape of Ted's chair as he rose, the heavy tread of his feet coming toward her. His hands came down on her shoulders, lightly, tenderly, and his grip sent strength into her.

"I wish I saw my way clear in this." His voice was husky. "I don't want you to get hurt, Fiona."

She gave in to the longing to lean back against him, feeling the thud of her heart, the protectiveness of his arms around her.

He pressed his cheek against her temple, and his breath feathered across her skin.

"I don't want to get hurt either, but I think it may be too late for that. I just hate to think how my grandparents will feel—"

"You can't tell them." He turned her to face him, and he was back to being the in-control cop again. "Not now. Not until I know for sure what the truth is."

She swallowed the argument she was tempted to make. Of course he was right. There was little sense in alarming them. Perhaps Ted would find that Levi hadn't been involved. She needed that to cling to.

"I won't." She took a step back, and his hands fell from her shoulders. "But you told me. Why?"

"Only because you were already involved, and—" He stopped, his frown deepening until it set deep furrows between his straight brows.

"What is it?"

"Something was said when the three boys were together. Something I wasn't meant to overhear."

"Are you going to tell me what it was, or do I have to guess?" At his expression, a chill went down her spine that had nothing to do with the temperature.

His blue eyes darkened when they rested on her. "You were mentioned. The others hushed him up pretty fast when they saw I was there, but I'm sure of it."

"Me? How would they even know me?" She didn't want to admit being frightened at the thought.

"I don't know what it means, but I don't like it. Maybe it was something about you being Levi's kin. Maybe they figured out that you spotted them that night at Ruth's store. I don't know, but I had to warn you."

"You can't think they'd try to do anything to me. That's ridiculous. What could they possibly gain?"

"Nothing, but I'd say rational thinking isn't exactly their strong suit." He clasped her hands in a quick, hard grip. "Look, it's probably nothing. Use some of those urban smarts of yours and take precautions—lock your doors, keep the outside lights burning."

She nodded, less concerned for herself than she was for Levi. And for Ted. "What are you going to do?"

"Investigate. Try to find out the truth." His

face was somber. "I love that boy, too, you know. But if he broke the law, he has to be held responsible."

Fiona was double-checking the contents of her delivery bag when she heard a soft sound—so soft, she couldn't be sure what it was. She glanced toward the office window. Darkness pressed on it.

Time had slipped away while she'd sat in the office after Ted left. Praying. Thinking. Trying to see her way through this difficult situation.

Keep your doors locked and your outside lights on, Ted had told her, and she'd forgotten those precautions already. He'd been overreacting, surely. This was Crossroads, not the big city.

Still, her heart thumped as she walked softly out into the hallway and peered into the waiting room. No one was at the front door—she'd be able to see that, even without the porch light on. She went quickly to the switches and turned the porch light on, just to be sure. Nothing.

The sound came again, and this time she recognized it—someone was tapping at the back door. Well, the vandals would hardly knock on her door. She stepped into the kitchen and saw a dark figure outlined against the glass. Her heart jolted before she realized that it was a woman in Amish dress.

She went quickly across the kitchen to open the door.

"Fiona." It was her grandmother. "I must talk with you, ja."

"Come in."

She caught her grandmother's hands and drew her into the warm kitchen. Louise's hands were cold in spite of the black woolen cape that covered her, and as she came into the light, Fiona was shocked by her expression. Her face was drawn and pale, her gray eyes red-rimmed.

"Please, sit down." She hadn't yet found the right thing to call her grandmother. She couldn't say Louise—it seemed too presumptuous, but Grandmother was a title she didn't want to use until she was invited to do so. "You're welcome in my house."

"I cannot stay long." She took the chair Rachel usually sat in and pushed the cape back off her shoulders, revealing the now-familiar dark dress and apron. "I came because someone said that you were the one who saw."

"Saw what?" She sat down opposite her grandmother, tension tightening her nerves.

"The people who broke into Ruth's store." Louise's eyes were dark with apprehension, her face taut. "Emma heard that you were the one who saw that night. Who called the police. That is true?"

Apparently there was little point in trying to keep it secret now. Everything was out in the open, or would be soon. "Yes. I heard the intruders, and I called Ted."

"And you saw." Her grandmother reached across the table to grip Fiona's hand. Her fingers seemed worn to the bone but still strong. "You saw them."

"Not to identify," she said quickly. "Just shadows, running away in the dark."

"It is true?" Her voice held anguish. "One of the boys, the one who kept watch, he was Amish?"

Fiona's heart twisted. Everything she'd feared about this was coming to pass, and there was no way to avoid it. She nodded.

Her grandmother took a shaky breath, and her face tightened until it seemed the wrinkled skin was a roadmap of all the grief of her lifetime. "Was it Levi?"

Pain ricocheted through her. "I couldn't see, honestly. Only an outline of a boy in Amish clothing. It could have been anyone." She tried not to think about what Ted had said, about how the circle of suspicion seemed to be narrowing around her young cousin.

Her grandmother stared at her, gray eyes boring into her, as if searching past all evasions for the truth. "There is more, Fiona. I can see it in your face. Tell me what it is that you know."

Pain gripped her heart. Ted had ordered her not to tell, but she couldn't lie to her grandmother. Ted should know that. She couldn't pretend that she didn't know where the police investigation was headed and let the family find out in some other, more painful way.

"I'm sorry," she whispered. "I understand that one of the boys they've identified mentioned Levi's name. There's nothing certain, no one's come right out and accused him—"

But her grandmother's expression collapsed in grief. Tears welled in her eyes, and she put work-worn hands up to cover her face.

"Please, don't." Fiona sprang from her chair and rounded the table to put her arms around the bent figure. "I'm so sorry. Nothing is certain—we don't know that he's done anything."

For just a moment her grandmother clung to her, arms tight around Fiona's waist. Then she pushed to her feet and wrapped herself in the black cloak.

"I must go." Louise turned toward the door.

"Grandmother—" The word was out without her thinking about it.

Her grandmother clutched her hand briefly. "It is in God's hands now."

She rushed out, leaving Fiona staring after her, her eyes wet with tears.

Chapter Fourteen

Saturday morning was usually Fiona's time to catch up with laundry and household chores, but she couldn't seem to settle to anything. Her mind kept returning again and again to the situation with Levi. What was happening with the family? What had her grandmother done when she'd run out the previous evening?

She couldn't keep Ted out of her thoughts, either. This was so difficult for him, too. He had such protective loyalty to his Amish roots, but an equally strong duty to his job. The conflict had to be tearing him apart.

She'd made a promise to him that she hadn't kept, agreeing that she wouldn't tell anyone about the accusation against Levi. She'd meant it when she'd agreed, and she didn't take breaking her word lightly.

But what else could she have done in the face of her grandmother's pain?

Bracing her hands against the washer lid, she stared blankly at the controls, unable to focus.

Lord, I don't know what to do, or even how to pray about it. Please, no matter what the truth is about Levi's involvement, work in this situation to bring good for him and his family.

She put her hands to her face, surprised to find it wet with tears. She dashed the tears away, straightening. She had been caught unwillingly in this situation, but she wouldn't let it control her. For all she knew, it might be days or even weeks until the investigation was concluded.

Switching on the washer, she turned and walked quickly through the house to the front door. With no clients to see, her day was her own unless Susie Yoder went into labor. She wouldn't spend it moping in the house. Grabbing her bag and jacket and checking to be sure she had her cell phone, she hurried outside.

The crisp autumn air had a bite to it, and the chrysanthemums glowed golden. It was a day that made one think of orange pumpkins, corn stalks and apple cider. Probably Ruth's store carried the apple cider, if not the pumpkins and corn stalks. She headed for the store, feeling better now that she had a destination.

As she approached the door she glimpsed, through the glass, an Amish couple standing with Ruth near the counter, heads together, deep in conversation. She opened the door, the bell jingling, and all three turned to look at her, faces as startled as if she'd been the subject of their conversation.

She was being paranoid, thinking such a thing. She pinned a smile to her face and advanced toward the counter.

The couple turned, faces grave, and nodded as they passed her. Ruth stared blankly for a moment before managing an unconvincing smile.

"Ruth, what's wrong?" Fiona felt as if a cold wind had swept through the store. "You look..." She wasn't sure how to finish that thought.

"You haven't heard?" Ruth's gray brows lifted. "It's all over the township. I thought surely you knew."

Her nerves prickled, but she tried to speak

lightly. "I must be out of the loop. What's all over the township?"

"The police have charged four boys with the vandalism. Three English teenagers." Ruth blinked, looking away. "And Levi Stolzfus."

Telling herself she'd expected it didn't seem to do much good. Tears welled in her eyes, and she blinked them back. "No. I didn't know."

How could she? No one had come to her—not Ted, not someone from the family. That was a separate hurt in her pain over Levi.

Ruth looked at her, frowning a little. "But wasn't it you who saw them when they ran away from here? That's what everyone is saying."

"No. I mean, I had a glimpse of them running away from the store, but I didn't see enough to identify anyone."

"Why didn't you say anything to me then?" Ruth tipped her head to one side, considering. "Ach, I see. Ted told you to be still about it. Well, it's out in the open now. Poor Louise."

Her heart clenched at the mention of her

grandmother. "Have you heard anything about how she's doing?"

"Not a word about any of the family. But surely they've been in touch with you."

"Not yet." It took an effort not to let pain show in her voice or her face. Maybe they wouldn't be in touch at all. The family would close in on themselves in a crisis, she already knew that. And she was on the outside.

She tried to swallow the lump in her throat. She could go to them, but their relationship was too new to test it in this way. And she knew in her heart she didn't have the courage to face the possibility that they would turn her away.

There was one other person who knew what was happening. She had to see Ted.

Fiona approached Ted's office door, her steps slowing. She could see him through the window, much as she'd seen Ruth and the Amish couple at the store.

Ted sat at his desk, perfectly still, frowning at something in front of him. His expression froze her hand on the knob. His face was taut with pain, maybe even grief. And it struck her that no one should be watching that private display of feelings.

No one, including her. Especially not her. No matter how close they'd drawn to each other in the past weeks, she didn't have the right. In the midst of her own pain over what had happened, she couldn't let herself forget that he was hurting, too.

And if he knew she'd told Louise what she'd promised not to tell, he'd be angry with her. Well, she'd just have to face that.

She took a breath, trying to still the pounding of her heart, and fumbled deliberately with the knob, giving him warning of her approach. By the time she had the door open and had stepped inside, his face had smoothed into its usual stolid expression.

"Fiona." There was no welcome in the way he said her name. He stood, as if good manners compelled that, but he didn't ask her to take the chair in front of his desk.

That steady stare made her nervous. "I...I'm sorry to interrupt. I wanted to find out about Levi, and I didn't know who else to ask."

For a long moment she didn't think he'd answer at all. Finally that rocky facade cracked just a little.

"All four of the boys have been charged and released into their parents' custody." His tone was cool and formal.

Relief washed over her. "He's home, then." At the back of her mind there'd been an image of her young cousin locked in a cell somewhere.

He gave a curt nod.

Thank You, Lord.

"What will happen next?" She took an impulsive step toward him, but stopped when he seemed to tighten in response.

"It's in the hands of the district attorney now. There will be a hearing in juvenile court, although it's possible that Jared could be charged as an adult."

"But Levi—surely, if he was only a lookout..." She still found it impossible to believe that he'd willingly participated in destruction.

If it were possible for stone to harden, Ted's face did just that. "I can't discuss an ongoing case with you."

"An ongoing case? This is my cousin, not just any ordinary case."

"Not in the eyes of the law. I can't talk about it with you, Fiona."

A shaft of anger pierced her. "Why not?

You weren't so reluctant to talk about the case when you wanted my help, were you?"

His fists braced against the desk so hard that the knuckles were white. "You were a witness. It was your duty to help in the investigation."

"I did help." Her voice wavered, and she fought to control it. "I helped, and now a member of my family is charged with a crime, and you won't even talk to me about it. I have a right to know—"

"I had a right to expect you to keep your promise, didn't I?" His eyes blazed with more emotion than she'd ever seen in him. "I trusted you with police information, and you broke that trust."

So, he knew about her grandmother's visit. Of course he'd see it that way. She'd been a fool to think he'd understand. "My grandmother came to me. She'd already heard rumors about me, about Levi. What else could I do?"

"You could have kept your word." A muscle in his jaw twitched, as if he tried to hold back and couldn't. "I went out to the farm expecting to have a private conversation with Levi and his parents. Instead, thanks to you, I had to face the whole church."

Her breath caught. "They didn't try to stop you—"

"They wouldn't do that." His eyes darkened. "They just watched while I arrested one of their own."

His pain reached out and clutched her heart. She could see the scene in his eyes— those dark, motionless figures, the faces of people he'd known and loved all his life, watching while he did what he knew was his duty, the act that sliced apart his roots and his calling.

Trust. He'd come back here after that horrible experience in Chicago, because here he could trust and be trusted. Now, as he saw it, she'd betrayed his trust. That was the one thing he'd never be able to forgive.

"You really don't have to help with this." Nolie took the stack of dishes from Fiona's hands. "You go back in and talk to Siobhan while I get the coffee and pie ready."

"No use." Siobhan came through the door from the dining room into the kitchen at Gabe and Nolie's farmhouse. "I'm here. Those men are talking fire department business again, and I don't have a thing to contribute to the conversation. I may as well help with the dishes."

Nolie laughed, setting the dishes in the sink that was ready with hot, soapy water. "That's all this family talks about, Fiona. You should know that by now. Unless we have the medical contingent together, that is. With you, me, Terry, her fiancé and Mary Kate, we ought to be able to outtalk the fire department once in a while."

"The rest of them aren't here," Siobhan said, measuring coffee into the coffeemaker. "You may as well be resigned to hearing firehouse talk."

Fiona busied herself with setting out the plates for the cherry pie her aunt Siobhan had brought, letting the other two women carry on with their laughing chatter. The invitation to dinner with Nolie and Gabe and her aunt and uncle had saved her from another lonely, depressing evening like the one she'd spent last night.

Yesterday Ted had cut away their promising relationship as if it meant nothing at all. As if the moments when he'd held her in his arms and kissed her hadn't existed.

And none of the Stolzfus family had come

near her since Levi's arrest. It seemed they too had shut her out.

She surely had grounds for sorrow. Small wonder she welcomed cheerful company.

Unfortunately, the clatter of dishes and chatter of women's voices was too reminiscent of being in her grandmother's kitchen, feeling a part of her mother's family at last. Now that was an illusion.

At least she had her practice. So far none of her patients had left her, and she could only pray that continued.

She'd come here to establish her midwife practice, not to look for relationships. If she had that, she shouldn't ask for more. Besides, she still had the Flanagans.

Nolie went through into the dining room with a tray of cups and silver. Aunt Siobhan put her arm around Fiona's waist. "Are you all right, dear? You seem very quiet tonight."

She managed a smile. "Just enjoying the talk, even when it is about the fire department."

"I thought perhaps you were worried about that cousin of yours. Does he have a good attorney?"

So Siobhan knew about that. It had probably been in the Suffolk newspapers already. The arrest of an Amish teen made news. "The Amish don't believe in being entangled with the law. Ruth says they're not likely to hire a lawyer."

"The court will appoint someone then." Concern filled her aunt's face. "We know a fine young attorney—someone who's helped Brendan with some of his parishioners. Maybe we could get her to volunteer to take the case."

"Would you?" Tears stung Fiona's eyes at the unexpected offer of help. "I'd be happy to pay an attorney, but I don't want to seem to interfere."

"I'll talk to her." Siobhan looked at Fiona, a question in her eyes. "Has this created problems for you with Ted Rittenhouse? It seemed the two of you were getting fairly close."

"We're—we're just acquaintances, that's all." She couldn't tell her aunt the truth about Ted without tears, so it was best if she said nothing.

Siobhan hugged her, as if she heard all the things Fiona didn't say.

Nolie came back in from the dining room, shaking her head. "You won't believe it. Gabe's radio went off with a fire call, and they're both hanging over it as if they're still on active duty."

"My husband's like an old fire horse," Siobhan said, crossing to the coffeemaker. "Ready to run the minute he hears the alarm. I suspect Gabe is just as bad."

They were still smiling at the image when Gabe appeared in the doorway, Uncle Joe right behind him. The expression on Gabe's face wiped away the smiles in an instant. He looked at Fiona.

She grasped the back of a kitchen chair, somehow knowing she needed its support. "What is it? What's happened?"

"It's a three-alarm from the Crossroads volunteers. Two companies from Suffolk are responding." He took a step toward her. "I'm sorry, Fiona. The building that's burning—it's your house."

She lost a few minutes then, probably from shock. She found herself being propelled toward Gabe's car by Siobhan and Nolie. Nolie gave her a fierce hug.

"I'm sorry I can't come, but someone has to stay with the baby. You're better off with Gabe."

"It's all right." Her aunt pushed her gently

into the back seat. "Joe and I will be with you. It's going to be all right."

Was it? As soon as he and his father were settled in the front seat, Gabe took off, lights flashing from the top of the car and a siren wailing in the night.

"I guess it helps to have firefighter relatives at a time like this." She tried to say the words lightly, but her voice was choked with emotion.

This couldn't be happening. It couldn't. It must have been a mistake. *Please, God—* Somehow she couldn't even find the words to pray.

Aunt Siobhan clasped both her hands, holding them warmly. "Let's pray," she said softly, and Fiona nodded.

"Father, You know we're in trouble now." Siobhan's voice was as conversational as if she spoke to a dear friend. "We ask for Your help in this situation. Be with those who are fighting this fire. Grant them Your protection and surround them with Your love. We pray for the preservation of Fiona's practice. She's doing Your healing work in the world, Father. Please be with her and help her now. Amen."

"Amen," the men said together from the front seat.

"Amen," Fiona whispered.

Her aunt's first thoughts had been for the people who were in danger, fighting the fire. Shame filled her that she hadn't thought of them first, too.

Please, Lord, be with them. Ted would be among them—she knew that as if she were there watching. He'd be a part of the volunteer force. *Please, protect him.*

Chapter Fifteen

"Start wetting down the side and roof of the general store!" Ted shouted the orders to the crew of the tanker truck that had just pulled up at the fire scene. His personal feelings might tell him to direct every weapon toward saving Fiona's house, but as chief of the volunteer fire company, his duty was to the entire community.

His jaw tightened. He'd been telling the township supervisors for years that they needed a new tanker, but no one listened. He wanted to have them here this instant, to see how inadequate their small tanker was. Crossroads was lucky to have good neighboring companies to call on.

Thing was, he was angry at everyone and everything, especially the fire, for what this was going to do to Fiona.

The crew chief, head of one of the other small volunteer companies in the county, nodded. He gestured to his crew to drag the heavy hoses toward the general store. It was safe at the moment, but a brisk autumn breeze, blowing now toward the rear yards, could switch directions at any moment.

Townsfolk already swarmed into the store, carrying everything they could to safety, and the auxiliary was working just as quickly, setting up coffee and water in the sheltered area in front of the barbershop.

Mac Leonard, one of his volunteers, paused by the rig. Mac's breath was coming too fast. At nearly seventy, he shouldn't be on the fire line, but it was almost impossible to turn away volunteers.

"You want us to try and get anything else out?" Mac nodded toward the meager pile of furnishings they'd pulled out of Fiona's house.

Ted hardened his heart against the thought of Fiona's grief, knowing he couldn't risk lives for her beloved possessions. "No. It's spreading too fast. If those other units from Suffolk get here in time, maybe we can save something else."

Even as he said the words, he heard the

welcome wail of the sirens. Suffolk's professional force provided training and much-needed support to the volunteer companies in the countryside.

The sight of the crews pouring off the hook-and-ladder and tanker he'd requested seemed to energize the volunteers, and a ragged cheer went up. He recognized the company commander headed his way— Seth Flanagan. He'd known Seth in a professional capacity for a couple of years, and now he knew him as Fiona's cousin.

Flanagan's face was tight as he watched smoke pouring from the windows of his cousin's house.

"Fiona wasn't home," Ted said quickly.

"I know. She's at my brother's. They're on their way now. Where's the water source?"

"Creek about fifty yards behind the house." He pointed. "Just follow our lines back."

Flanagan nodded and turned to his crew, giving rapid orders.

Fiona was on her way. His heart twisted. He couldn't kid himself. Seth Flanagan knew as well as he did that the structure was already too involved. All that dry old wood had gone up like so much tinder.

They'd give it their best battle, but in the end, they weren't going to save the house.

The fire broke through the front wall, erupting upward as it met the wood of the porch. People gasped, stopping to watch, faces somber.

One of the men on the hose line stumbled, and Ted leaped forward to drag him away.

"Take a break," he urged. He grabbed the line himself until another volunteer came forward to take his place.

He'd barely turned away from the hose when a stir went through the crowd. A car pulled up, stopping just beyond the tanker. People spilled out the doors. In the eerie orange glow of the fire, he saw Fiona. Her mouth opened in a cry. She darted toward the building.

Heart pounding, he started to run toward her, but the people who were with her—her relatives, he realized—held her back, surrounding her with loving arms.

Foolish, that instinctive need he'd had to race to her. She had family to take care of her.

An ominous crack sent him spinning back to the fire. "Get back! Everyone back!"

His shout was drowned in the roar as the

roof caved in. He did a quick count, making sure his people were safe. He couldn't bear to look at Fiona, but he felt her grief as surely as if he held her in his arms.

The next hour passed in a haze of activity, until finally they were wetting down the embers and he could take stock of the damage. Not good, but he guessed it could have been worse. No one had died. Fiona's house was a total loss, but there hadn't been any damage to the surrounding buildings except for a few broken windows and a layer of soot to be cleaned away.

Still, he didn't suppose Fiona was in any shape to hear that this could have been worse. Her work, her home, had been destroyed. He forced himself to look toward her.

At some time during the past hour, the Stolzfus family had arrived, too. Family from both sides clustered around Fiona, trying to comfort her. His throat, already raw from the smoke, tightened as he saw Fiona folded in the arms of her grandmother and grandfather Stolzfus.

In everything, God works for the good of those who love Him. It was tough to understand how God was bringing good out of this circumstance, but if a man didn't have faith, he didn't have anything.

Maybe it would cheer Fiona to know that they'd saved a few things. He bent, picking up the wooden dower box he'd spotted on her dresser when he'd done a sweep of the house, and carried it over to where she stood. The cluster of family members parted, letting him approach.

"Fiona, I'm sorry." His voice rasped on the words. "I wish we could have saved the house for you."

She didn't seem to hear him. Her gaze was focused on the smoldering remains of her life, her eyes wide with what he knew was shock. Gabe Flanagan, the cousin he'd met at the farm, put his arm around her shoulders.

"Come on, Fiona. There's nothing you can do here. Let's go back to our place."

She shook her head, not moving. Gabe looked at him, helpless, clearly not sure what to do. He seemed to be expecting something from Ted.

Small help he could be, but he had to try. "We managed to pull a few things out before it got too bad."

Fiona still didn't react. He wasn't even sure she heard him.

"This was on your dresser." He shoved the box into her hands. "I thought it might be important."

Her hands grasped the box instinctively. She looked at it, and suddenly tears streamed down her face. Her body shook with sobs.

Aghast, he reached for the box, but her grandmother stopped him, shaking her head. "No. This is good. She needs to weep now."

All he could do was nod and turn away. Fiona didn't need him—not now that she had the family she'd always wanted.

But as he looked at the smoking rubble, unexpected fury surged through him. The arson squad would be here in the morning, and he'd be right at their heels. He would know the truth about this fire, no matter what.

"Maybe you should go back to Crossroads today." Nolie sat down opposite Fiona at the sturdy pine kitchen table in the farmhouse, her face concerned. "It's been over a week. Wouldn't you at least like to see what things they were able to save from the fire?"

Fiona wrapped her fingers around the steaming mug of tea in front of her, trying to absorb some of its warmth. She stared past Nolie's worried face, out the kitchen window. As if to echo the devastation in her heart, the weather had turned colder, and frost had nipped all but the hardiest flowers in Nolie's garden.

"Not today. Maybe tomorrow I'll go."

It was the same thing she'd said every day for a week, and Nolie had accepted the words. But her expression grew more worried each day.

"So many people have been asking for you." Nolie coaxed her as if Fiona were her toddler daughter. "Don't you want to see them?"

Fiona's mind winced away from the thought. To see the people of Crossroads, to see the ruins of the life she'd tried to build there—no, she couldn't. She wasn't ready.

You're hiding, the voice of her conscience said. *That's what you always do.*

"I can't. Not yet. Not until I've decided what I'm going to do. The birthing center will handle my patients until then."

That was what kept her frozen, unable to move from the comfortable hiding place she'd found at Gabe and Nolie's farm. What would she do? What could she do?

"You'll rebuild, of course." Nolie sounded confident. "You own the land, and your insurance—"

She shook her head. "My insurance wasn't enough to cover all that I've lost, and I'd invested everything I had in the practice. In a year, I'd have been out of the red, but as it is—"

As it was, she felt crushed beneath a load of mortgage payments for a house and a business that weren't there any longer.

"Everyone wants to help." Nolie covered Fiona's hand with hers, and Fiona felt the warmth of her caring. "We'll find a way for you to rebuild. Just tell us what you want to do, and we'll help."

Her throat tightened. They were all so loving and helpful, these two families she'd so unexpectedly come to call her own. It wasn't fair to hold them hostage to her inability to make up her mind.

"I know. I'm sorry." Her throat tightened. "I guess I didn't realize how much that place had become home to me until it was gone." The furniture she'd picked out with such care, the cozy office, the living room Siobhan and Nolie had helped her paint—all of that was turned to ash. She tried to focus. "I know that's not an excuse to mope around, but I can't seem to get moving."

The telephone rang. With a sympathetic pat on her hand, Nolie went to answer it. In a moment, she turned back to Fiona, an odd expression on her face.

"It's for you," she said. "It's your father."

Fiona gingerly took the phone Nolie held out to her. Maybe Nolie had misunderstood who was calling. Her father hadn't spoken with her in over a month—not since he'd made clear what he thought of her foolish plan to relocate to Pennsylvania. It was as if, once she'd left California, he'd wiped her from his thoughts and his life.

"Hello. Dad?"

"How are you, Fiona?" Her father's voice was unexpectedly gentle. "I heard about the fire. Are you all right?"

"Fine." Well, she wasn't, but he wouldn't want to hear that. "How did you hear about it?"

"My brother called me." He cleared his throat. "Funny, to hear his voice after all these years. He sounds well."

"Yes." They could have talked to each

other at any time in the past twenty-five years, if they weren't both so stubborn, but it wasn't her place to tell him that. "The whole family has been very helpful."

I've found a place here, Dad, that I never found with you. Why was that? She'd probably never know the answer to that.

"Well, I..." Surprisingly, her confident father sounded unsure of himself. "Your step-mother and I wanted you to know how sorry we are about your troubles. We want to help. Whether you want to rebuild or come back to California, you can count on us for financial support."

The offer was so unexpected that her throat closed for an instant. She hadn't asked, or been offered, any help since the moment she'd graduated from college. It had simply been understood that her father had discharged his obligation to her and that she was on her own.

"Thank you." She managed to get the words out, even though they sounded rather choked. "I—I haven't decided yet what I'm going to do, but I'll be in touch."

"Good." Her father's voice had that hearty tone it always took on at any display of emotion. "I'll talk to you soon, then. Good-bye."

She hung up, knowing the face she turned to Nolie must express her total bewilderment. "Uncle Joe called him. And he wants to help."

"Well, it's about time." Nolie's blue eyes shone suddenly with tears. "Siobhan must be so glad that they're talking again, even if it took a disaster to accomplish it."

Fiona nodded, feeling like smiling for the first time in a week. "At least something good came out of this."

Her own words startled her, and she blinked. Was she actually able to admit that God was bringing something good out of the grief that overwhelmed her?

The telephone rang again. Shaking her head, Nolie picked up. Her expression changed in an instant. "She'll be right there," she said.

"What is it?" If this was another effort to get her to Crossroads—

"That was Susie Yoder's neighbor. Susie's in labor. I guess it's time for you to saddle up and get back to delivering babies."

Fiona could only stare blankly at Nolie. "But I—I referred Susie to the birthing clinic in Suffolk. I thought she was going to go there."

"The neighbor says she's determined about this, and Aaron can't budge her. She's having her baby at home, and you're going to deliver it."

"I don't have anything. My delivery kit was in the house."

It was more than that, and she knew it. It was as if the fire had burned away her confidence when it burned her belongings.

"Well, then, I guess it's lucky that the staff from the birthing clinic dropped off a new delivery kit to replace the one you lost." Nolie tossed a jacket toward her and hustled her toward the door. "It's in your car, ready for you. Babies don't wait for anyone, not even the midwife."

Nolie's words seemed a catalyst, sending energy surging through her, chasing away the inertia that had held her paralyzed. Fiona grabbed her bag and cell phone and thrust her arms into the jacket sleeves.

"You know, you're right." She smiled, suddenly feeling like herself again. In this, at least, she knew what to do. "I guess the midwife had better get moving."

*   *   *

"You're definitely in labor."

Fiona's assurance seemed to take some of the tension from Susie's face. She leaned back in the rocking chair, reaching out to touch the hand-carved cradle that was a new piece of furniture in the simple bedroom since the last time Fiona had been to the house.

"Ja, *gut*." The stress of the moment seemed to send Susie back to the Low German that was everyday speech for the Amish. "I thought yes, but I didn't want to call you out for nothing, slow as this baby has been to decide to come."

Fiona patted her shoulder. "That's fine. I'd rather be called out on twenty false alarms than miss the real thing."

The numbness that had gripped her since the night of the fire had vanished in the need to do the thing she was trained for—the thing she was meant to do.

"How soon?"

"It's going to be a while." She smiled reassuringly at Aaron, who hovered in the doorway, as if not sure whether to stay or run. "Quite a few hours, probably. Right now, I think it would be good for Susie to take a walk. Why don't you go with her?"

His Adam's apple bobbed. "But—what if the baby starts to come?"

"The baby won't come that suddenly. Trust me. Just let Susie stop walking and lean on you when a contraction occurs. You'll be fine."

He didn't look so sure, but he nodded and came to take Susie's arm, hoisting her out of the chair. "We will walk, then."

She waited until they were out the door before setting about getting the room ready for the new little life who'd soon be taking up residence here. The familiar routine of laying out supplies and putting clean sheets and plastic—another gift from the birthing clinic—on the bed soothed away the last edges of strain.

Nolie was right. She was still a midwife, whether she had a building for her practice or not. She'd been paralyzed by the enormity of making decisions about her future, but here, with a baby on the way, she need only take the next step.

Thank You, Lord. Thank You for reminding me of who I am.

When she'd finished with the room, she

went out to the porch to see how Susie was progressing with her walk. She found them coming slowly back to the house. A car was pulling out of the driveway—a police car.

She shielded her eyes against the red glow of the setting sun. "Was that Ted?"

Her heart gave an extra thump at the thought of him. He'd called every day during the past week, apparently accepting without comment Nolie's explanation that she didn't feel like talking yet.

In truth, she hadn't known what to say to him. She still didn't.

"Ja, Ted." Aaron rubbed Susie's back as another contraction started. "He heard that you were here and just wanted to be sure everything was all right."

He hadn't asked to see her, apparently. Well, that was to be expected. She understood that the bright promise of something between them was gone. And if she hadn't quite accepted it, she would. It would take time, maybe, to put away that dream, but she could do it.

She managed a smile as she helped Susie up the steps. "Everything is fine. I hope you told him that." ·

* * *

"Everything is fine." Fiona adjusted the flame on the oil lamp so that she could see a little better. She hadn't thought about how dark it would be in an Amish farmhouse in the middle of the night. "You're progressing just as you should."

"Ja, fine." Susie's mother, who'd arrived before Susie had gone into the second stage of labor, echoed the assurance. "First babies take some time to come."

Thank heaven Susie's mother was a sensible woman who took the birth of her grandchild in stride. Susie had gained strength from her presence.

Susie leaned back against Aaron, resting between contractions, her face pale. "I'm so tired. Too tired. I can't do it."

Fiona had heard that before, so often, and usually at just this stage. "You *can* do it. It's almost time to push. Your baby's about ready to be born."

Susie shook her head. "I can't. I can't." She was distracted, weary, losing the concentration she needed to get through the next few minutes.

"I know you're tired." Fiona kept her tone soft and soothing. "Don't think about that. Think about the happiness that's waiting for you. Think about having your baby in your arms." She leaned forward, holding Susie's gaze with hers. "That's worth fighting for, Susie. Isn't it?"

Slowly she nodded. "Ja. It is worth fighting for." She gripped Aaron's arms. "I am ready."

Chapter Sixteen

"You are beautiful. Yes, you are." Fiona crooned to the tiny baby boy and then settled him in the waiting arms of his mother.

"He is." Susie's plain face was beautiful, too, as she looked at her son.

Aaron leaned on the bed, watching his wife and newborn son with an expression of sheer wonderment on his face. "Our son. We have a son." It was as if he hadn't really believed it until this moment.

As often as Fiona experienced this moment, it never became old. Her heart swelled, and tears pricked her eyes. Always the birth of a new child was an affirmation of God's presence in their lives, a reminder that His miracles happened in just such everyday ways.

Susie's mother stood, tucking the quilt

around her daughter. "The sun is already up. Time for a good breakfast for all of us."

She glanced at Fiona, and Fiona nodded, knowing what she meant. It was the right moment to leave the new little family alone together.

"That sounds like a great idea." She followed the older woman out of the room. "We can all use something to eat, and then maybe Susie can sleep for a bit."

"Ja." Susie's mother paused, looking at Fiona, her eyes soft behind the wire-rimmed glasses she wore. "You did good. Is good that you are come to us."

Fiona nodded, unable to speak for the lump in her throat. It *was* good that she had come here, to these people. Despite the trouble she'd encountered, even despite the loss of her house, she was at home here.

The decision she'd struggled with for the past week had already been made. She would stay in Crossroads. She didn't see her way clear yet, didn't have any idea how or where she would set up her practice again, but at least this much she knew—she was meant to be here.

She followed the woman into the kitchen, standing at the window to watch as the sun chased the shadows away. The sizzle of bacon in the pan reminded her of how long it had been since she'd eaten, but even without food, she felt energized. Strong. As if she could face whatever came and deal with it.

She hadn't been dealing with anything lately—not the loss of her house, not the situation with Ted. Instead she'd hidden, letting her family coddle and protect her.

The words she'd spoken to Susie came back to her. *Happiness is worth fighting for.* She'd been trying to encourage the tired young mother, but the words were true. And they applied to her, didn't they?

In the past week, she hadn't fought for anything. She'd withdrawn, just as she always did when faced with the risk of pain and rejection.

Understanding why she did that didn't make it right. She'd risked rejection when she'd approached the Flanagans, and she had a whole, loving family as a result. She'd risked again when she'd tried to mend the breach with her mother's family. She still wasn't sure how much the pain of Levi's arrest would affect them, but they'd stood by her while her house burned, and that was something.

Risk. Pain. Happiness. With every step toward belonging, there was a risk. There was a cost. Was she ready to face that?

Maybe the answer had been deep inside her all along. She had to face Ted once again. She had to risk hearing him say that it couldn't work between them. If he did, well, she'd live with that. But she wouldn't hide from the risk. Happiness was worth fighting for.

It was midmorning by the time Fiona arrived in Crossroads, having left the happy family enjoying their time together. She'd promised to check in on Susie in a few hours, but she had plenty of time to track down Ted.

Her stomach quivering with nerves, she approached Ted's office door. She opened it quickly, afraid that if she delayed for even a moment, she'd turn away.

The office was empty. She stood in the center of the small room, looking around. Odd that Ted would leave the door unlocked when he wasn't here, but maybe he figured Crossroads was safe again now that the vandals had been identified. Even the coffeepot was cold and empty.

She'd keyed herself up to face him, and now she was totally deflated. What should she do now? She turned to the door and there he was, hand on the knob.

She took a breath, trying to still the nerves that danced at the very sight of him. "Ted."

"Fiona, I thought you were still with Susie." He shoved his hat back on his head. "Is everything okay out there?"

"Just fine. They have a beautiful little boy." The memory curved her lips into a smile, easing her tension. "Susie is doing great."

"And Aaron? He didn't pass out on you, did he?"

They were actually smiling together, something she hadn't expected to see again. "He turned white a couple of times, but he held up beautifully. I'm sure he'll soon be bragging about it."

"I'll bet he will."

Silence fell between them. She couldn't seem to look away from him, but neither could she find the words she wanted to say.

"Ted, I—"

He stopped her with a quick shake of his

head. "Look, before you say anything, there's something I want to show you. All right?"

She blinked, surprised. "All right."

"Good." He held the door open, ushering her out. "I'll drive. It's not far."

She slid into the front seat of the patrol car that waited at the curb and looked curiously at the array of gadgets on the dash. "I've never been in a police car before. I'm very impressed."

He smiled as he turned the ignition. "Don't be. This is pretty low-tech compared to most modern departments."

He pulled out into the street. Crossroads was never busy, but today it seemed more deserted than usual. Only one car was parked in front of the café, and even the post office didn't appear to be doing any business.

"Where is everyone?" She glanced back along the street.

"Guess they're all busy." He tried to say it casually, but there was suppressed emotion in his voice that drew her attention.

"Is something happening that I should know about?"

He shot her a glance she couldn't read.

"Could be. Just be patient a second, and then you can tell me."

He rounded the corner. Ruth's general store appeared, looking none the worse for wear since the fire. Fiona's stomach tightened. In an instant she'd see the place where her home had been. She couldn't do this—

Her breath caught. She closed her eyes for a second, then opened them again. No, she wasn't dreaming. Where there had been a mass of smoldering ashes and charred timbers, raw new wood framed in a building that appeared like a ghost of what had once been there.

No, not a ghost. This was real.

People swarmed over the structure, some Amish, some dressed in jeans and sweatshirts. Hammers pounded and saws churned. Amish buggies stood next to dusty pickups and shiny SUVs. A long table laden with coffee urns and what looked like platters of food was set up next to Ruth's store.

"What...what's happening?" She leaned forward, one hand braced against the dash. "I don't...I don't understand." She looked at Ted, unable to take it in.

"What's to understand?" He shrugged, as

if to dismiss this as something quite ordinary. "If a barn burns, the Amish will replace it in a day. Now, your house is going to take a little longer, since you won't be content with stalls, but then, we've got quite a lot of help."

"I can't believe this." She fumbled with the door, until finally he reached across her and opened it, his big hand warm against hers.

"Believe it." His voice was a low rumble that set her nerves quivering. "It's real."

Quickly, as if afraid he'd gotten too close, he slid out of the driver's seat, coming around the car to join her. People paused in their work when they saw her, raising a hand in welcome, and then turning back to the job at hand.

She glanced from one person to another, recognizing her Flanagan cousins working side by side with her Amish kin. That was why Nolie had been trying so hard to get her to Crossroads, obviously. She'd known all about it.

Her heart caught. Levi was there, working next to his father, his face solemn and intent.

"Levi—" Her voice choked as she remembered what had happened the last time she'd asked Ted about the boy.

"He's doing all right," Ted said quickly. He didn't look at her, and she wondered if he was remembering that, too. "He came clean with his parents and the church about everything that happened, and he accepted the punishment they meted out. I expect he's learned enough from this experience to last him a good long time."

It was a relief to know that Levi was right with his community, but that wasn't everything. "What about the court? Did he get a lawyer?" Siobhan's promise to find an attorney for Levi had been swamped by everything else that happened.

Ted nodded. "He has representation, and the other boys admitted he just acted as a lookout on a couple of their pranks. He refused to go the nights they tried to torch the barns—maybe he'd figured out by then that he was in too deep."

"Will the court see it that way?" She was looking to Ted for answers again.

"He'll get off with probation. The other two will get community service, I imagine."

"Two?" She looked at him, confused. "There were three, weren't there?"

"Yes, three." His voice sounded grim. "Our friend Jared isn't going to get off so lightly." His hand closed over hers, as if he thought she needed some support. "Jared torched your house."

She could only stare at him, amazed that she hadn't even wondered until this moment how the fire had started. "Are you sure?"

He nodded. "We were already on his trail when his parents brought him in. They'd found the evidence. To do them credit, they were appalled. Maybe they'll finally face the truth about that kid."

Surprisingly, there was little anger in her heart when she thought of the boy. *I forgive him, Father. Help me when I feel resentment or anger toward him.*

"Come on." Ted tugged at her hand. "See what you think of your new home and office." He drew her toward the building, holding her steady while she walked up a plank that led to the first floor. "Mose had a lot of good ideas after working on the renovation. We thought you could use a waiting room that's a little larger, seeing as how you'll probably have a lot of new clients in the next few years."

She stood next to him in what would be her waiting room, her throat tightening. "You've thought of everything, haven't you?"

But that wasn't what her heart was saying. What about us, Ted? You've taken care of everything else, but what about what went wrong between us?

As if he felt her thoughts, Ted's grip on her hand grew stronger. He nodded toward the Amish man working nearby, and she realized it was his brother.

"You know, every once in a while, my big brother Jacob thinks he has to straighten me out about things." He sounded casual, but she sensed the undertone of emotion in the words. "Seems like he felt compelled to tell me that a man had to be a blockhead to turn away from the woman he cared about because she acted out of the warmth of her heart to save another person pain."

Her heart was thudding so loudly she could hear it. "Do you listen when your big brother gives you advice?"

"Not always." He swung to face her more fully, clasping both her hands in his. "But sometimes, like now, he's right." The warmth from his hands flowed through her, unlocking the emotions that had been frozen for days. "I guess you know why I acted the way I did. Does knowing that mean you can understand and forgive me?"

She did know. He'd used the trust issue as a barrier between them, caught as he was between his own need to protect his community and fulfilling the law.

Her fingers moved on his. "You're not betraying anyone by doing the work God called you to, you know." She kept her voice soft, even knowing no one could hear them over the clatter of work going on around them.

"I know that now."

"I'm glad."

Ted's blue eyes seemed to have a flame deep inside them when he looked at her. "And I know it's not wrong to love the woman God brought into my life, either," he said softly. He drew her closer, until anyone who looked at them could guess what was happening between them. "Some people might say I'm a little old to go sweethearting again, but I'll risk it if you will."

Risk. There it was again. She understood now. She didn't get the reward without being willing to risk everything, in faith and in life.

She took the step that separated them, feeling his arms close around her, feeling the warmth of friends, family, community supporting them.

She was home. God had truly brought her home.

* * * * *

Dear Reader,

Thank you for picking up this newest book in the story of the Flanagan family. I hope you enjoyed visiting old friends and meeting new ones.

It was a tricky business to introduce a previously unknown cousin to the Flanagans in this story, but I hope you'll feel it worked. In this case, the story came first—I knew I wanted to write about the Amish in Pennsylvania, so I needed a heroine, such as Fiona, who had a very good reason for being there and struggling for acceptance. And the character of Ted, with his need to create a life between two worlds, really touched my heart.

I owe profound thanks to my friend Winona Cochran, professor of psychology as well as a nurse-midwife with experience in the Amish community, for her invaluable contributions to *Restless Hearts*.

I hope you'll let me know how you felt about this story. I'd love to hear from you, and you can write to me at Steeple Hill Books, 233 Broadway, Suite 1001, New

York, NY 10279, e-mail me at marta@martaperry.com, or visit me on the Web at www.martaperry.com. Please come back for the next Flanagan story, *A Soldier's Heart,* coming in May 2007.

Blessings,

Marta Perry

QUESTIONS FOR DISCUSSION

1. What qualities in Fiona make her a good nurse-midwife? Do you think she could be as effective without those innate qualities?

2. Ted struggles every day with the inherent conflict between his upbringing and his calling to be a policeman. Do you sympathize with his need to succeed? Do you feel he makes the right decisions in balancing that conflict?

3. Fiona reacts to the problems of her childhood by avoiding emotional risk. Were you able to sympathize with her attitude, even if you didn't approve if it? Why or why not?

4. Ted wants to protect his friends from the trouble he feels would come with Fiona's presence. Have you ever had similar feelings of longing to protect a friend?

5. Nolie tells Fiona that she feels God has brought her to Crossroads, and that thought is echoed by several other

characters. Have you ever felt that God has led you to a particular place or situation?

6. Fiona's acceptance in the community comes when people see the depth of her caring for others. How do newcomers become accepted in your community?

7. Ted quotes the story of Joseph in the Old Testament when he tries to explain how God has worked in his life. Have you ever had an experience in which God brought good out of a situation where another person intended harm?

8. Fiona sees the similarity between the message Ted takes to heart and her own special verse, but she struggles to see how God is working for good in the troubles that come to her. Have you ever faced that same struggle?

9. "Happiness is worth fighting for," Fiona tells Susie as she encourages her through the birth of her child. But she has to learn for herself that happiness only comes when she is willing to risk